# Harry's Game

## Winds of Change

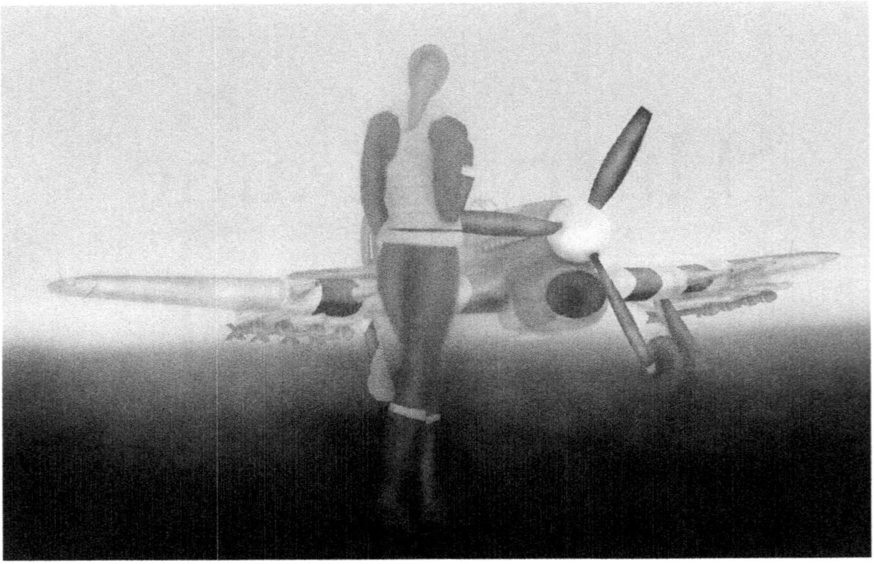

# Harry's Game

## Winds of Change

Karl Jackson

Alpaca & Goose
2022

*Harry's Game – Winds of change* is a work of historical fiction based on significant events that took place during 1944. Any names, characters, places, events, or incidents within the story are either the products of the author's imagination or inspired by similar actual events and used in a fictitious manner. Any references or opinions related to any organisations or entities exist only within the fictitious realms of the story, and any resemblance to actual persons, living or dead, is purely coincidental.



karl@harrysgame.com

*Book design & Illustration by Karl Jackson*

First published – May 2022 by Alpaca & Goose

www.alpacagoose.com

**First Edition**

ISBN 978-1-9162651-7-2

www.harrysgame.com

# *'Friends'*

*Dedicated to those who fought to free Europe on the ground, at sea, and in the air.*

## Chapter 1

## Going Home

The sun was just rising in the misty pale blue sky as Harriet walked through the manicured grounds of the large stately home she'd arrived at, following an early morning drive from her airfield near Cambridge. It was cold, and she was happy for her long, thick overcoat and soft brown leather gloves, which protected her from the worst of the chilly February morning. As always, she'd have preferred to have been wearing trousers in cold weather, but the telegram she'd received while at home in East Yorkshire on leave, where she'd been sent to recover after her experience in France, had been very clear in stating that she was to be in her best uniform when she reported to the Air Officer Commanding Air Defence Great Britain, the organisation which had previously been known as Fighter Command. It had come as a surprise to be summoned to the beautiful North London mansion, which had been taken over by Fighter Command before the war, and had been their very exclusive seat of their power since. She'd only been back in the country for just over a week. After a couple of days in London being debriefed by Atwell, who turned out to be rather more than just an agent who trained operatives for undercover work in France, her commanding officer had sent her on leave until the end of the month. The timings in the telegram had been so tight that she hadn't even had time to see Nicole when she called in to change into her best uniform, and take the MG Roadster that Cas had given them on what he referred to as a 'long term loan', so she could drive to North London. Fortunately, Archie had been available to fly her south in a Mosquito, but nobody was around when she landed. All were on a mission, Nicole included, and the CO was down at the cottage with them. So, she'd had a quiet drink in the bar by herself, then had an early night, before getting up and leaving long before breakfast.

It was early, but there was already lots of activity at the headquarters. To her irritation, Harriet had to leave her car in a car park further down the drive and walk to the main house, while jeeps and staff cars were buzzing back and forth, carrying senior officers of all services and nationalities. The heightened state of activity was mirrored inside the building. After having her identity documents checked by the RAF Police Sergeant guarding the entrance, she was shown into the magnificent building with its high ceilings and luxurious appointments, and shown to an office opposite a vast grand staircase, which swept elegantly upwards, and had what seemed like a constant stream of WAAFs heading in each direction, carrying papers, cups, maps, and whatever else. Once in the office, she was asked by a Squadron Leader to take a seat, which she did after hanging her coat on the stand in the corner while he continued his work. She waited patiently, and waited, and waited, listening to the Squadron Leader mutter under his breath every now and then when he read something clearly disagreeable, or made a mistake on whatever it was he was writing. He'd been pleasant enough when she'd introduced herself, even offering her a cup of tea, which she politely declined, before going back to his work and generally carrying on as though she wasn't there. He had a couple of medal ribbons below the wings above his left pocket, one of which was the Distinguished Flying Cross, a highly prized award for courage and bravery in the air. He'd also been awarded the 1939 - 1943 Star for his services in the war. Harriet had received the same medal in November, along with the Africa Star for her time in Malta. Two more ribbons to add to her expanding collection, which made people's eyebrows raise and her eyes roll. She'd also been presented a small silver winged boot, which she wore on her left pocket, having made a member of the Late Arrivals Club when tales of her escapades in the desert had got back to the club founders in Cairo. It wasn't an officially sanctioned club, though there were some quite senior officers among the members. Membership was exclusive to those who'd come down in the desert following enemy intervention or action, which usually meant they'd been shot down and had to make their way back by other means, often arriving much later than scheduled. Both the badge, and the certificate which accompanied it, had been presented to Harriet when an officer posted home from the desert had dropped by her airfield. She didn't have a clue what it was at first, but the very thought of it made her smile. It was very eccentric, and very English, and to know that those at the top of the RAF had condoned the wearing of the badge, even though it was unofficial, just made her smile more. The officer presenting it to her had said it was a great talking point, and it certainly was. Anyone seeing it asked about it, and as with every other pilot in the RAF, the story got longer and a little more elaborate each time she told it. She'd also been made a member of the Caterpillar Club for having taken to her parachute to escape a damaged aeroplane, and the Goldfish Club for having ditched in water and used a life jacket and life raft to stay alive. For reasons nobody seemed to know, neither of these awards were as well tolerated by the upper echelons of the RAF as the winged boot, so neither could be worn anywhere near the uniform. However, most members, Harriet included, had them stitched under the flap of the left breast pocket on their tunics, just for good luck. She laughed to herself as she looked down at her medal ribbons and decorations, she'd never been a Girl Guide, but she'd certainly collected lots of badges.

Her daydreaming was disturbed by the door to the inner office opening, and the AOC walking out with an American General and a British Air Commodore. Harriet rose from her chair as they finished their conversation in hushed tones, not paying her the slightest bit of notice, then said goodbye. The two left, and the AOC turned to look at Harriet.

"You must be Cornwall," he said as she stood smartly to attention. He had a big moustache, pilot's wings, and a couple of rows of medals from the last war. She didn't know him, or much about him; he'd only taken over Fighter Command the previous year, and she'd been out of the country for a while, or hiding away flying Lysanders, and hadn't had much to do with fighters in England since 1940.

"Yes, Sir," she replied.

"Well, we'd better get this over with." He nodded his head towards his office door, signalling for her to join him, and she quickly followed him into his office and stood in front of his desk. "Commissioned into the Volunteer Reserve, weren't you Cornwall?" he asked as he took his seat.

"Yes, Sir. 1940."

"Yes..." He frowned as he looked her up and down, making her heart race and her tummy flip uncomfortably. She had absolutely no idea why she'd been summoned; the telegram didn't say anything other than where she was to be, and when. His suggestion that whatever she was there for was something 'to get over with' didn't fill her with warmth, and neither did his frown. "I'm not sure that winged boot on your uniform is within King's Regulations..."

"Sir..." She looked down at her chest and felt her temperature rise, as she fought the overwhelming urge to run away and hide. "I... I was told it was permissible to wear it, Sir..."

"Were you indeed?" He let out a sigh. "Word to the wise, Cornwall. Whatever you were allowed to get away with in Malta should probably stay in Malta, and standing in front of an Air Chief Marshal while wearing incorrect uniform would, more often than not, be an entirely unwise decision.

"Yes, Sir. Sorry, Sir. It won't happen again."

"Good. Now, we'd better get down to business..." He fixed her in his stare for a moment. "The Air Ministry, in their infinite wisdom, have made a decision to try and deal with several of their problems at once, which is why you're here, and I'm having to do something I'd rather not! At least not while we're so busy with other, much more important things. However, orders are orders, so neither of us have much say, other than to get on with it." He lifted a folder from his desk and checked it, all while Harriet's heart was in her mouth. She felt she was in trouble, but she couldn't for the life of her think what she'd done. Her fear that the RAF would find out they'd made a massive mistake in making her a pilot had eased a long time ago. She'd been decorated and promoted since then, and any mistake would have been long since discovered and rectified, or so she thought. "508 Squadron, wasn't it?" he asked, after snapping the file closed again. "Where you started, I mean?"

"Yes, Sir. Unfortunately, the squadron was decommissioned in 1940."

"Mothballed..."

"Sir?"

"Put on the inactive list, so to speak. As we do with officers who we don't necessarily need at the time." Her heart was now pounding. Atwell had recommended a period of rest for Harriet in her debriefing report to the RAF, following her time at the hands of the Gestapo, but she wasn't expecting to be retired. She was in her early twenties, and she was a good pilot. Surely, they could find something else for her. Something other than being sent home. Her mind was spinning, and she didn't know what to do or what to say. "Anyway, I digress. You're to report to RAF Leconfield in East Yorkshire tomorrow, where you'll establish and train a new fighter squadron, with the express purpose of contributing to the national defence. You'll have a month to get them into shape, and then you'll be made operational and join us in keeping the skies above England clear of German interlopers, of which there are a great many at the moment. Understood?"

"Sir…" she replied. Her eyes were wide open in shock.

"Your pilots will be receiving their orders today, and all should be with you by the end of the week. Their personnel files will be sent to your office, but I've taken the liberty of putting together a list so you can choose your flight commanders and start putting a plan together. I expect you'll recognise some of the names." He leant across his desk and handed her a sheet of paper, which she looked at, running her eyes down the list of twenty one names.

"Sir…" she said firmly as she looked him in the eyes. "A lot of these names are…" She wasn't sure she'd read it right, and had to check it again before continuing.

"All of them are female." He gave her the slightest smile. "You gave the Air Ministry a headache the day you arrived, and it hasn't eased any since... I don't need to tell you that the very idea of female combat pilots leaves a bad taste in a lot of very senior mouths, not forgetting the most upset ladies who don't like the idea of their husbands and sons serving alongside young women, so the decision has been taken to put you all together in the same place. It keeps the dinosaurs happy because you're no longer in their squadrons, and it keeps the feminists happy because you're still flying. Personally, I think it's nonsense. I have better things to do with my time right now than play politics, but orders are orders. I have mine, and you have yours. Ultimately, if by putting you together I get an extra squadron for national defence, and I can release another squadron for front line duties, I'll be happy."

"Yes, Sir." It was taking every effort not to scream with excitement. Finally, her wildest dreams were coming true.

"That's all. See Squadron Leader Thomas on your way out; he'll give you your orders."

"Thank you, Sir. I won't let you down."

"It's not me you'll be letting down if it all goes wrong, Cornwall."

"Yes, Sir."

"Oh, and apparently, you've been written up for the Distinguished Service Cross by the skipper of a tanker you were somehow on in the Mediterranean. There'll be an investiture at some point, but you can wear the ribbon as soon as it's in the London Gazette, which should be some time in the next few days. May as well get the ribbon on before you go north. Good luck, Cornwall." He stood and handed her a notice confirming the medal, then offered his hand, which she shook before saluting and leaving his office. Her hands were shaking as she pulled the door closed and tried to control her breathing.

"The AOC said you have my orders for me?" she said quietly to the Squadron Leader sitting behind the desk, while doing her best not to appear as shell shocked as she felt.

"Of course, here you go." He stood and passed her a large, sealed envelope. "Not many know of the plans, but I wish you all the best."

"Thank you... I don't suppose you know where I could find Wing Commander Salisbury?"

"I imagine he's probably on duty. I can call the bunker and let him know you're here if you'd like?"

"Please…" She gave him a smile, then went back to reading the list of names she'd been given. It made her happy to know that Nicole was on it, and she couldn't wait to tell her.

"Wing Commander Salisbury says he'll be up in a few minutes, and asks if you wait for him in the canteen."

"I will if you let me know where it is?"

"I'll show you the way. I need to go there myself anyway."

"Before we go, the AOC said you'd be sending out posting orders to my pilots today?"

"Yes. I have them all ready to go. The written orders will follow the telegrams that we'll be sending later this morning."

"If you have Flight Lieutenant Delacourt's orders, I can deliver them in person. She's in my current unit."

"Saves me a job." He smiled as he checked through his out tray for Nicole's posting orders. He put them in an envelope and handed them to Harriet. "Right, let's go to the canteen." Harriet grabbed her coat and hat, and followed him out into the increasingly busy hall, where they dodged officers of all types to get to a staircase that led downwards. She cringed as she started down the stairs, and her mind immediately jumped back to the basement in the Gestapo headquarters. She'd been dragged up and down the stairs to and from her cell in the basement so many times, and other than being released from captivity, there were absolutely no happy memories from the place. Heading downwards on the stairs from a ground floor filled her with dread. To her surprise, the basement wasn't what she thought. The rear of the house was at a lower level than the front, and she was led to a small canteen with long glass doors leading out to a terrace, and an expanse of what looked to be quite magnificent gardens. She took a cup of tea and slipped out of the door onto the terrace, leaving the noise of the busy canteen behind her. The view was incredible. Even though it was winter and in the middle of a war, the gardens were in pristine condition, with an ornate fountain as the centrepiece. In the distance was the city of London, complete with smoke rising up from chimneys, and barrage balloons scattered across the sky. It was cold, but it was worth being outside just for the view. That and the quietness away from people, so she could think through what had just happened.

"What are you doing here?" Cas asked as he joined her.

"Can you never just say something nice when you see me?" she replied with a frown. "Like 'hello', or 'it's nice to see you.' I'm sure it wouldn't be too difficult!"

"You're feeling better, I see," he replied with a warm smile. He'd visited her at aunt Mary's when she was on leave. It was an unexpected surprise that had made her smile, despite her feeling so low and broken that she was embarrassed at him seeing her that way at first.

"With good reason!" She smiled excitedly as she waved the list of names in front of him.

"What's this?" He snatched it from her after she'd mischievously moved it just out of reach every time he went to take it. He narrowed his eyes at her, but couldn't help smiling at her mischievousness.

"I've been given command of a squadron.'

"You've been given command of 'the' squadron…"

"What?"

"What?"

"Stop it! What are you talking about?"

"Pilots posted to 508 Squadron Auxiliary Air Force…" He stood next to her and pointed to the sentence above the list of names. "Commanding Officer: Squadron Leader H Cornwall."

"Oh my God… They've given me command of the Black Sheep?"

"What else? I thought that was what you were showing me?"

"Look at the names..."

"The what?"

"The names. Look at them."

"Delacourt... Nicole too?"

"Cas!" She rolled her eyes. "They're all female. Every pilot is a girl. The AOC has told me I'm setting up an all female squadron!"

"Bloody hell!"

"Watch it!" She nudged him with her elbow.

"What? I mean bloody hell, I never thought I'd see the day... Well done, Harry. Well done!" He put his hand on her shoulder and squeezed. "When do you leave?"

"Tomorrow. The squadron is forming in East Yorkshire."

"It'd have to. It's the spiritual home of 508. Harry, I really can't tell you how happy I am for you."

"I just want to jump up and down and scream. I can't believe it."

"This needs a proper party to celebrate. Tonight, the American Bar?"

"I'll be there!"

"Why not pack your car and bring it down to London? I'll make a few calls and see if I can get you a room at The Savoy. That way, you won't have to rush off, and you can head north after a good breakfast and a bit of shopping?"

"Because it's your car, which you loaned to us while we're down here near London, and now we're leaving..."

"Oh, don't be ridiculous. I don't need it, do I? I've got my Aston."

"OK..." She felt herself blush. "If you think you can sort a room? I know the Americans book everything these days."

"Leave it to me." He checked his watch. "I need to get back; I'm the duty controller."

"You never said you worked somewhere so luxurious... When you said you were a controller, I imagined the tunnels in Malta. Not a stately home."

"The house is for the senior officers. I still work in a bunker."

"If you say so."

"Do you have anything else to do while you're here?"

"No... I'm heading straight back to let Nicole know. We need to get packed."

"OK, I'll walk you out if you like?" She nodded, and they walked back through the house, then out of the main entrance. "Where's your car?"

"Down in the car park. They wouldn't let me bring it up to the house. Authorised vehicles only, apparently.

"That makes sense, I suppose. Got to keep the riffraff out..."

"You're not as funny as you think you are."

"I'm hilarious."

"I'll see you tonight."

The drive out of London and back to the airfield flew by in a blur as Harriet raced along the roads smiling to herself, and planning how things were going to be. She hadn't even read her orders yet, and didn't know half the story, but she had enough to daydream her way north. Memories of France didn't even feature. She was going back to a fighter squadron, her own squadron, and she was going to be assigned to national defence. It wasn't 1940, and the Germans weren't raiding every five minutes; those days were long gone, but she wouldn't be flying over France either. It was the best job she could imagine. She breezed through the front gate and called by the CO's office to let him know her orders. The AOC had called in advance to let him know, so it wasn't too much of a shock, but he was disappointed to be losing two of his pilots, especially as things were getting busier than ever. He was gracious enough, though, and thanked Harriet for her work, and apologised again for what had happened to her in France as though it was his fault.

"Why are you making so much noise?" Nicole complained from under her covers, as Harriet went about emptying her locker and packing her kit. It had been a long night, according to the CO. Take off had been delayed, and Nicole hadn't landed in England until gone four in the morning. To make things worse, the cottage was in demand. So, instead of sleeping off her mission there, she'd been instructed to fly back to her home field at first light, having spent the remaining hours of darkness snoozing in the cottage living room. By the CO's estimates, she'd been asleep two hours at the most.

"Have you missed me?" Harriet replied chirpily.

"No! Now keep the noise down. I have to fly tonight."

"No, you don't."

"What?"

"You're not flying tonight."

"What are you talking about?" Nicole lifted onto her elbows and looked at Harriet through one tired eye, keeping the other tightly closed. Her hair was a mess, and she looked tired, and certainly not in the mood for a conversation.

"You've been posted."

"I don't have the energy for this. I'm too tired."

"Read it yourself." Harriet threw the envelope containing Nicole's posting onto her bed, then turned back to her locker and carried on sorting her things, making an extra effort to drop and clatter coat hangers, smiling to herself while she did.

"You're not funny...." Nicole grumbled, as she pulled at the envelope and removed the paper inside. "508 Squadron?" she asked. She was suddenly wide awake, and her voice had a ring of excitement.

"It's reforming in East Yorkshire, and you're the new commander of A Flight, and Second in Command of the squadron. We've been released from duties, and as soon as you've packed, we're heading to London for a party. Cas is sorting rooms for us at The Savoy."

"We're going together?" Nicole asked excitedly, as she read through the orders for herself.

"We are if you ever get out of bed." Nicole jumped up and threw herself at Harriet. Wrapping her in a warm hug.

"We're going home!"

"Get dressed!"

"Which flight will you command?" Nicole asked, while rattling through her locker and pulling out her clothes.

"All of them."

"You're the new CO of 508?" Nicole turned and looked at Harriet. Her eyes were wide open with excitement.

"Apparently."

"Harriet, this is incredible! It's our squadron!"

"Get dressed!"

"We're going to London right away?"

"As soon as you're ready."

"I didn't eat breakfast yet."

"If you stop messing about and get dressed and packed, I'll buy you lunch in London."

"We can go to Harrods for coffee! They have the proper stuff, not the dust they have in the RAF!"

"I said I'd take you out for lunch. I never said at Harrods! I'm not rich!"

"You're a Squadron Leader. You're paid more than me. Besides, you didn't get me a Christmas present."

"I was in France…"

"Which means you have over a month of back pay that you haven't spent." Nicole shrugged casually while pulling on her uniform. "How are you feeling?"

"Nice of you to ask... After you'd asked me to take you to Harrods."

"I have my priorities."

"I'm better than I was. Some time at home helped. Which reminds me, we're posted not far from home, so we can stay with aunt Mary when we have time off."

"Hopefully, the new CO gives us a few breaks, in that case…" Nicole smirked. "What about the other pilots already in the squadron? Won't they be annoyed at us turning up and taking senior positions?"

"The other pilots will be arriving at the same time. It's the first time the squadron's reforming since 1940."

"You have to select new pilots?"

"It's already been done for me." Harriet handed her the pilot list, and Nicole's eyes opened wide.

"They're..."

"All female." Harriet smiled.

"Mon Dieu..."

"I know. Now get dressed, or they're going to be an all female squadron without a CO and senior Flight Commander, because they're busy standing around talking instead of moving."

"You're going to be a nightmare as CO."

"I was your CO in Malta."

"That's how I know!"

After packing, they stopped at the office to say goodbye to H one last time, then had a quick drive around the station to hunt down their WAAF friends so they could let them know they were leaving. All were happy for them, and a little sad to see their flying friends go. Goodbyes done, and they were on the road to London, where they arrived with time to check in to The Savoy, who were expecting them thanks to Cas, before heading out to Harrods for Harriet's promised treat. Following that, they spent the afternoon shopping, with the now traditional trip to Fortnum and Mason for tea and tinned goods. They even had time to catch a West End show before heading back to the hotel and getting ready for their night in the American Bar. Once dressed in their best uniforms, they had a light dinner in the restaurant before heading to the bar for martinis. Cas joined them, and Ralph, and even Atwell put in an appearance. It was a night of proper celebration. The drinks flowed, they danced, and they all laughed so much that they were in tears. It was the type of night that had kept Harriet going while she was in France.

"Everything OK?" Atwell asked, as she joined Harriet outside in the cold night air. The smoke and excitement had got too much, and she'd slipped out to get some fresh air when she thought nobody was looking.

"Just cooling down a little," Harriet replied with a smile. Her cheeks were burning from the martinis, and her head was light.

"It is a little stuffy in there, I suppose."

"I didn't think anyone would notice my escape."

"I notice everything. I thought you knew that about me by now?" She gave Harriet a rare smile. "So, you're going to lead a fighter squadron…"

"Yes… I can't wait. It's something I've dreamt about. I mean, I've done the job before, but this is different."

"You'll be good at it."

"How do you know?" Harriet smirked.

"I know everything. You should know that too."

"I'm learning…"

"Me too."

"Oh?"

"Yes… I seem to remember giving you a bit of a hard time when we first met."

"I hadn't noticed…"

"Indeed. Anyway, it wasn't because you were a woman, or because of anything you said, just so you know. I've been around pilots for years. Trained with them, been on operations with them, the works, and you won't believe how many I've met who think they're God's gift."

"To what?"

"Everything! To the country, to women, to the world!" She rolled her eyes, and Harriet laughed. "I just learned to be direct with them. It's the only way to keep them under control."

"Something of a generalisation, but you're not too far off."

"Oh, I know. You wouldn't believe the number of propositions I've had from pilots."

"They wouldn't dare if they knew you."

"I don't know how to take that." She frowned mischievously at Harriet.

"They're easily intimidated, or so I've found. Pilots love to showboat, until they find out a woman can handle herself, that is. Then they tend to go all quiet."

"Speaking from experience?"

"I've been a pilot with the RAF for almost four years…"

"Point taken," Atwell laughed. "Anyway, you've taught me that it's not right, or fair, to generalise. The way you kept us alive when we were jumped by those German fighters over the Thames Estuary really made me stop and think. Then, when I learned of everything you went through in France, and what you did there, I learned not to tar everyone with the same brush."

"I didn't do much." Harriet felt herself blushing, while trying to be as casual and dismissive as possible.

"I debriefed the young resistance girl you brought home with you, so I know you're talking nonsense… She told me how you wouldn't break and tell the Gestapo what they wanted to know, not even when they pushed you to the limit, and she told me that when it came to the end, you traded your life for hers in return for a pack of lies that you sold to them so convincingly that they swallowed it hook, line, and sinker."

"She was delusional from the pain."

"Not so much to be very, very accurate in every detail of your stay with the Gestapo. You know, if you'd have talked, they'd have rounded up the entire Resistance network in the area. More would have talked under torture, and we'd have lost everything."

"You can stop now."

"As I said, I learned not to judge a book by its cover."

"That goes both ways, I suppose," Harriet shrugged. "I had you down as intimidating, confident, and somebody who could take care of themselves in a fight, and... Well..." She couldn't hold in her laugh, and neither could Atwell, despite doing her best to try and look insulted.

"I'm going to miss you when you head up north."

"You're welcome to visit us anytime. In between your secret missions."

"Careful, I may just take you up on that. Right, shall we go back in? It's freezing out here, and Cas was at the bar buying martinis when I came out." She turned and headed back towards the door.

"Atwell..."

"Yes?"

"Thanks for rescuing me..."

"What else was I going to do?" She gave Harriet a smile.

## Chapter 2

### Uneven

"Squadron Leader Cornwall, Sir," Harriet said, as she stood in front of the Station Commander's desk and gave him a smart salute. It had been a long drive from London, which she and Nicole had shared after a good breakfast and lots of coffee, both of which were needed after the previous night's celebrations.

"Of course! Who else would you be?" he replied while jumping from his chair, before walking around his desk with his hand extended. "Alan Battle. Welcome to Yorkshire."

"Thank you, Sir."

"Al will do when we're not in company, Harriet?"

"Harry. Sir."

"Harry it is. So, you've come north to form a new fighter squadron."

"Yes. My pilots are due over the coming days, but I wanted to get settled in before they get here."

"Good plan. One of our other squadrons moved down south last week, so I've had their hangar and office space cleared out for you. I'll have Charlie show you around once we've finished chatting, so you can make yourself comfortable. I've arranged for an accommodation block to be put to one side for your officers, though the NCOs will have to stay in the WAAF block, I'm afraid. I've also arranged for a cottage for you off the station. Doesn't do to have you in the same accommodation as your pilots; you need some space to think and clear your head. Again, I'll have Charlie show you down there once you've had a trip to your office."

"Thank you." Harriet smiled warmly. She was expecting to be an inconvenience, and to be greeted by a Station Commander who wouldn't have much time for her, or the Air Ministry's latest plan for dealing with female pilots, so it was a pleasant and very welcome surprise to be greeted by somebody so welcoming, who'd done so much to prepare for her arrival.

"Now, some of your ground crew have already arrived. I stood them down for today, so you'll get to meet them tomorrow morning. It was pointless them hanging around when you don't have any aeroplanes."

"Sir?"

"Al."

"Al?"

"They're being prepared at a Maintenance Unit, and should be ready in the next couple of days. I'll have an Anson put on to taxi you around to collect them when the time comes, so don't worry there."

"Thank you." Harriet smiled again, while feeling a little inconvenienced that she'd been sent to form a fighter squadron that didn't have any fighters.

"So, once your pilots are here, I'll expect you to keep me updated on your progress, but otherwise, I'll give you free rein to train them as you see fit. It's not an easy job forming a squadron. Cohesion and esprit de corps are key! Get them fighting for each other, and they'll be a force to be reckoned with. I expect to see you all in the Mess, and I expect the best behaviour. Pilots will be pilots, but we have standards, especially for the officers. We need to set an example. You understand, of course. You wouldn't have got where you are without knowing that." He gave her a warm smile as he clapped his hands on his thighs with the same light eccentricity many senior officers seemed to have. "Right, I won't keep you. Let's get you shown around, then you can get over to your cottage and get settled in You won't know anyone on the station, so you can join us for dinner tonight." He gave her a wink as he stood and picked up his phone. "Charlie, come up here, would you."

"I wonder if you'd mind if I ate in the Mess tonight?" Harriet asked.

"I assure you; my wife's cooking is better than you may think. I was fortunate enough to marry a Frenchwoman, and she's a fantastic cook.

"It's not that…" Harriet found herself blushing at the thought of inadvertently insulting her new boss on the first day. "I brought one of my flight commanders with me, Flight Lieutenant Delacourt. I'd hate to leave her in the Mess by herself on her first night."

"Oh, that's a relief. The wife would have been furious. Bring Delacourt with you; she's more than welcome." The door opened, and a tall, slender, WAAF Sergeant with copper red hair stood smartly to attention in the doorway. "Ah, Charlie, there you are. This is Squadron Leader Cornwall, the new CO of 508 Squadron. Take her down to the lines and show her around, would you?"

"Yes, Sir," Charlie replied formally.

"Once they've had a look around, show her to the cottage you arranged for her, and have the Duty Driver collect her at seven."

"Sir."

"I'll see you later, and welcome to the team." He shook Harriet's hand again, and she gave him a smart salute before following Charlie from the office and through the building, back to the cold afternoon air. The light was already starting to fade, and Harriet was starting to feel tired from the drive, and the excesses of the night before.

"I can drive you in the CO's car if you'd like, Ma'am?" Charlie said.

"Lead the way, and I'll follow you in my car," Harriet replied, and walked over to the MG.

"Are you done?" Nicole asked as Harriet climbed into the driving seat. "I'm tired, and could sleep for a week."

"We've got a tour to go on first."

"What? Where?"

"Our new office."

"Can't you just drop me at the Mess?"

"No. We need to go and have a look around. Then we're eating with the Station Commander and his wife at seven, so you'd better wake up."

"I hate the RAF," Nicole sighed, while slumping in her seat. "I just want to sleep."

"You really are such a baby at times." Harriet rolled her eyes as she started the engine and followed Charlie.

"I'll remind you that the night before last, I was flying over France, and had only been in bed an hour when you came in like a bull in a Chinese shop and dragged me out of my sleep."

"Bull in a china shop."

"Same thing."

"Why would a bull in a Chinese shop make any sense at all? It's a china shop. Fine bone china."

"I don't know. You English make up stupid things all the time. Anyway, you made lots of noise and woke me, then dragged me to London and had me partying all night. So it should be no surprise that I'm tired."

"Your pilots are going to love you."

"Of course they are; I'm a delight… Anyway, who's going to be in my flight? You showed me names, but that's all."

"It hasn't been decided yet."

"I can tell you who I want, if that would help?"

"And how would that be fair? The other flight commanders wouldn't have any say."

"The other Flight Commanders aren't family. We're sisters. You should let me choose first."

"Are you going to be like this all night?"

"I'll decide later… I hope the Station Commander's wife can cook. English food can be so bland."

"I'll tell aunt Mary that when we go home to visit."

"Aunt Mary can cook. Not like a Frenchwoman, of course, but she's good."

"I'm not sure that's quite the compliment you think it is. Maybe don't tell her that. Anyway, the Station Commander's wife is French, apparently, so you're in luck. At least you are if you stop whining; otherwise, I'll leave you in the Mess and go myself."

"French?" Nicole asked as her ears pricked up, and she sat straight. Totally ignoring everything else Harriet had said.

"Yes. Now smile and be nice." They pulled up at the dispersal hut outside a large green hangar, and they both stepped out to meet Charlie.

"This is your dispersal, Ma'am," Charlie said. "That hangar is yours, and the offices and stores have been cleared for you. Unfortunately, nothing much has arrived yet. The basics are in. The phones, furniture, and stationery, but your stores aren't due until the end of the week. I'll chase them when I get back."

"Thank you…" Harriet walked around and looked at the hangar and dispersal hut. It was all hers, and that made her smile. Charlie showed her to her office in the dispersal, and around the hangar. It was big and empty, and their footsteps echoed, and she couldn't be happier at the smell of oil and aviation fuel. She stood in the silence for a moment and closed her eyes. There was so much to come and so many unknowns, but she couldn't be more excited to get started.

"It's going to be incredible, isn't it?" Nicole asked as she stood by Harriet's side.

"I hope so."

"Think of those two girls sunbathing back in France, when Sully's Hurricane landed in grandpa's field. Did you ever imagine that they'd be here doing this?"

"It's a miracle we made it out of France!" Harriet smirked, and they both found themselves laughing. It was true enough. France was chaos, and they escaped through nothing more than pure luck.

After their tour, they were shown to Harriet's cottage, which was much larger than she expected, with a roaring log fire, smart kitchen, and huge garden. Nicole was naturally furious that Harriet would get a cottage to herself while she had a room in the Mess, and the fury didn't ease any when Harriet explained that it would be blatant favouritism if she allowed Nicole to move in too, despite Nicole's repeated requests from that moment onwards, which quickly became demands that received exactly the same answer. The bickering was put on the back burner for dinner with the Station Commander and his wife, Lina, who took an instant shine to Nicole. It turned out that Lina was from the much disputed Alsace region of France, which was a German territory for decades, right up until the end of the Great War, when it was handed back to France. This meant that Lina was technically German, though she couldn't be more French in every way, and she'd missed having a fellow Frenchwoman to talk to. The moment Lina saw Nicole's 'France' shoulder titles on her uniform, she became an instant surrogate mother, and Nicole enjoyed every moment of being the favourite. She helped prepare dinner, poured the wine, and talked in fast and excitable French, which Lina absolutely loved. Max explained that Lina missed France, and often talked about how she missed being able to just sit and talk with somebody in French other than him, whose French wasn't quite what she'd hoped it would be, despite him having spent time there during and after the last war. The conversation continued over the finest

French Cognac, while Harriet and Max talked about her time in Malta, and his time in France during the last war. He'd flown the Sopwith Triplane with the Royal Flying Corps until he was shot down and badly injured, and evacuated to a hospital outside a small French town, which is where he met his wife to be. He missed flying, but after the war, the opportunities became fewer and fewer, especially with his injury, so he accepted a job in France as a liaison officer, before coming back to England to work in a number of staff jobs. He was eventually promoted to Group Captain and given command of a station, which kept him connected with flying and suited him just fine. As interesting as his own story was, he was fascinated by Harriet's. She didn't go into too much detail, but what she did say was enough for him, especially her time with the Americans, which he questioned her about in fine detail. It was the perfect night, and the perfect welcome to a new home, and it finished with Nicole getting her way and spending the night with Harriet in her cottage, where they lay awake in the glow of the fire, talking excitedly about the future and drinking brandy, which wasn't quite to the same standard as that she'd had with Al and Lina.

"Squadron Leader Cornwall, you do know that I'm not your personal assistant in this war, and you can't simply demand that I'm dragged across the country on a whim just to serve you!" a familiar voice demanded from behind Harriet and Nicole, as they sat at their table in the Mess where they were waiting for their breakfast.

"Ginny…" Harriet gasped as she turned to see the tall, athletic looking blonde standing in the doorway with her hands on her hips, and staring through narrowed eyes.

"I'll Ginny you! I was enjoying myself in Scotland, thank you very much. At least I was until a telegram arrived dispatching me to the wilds of Yorkshire. I half expected it was the hand of my oaf of a brother, until I saw your name all over it…"

"Ginny!" Harriet ignored the rant as she jumped up from her seat and walked over to her friend, trying to compose herself and not appear quite as overexcited in front of the other officers in the Mess, some of whom were already frowning at the noise. "When did you train as an Observer?" she asked as she looked at the single wing brevet and letter

'O' above the left pocket of Ginny's tunic. "Or get awarded the Air Force Cross, for that matter?" she added, as she noticed the red and white diagonal striped medal ribbon below the brevet.

"Pietersen, that idiot you left in charge of your Norwegian Squadron, sent me on the course, and no sooner did I get back, he went and crashed on the coast, just where I happened to be! I had to drag his stupid carcass out of his Mosquito, and to punish me for the good deed, he went and recommended me for the AFC. Anyway, stop deflecting! Why was I summoned to Yorkshire?"

"I've got absolutely no idea... Do you want to join us for breakfast?" Harriet waved her hand towards their table.

"I see she's dragged you into whatever charade this is," Ginny said to Nicole.

"I'm always the first in line for her games. It's my punishment for being her friend," Nicole shrugged, then sipped on her coffee. "It's nice to see you. I'm happy it's not just me she's pulled into this."

"Whatever this is... So, Squadron Leader Cornwall, why have I been sitting around in Yorkshire for the last couple of days, staring at an empty squadron hangar and offices?"

"You don't know?" Harriet asked, genuinely surprised.

"No! I don't generally get involved in conversations about what I'd like to do or where I'd like to go; it's not how the RAF works. I just get dragged around the country to be your dogsbody."

"I think that's me," Nicole added.

"Will you both shut up and stop giving me a hard time?" Harriet sighed. "You've just been made a flight commander and Second in Command of the squadron," she barked at Nicole, who smirked in reply as Harriet turned on Ginny. "And as for you, I've got absolutely no idea why you're here! I didn't even know I was coming here until the day before yesterday. I certainly didn't ask for you... And the way you're giving me a hard time, I'm not sure I want you!"

"Well, it looks like you're stuck with me. My orders were to report to the Commanding Officer of 508 Squadron, a Squadron Leader Cornwall, to take my post as Adjutant."

"Looks like they're serious," Nicole said.

"About?"

"We're putting together a new fighter squadron," Harriet replied. "Apparently, you're the Adjutant," She let herself smirk after the barrage of attitude she'd just given, which had some of the other officers frowning even more. "I mean, if I was to choose somebody, it'd maybe not be..."

"I can always go back to Scotland? They have proper whisky, and lots of meat." Ginny frowned as she looked at the meagre boiled egg and toast that was delivered to her, not the eggs and bacon that were served to Harriet and Nicole. "Don't I get bacon?" she frowned at the steward.

"Sorry, Ma'am. Aircrew only," the steward replied.

"I'm an Observer!" She pointed to her brevet.

"Are you flying today, Ma'am?"

"No..." she sighed. "Neither are they..." she muttered irritably under her breath while looking at Harriet and Nicole as the steward walked away in apparent blissful ignorance. Both smirked, then donated a piece of bacon each, putting it on Ginny's plate before she could argue.

"Welcome to the squadron," Harriet said, then poured Ginny a cup of tea from the pot that had been left on the table.

"So, when are the rest of the squadron arriving?"

"Over the next few days. We haven't even got any aeroplanes yet."

"Some squadron."

"You don't know the half of it."

"Oh well, it's nice to know the RAF hasn't changed. Still making half thought through decisions."

"Are you settled in the Mess?"

"Yes, the room's quite nice, though there's only two of us in the whole block at the moment."

"Who's the other?"

"Jo Bird."

"Who?"

"Of course. You have as much idea of what's going on as I do... Flight Officer Jo Bird. A WAAF Engineering Officer. She's one of yours, too. Apparently."

"They're putting all of the women in one place," Nicole said. "If the airfield gets bombed next week, you know why." They all smiled as they went about eating their breakfast, knowing full well that while she said it in jest, they wouldn't be surprised if it happened.

After breakfast, they squeezed into the two seat car and raced down to the dispersal, ready for a day of the unknown. There were no pilots, no aeroplanes, no spares, and no orders, other than to train a squadron that so far only existed on paper. The AOC had given Harriet a month to get the squadron operational. If the first day was anything to go by, it'd take a month just for them to materialise, let alone get them flying.

"Jo!" Ginny shouted, as she stepped out of the car and waved at the uniformed blonde woman walking out of the hangar. She waved back, and walked over the Ginny with a smile on her face.

"Didn't realise you had such a nice car," Jo said as she looked at the MG, not noticing Harriet and Nicole bickering inside.

"I don't; it belongs to the new skipper." She turned and nodded in Harriet's direction as she climbed out of the car.

"Ma'am," Jo said as she stood smartly to attention and saluted.

"You must be Jo Bird," Harriet said as she returned the salute, then offered her hand.

"Yes, Ma'am."

"At ease. This is Flight Lieutenant Nicole Delacourt, my Second in Command." Nicole shook Jo's hand politely. "I'm told you're my new Engineering Officer?"

"Yes, Ma'am."

"Harry will do when nobody else is around. These two excepted, they've known me long enough not to care. So, as our engineer, I'm assuming you know when our aeroplanes will be arriving?"

"No idea. We're ready for them, though. Most of the girls have come from operational squadrons or maintenance units, and we're all keen to go."

"Well, that's something... Did you say girls?"

"Every last one of us."

"Good..." Harriet smiled.

"Watch for the bombs..." Nicole said as she rolled her eyes.

"Bombs?" Jo asked nervously.

"Ignore her..." Harriet said with a smile. "So, other than having no aeroplanes, is there anything else I need to worry about?"

"I don't have any spares. We've got tools, but nothing to fix, and no spare parts to fix it with."

"That seems to be par for the course today. We'll see if we can find out what's going on, then we can get busy ordering spares."

"I've got the ground crews scrubbing the hangar and offices for the time being. The last lot left it like a pigsty." At that, the unique and distinctive sound of Merlin engines hummed in the distance, and Harriet scanned the blue sky. "Ours?"

"I don't know... Maybe?"

"There!" Nicole said, pointing to the south at a line of tiny dots.

"Well, the other squadron based here is on Halifax bombers, so it's not them," Jo said.

"Could be passing, on their way somewhere else."

"No, they're coming in," Harriet said, as the line of dots started a curved approach towards the airfield. "They're not ours, though."

"How do you know?" Ginny asked.

"They're Hurricanes, obsolete as fighters. Even the RAF don't hate us that much." They watched as one after the other, the line of Mk2c Hurricanes with their twin 20mm cannons on each wing landed and rolled down the runway. "A ground attack squadron passing through, no doubt. Oh well, let's get to work. Ginny, do you want to work your magic on the phone, and see if you can find out what's going on?"

"Anything in particular you want me to work on first?"

"Finding us some aeroplanes would be nice..."

"I'll see what I can do. Short of that, I'll get us all a transfer to the Navy. At least they have rum."

"That's more than we have," Nicole said, as the first of the Hurricanes taxied up to the control tower in the distance and shut down.

"Help Ginny if you're bored," Harriet replied. "Maybe call the NAAFI, too, and ask them what time the tea truck will be coming around?" Nicole shrugged and walked off towards the dispersal hut, leaving Harriet and Jo. "Right, let's go meet your crew." They walked into the hangar, where an army of women in overalls were brushing, polishing, and dusting from the top down. There were even some more acrobatic types at the top of the hangar, hanging off beams and cleaning lights, which had Harriet watching them nervously in case they fell. Jo gave the loudest wolf whistle Harriet had ever heard, which echoed around the hangar and got everyone's attention. She waved at them to join her, and they all quickly formed a squad, which Jo brought to attention. Even the acrobats managed to get down in record time.

"I'd like to introduce you to our new Commanding Officer," Jo started. "Squadron Leader Harriet Cornwall." She paused for a moment to let her WAAFs digest what she'd said. "As the more astute of you will know, Squadron Leader Cornwall is a fighter ace with victories in France, Malta, and the Battle of Britain, and she's the best fighter pilot in the RAF by a long way. She's fought and won against Germans, Italians, and even the Japanese, and we're honoured to have the opportunity to maintain the aeroplanes that will take her and her pilots into battle." Jo turned to face Harriet, who was doing her best to stop herself blushing, and gave her a smart salute, which was returned with as much confidence as could be managed.

"At ease," Harriet said, and the parade of WAAFs stood at ease. Every one of them stared at her, and she felt her throat go dry. "Thank you..." she said to Jo before addressing the amassed ground crew. "Whatever stories you've heard, however many pilots you've talked to, the truth is that absolutely nothing could have happened in France, Malta, or anywhere else if it wasn't for the ground crews. Fighter pilots are in the air for an hour, maybe, two at the most, and they're in combat for seconds, but it's the hours of hard work put in by the fitters, riggers, armourers, and every other trade on the ground that make the magic happen. Remember that, and remember that the aeroplanes we fly belong to you. As do our victories and successes.

I'm looking forward to working with you all." To her surprise, a round of applause started. She wasn't expecting it, but before she could blush, she was saved by the roar of a Merlin engine outside the hangar. "Right, get back to work. I'd better go and see what that's all about." She turned and marched away as quickly as she could, desperate to escape the unscripted applause, and stepped outside to see a Hurricane shutting down on the dispersal, and others following from the direction of the tower.

"Squadron Leader Cornwall?" the Air Transport Auxiliary pilot asked as he jumped down from the wing. He was an older man, as many in the ATA were. Pilots too old or too broken for combat service, but still wanting to do their part in delivering aircraft around the country. Ancient and Tattered Airmen, as they were known in the RAF, except for the female section, which had grown to well over a hundred strong since the days that Harriet was one of their number, and mostly young, glamorous, and anything but tattered. They even featured on the covers of magazines, and could often be found at some of the most exclusive parties in London.

"Yes..." she replied as she walked over to meet him. Nicole and Ginny were on their way to join them, too, and as she looked over her shoulder, she saw that Jo and all of the ground crew were watching from the hangar.

"Good! Found you at last! I'm told you were expecting us."

"What?" She was dumbstruck, and couldn't think of anything more eloquent to say.

"Squadron Leader Cornwall, 508 Squadron Auxiliary Air Force?" He checked his paperwork to be sure he'd got the right place.

"Yes...?"

"Well, these fine machines are yours. Hurricane Mk2c. Sixteen of them altogether, with more on the way this afternoon."

"Hurricanes..."

"That's right. If I can get you to sign for them? We have a couple of Ansons following us in, and we need a quick turnaround so we can get the rest to you." He handed Harriet the delivery chit, which she reviewed, as one by one, the other Hurricanes cut their engines after forming two neat lines on the dispersal. Harriet sighed as she watched a pair of Anson transports swooping in to land, just as he'd said.

"You're sure these are for us?"

"Positive. Says so right there." He tapped the paperwork, which she read for the fifth time before reluctantly signing it. The pilots formed a queue for her to sign their delivery chits, and as soon as she'd signed them all, they were heading over to the waiting Ansons. "We'll have the rest to you this afternoon at the latest. Cheerio!"

"Bye…" Harriet said quietly as she watched them leave.

"They're giving us Hurricanes?" Nicole asked, as she stood beside Harriet and looked at the neat lines of aeroplanes.

"Looks that way…"

"Hurricanes haven't been used as fighters for years. Not in this country, at least. They're not fast enough."

"Hush…" Harriet whispered as she turned to see the shocked expressions on the faces of the ground crew. "Whatever happens, they've got to believe that we're confident. Like we expected it, and it's part of the plan. They can't think we're being treated differently to other squadrons."

"We are…"

"I know!" She turned to face Jo and the ground crew. "Right, I want them stripped down and checked over, and a serviceability report on my desk by lunch", she shouted confidently. "Flight Officer Bird, get on to headquarters and order all the spares you think we'll need!" Jo nodded in response, and at a shout, the ground crews formed a squad, ready for her to assign them to their steads. "I'll be back…" Harriet whispered to Nicole and Ginny. "Let them see you being positive. I'll talk to you in a while." She marched away to her car, jumped in, and sped off towards station headquarters, scattering a squad of airmen marching along the road as she passed, then screeched to a halt before heading up to Al's office.

Al held up his hand as Charlie showed Harriet into his office. He was sitting behind his desk with his phone glued to his ear, while shaking his head and rolling his eyes at her in frustration.

"Tea?" Charlie whispered to Harriet, who shook her head. She felt herself shaking, and it was taking every effort not to put Al's phone down for him so she could say her piece, which was bursting to get out of her.

"I know what you're going to say," Al said as he put the phone down. "I've just been on to Group Headquarters, and the official word is that we're to shut up and get on with it. I say we, but of course, they mean you."

"Hurricanes?" Harriet asked, as Charlie backed out and closed the door, knowing when it was best to make herself scarce.

"Apparently."

"We're supposed to be a fighter squadron. If we go up against 109s in those old buckets, the RAF will very quickly have one less squadron, and you'll have lots of letters to write to the pilots' next of kin!"

"Harry, what can I say? As soon as I got word from the tower, I was on the phone to Group HQ. Apparently, all spare Spitfires are being prioritised for the 2nd Tactical Air Force for operations over Europe. Bomber escorts, fighters sweeps, that sort of thing. All there is available for you is Hurricanes.'

"Sir!"

"Al..."

"We'll be massacred!"

"Not necessarily… You're assigned to air defence. I can't see there being many 109s swanning around England these days; the most you'll bump into is a stray bomber here and there, and the Hurricane can more than handle itself against them." He stood and walked around his desk, trying his best to calm her, as he could see she was physically shaking with anger. "Look, it's not ideal, I know. I'll have words and see if I can get some more sensible answers, but for now, we'll have to make do."

"Bloody Hurricanes!" she barked, then left his office and went back down to the car. She was furious. The RAF really were trying to deal with their problems all at the same time. There wouldn't be any female pilots to worry about if they were all dead. She sped back to the dispersal, where she took a deep breath to compose herself before stepping out of the car. The ground crews were a hive of activity around the aeroplanes. Cowlings were off, cannons were being checked, and a fuel bowser was topping up the tanks. She took another deep breath and smiled, remembering her own words to Nicole, then went into the dispersal hut and closed the door behind her, before heading into her office.

"Well?" Nicole asked.

"You already know the answer… Look, we need to make this work. The three of us can talk about it when we're alone, but in front of everyone else, we've got to put on an act. The squadron has to believe that us getting Hurricanes is the best possible outcome. Nicole, you and I have flown Hurricanes in combat, and we've shot down Messerschmitt 109s in them. We can do this."

"The 109s were old models, Harry, you know that!" Nicole pleaded. "The new models will run rings around us; we won't stand a chance."

"No! The Hurricane is a good aeroplane, and the ones we have are armed with four 20mm cannons. With a good pilot behind the controls, we'll more than hold our own. We're just going to have to be smart with our training, that's all. As soon as the pilots are here, we need to drill them in tactics and combat flying. The stuff we did in Malta, not what they get taught in training. We're going to do this, and we're going to show the bloody Air Ministry that they're not going to make us go away!" Harriet boomed. "They want us to quit. They want us to say no to flying Hurricanes, so they can say they tried, but female pilots refused to fly, and I'm not letting them get away with it!" She was shaking with defiance as she slammed her hand on the desk.

"OK," Nicole said with a smile. "If that's their game, I'm in."

"Me too," Ginny said. "We can do this."

"OK…" Harriet looked around while thinking. "Nicole, you were an instructor, and you flew Hurricanes in Malta. Create me a training plan that will give our pilots the edge. We can't outrun a 109, and certainly not a Focke Wulf 190. We can't out climb them, or out dive them. That means all we've got are our turns. Whatever you put together, that has to be our main tactic.

"I'll start right away."

"Ginny, we need all the supplies we can get our hands on. I don't want the pilots wanting for anything. Their time and energy need to be focused on flying and training; we can't afford for them to be distracted by anything else. I ll give you the list of names we're expecting. Get the rooms assigned, and get the ground crews to make sure they're set up. I want breakfast served first thing, before anyone else is up and about, and we'll have lunch down here at the dispersal. Talk with the chefs, make sure everything's here on time, every time. We're going to have a lot of work to do…" A cough from the main room in the dispersal hut caught Harriet's attention, and she walked through to see a short WAAF Corporal. "Yes?"

"Corporal Deutsch, Ma'am. I was told to report here." She had a soft voice with the slightest of accents.

"Deutsch? As in German?" Harriet frowned; she wasn't expecting visitors, and had a lot more on her mind.

"Yes, Ma'am... Most people call me Dutch."

"What do you do?"

"I'm a clerk, Ma'am. I was told I'm assigned to your squadron."

"Good. Ginny, your right hand's just arrived." Ginny walked through and looked at the tiny young woman. "Flight Lieutenant Russel is the Adjutant; you'll work with her to make sure the squadron stays operational. You're going to have to be sharp, or we'll need a replacement."

"I can do sharp, Ma'am."

"We'll soon see…"

## Chapter 3

## Back In The Saddle

After two days of frustration, the squadron's Hurricanes were as ready as they could be. Twenty had arrived in total, one of which gave up as soon as it arrived, and no matter what Jo and her engineers tried, there was no getting it to work consistently. Sometimes the engine would misfire, sometimes it would cut out, and other times, when the engine actually worked fine, the undercarriage would stick, or the flaps, or any of a hundred different things that could go wrong, did. It was what the ground crew called a hangar queen. When there were no obvious answers left, Harriet requested a replacement and was told to wait, so she and Nicole went flying instead. Nicole had written a training programme that was as technical as it was intense. The pilots were going to be eased in with formation flying and basic tactics, and once they were warmed up, it was simulated combat morning, noon, and night. Instead of spending any more time arguing with the RAF, Harriet thought it would be better if she and Nicole got to grips with the Hurricane again themselves, while testing out some of Nicole's training sessions. They went up three times in the morning, each time heading up to twenty thousand feet and getting stuck into each other. Taking it in turns playing enemy, while the other twisted and turned to try and get away. It was tiring work, but Harriet couldn't help but smile all the way through it. The Hurricane was her first love, and she'd developed an instinct for flying it to the limit of its performance. A skill that came from knowing she'd have died over Malta if she didn't. After the first sortie, she felt she was back as a confident fighter pilot, as was Nicole, and they went at each other as though they were back in the Mediterranean taking on the Luftwaffe's finest. Nicole's extended time as a combat instructor showed, and she had Harriet on the ropes a few times, though every now and then, she tried to fly the Hurricane like it was a Mosquito, which opened the door for Harriet to take advantage of a slow reaction or silly mistake. As a treat after their third sortie, they went visiting and landed at Archie's airfield, where they were welcomed like long lost relatives and taken to lunch while they talked about the old days, and the new, and got Archie's agreement for his Mosquitoes to play enemy for the pilots when time allowed.

After lunch, they took a flight east and did a couple of circuits around aunt Mary's house before heading back to the airfield. Harriet had called and let aunt Mary know she and Nicole were going to be local for a month and promised to visit when they got time, and even stay if there was enough time off. She was in the garden when they circled, and waved up at them, getting a wing waggle in return. It was something that made Harriet smile. She liked being able to fly over her home and wave to her family; it was something many didn't get to do. As they finally returned, they did a pass of the airfield before coming in to land, and shutting down as they stopped at the dispersal.

"How is she?" Jo asked, as she met Harriet at the wing.

"Perfect," Harriet replied with a smile. "I could do with another fifty miles per hour, if you could manage that...?"

"I might be able to squeeze another two or three at best, if that'll do?"

"I'll take it..." She smiled at the two young women who'd come to check the Hurricane over. A Corporal, Beth Morgan, and a Leading Aircraftwoman, Grace Billington. Jo had assured Harriet that they were the best when she assigned them as her ground crew, and so far, she'd been right. "Get her ready. We may go up again later."

"I think you may be busy, Ma'am," Jo said, as she pointed to the sand and blue uniformed bodies extracting themselves from the back of the truck that had rolled to a halt outside the dispersal hut.

"Pilots?" Nicole asked as she joined Harriet.

"Let's go see," Harriet replied with a smile. Dutch was at the truck's tailgate, standing with a clipboard and scribbling details as she talked to the four women, who were surrounding her wearing long blue coats and sandstone coloured skirts. She looked up and pointed in Harriet's direction, and the four turned their heads to look. Harriet was already smiling so much that her jaw was hurting by the time she was in front of them.

"Flight Lieutenant Lexington reporting for duty, Ma'am," the golden American said formally while saluting Harriet.

"Lexi…" Harriet replied. It was the first time she'd seen her American friend since 1940, when she and the other ATA girls were sent to train as fighter pilots, and she hadn't heard much of her since. She'd always been golden. Her skin, her hair, her personality even, always perfectly Californian, but she was more tanned than ever, her almost mahogany skin lighting up her blue eyes and brilliant white teeth, and her hair was shimmering like spun gold. "Gabi," she gave a nod to the smiling and equally as golden ice blonde standing by Lexi's side. Another of her ATA friends, a Polish girl who'd flown an unarmed communications aeroplane out of Poland to escape the Nazi invasion, and was always so angry that when she got to England, the RAF wouldn't let her fight.

"Flight Sergeant Alice Adams, Royal Australian Air Force," Lexi introduced the tall, lean blonde next to her, "and Flight Sergeant Puck Van de Windt of the Netherlands East Indies." She pointed to the next blonde. Each of them was deeply tanned, and their hair bleached different shades of gold.

"Harry Cornwall." She shook their hands in turn, as did Nicole. "Nice to meet you both; this is my second in command, Nicole Delacourt. Welcome to the Squadron." She gave them a smile, while looking them up and down. "Though I'm not sure you're dressed for England in winter…" She looked to Lexi enquiringly, raising her eyebrow.

"It's what we have," she shrugged, lifting her dusty half empty kit bag. "We've been in the desert the last couple of years, and lost most of our possessions. The first civilisation we've seen was the train here from London."

"You've come from the desert?"

"Yes, Ma'am, North Africa. We got orders a couple of days ago telling us to pack up and get our asses to England, and here we are. We didn't have time for much more than a quick wash up, and certainly no time for shopping. Some officer took pity on us when we landed and gave us these coats. Otherwise, we'd be blue in a different way."

"I'm so sorry... I didn't know. When did you last eat?"

"Before we left North Africa."

"Dutch, call the Mess and tell them to put food on for four pilots right away, my orders." She turned and waved at the dispersal hut, and Ginny came out to join them. "Ginny, this is Lexi. She and her friends have just arrived from the desert. Can you get their measurements down to my tailor in London right away? Give him my regards, and ask if he'd please provide them with uniforms as soon as he can. Let him know it's urgent, and I'll call him later to settle the bill."

"Ma'am," Ginny replied as she turned to leave.

"And Ginny, can we send a car into town to go and fetch some toiletries for them, and any other personal bits and pieces they need."

"I'll get on it."

"Lexi, Ginny's our Adjutant. You and your girls give her a list of the personal effects you need, and she'll have them to you before dinner. Ginny, call the stores, see if they have some WAAF issue uniforms for the time being."

"Right, let's get a list. Dutch?" Ginny said, and the young Corporal turned a clean sheet of paper on her clipboard, and stood ready with her pencil.

"Lexi, I can't tell you how good it is to see you," Harriet said with a warm smile. "Get settled in, and we'll catch up at dinner. Corporal Deutsch will take you down to the Mess so you can clean up and have lunch.

"I almost daren't ask why we've been summoned here?" the glamorous Californian asked with a mischievous smile.

"I'll tell you all at dinner. It's nothing bad though, I promise," she said as she gave Lexi and the others a reassuring smile. "Dutch, I'll call the

Mess for you. You get the shopping list and get them down to the Mess."

"You know, they didn't even pay us before we left..."

"Don't worry about it; we'll put it on the squadron account. It's the least the RAF can do for you."

"You have an account?"

"We'll soon find out."

After seeing them off, Nicole joined Harriet in her office, and they had tea from the flask that had been delivered from the Mess. Nicole repeated her misgivings in a more genuine tone than she had previously, keeping her words hushed so Ginny wouldn't hear while she was on the phone in the next room. The lack of care the RAF had shown to Lexi and her group was just another nail in the coffin after the Hurricanes. Harriet agreed, though she wasn't about to say it out loud. She was beyond furious that four female pilots would be dragged out of the desert and sent home to England in winter with hardly any kit, not even warm coats. More than that, she was disappointed. When she'd first been told about the squadron, she believed that finally women had been accepted, but even though it had only been a few days, she was starting to come around to Nicole's way of thinking.

Another handful of pilots arrived during the afternoon, while Harriet and Nicole were fine tuning the training schedule. Harriet hadn't met any of them, and they didn't know each other that well either. They'd come from units scattered across the country. Some had been used as ferry pilots; others towed targets for the anti aircraft artillery to shoot at in training. Two had been in fighter squadrons, but neither had done much flying. They were quiet and nervous, and their arrival just added to Nicole's sense of foreboding.

"I'm hungry..." Nicole said, as she smoked a cigarette while watching the sunset.

"You're always hungry," Harriet replied. "And you should stop smoking those things; they're not good for you."

"Less dangerous than a Hurricane right now."

"You're going to need to stop that."

"What? It's true," Nicole shrugged.

"I know, but that doesn't help anyone. Lexi's lot have something about them, but the others that arrived look like they've been kept a long way from any action. We need to focus on making them feel better, not making us feel worse."

"I don't feel worse; I feel hungry."

"You're going to be hard work…"

"Nonsense, I'm a delight."

"Well, take your delightful self inside and tell Ginny and Dutch we're knocking off."

"Then we can go eat?"

"I suppose." Harriet rolled her eyes as Nicole threw her cigarette into the sand filled tin by the door, and ran into the dispersal hut. Harriet checked her watch, then looked up to see a truck rolling towards her. She watched and waited to see who was dispensed from it this time, and felt a little weary at the thought of more inexperienced pilots being sent to the slaughter. A single figure jumped out of the cab, and dragged a large kitbag out with them, then waved the truck off as it left before walking over to Harriet.

"There had better be a good reason I've been posted away from my job flying photographic reconnaissance," AP said with narrowed eyes as she stood in front of Harriet in her long overcoat, with her kitbag slung over her shoulder.

"I was wondering when you'd get here..." Harriet replied, unable to keep her smile in. She stepped forward and threw her arms around AP; after the previous few days, she was happy to see a competent, confident, and appropriately dressed face.

"I'm not sure you're allowed to hug your subordinates," AP replied, while patting Harriet on the back.

"I'm not sure I care," Harriet replied, while giving AP a tight squeeze. "We're about to go to the Mess for dinner. Hungry?"

"I'm sure I'll force something down. Then you can tell me why I'm here."

Dinner was filled with conversation about where people had been and what they'd been doing, and Harriet felt herself glowing to be surrounded by her friends. Ginny had joined them after finishing up at the dispersal, and when they'd finished their meals, Harriet asked her, Nicole, AP, and Lexi to join her for a drink in the Mess anteroom. She bought them a whisky each, and they moved to a quiet corner of the room, where they pulled their deep leather armchairs into a circle.

"So, if you haven't already realised what's going on," Harriet started. "The Air Ministry have made the unlikely and unexpected decision to raise an all female fighter squadron. I won't get into the politics of it, but as a result, I've been ordered to form the squadron, and the three of you are my new flight commanders." She looked at Nicole, AP, and Lexi in turn, and watched as they fought the smiles that were turning up the corners of their mouths. "I'm going to run the squadron the same way as we did it in the Battle of Britain. Three flights of four, with two sections of two in each flight, flying in loose pairs. It's how the Luftwaffe do it, and it works. Nicole, you'll lead A Flight, and you'll be my Second in Command. AP, you get B Flight, and C Flight's yours, Lexi."

"What about you?" AP asked. "Retired from flying?"

"I'll lead the squadron with my number two, and I won't get in the way of you leading your flights." She pulled a piece of paper from her pocket and placed it on the table between them. "I'll leave you to decide between you who's in who's flight." She downed her whisky and stood to leave. "Training starts first thing tomorrow morning. We've only got a little over three weeks to get ourselves operational, so it's going to be hard work. Better get an early night." She gave them all a smile, then left the anteroom. A little bit of her was disappointed that she wasn't staying in the Mess, but she knew that she needed to separate herself a little, not only because she was in command, but because it was vitally important that they spent time with their pilots and developed their teams.

It was hard to sleep when Harriet finally settled in the cottage. It was cold. The fire hadn't been lit, so instead of sitting up and shivering, she went straight to bed, where she lay tossing and turning for hours as she thought through what was to come. Only half of her pilots had arrived, and most that had got there didn't have a clue what was expected of them. Then there was the issue of their skills. Lexi told her over dinner that she and the three that arrived with her and flown together in the desert for a long time, taking Hurricanes into action against the Germans and Italians over the desert; though they spent most of their time flying ground attack sorties, and shooting up tanks, trucks, and anything that moved. They had the most experience, and they were going to be useful, but some of the others had done nothing more than ferry flights or instructing basic flight, and had never been anywhere near combat. Then there was the Hurricanes. She was determined to make the best of the situation, but having outdated aircraft for fighter defence was asking for trouble. The thoughts haunted her until finally, she fell asleep sometime after midnight, leaving her to feel rotten when she woke with her alarm.

It was still dark when Harriet arrived at the dispersal. Unsurprisingly, Ginny was waiting for her, and greeted her with a cup of tea made with fresh leaves she'd bought from Fortnum's on her shopping trip before departing for the north.

"Good morning, sunshine!" Ginny said cheerily as she handed over the tea. The dispersal hut was warm; the potbellied stove had been lit and stoked, and it radiated a welcome heat.

"Is there ever a time when you're not painfully pleasant?" Harriet asked after sipping on the warm, sweet tea.

"It's a new day; what's not to be happy about?"

"It's far too early for you..."

"For me to what?"

"For you in general!"

"I have some good news for you."

"Go on..."

"All of your remaining pilots arrived overnight, and all are sorted into their flights." She pointed to the board on the wall with the pilots' names listed under their flights. "The stores will be open at seven for them to collect their flying kit and anything else they may need, and there's an early breakfast for them as requested. We've even got a truck to cart them around in, so they don't have to lose valuable training time walking here and there."

"Do you ever actually sleep? Or do you just spend your nights badgering storemen and cooks?"

"You're welcome." She gave Harriet a wink.

"I may just go back to bed and leave you to run the show."

"You could, but I don't fly. You're needed."

"You have a pilot's licence and an Observer's brevet. You can fly; you have flown."

"Not fighters, no thanks. Give me a little Gypsy Moth, and I'll be fine. Even the right hand seat of a Mosquito was a bit questionable, especially when people started shooting at me. I think I'll stay on the ground, but thanks for the consideration."

"What time are they due here?'

"An hour. I told the driver to take them to the stores on their way here. Save having to go back again."

"Makes sense." Harriet walked through to her office, where she slung her flying jacket and hat on the stand in the corner, then sat at her desk and looked at the pile of paperwork waiting for her. "This makes less sense..."

"Stores orders, parts requisitions, daily reports, personnel reports. All need a Commanding Officer's signature if this squadron is going to get past the first week."

"Thanks..."

"You're welcome. The personal files for all the pilots arrived, too. They're in your filing cabinet if you want to have a read."

"Aren't you missing Scotland?"

"Dreadfully. Why, are you going to send me back there?"

"No. I just like to know you're suffering as much as me sometimes." She smirked at Ginny, who did a polite curtsy, then took a seat at her own desk and started on her paperwork with a smile. Harriet sat for a while and watched her in the dimly lit room. It was quiet and peaceful. Cas had once said it was the best time of the day. Before sunrise, when the air was cool, and you've no idea what the day will bring. She put her pen down and took her cup of tea outside, and walked along the line of Hurricanes, their dark silhouettes standing black against the royal blue of the dawn twilight sky. Despite the peacefulness, the aeroplanes stood proud and confident, like they were ready for battle, and she couldn't help but smile, despite her concerns that they were past their prime. She climbed up on her own aeroplane and sat on the wing while drinking her tea and watching as the ground crews jumped from their transport truck, and went about opening up the hangar doors and preparing for their day. She knew she had her paperwork to do, but right at that moment, it was the last thing on her mind. It was just nice to be outside in the cool morning air and not overthinking things. "Good morning, ladies," she said as her ground crew approached the Hurricane.

"Morning, Ma'am," they replied in unison. They looked at each other, a little surprised that Harriet would be there waiting for them.

"We're going to have a busy flying day today, so she's going to need to be at her best."

"Yes, Ma'am," came the reply, as Harriet pulled herself to her feet, then jumped down from the wing without spilling what remained of her tea. She gave them a smile, then walked over to the hangar, where she found Jo checking through service logs for the aircraft.

"How are things looking?"

"Surprisingly good," Jo replied. "All except the hangar queen are serviceable and ready to go. They're old, but they've been looked after. Engines are running fine, airframes are in good condition, and guns are looking good. They'll need an air test, of course, but they got here, so we know they fly."

"Good. Have your ground crews get them ready; we're going to have a busy day."

"Already on it. I've written up the service schedules, and if we can get the queen repaired." She nodded at the malfunctioning Hurricane in the corner of the hangar. "I'll be able to give you sixteen flying most days. It'll be tight, and we'll be pulling some night shifts, but I think we can do it."

"Thanks. It's going to be hard on your people, but we don't have long to get the pilots up to speed, so every hour is going to count."

"We won't let you down. Just try not to break any."

"No promises..." She smiled, then left, heading back to her desk.

"Better?" Ginny asked, without looking up from her work.

"Much," Harriet replied, then went about signing the documents piled in front of her. The cool air had chilled her a little, enough to wake her up with the help of the tea. The work was tedious but essential, and she thought back to her time in Kent when Max had been shot down. She'd been left in charge of the squadron, and after a day of being called up to fight, again and again, she'd spent the warm evening sitting at a desk and filling out paperwork under Cas' tuition, while Nicole sat outside smoking and soaking up the sun. She'd never imagined back then that she'd actually be commanding a squadron. She'd had Command in Malta and Scotland, but this felt very different. She wasn't a caretaker, it was all hers, and there was a lot of pressure that came with it. As tests went, it was a big one. Maybe the biggest she'd faced, in a way. The sound of a truck pulling up outside disturbed her daydreams, and she walked over to the window and watched as the tailgate dropped, and one by one, the pilots jumped to the ground.

"Showtime…" Ginny said as she stood beside Harriet and watched.

"Something like that," Harriet smirked, then headed outside as the truck drove off and left the gathered pilots in the half light of dawn. "Good morning, ladies," she said as she approached, and they fell quiet and stood to attention. "Is there anyone here who hasn't flown a Hurricane?" She looked around the dark faces, and was relieved when no hands went up. "The sun will be up in half an hour, and we won't be far behind it. Today's evaluation day. If you can't handle a Hurricane, you'll be back at the unit you came from by breakfast tomorrow. We don't have room for passengers. Flight commanders, I'll see you in my office." She turned and walked away, with Niccole, AP, and Lexi following close behind. She nodded for Ginny to close the door, which she did, respectfully staying outside and leaving Harriet to talk to them. "Have you had a chance to talk to your pilots?" she asked, and they all nodded silently. "Good. I want you to evaluate your pilots this morning. Get them up, and see how they are with the Hurricane. I've marked a training area on the chart in the main room, and you're to keep within it. Handling is everything, and they need to be able to use their surroundings, whether that's hiding in the clouds or dropping to the ground and hiding between the hills. We'll meet at lunch and discuss how they're doing, then each flight will get the opportunity to show their stuff over the airfield this afternoon. Any questions?" They shook their heads. Each had a look of confidence that bordered on defiance, which made her smile as the hairs on the back of her neck stood up with pride and excitement. "Better get to it; you'll want to brief them before take off. Just remember what we're going to be asking them to do when we're made operational. Don't go easy on them."

Harriet watched and listened as each of her flight commanders briefed their pilots, staying far enough away not to be a distraction, but close enough to get a feel for the quality of the briefing, and how the pilots responded. She then walked around the Hurricanes, and watched as the briefed pilots went through their checks. Again, she stayed far enough from them to not be in the way, but close enough to see their attention to detail and the looks on their faces. Few of them looked at her, and when they did, it was nothing more than a fleeting glance with hardly an acknowledgement. They went around their work professionally and without mistake, and when it came to taking off, every one of them lifted from the ground with perfect ease. Not even a flinch or a wobble. She smiled to herself, then went back to her office to read through their files and better understand the young women she was leading. She'd been given twenty one pilots in total, seven to each flight, and those that weren't currently flying had been sent by their flight commanders to the hangar to work with the ground crews on refreshing their knowledge of the Hurricane, and as Harriet looked into the hangar when passing, all nine of them were sitting in a circle while Jo Bird gave them a briefing on the Hurricane's parameters and handling. Back in her office, she poured a cup of tea for Ginny and Dutch, then sat at her desk and started working through the files. Of the twenty one she'd been given, she knew six, Nicole, AP, Lexi, and Gabi, and two of the girls she'd trained in California. The others were a blank slate, quite literally in most cases, because their files were basic at best, with hardly any detail. Some had been instructors in Canada, some had been on maintenance units in England, transporting and testing newly refitted aeroplanes before they were taken to their squadrons. Others had been ferrying aircraft, the same as the ATA. A small number had been posted to fighter squadrons but hadn't done much while there, and all in all, there wasn't a great deal of combat experience, or at least none that was documented. Lexi and her pilots from North Africa had the most experience, though even their files were as sparse as everyone else's, and merely suggested that they'd been deployed in the desert. It made the whole exercise of reading the files a waste of time. To add to her irritation at the apparent neglect the files had seen, of the twenty one pilots posted to the squadron, all but six were non commissioned officers, Sergeants or Flight Sergeants. It didn't make a difference to the person, but in Harriet's mind, it showed that nobody had really paid much attention to them. Nobody had thought about their development or progression, and the reports in their files said as much. She put the files back in the filing cabinet where they belonged, and went about dealing with the steadily growing mountain of paperwork Ginny was merrily creating for her.

At the end of the first day of training, where the pilots had been evaluated in their handling skills on a series of flights designed to test them in every aspect of flying, it was time for the final assessment that determined whether they'd be staying. Nicole had created the training plan and shared it with AP and Lexi in the Mess, so they all knew what they were looking for from their pilots, and when Al unexpectedly joined Harriet standing on the control tower balcony in the late afternoon sun, she was confident that he would be impressed. Or at least she was hoping as much. There would be six sorties in all, two from each flight, giving all pilots the opportunity to show what they were capable of. The first was inbound, the four Hurricanes flying in a loose finger four formation as they raced towards the airfield.

"How are they doing?" Al asked. He was excited at the prospect of watching the display. He'd just so happened to be visiting the control tower for no apparent reason, and after talking to Harriet and finding out what was happening, he'd decided to stay and see how his new charges were getting on.

"We'll soon see," Harriet replied as she pointed to the approaching Hurricanes. Her heart raced a little in anticipation as they arrived at the airfield, hoping that Nicole's opening display wouldn't have Al questioning her ability to command a squadron. She needn't have worried. The Hurricanes gave a perfect flying display, breaking into pairs that split either side of the tower at high speed before joining together and playing follow the leader, as Nicole led them in a series of loops and rolls, before landing in pairs and rolling quickly to the dispersal to hand their aeroplanes over to the others in their flight. Next came AP's B Flight, who opened with a long and winding flypast of the tower, which extended into a steady climbing turn, circling the Hurricanes in perfect formation before rolling off the top of their climb and diving down elegantly, levelling and rolling before landing. It was difficult to see Lexi's C Flight, until they hopped over the perimeter fence at zero feet and raced towards the tower so low that they could have cut the grass with their propellers. Harriet's heart raced as they pulled up in front of the tower in a vertical climb, before peeling off into diving rolls towards the ground. It was an incredible display.

"That's a pretty good show, Harry," Al said while they waited for the pilots to switch, so the second round could get underway. "Seems they think so, too." He pointed down at the bomber crews gathering on the hard standing below the tower. "Being a bomber station, we don't get to see fighter displays that often. It seems the lads are enjoying the treat." Harriet looked at them for a moment, then turned her head as the twelve Hurricanes took off in their flights, and circled over the airfield before heading north to prepare for their displays.

"Squadron Leader Cornwall," Charlie said as she stepped out onto the balcony.

"Yes?" Harriet replied as she turned.

"Somebody to see you..." She stood aside, and a young woman stepped out in her best uniform and saluted.

"Flying Officer Stone reporting for duty, Ma'am," she said formally.

"Carrie Stone..." Harriet said with a smile, as she recognised the girl she'd first met in Kent when she was recovering from her experiences in France, and then again when she trained her in California. "I don't remember seeing your name on my posting list."

"No, Ma'am..." Carrie replied, swallowing nervously, but not offering anything else.

"Well?" Harriet raised her eyebrow questioningly.

"I was supposed to be on the list, Ma'am, but I was in hospital when it was finalised."

"Hospital?"

"Yes, Ma'am. I was involved in a crash, and the Medical Officer insisted that I be sent to the hospital. Unfortunately, that meant my CO wasn't able to release me at the time, but I'm here now…"

"What sort of crash?"

"A Blenheim. It lost an engine on take off, and I ended up in the woods. I'm OK, though." She squared her shoulders confidently as Harriet looked at her for a moment, while listening to the sound of approaching Merlin engines. She nodded to the railing beside her, and Carrie walked over and joined her in watching part two of the display, as Hurricanes roared and rolled, looping, diving, and slipping through the sky to the cheers of the massed army of bomber crews and ground crews that had now gathered below the tower.

"Can I keep her?" Harriet asked Al as quietly as she could, as a pair of Hurricanes rolled past the tower.

"She seems keen enough to be here," he replied in an equally quiet whisper, not taking his eyes off the Hurricanes.

"Thank you… Also... I need to make a few administrative changes to pull the squadron together into a tight team, something to get them over the Hurricane issue."

"Whatever you need, I'll support you." He gave her a wink as he briefly glanced away from following the Hurricanes. "If you can do this in a day, I can't wait to see what you've done in a month."

"We won't let you down."

"I know…" He kept his eyes on the Hurricanes, and Harriet smiled as she joined him watching. Her heart still raced, hoping nothing would go wrong at the last minute, but she didn't have a thing to worry about. Each flight delivered a flawless display, which got a huge applause from the bomber crews, who slowly melted away to prepare for their own night time mission after the Hurricanes landed. "Good show, Harry. My compliments to your pilots," Al said with an excited smile on his face. Harriet stood to attention and saluted him before he left with Charlie, and the other control tower staff followed him back inside.

"Why were you in the hospital?" Harriet asked Carrie when they were finally alone.

"I honestly don't know. Probably because I'm a girl, and they expected my fragile and delicate self to be broken after the Blenheim incident."

"If you say so... Come on, let's go." She led Carrie down to her car, and they raced back along the runway towards the dispersal hut. "You know that all of my flights are fully staffed at the moment."

"I can be a reserve; I don't mind. Or I can be duty pilot, or fly the communications aircraft. Whatever you need me to do." She talked politely, yet casually, without being overly familiar or excitable, to the point where Harriet was having to fight a smile at exactly how casual Carrie was being. Before she could say any more, Harriet was distracted by the sight awaiting her at the dispersal. The Hurricanes were lined up neatly, and the ground crews were crawling over them like ants, checking them and looking them over after a day's hard flying, and in front of the dispersal, the pilots were paraded in their flights. She smiled as she stopped the car, and prepared herself with a deep breath. "Where shall I stand?" Carrie asked.

"To my right and slightly behind." Harriet said as she climbed out of the car and marched over to stand in front of the parade, with Carrie hurrying to take up her post as instructed. Nicole brought them to attention, and Harriet took over, then stood them at ease. "We've got a little over three weeks until we're required to be operational, and today's flying gives me confidence that we'll achieve that target," she started. "However, as well as you flew today, this is just the start. The training will be rigorous, and has been designed to push you to your limits. Work together as a team, and trust your flight commanders. You need to learn to function as a unit and trust each other with your lives, and you need to learn fast." She paused for a moment and looked around the pilots, all of whom stared her in the eyes. "You're going to need each other in combat, and you're going to rely on each other. Remember that." She could see how proud they looked, their shoulders squared, and their heads held high. "Furthermore, we need to work together, know each other, and trust each other implicitly, and we can't have any inequality in the squadron. I'm therefore recommending all Non Commissioned Officer pilots on the squadron strength for commissioning to the rank of Pilot Officer, effective immediately." There was a gasp among the ranks of pilots as they glanced at each other while fighting the urge to cheer and smile. "The Adjutant will sort the paperwork, and you'll be supported in the process of your discharge from the ranks, and commissioning into the Volunteer Reserve, and we'll do what we can to help you with the formalities." She paused for a moment and looked over to Ginny, who nodded formally in agreement. "Before you go, I want to introduce you to Flying Officer Carrie Stone." She turned and looked at Carrie, who blushed a little. "Flying Officer Stone has the displeasure of being my Number Two, and she's going to have the hardest time of all of you. Make her welcome, and help her get settled in the squadron! Right, that's everything. Once dismissed, I want you to help the ground crew with your aeroplanes before you head off for dinner and an early night." She brought the parade to attention and handed it over to Ginny. "Come with me," she said to Carrie, then headed to her office. "Close the door..." she instructed, as she sat behind her desk, and Carrie stood in front of it. "Before I start getting phone calls, you need to tell me the truth."

"Ma'am..."

"I've known you long enough, Carrie, and I've known the RAF longer. You turn up here unannounced, and without any kit, and with a story that has more holes than a tea strainer. Come on, let's have it."

"I was in a crash, just as I said..." she explained awkwardly. "The port engine on the Blenheim flamed just after take off. I hadn't even had time to get the undercarriage up. I corrected best I could for the yaw, and adjusted the throttles, but there was no saving it. I just about managed to stop it rolling or stalling, but it was a heavy landing, and the undercarriage collapsed. I was knocked out, but we were OK."

"Having had similar in a Mosquito, I can say from experience that you did well to get it down the right way up. Being able to walk away from it is the icing on the cake."

"I didn't… I was knocked out and beaten up a bit, but my crew were OK, nothing more than a few cuts and bruises."

"Still a success."

"My CO didn't see it that way. He visited me in the hospital to tell me he was going to court martial me for poor aircraft control, and the reckless endangering of my aeroplane and crew."

"Excuse me?"

"I promise you that I did all I could to get the aeroplane down safely…"

"Carrie, the fact that you and your crew are alive is enough to support that, and any court martial would see that as clear as day. If it happened as you say, you're not at fault."

"He didn't see it that way… Anyway, I'd heard from one of the clerks that an order had been received asking for details of female pilots trained on fighters, and that they were being sent here to report to you, so I escaped from the hospital. My clerk friend met me in the park with my uniform and a travel warrant, and here I am."

"Carrie Stone…" Harriet rolled her eyes, then smiled at the nervous looking young woman. "Fortunately, the Station Commander said I could keep you, so that's one obstacle crossed." She looked to the door as a knock disturbed the conversation. "Yes?"

"Ma'am…" Ginny said as she opened the door and looked in.

"Just the person, come in." Ginny nodded and closed the door behind her, then stood by the side of the desk. "We need to make sure Flying

Officer Stone is on our strength as soon as possible. Groupie has given me the OK to keep her. Can you get the orders off to Group Headquarters and have the transfer sent to her former squadron?"

"I think I can do that."

"Unfortunately, she lost her kit bag on the way. Do you think you can talk to your friends in the stores again, and make sure she's got everything she needs?"

"Of course."

"She'll need a bed in the Mess as well."

"The truck is heading down to the Mess any minute…"

"Better get going then. Welcome to the squadron." Harriet stood and offered Carrie her hand, which she shook firmly while smiling happily. "Ginny will sort you out, and she'll book you in to see the Medical Officer in the morning, just to make sure you're OK to fly. I'll see you tomorrow."

"Thank you." She looked Harriet in the eyes for a moment, then left the office.

"Collecting strays already?" Ginny asked as she closed the door again.

"I got you, didn't I?"

"Touché… Anyway, I'm assuming her arrival here wasn't exactly scripted."

"Not exactly. If you can find out what you can about her former CO, I'd be grateful. She managed to get a damaged aeroplane down and save her crew, and he wanted to put her on a charge for it."

"I'll make a point of finding out everything I can. Now, I hope you're ready for a long night?"

"Why?"

"Because you've just recommended more than three quarters of your pilots for a commission, which means you and I are going to have a long night completing the paperwork and writing the type of commendations that make sure they don't get rejected."

"They won't get rejected."

"And why's that?"

"The Station Commander said he'd support it."

"I won't even ask how you managed to get him to agree to that. Either way, it has to get through Group Headquarters, too! So, we need to make sure we do it in such a way that it comes off, otherwise you're going to look ridiculous when you have to tell them they're being demoted again."

"If you were a halfway decent Adjutant, you'd find a way of guaranteeing it."

"I'm better than that, which is why you're in for a long night of writing. Now, you get comfortable, and I'll go make us a cup of tea." She gave Harriet a mischievous smile, while Harriet sunk into her chair and rolled her eyes.

## Chapter 4

## Incoming

"Hello Vixen Leader, Starfish control here," the message came over the radio as Harriet led the squadron on a sunset patrol, the last flight of their training before she reported them as operational. It had been a relentless four weeks, during which her pilots had been faultless. She'd asked a lot of them, and they'd delivered every day without fail. Not one of them had failed, or given her reason to question whether they should be there; if anything, they made her question why they hadn't been pushed before. The flight commanders had been tireless in their leading and training, while maintaining their own very high standards at all times, something they used to influence and motivate their pilots with great success. Lexi's pilots had also shown outstanding leadership, sharing their experiences from North Africa, and teaching their peers how to get the most out of a Hurricane. Those that hadn't seen combat soon learned what was expected of them, and were flying to the highest standard, far in excess of what Harriet had hoped for. To make the most of spring finally arriving, Harriet had decided that a squadron strength sunset patrol would be the best way to reward her pilots for a hard month of training, giving them a symbolic end to remember. She'd always enjoyed flying at sunset. The view was breathtaking. It was a luxury that so few got to enjoy, and in her mind, there wasn't a better way to celebrate flying.

" Vixen Leader receiving," Harriet replied with a frown. The sector controllers knew they were there. She had to let them know each time the squadron flew, but they never really bothered with her or any of her squadron, other than to answer requests for vectors or other mundane routine tasks. They'd never actually initiated contact.

"We've received reports of aircraft east of the Humber Estuary, and as you're in the area, we need you to go check it out. Save us scrambling the standby. It's likely the Navy getting jumpy again, as we're not expecting anyone, but it's best to check all the same. Make angels two five, and vector zero nine zero."

"Wilco," Harriet replied. "Vixen Squadron, turn zero nine zero, and climb to angels two five." She pushed her throttle forward and pulled back on the stick, starting a climbing turn and checking in her mirror to see the squadron following her in perfect synchronicity. The entire formation climbed together and turned together, without an aeroplane out of place. The skill and confidence of the display made her smile, despite her feeling mildly irritated that they'd send her squadron to chase ghosts, instead of bothering the fighters on standby to do precisely what they were on duty for. Still, it was recognition that the sector controller at least thought the squadron was ready, even if it was just to have a look around at an empty piece of sky. "Yankee, take C Flight up to angels three zero and keep an eye out for trouble," she said as they flew up the Humber Estuary, watching a convoy cut a silver line through the shimmering red and orange river as they made their way to the docks at Hull. There was some broken cloud rolling in from the east, sitting just a few thousand feet above the squadron. If there was anyone poking about, she thought it better to have some eyes up above and watching over them."

"Angels three zero, got it," Lexi replied, before giving her orders and leading her flight up in a steep climb. Harriet turned and watched them go, disappearing up into the cloud. Her heart was racing a little bit. It wasn't Kent, or even Malta, but the adrenaline was just about starting to flow at the thought of being on an operational flight again. As they passed Spurn Point, the thin strip of Yorkshire that stuck out into the North Sea, Harriet squinted as she thought she saw something in the distance, sitting just under the cloud base. "C Flight, see anything up there?"

"Nothing, the cloud's thinner, and visibility is good," Lexi replied.

"OK, stay on station and stand by." Harriet looked around, then focused on the dot again, and this time the hairs on the back of her neck stood up as other dots joined it. "Vixen Squadron, bandits twelve o'clock high. A Flight, left, B Flight, right, and let's climb to the cloud base." Her heart was racing as the squadron responded instantly to her instructions. "Starfish, this is Vixen Leader. Bandits, thirty plus, angels two five!" she said calmly into the radio, letting the Controller know that the ghosts were very much real. All the time, the dots were getting bigger, and soon they came close enough for their shapes to give them away. Heinkels. Twin engine long range medium bombers, thirty of them at least. "C Flight, keep your eyes open for long distance fighters. There'll be Messerschmitt 110s out there somewhere, no doubt. Don't take them head on, and watch for their rear gunners. Try and hit them from the side if you can. "A and B Flights, drop back and follow me in, and try to catch them on the break. Vixen Two, stay on me, and keep your eyes open." She looked across to Carrie, who was to her right and slightly behind, as she always was, and got a nod of compliance from her young Number Two. The bombers continued in their formation, creeping forward just under the clouds. Harriet switched her gun button to fire and pushed the throttle forward, snapping the engineer's wire and going through the gate to increase her engine speed to maximum. She wanted to hit the bombers as hard and fast as she could. "Here we go. Get stuck in, and watch for their gunners. Tally Ho!" She pushed her gun button for just a second as she closed on the leading bomber, and felt the four 20mm cannons rumble into life as they sent four glowing lines of tracer reaching forward like lances that pierced the greenhouse like nose of the enemy aircraft, making it sparkle as the ordnance cut the metalwork to pieces, along with anything or anyone that was in it. The bomber immediately slumped nose first into a spiralling dive towards the sea. Harriet sped through the gap it had left in the formation, with Carrie dropping onto her tail and slightly right, and she fired at the next bomber in line, igniting its port engine. "Stay with me, Carrie!" she shouted as she passed through the formation, then pulled up hard and away from the bombers, which were now scattering in every direction, just as she'd hoped. She rolled her Hurricane on its back and looked down at the mess she'd just passed through, and watched as Nicole led her flight in on the bombers that had broken right, and AP hit those turning left. The darkening sky was a mesh of tracer, but her plan had worked. With the bombers scattered, they were easy prey for her Hurricanes, and not able to cover each other to fight off the attackers. "Lexi. Fighters?" She shouted as she got a picture of the battle, and planned her next move.

"Nothing up here," Lexi replied.

"Get down here and help yourself in that case."

"Yes, Ma'am! C Flight, let's go get us some scalps," she whooped, and Harriet looked up to see the four Hurricanes diving straight down through a hole in the broken clouds.

"Carrie, see the two below us and to the right, turning hard side by side?"

"I see them," Carrie replied, in a calm and calculated manner.

"Go get them. Get the one on the inside; I'll watch your tail."

"Wilco. Tally ho!" Carrie called as she dived and turned after the bombers.

"Keep your height, and watch your angle," Harriet shouted after her, while spinning her head and making sure their tails were clear. Lines of tracer came up from both bombers, converging on Carrie's Hurricane. She rolled to dodge the bullets, then levelled out and let out a burst of cannon fire into the closest bomber's right engine. It exploded almost instantly, blowing the wing off and flipping the bomber on its back, forcing her to pull up to avoid both it and the burning explosion that consumed it. She continued her turn, and Harriet stayed with her as the second bomber dived and turned the other away. "It's OK, let him go," Harriet said as she saw Carrie searching for her target. "Good shooting, now let's go back and join the others. I'll lead." She rolled and pulled back on her stick, pulling the Hurricane down and around to face west. Bombers were everywhere, some running home, others burning and smoking, and one heading straight down nose first for the sea. To the north, she could see a pair of Hurricanes at wave top height chasing a smoking bomber, while two more were chasing hard on their tails. A blast of cannon fire knocked it down into a massive plume of water, and the four pulled up together. To her right, a bomber was racing up towards the thickening cloud, which was slowly descending. Too slowly, it turned out, as a pair of hurricanes cut into it just at the last moment, leaving it to roll into the cloud and explode. "Alright, everyone, that'll do," she said as the battle broke up, and the remaining bombers either ran for the waves or hid up in the clouds. A group of enemy aircraft, maybe a squadron of them, had managed to turn away and run, but they were so far away that it was pointless and risky giving chase. Besides, ammunition would be running short. Their Hurricanes being armed with cannons meant they could do more damage than they would with machine guns, but it also meant they had less ammunition. It was also getting dark, and if the Germans were daring to risk a raid in daylight, they could be up to something else, and it wouldn't do to be caught in the dark with no ammunition. She circled, with Carrie keeping her station, while other Hurricanes came to join her as they broke off the hunt.

"Vixen Leader, Starfish Control. Spitfires vectored to intercept. Keep your distance, and report enemy positions," came the call from land over the radio. Making Harriet shake her head and smile and laugh to herself at the absurdity.

"Starfish Control, Vixen Leader. Enemy engaged and remaining aircraft running west, we're heading home," she replied with a happiness that almost consumed her. She was so full of adrenaline and excitement that she didn't even have time to be annoyed at being told to keep her distance and watch while others were sent to do the fighting. "Vixen Leader to Vixen Squadron, form on me and let's go home. Flight commanders report in."

"A Flight all accounted for," Nicole replied, as her four Hurricanes formed on Harriet's right.

"B Flight all accounted for," AP added as the next four took station.

"C Flight running hot and ready to rock," Lexi said, making Harriet smile. She looked across the sky as the Hurricanes stretched out to her left and right in a perfect v, with her and Carrie at the front. No smoke, no erratic movements, not a thing out of place. Her adrenaline was flowing so much that she was shaking. It was only as they entered the Humber Estuary again, following the dulling red of the sunset lit river, that she realised her mouth hadn't dried out once during the brief yet incredibly violent battle. She'd seen at least five enemy bombers go down, and the sky was full of smoke trails from others, yet she'd been so distracted by leading that she hadn't had time to even break a sweat. As they approached home, she had the squadron form in flights behind her, then led them in a low level flypast once she'd confirmed there was no traffic on the runway. They peeled away and landed in their flights, while she circled and watched them roll to their places on the dispersal. Finally, once Lexi's flight were down and taxiing in, she and Carrie landed side by side, and were the last to take their places and shut down. As her engine stopped and she pulled off her helmet, she could hear the excited conversation already filling the dispersal.

"Everything OK, Ma'am?" Beth asked as she jumped onto the wing to welcome her home.

"Couldn't be better!" she beamed with excitement.

"Did you get one, Ma'am?"

"I certainly did! Good work to you both on making sure she was up to the fight!" Harriet jumped down from the Hurricane and was immediately joined by Nicole, who excitedly jumped at her and wrapped her in a hug.

"That was incredible!" Nicole shouted excitedly. Harriet hugged her back, laughing, almost deliriously with relief.

"Well, that sure showed the Germans," Lexi added as she joined them.

"I've had worse days," AP said, in her usual underwhelmed and casual way.

"The Station Commander's here," Ginny said as she made her way to Harriet, squeezing through the pilots who'd circled her, all chattering excitedly and talking through the battle.

"Fall in!" Harriet shouted, and the pilots quickly fell silent and formed in their flights, where they stood smartly to attention. Harriet stood in front of them and saluted as Al walked towards her. "508 Squadron present and correct, Sir," she said as he stood in front of her. He looked a little confused, bewildered even, as he looked first at her, and then at her pilots.

"I've just got off the phone with Group Headquarters..." Al said, clearing his throat and making sure he could be heard by everyone present. "There's a story doing the rounds that this very evening a squadron of Hurricanes intercepted, and turned back, a surprise German raid heading for the Hull docks, inflicting significant losses on the enemy in the process." He paused for a moment and let out a smile. "As you're the only Hurricane squadron in the area, I think we can safely say that 508 Squadron Auxiliary Air Force is now fully operational, and I've told Group as much. Congratulations, ladies. Once your CO has stood you down, I'll have a drink waiting on the Mess bar for each and every one of you. Welcome to the fight!" He gave Harriet a nod. "I've brought the Intelligence Officer over from the bomber boys, seeing as you don't have one of your own. He'll take your combat reports, then you can stand your girls down. Well done, Harry. Very well done!"

"Thank you, Sir." She saluted him, then turned and dismissed the squadron, who immediately erupted in a huge cheer that echoed around the dispersal. "Report to your ground crews, then into the dispersal hut for combat reports. The sooner you get it done, the sooner you can get to the Mess. Best uniforms tonight, ladies, we're celebrating." Another cheer went up, and the pilots ran off to their aircraft to brief their ground crews on performance and snags, while Harriet walked with Al towards his car. "I appreciate you coming down here to speak to the squadron; it'll mean a lot to them to be recognised."

"Honestly, I wanted to hear it from the horse's mouth. When Sector Control called and said you were getting stuck into a German raid, I didn't know what to think. If I'm honest, neither did they. There was a terrible flap on that went all the way to the top. You're not operational yet, or weren't, anyway, and you certainly shouldn't have been sent into combat. The controller who tasked you would have been for the high jump if the result had gone the other way."

"Lucky we're not a bunch of novices in that case."

"Quite... Everyone get back OK?"

"All safe and accounted for."

"Good. You know, it set a cat among the pigeons at the Air Ministry when you promoted all of your NCOs. 'We don't need some jumped up girl challenging tried and tested RAF doctrine' is how it was put. At least that's the polite version."

"I didn't know…? Harriet frowned in disappointment, not that it surprised her. Despite all that she'd done, attitudes towards any form of equality were moving at a glacial pace in the corridors of power.

"That's because the type of people who say such things have one eye on their careers and future peerages when they say them. Misogyny is perfectly acceptable when you're with the boys, but if you're going to put your head above the parapet in public life at some point, you need to remember that women have the vote these days…" He gave her a forced and uncomfortable smile. "Look, Harry, I couldn't be more proud of what you and your squadron have achieved, despite the best efforts of some to undermine you, but it's important you know that the future isn't going to be plane sailing. I know you haven't had the easiest time, but I fear it may get worse, especially after this evening. You were supposed to fail, or stay quietly out of the way, not shoot down half a dozen German bombers before you're even made operational." He gave her a wink and a warm smile. "I'll see you in the Mess." He got into his car, and she stood and watched as he was driven away. He was right, and she knew it. Some in power were going to be furious when they found out what had happened, but right at that moment, she couldn't care less. In fact, if anything, it made her all the more proud of what her squadron had achieved.

After dinner, the squadron pilots, with Ginny and Jo, paraded outside of their accommodation block and checked each other over in their best uniforms. They were excited and still buzzing with adrenaline, and they were ready to celebrate. Harriet couldn't have been more proud as she marched them the long way around the station, making sure everyone who was watching got to see the twenty five immaculately dressed and very proud young women march in perfect unity. Their step in time, and their arms swinging uniformly, giving a display of the highest standard of parade drill that got cheers as they passed the WAAF accommodation. Al was standing on the steps of the Officers' Mess to receive them, and after having Harriet dismiss the parade, he asked them to follow him into the Mess bar. Harriet's cheeks burned as he led her through the doors. The bar was packed with every officer on the station who wasn't on duty, and as the squadron finished filing in, Al stood facing them, and looked each of them in the eyes.

"To the fighting 508! Praise God we're on the same side." He raised a glass, as did the other officers.

"The fighting 508!" they repeated, then drank the toast.

"Ladies, the drinks are on me!" He pointed to the bar, which was lined with large whiskies, and a loud cheer went up.

"I wasn't expecting that," Harriet said in a whisper as he handed her a drink.

"Good. That means I'm still able to keep some secrets from that Adjutant of yours, who seems to know pretty much everything that happens on this station long before I do."

"Yes, she's annoying like that…" Harriet said as Ginny joined them. "Ears burning?"

"Me? Not at all. Though it's going to take more than one drink to celebrate us being posted."

"See…" Al said, with a sigh and a roll of his eyes."

"We're being posted?" Harriet asked excitedly.

"Kent," Ginny replied.

"When you're quite finished, Miss Russel…" Al said, getting a politely innocent smile from Ginny. "Kent…" he added. "You'll be formally made operational tomorrow, and following two days leave, you'll fly your Hurricanes south to fly with 11 Group."

"Your old stomping ground," Ginny said to Harriet, giving her a wink.

"Really?" Harriet asked excitedly.

"Apparently, the Luftwaffe are stepping up their raids again, particularly in the southeast, and home defence squadrons are in demand... Personally, I can't wait. I can go back to having secrets on my own station..." He looked firmly at Ginny, who simply smiled once again. "It'll also reduce the number of transfer requests I'm getting!"

"Transfer requests?"

"Every WAAF on the station is wanting to join your squadron, even Charlie asked!"

"Sorry..."

"Don't be. It's a sign that you're getting it right."

The night was a huge celebration, and the drinks flowed. The piano was played into the early hours, and there was a lot of singing and dancing. The atmosphere was euphoric. Nobody was down, nobody left early, and every last one of the squadron had to be almost dragged from the bar when the night was over. Harriet had followed Al in buying a round of drinks, or two, though she did her best to drink plenty of water through the night so she didn't totally lose control, despite which she still woke in Nicole's room with a hangover that could only be shifted by a plunge in an ice cold bath, and a visit to the hangar for some oxygen, before parading the squadron and standing them down for a couple of days leave. The pilots scattered in all directions. Lexi and her group headed to London, while AP went home to Lincolnshire to visit her family. Al even put on an Anson to shuttle them around the country to save time messing about with trains and losing valuable leave time. Ginny and Nicole ended up squeezed into the MG with Harriet as they raced to aunt Mary's for a couple of days of well earned leave. Despite being less than twenty miles away, they hadn't visited aunt Mary once, other than to fly overhead, due to the packed training schedule that Nicole had put together, which had seen the entire squadron either training, eating, or sleeping the entire time. No days off, and no nights drinking in the

Mess. Pilots from the bomber squadron on the same station had tried to be sociable. They attempted to arrange drinks, or parties, or nights out, but not one pilot took them up on the offer. All preferring an early night in with their heads in the books instead.

"Why do you never call to let me know you're coming home?" Aunt Mary demanded, as she ran out of the front door after Harriet had rolled up the gravel drive honking the horn of the overloaded MG.

"I thought it'd be a nice surprise," Harriet replied.

"It always is." She hugged Harriet and then Nicole, and much to her surprise, Ginny got a hug too. "How long are you here for?"

"Only a couple of days, then we're heading down to Kent for a while."

"We'd better make the most of it in that case. I'll cook us a nice meal tonight, and then we can go to the pub."

"I brought some tea." Harriet handed her a bag of goodies she'd picked up from Fortnum's the last time she was in London, and Mary's face lit up.

"Well, go and get settled in your rooms, and I'll put the kettle on. Ginny can have the spare room she used Christmas before last." She ushered them in, and as Nicole and Ginny headed upstairs, Harriet followed Mary through to the kitchen. "It's so nice to have you home, though it would be nice if it was for longer."

"I know… I look forward to a time when I can just come and stay without having to be back somewhere."

"It's been almost five years. Longer than the last war, and that was the war to end all wars, or so they said. It sometimes feels like it'll never end. We don't get as many air raids these days, and the news reports say the tide is turning, but it's hard to believe."

"It is. Turning, I mean," Harriet said as reassuringly as she could. "I've seen it. I was there to see them kicked out of North Africa, and to see Sicily invaded. We've just got to stay positive."

"We do," Mary gave her a warm smile. "Just make sure you stay safe; it'd be a shame for something to happen now you've made it this far."

"I will. I fly with the best."

"Good. Before you go upstairs, there's somebody out in the garden who I know will be happy to see you." Harriet nodded and headed out of the door into the courtyard, then into the large garden, where the spring flowers were blooming.

"Harriet…" Eloise said as she saw her from across the garden, where she'd been tidying the fruit bushes Mary had planted at the start of the war to help supplement the household food supplies.

"Hello," Harriet replied as the young woman ran across the lawn and threw her arms around Harriet, hugging her tight.

"I've missed you!" she said excitedly in accented English, between kissing Harriet repeatedly on the cheeks.

"You're looking well," Harriet said with a smile while looking her friend over. Most of the bruising had faded, and she was looking healthy and vibrant.

"Your aunt looks after me, and she feeds me well."

"A French girl complementing English food. I never thought I'd hear it…" Harriet laughed.

"It's true; she's a good cook."

"Careful, say that too loud, and they'll never let you back in France."

"I don't mind. I have nothing there. Maybe I'll stay in England." She shrugged casually.

"I didn't know your English was so good."

"It wasn't. Your aunt is teaching me. Her French is better than my English, and she's very patient."

"How are you recovering?"

"Not bad. How about you?"

"Not bad… It's good to see you again."

"And you. Will you stay long?"

"Two days, then we're heading south."

"Back to the war?"

"Yes." She forced a smile, then caught herself and shook out of the darkness that suddenly started to creep up on her. "I should go and get unpacked. We're going to the pub tonight if you'd like to come?"

"I'd like that," Eloise nodded and smiled, then after giving Harriet another hug, she went back to tending the garden, while Harriet returned to the house and went up to her room. She was happy to see Eloise again, and relieved to see that she was recovering from her experience at the hands of the Gestapo. There was a sadness, too, that had descended when going back to the war was mentioned. There'd been a great success the previous night when they bumped into a raid of German bombers that were trying to sneak in undetected, with seven enemy aircraft confirmed shot down, another five probables but not witnessed, and more damaged, all for no losses among the squadron. It was a success, but she couldn't help thinking that Kent was going to be different. The last time she was in action there, it was life and death for even the best pilots every time they went up, and bombers were never left unescorted. She shook it off again after Nicole appeared to drag her from her room, and they had tea with Mary and talked about the war. It was nice to be home, and just as nice to visit the pub in the village, where their uniforms ensured they didn't buy a drink all night. When they finally got home to their beds, Harriet and Nicole laid talking for hours, about the war, about home, and about France, before sleeping long into the next morning. The following day they went into the town to do some shopping with

Ginny, before having a relaxing evening at home with Mary and Eloise, enjoying a meal together and playing cards, and making the most of their last evening, with the help of a bottle of very nice whisky that Mary had managed to talk out of the landlord of the pub. A warm fire and good company made it difficult to leave the next morning, but they had to be at the dispersal bright and early to prepare for their flight south. Most of the ground crews had left a couple of days earlier, to drive down and get settled before the aeroplanes arrived. The majority of the pilots' kit had gone with them, so all they needed to do was change into their flying gear, put their best uniforms in the Anson that would be taking Ginny, Dutch, the paperwork, along with some stores, then fly their Hurricanes down to Kent.

"Thank God you're here, Ma'am," Dutch said as Harriet pulled up outside the dispersal and climbed out of her car. She was already in her flying kit, and was hoping to get straight on with the route planning and briefing, but the urgency in Dutch's voice suggested there was something not quite right.

"What's wrong?" Harriet asked, while frowning in anticipation.

"The Station Commander wants to see you right away. Flying Officer Stone is up there, and I think there's trouble."

"Stone? What's going on?"

"Honestly, Ma'am, I've no idea. There was an officer here waiting for Stone when she arrived back from leave, a Squadron Leader, and he took her straight to Station Headquarters. He wouldn't tell me who he was, and there were no other officers around senior enough to deal with him."

"OK, I'll go and see what's happening." She turned to Nicole. "Get started with the route planning; we'll need to get off as soon as I've dealt with whatever nonsense is going on."

"The challenges of power," Nicole sighed mischievously, getting a sharp look in reply from Harriet as she jumped back in the car.

"I won't be long..." she shouted out of the window as she sped away, before whizzing around the roads to the headquarters while feeling both nervous about what was wrong with Carrie, and irritated because her plans had been thrown out by something beyond her control. She was supposed to arrive, confirm the route, brief the pilots, and go, and somebody getting in the way of that was infuriating. She screeched to a halt and jumped out of the car, then marched through the headquarters in the direction of Al's office.

"Ma'am..." Charlie said as she intercepted Harriet's advance, and waved her into a small room where Carrie was sitting on a chair and looking distraught.

"What's happening?" Harriet asked, as Charlie closed the door behind them.

"It's my old CO," Carrie replied. She was clearly doing her best to hold herself together, and not let out the emotion that was bubbling under the surface.

"What about him?"

"He's here," Charlie said. He's in with Groupie at the moment, and he's causing all sorts of problems."

"About what? Carrie?"

"He's saying I'm AWOL..."

"What?"

"Absent Without Official Leave," Charlie explained.

"Yes, I know what it means..." Harriet replied, trying to keep the sharpness from her voice.

"I'll let Groupie know you're here..."

"Don't worry," Harriet said as she put her hand on Carrie's shoulder. "Stand up and straighten yourself out, and when we go in there, I want to you stand tall and look straight ahead." She helped Carrie up and straightened her uniform.

"What do I say?"

"Nothing. Leave the talking to me."

"Groupie would like to see you both," Charlie said as politely as she could, trying not to irritate Harriet further.

"Right, remember what I said. Stand tall and be confident," Harriet said, then led Carrie into Al's office. They both stood smartly to attention in front of his desk, while Carrie's former CO stood to the side of them. He stared at them both over the end of his long nose, which sat above a very narrow and quite ridiculous looking moustache.

"Thank you for joining us, Squadron Leader Cornwall," Al said formally, yet politely. "This is Squadron Leader Smith." He gestured at the tall, thin man still sneering at Carrie. "Unfortunately, he brings rather disagreeable news, and is suggesting that young Flying Officer Stone is AWOL from her unit, and here under false pretences… Is that right?" He looked over to Smith, who nodded quickly.

"Yes, Sir, quite right," Smith said. "Stone was in the hospital following a crash, and awaiting trial by court martial for negligence and incompetence, resulting in a valuable aircraft being written off."

"Yes…" Al frowned at him a little, then turned back to Harriet. "So, you see, something of a difficult situation."

"One which I'm sure we can resolve, Sir. I'm happy to escort Stone back to her unit and place her under Mess arrest pending the Court Martial, and I don't think we need to say anything else about it," Smith said in an almost friendly manner. "I can't imagine Squadron Leader Cornwall knew a thing about it; she was likely hoodwinked by Stone, too. I wouldn't want to make trouble for another squadron commander. It's a tough enough job as is. What do you say, Cornwall?" He looked at Harriet and smiled. She stared at him a moment, with the same frown she'd had since she'd entered the office, then looked back to Al.

"Well?" Al asked.

"Flying Officer Stone has been posted to my squadron, Sir, and she flies as my Number Two. I'd rather keep her if it's all the same," Harriet replied confidently.

"I think you'll find that the posting was irregular," Smith said. "Again, you weren't to know that she was AWOL, and I have absolutely no intention of making a noise about that, but you do see that Stone's place is back where she came from? So she can face the consequences of her actions."

"Oh, I knew all about it," Harriet replied, fixing him firmly in her stare as Al raised his eyebrow, and joined her looking at Smith. "I know that she managed to land a twin engine aeroplane that lost one of those engines on take off, and that without her fast thinking and quick responses, it would likely have crashed and killed everyone on board. I've read the report, and the witness statements of observers and her crew, who walked away with minor injuries; and as an instructor on Mosquitoes who has experienced an engine failure on take off, I'd be more than happy to provide professional testimony in support of her in any court martial."

"Excuse me?"

"She saved lives, and you know that. However, you're trying to throw the book at her because since the day she turned up on your squadron, you've pestered her relentlessly, and often inappropriately, propositioning her more than once to engage in an unprofessional and strictly forbidden relationship with a senior officer, specifically her CO, and when she declined, repeatedly, you did everything you could to make her life hell. I have those witness statements, too..." Harriet smirked at him.

"How very dare you!" He turned all shades of red, then bellowed at Al. "Sir, I must protest! This is an obvious attempt to slander a senior officer to deflect from very serious accusations!"

"It's only slander if it's untrue," Harriet shrugged before looking back to Al, who was looking intrigued, but otherwise unperturbed by the whole situation. "The posting is all above board, Sir, and done with the knowledge of Fighter Command Headquarters. I arranged it when I found out what had been going on, and thought it better to remove Flying Officer Stone from the situation. For her own safety, if nothing else." She looked at Smith again, fixing him in her stare. "Besides, I thought it better to do things quietly, so Squadron Leader Smith's wife didn't find out about his penchant for young women under his command. Especially after the incident with the WAAF last year..." She let the slightest smirk turn up the corners of her mouth while Smith's eyes bulged, and he continued to turn red while sweating profusely.

"Sir..." he stammered. He was shaking, not entirely sure how to answer.

"An intriguing story," Al said.

"With evidence to support it, Sir," Harriet replied.

"Quite the argument, Smith. Anything you'd like to say?"

"No, Sir..." Smith replied, shaking his head, and looking incredibly uncomfortable.

"No, Sir..." Al repeated. "It's not enough for you to behave in a predatory, and frankly unacceptable way towards female personnel, Smith. You bring the RAF into further disrepute with your misuse of disciplinary processes. I'm assuming the paperwork for the court martial hasn't actually been submitted to your CO?"

"No, Sir..."

"No, because that would put you in a precarious position given the statements of Stone's crew, which contradict your charge, and your CO wouldn't be pleased if all this came out in public..." Smith shook his head. "The RAF doesn't need that; we have a war to fight. What it does need, though, is good pilots and senior officers who don't take advantage of them, and most of all, it needs the public behind it. If the people we serve fear us and fear what we'll do to their daughters, we're no better than the Nazis. This will come out, Smith, but it'll be done properly. You can wait outside while I talk with your CO and Group HQ." Smith nodded, saluted, and left in silence. His head bowed in shame. "You should have told me," Al said to Harriet after he'd left.

"Yes, Sir. Genuinely, I thought it better to just arrange the posting and hope it would blow over. I didn't want to cause any trouble."

"I know." He gave her a warm smile. "And don't worry, I'll make sure it's dealt with properly, and discreetly. I'll keep your names out of it."

"Thank you, Sir."

"Stone, you have my apologies."

"Sir?" Carrie looked at him, a little confused.

"You deserve better from the organisation you've served so diligently. Fortunately, I'm quite sure that you've found yourself a CO who will go to great lengths to protect her people, and I doubt you'll have any more problems."

"Thank you, Sir." Carrie smiled, and blushed a little as she looked at Harriet. "Does that mean I can stay with the squadron, Sir?"

"What do you think, Harry? Want to keep her?"

"I'd need to find another Number Two if I gave her away, Sir, and we're about to leave for Kent."

"You'd better keep her, in that case. Get yourselves down to the squadron, and I'll come down and see you off before you leave. You'd better send Smith in. I think we need to have one of those awkward conversations with his boss."

"Sir." Harriet saluted, and they both left. "Charlie, where did you put Squadron Leader Smith?" Harriet asked as they left.

"In the same room where you were waiting, Ma'am," Charlie replied while quickly standing, and heading over to the door.

"Charlie," Harriet put her hand on the Sergeant's arm. "I'm sorry if I snapped at you earlier; I didn't mean to. I was a little irritated, but not by you."

"I know, Ma'am. Good luck in Kent; all of us WAAFs are behind you and wishing you the best."

"Thank you." Harriet smiled, and blushed a little, then walked into the office where Smith was waiting and looked at him for a moment. "The Station Commander wants to see you..." He stood and nodded, then went to walk past her. She stood in his way and looked him in the eyes. "The Station Commander's a good man, and I don't doubt that he'll try and spare too many blushes when he deals with you, but you should know that if I ever hear of you mistreating another woman, I won't be anywhere near as kind." She stared at him for a moment, letting her words sink in. "Your wife will know every filthy detail, as will everyone who knows you. Oh, and if they still let you fly, I'll come and find you and shoot you out of the sky myself." She gave him a smile, then stepped aside and let him go without a word. "Right, come on, Carrie. We've got aeroplanes to fly!" She gave Charlie a smile, then marched confidently back to her car with her head held high.

"Ma'am... How did you know all that about him?" Carrie asked as they drove back to the dispersal.

"I'm pretty sure we agreed it'd be Harry when nobody's around..."

"Sorry..." Carrie smiled and blushed a little.

"I didn't. You should just be happy that our Adjutant thinks of herself as something of a Sherlock Holmes, and never does anything without getting the full story," Harriet smiled. "When I asked her to arrange your posting to us, she did a bit of digging to see what had happened with your crash, and it seems that people like talking to her, because she got chapter and verse from a small army of people Smith had wronged. They were all too happy to talk to somebody independent of the unit. So, we put a file together and kept it handy just in case we needed it…"

"I'm happy you did."

"Me too. Where would I get another Number Two at such short notice? Let alone one I trust enough to keep my tail clear in battle."

"I'll keep it clear; you have my word."

"I know."

## Chapter 5

### Meet The New Boss – Same As The Old Boss

Harriet looked down at London and smiled as she led the squadron south to their new home. It was a crisp and clear spring day, and the visibility was perfect, as it often was in spring. A little haze and clear blue skies as far as the eye could see, with the only cloud being the smoke and smog rising over London, hanging around the barrage balloons that hung thousands of feet below as the Hurricanes passed. The only downside was the temperature, which above 25,000 feet was more than a little cool, though nowhere near as cold as she remembered being in the American P38 Lightning. Having a roaring Rolls Royce Merlin engine right in front of her feet meant that some of the heat came into the cockpit, though not by design, but it was enough to keep her from being uncomfortable. Especially with her sheepskin jacket, thermal underwear, and the white sailor's roll neck pullover she'd been given when in Scotland. The flight had been quiet and incident free, with Nicole's route taking them to the east of London on their way to their new home. The majority of the time, Harriet found herself daydreaming, thinking of a hundred and one scenarios while wondering what would come next. The squadron had done all that had been asked of them, despite the best efforts of some to derail their mission, and now it was time to prove themselves on the front lines. She had confidence in her pilots; they'd proved their worth when they ripped apart a German bombing raid without loss; it was the aeroplanes she was worried about. No matter how hard she tried, she couldn't shake the feeling of dread that came with the thought of heading south in outdated Hurricanes. Unescorted bombers were very different creatures to the latest Luftwaffe fighters, which could put up a good fight against even the best Spitfire. As London fell behind them and they passed over the light rolling hills of Kent, she shook the thoughts from her head and paid attention to what she was doing. They were well within the range of enemy fighters, and while the Germans didn't tend to visit as much as they had in 1940, there were still regular fighters sweeps designed to keep the RAF on their toes, while shooting up and bombing key installations. Harriet thought back to her incident in the Lysander, where she'd had just such an experience when she was jumped by four

Messerschmitt 109s and knocked down over the Thames Estuary. The memory was enough to keep her sharp, and she warned the Squadron to keep their eyes open as she guided them over the last part of their journey to their station on the south coast. The station she'd been based at throughout the Battle of Britain.

After calling Control to announce the squadron's arrival, Harriet was instructed to hold and wait, where she circled and watched as Hawker Typhoon fighter bombers came in to land in ones and twos, bouncing down onto the ground and running to a dispersal which was littered with tents at the far end of the airfield. Finally, when the last of the Typhoons had landed, Harriet was given permission to bring her aeroplanes in. She sent the squadron in by flights before she and Carrie touched down and followed the signals to their dispersal, where she shut down the engine and quickly stood and stretched her tight back and legs. She was excited. It felt like coming home, and while she'd been away for almost four years, there was an irrational hope that at least somebody she knew from the old days would still be there. Her ground crew were there to greet her, and quickly got on with checking the Hurricane over while she walked over to her old dispersal hut, where Jo Bird was waiting for her with Dutch by her side.

"Welcome home, Ma'am," Jo said, as Harriet looked at the scramble bell hanging outside the dispersal door, and smiled as she ran her finger over it. By the time she'd finished in 1940, the sound of the bell ringing was enough to turn her spine to ice, and it frequently made others vomit. Even the most stoic and steadfast had a sudden and uncontrollable rise in their heart rate and a sinking feeling in their stomach when it rang. Three, four, or even five times a day it would clatter, and the pilots would sprint to their waiting Spitfires to intercept an incoming German raid, knowing that each flight could be their last. At the time, Harriet had remembered saying that she'd never have a telephone in her house if she made it through the war, as that was always the herald. The ring came before the bell, when the duty controller called to scramble the squadron.

"Thank you," Harriet replied, having pulled her attention back to the present, and out of the distant, yet strikingly vivid memories of 1940. "Everything set?"

"I think so. We've got the hangar ready, and now the aeroplanes are here, we can get to work preparing them. Were there any difficulties on the flight down?"

"Not that I know of. We all got here in one piece, at least, so that's something."

"We'd better have a look all the same. I want as many ready as possible by tomorrow, assuming we'll be on duty from first thing in the morning?"

"You've been here longer than I have, you tell me?"

"I wouldn't know, nobody talks to us. The Station Adjutant told us where to set up, and showed us the accommodation block, but that's about it. Other than to say that you're to report to the Station Commander at eleven. That's right, isn't it?" She looked down at Dutch, who looked at her clipboard and nodded.

"Yes, Ma'am. Squadron Leader Cornwall to meet Group Captain Stanley," Dutch replied confidently. Everything about her was lists, and nothing escaped her. She was a tremendous asset to the squadron, and Harriet was very happy that Al had let her keep the young Corporal when the squadron got its marching orders.

"A traditionally warm RAF welcome..." Harriet sighed.

"Something like that," Jo replied. "Though we don't have much in the way of stores and spares, if you could mention it when you meet him? What we've got won't get us through a week, especially if we get caught up in any action."

"I'll mention it. Anything else?"

"The accommodation block put aside for the officers is a tip. Damp and cold at best, and there isn't any hot water."

"What?" Harriet frowned, feeling irritated at the news that the accommodation wasn't up to standard. "What about the other ranks? Is theirs OK?"

"They're in the station WAAF accommodation, so I think so?" She looked at Dutch again.

"Yes, Ma'am. It's a bit cramped, as there isn't space, so we've had to squeeze more into a room than they're designed for, but we can make it work."

"That's something, at least," Harriet sighed. "Hot water?"

"Yes, Ma'am."

"Good. I'll have a word with the Station Commander about the overcrowding at the same time as I address the officers' accommodation. Anything else I should know about?"

"I'm sure something will come up..." Jo said with a smile. "Right, I'd better get to work. Aeroplanes don't look after themselves."

"Never let me recommend you for a commission, Dutch. Stay where the water's warm."

"Yes, Ma'am," Dutch smiled. "Shall I show you to your office?"

"No, that's OK. I know the way..." The dispersal hut had hardly changed since 1940, and she was pretty sure that many of the chairs were the same ones she'd sat on when she was last there. She smiled as she headed through to what had been Max's office, and Singh's before him, then found herself letting out a laugh as she remembered how angry she'd been when she was grounded, and how Max had thought she was going to stab him with the ceremonial sword she'd been presented by the King. It hadn't changed much either, and she shook her head in amazement that she was back home, and the office was now hers. She glanced at the clock and noticed the time. She didn't have long until she was due to meet the Station Commander, and she didn't want to get off to a bad start by turning up in flying kit.

"Is there a truck to take me to Station HQ?" she shouted into the main room, where Dutch was working on one of her many lists."

"Yes, Ma'am. I'll drive you down myself."

"Ten minutes." She pushed the door closed, then threw her kitbag on her desk and unpacked her best uniform, which she'd rolled carefully and neatly so as not to crease it, before sticking it in the Hurricane's fuselage next to the radio, a space just big enough for a pilot to store a small bag, and hopefully out of the way of any oil or petrol which could dirty the contents. She pulled the curtains across the windows and quickly stripped, grateful for the warmth of the potbellied stove in the main room that had thankfully been lit long enough ago to heat the entire hut. Midway through changing, she bent over her desk to grab her skirt, and to her horror, the door opened behind her. She spun around to see Nicole standing in the doorway and smirking. "Shut the door!" she yelled.

"What are you doing?" Nicole asked with a frown, while Harriet desperately tried to cover herself with her overcoat.

"Trying not to stand half naked in front of the whole squadron!"

"Who's naked in front of the whole squadron?" Lexi asked as she joined Nicole in the doorway. "Oh, honey, y'all need to do that somewhere more private," she laughed.

"Oh, God!" Harriet felt herself blushing as she looked at them. "I would! If you'd all bugger off and leave me alone for five minutes, now get out!"

"What on earth's going on…" AP asked with her trademark frown as she joined them. "Oh… Whatever this is, can we not?" She shook her head in disappointment.

"Out!" Harriet bellowed, and the three backed away, with Nicole still smirking as she closed the door, leaving Harriet flustered and sighing. She checked her watch. She didn't have time to waste, so she finished dressing, then with a deep breath, she pulled the door open and marched out into the dispersal hut. "I'm going to Station HQ to report in. I want a status report on aeroplanes and pilots when I get back, and a flying rota for your flights so we know who'll be on standby. Get everyone settled into their rooms, and we'll have a briefing here after lunch!" she barked at Nicole, AP, and Lexi, without looking at any of them, knowing she'd turn bright red if she did. She quickly left and jumped in the truck before her blush came back with a vengeance, and tried to relax as Dutch drove her to her meeting. She found herself smiling as she watched the station's buildings go by. She'd had lots of good times there, scattered amongst the bad of 1940. For every pilot lost, and every night of sleep that didn't even begin to touch the exhaustion, there was a party in the Mess, a game of football, or even just laughing and joking with her friends. Even visits to HQ were pleasant. Alastair had been the best Station Commander she could have asked for, and he'd become a good friend when they'd met again in Scotland. He'd found it most amusing when she'd corrected the King of Norway during his visit to present her with the Distinguished Flying Cross, and never let her forget it.

She left Dutch and went into the HQ, sending the young Corporal to the NAAFI for a cup of tea while she waited. The atmosphere in the HQ building was a little different to what she'd experienced before. People were busy, with their heads down at their desks, and there wasn't the lightness and joviality about the place that there had been in 1940, despite England being a breath away from invasion at the time. She shrugged. The world had moved on. The war had turned, and it had lasted four and a half long years. It would be reasonable to assume that people maybe weren't as lighthearted as they were at the start was because they were tired of the war. 1940 was referred to as the summer of love. Many service personnel, especially the RAF, expected to be dead by the winter if the invasion went ahead, and everyone else expected a life of misery. If, on the other hand, the invasion was held off, everyone would be happy. That was the theory, at least, and explained why despite being as close to the end as it was possible for a country to get without enemy troops actually landing on the beaches, people weren't so depressed. It was one last hurrah, live or die. She was shown to a chair outside the Station Commander's office, where she joined another Squadron Leader, a young man with golden hair and a 'Netherlands' patch on the arm of his tunic. He stood when she approached, and bowed his head slightly.

"Hello," Harriet said politely. "Am I joining a queue?"

"I think so. Jan Versluys, nice to meet you." He offered his hand, which Harriet shook with a smile.

"Harry Cornwall. Are you stationed here?" she asked as they took their seats.

"Yes. Kind of. I run one of the Typhoon squadrons. We live in the tents down the end of the airfield."

"I saw those when we came in earlier. What on earth are you doing living in tents? Don't tell me there's no hot water in your accommodation either?"

"No, we have plenty of hot water; our ground crews are very good at looking after us," he laughed. "We're with the Second Tactical Air Force, and our boss has us living in tents so we can move around quickly. At least that's the logic; we haven't moved much in a while."

"Second Tactical Air Force? You mean you're flying offensive operations?" Her eyes filled with excitement at the thought. When Fighter Command was renamed Air Defence Great Britain and tasked with the defence of the realm, the offensive fighters were all bundled into the Second Tactical Air Force, an organisation which had been born in the Western Desert, and become experts at ground support operations.

"Yes, over France most of the time. It's dangerous work, but it feels good to take the war back to the Nazis. Soon we'll kick them out of our country, and we can go home."

"You're Dutch." She nodded at the badge on his arm.

"Yes," he replied proudly. We all are. My entire squadron is made up of free Dutch pilots. It makes a difference when you all have the same motivation. What about you? What's a Norwegian doing here?" He pointed at the shoulder title on her own uniform.

"Honestly, I don't know just yet. My squadron has just been posted in today as part of the home defence force."

"You're the ones we saw landing earlier in the Hurricanes?"

"Yes..."

"That sounds more dangerous than our job. Hurricanes are a little old for this corner of England, aren't they?"

"Just a little."

"Good luck!"

"Thank you."

"So, when did women start flying fighters? I have no problem with it, I should say. If a pilot can do their job, I don't care who they are." He pointed to the pilot's wings on Harriet's chest.

"I started in 1940..."

"Really? Wow! I didn't know; they certainly kept you a secret. How is it being a female pilot in your squadron? Do they accept you?"

"I certainly hope so." She gave him a smile, but before she could say anything else, a barrage of shouting came from inside the Station Commander's office. It got progressively louder, almost to the point of screaming, and Harriet found herself staring at the door with her eyes wide open. It was suddenly silent, and footsteps came closer. The door opened, and a WAAF officer marched out and closed the door. Her eyes were red like she was fighting to hold in her tears. She looked at Harriet briefly and gave an uncomfortable half smile, then quickly walked away. "What on earth was that?" Harriet whispered.

"The Station Commander..." Jan replied quietly. "A warning to a friend. There's only one thing he hates more than having foreign pilots on his air station."

"What's that?"

"Women in uniform."

"Great..."

"He doesn't like us, but he doesn't have a great deal of sway over us because we come under a different command, but he can still make life here uncomfortable. You, however..."

"My day just gets better," she sighed, then sat up straight as the door opened, and an older bald man with glasses stood staring at her.

"You must be Cornwall," he said.

"Yes, Sir," Harriet replied, as both she and Jan jumped up and stood smartly to attention.

"Norwegian?" He looked at the shoulder titles on her tunic.

"English. Of Norwegian descent, Sir."

"You'd better come in first. Vergil, you can wait."

"Versluys," Jan muttered under his breath as Harriet followed the Station Commander into his office. He pointed to a place in front of his desk, where Harriet stood obediently while he took a seat at the other side, and reclined in his chair while staring at her through his dark rimmed round glasses.

"Let me make things very clear, Squadron Leader Cornwall, so there can be no ambiguity. I'm not happy that you're here!" he hissed.

"Sir?" Harriet replied, frowning with disbelief at his combative attitude. There was very little chance of any ambiguity. He held up his finger to silence her, making her feel like a chastised schoolgirl standing in front of the head's desk, not to mention making her feel all the more irritated.

"Whatever the RAF are playing at, I don't like it. I don't believe women have a place in the service, and I certainly don't think they have a place flying aircraft. So, let's be clear. You've heard of the old adage about being seen and not heard?"

"Yes, Sir."

"Well, in this case, I want you to make sure that neither you nor your pilots are seen or heard for the duration of your stay on my station. You'll do your jobs, and you'll stay out of my way, understood?"

"Yes, Sir."

"Good. Now the formalities are over with, we can get down to tactics. Your squadron has been allocated to air defence, which means that you'll fly standing patrols along the coast of Kent four times per day. Sunrise, mid morning, mid afternoon, and sunset. You'll have a flight on standby at all other times between daybreak and night."

"Standing patrols, Sir?"

"You heard me. You'll fly a patrol line between set points, and intercept any enemy aircraft you encounter. I'm sure you've heard of the concept. You're a Squadron Leader, apparently. I'll be disappointed, but not surprised, if you don't."

"Of course I know what they are, Sir, it's just that they were proved ineffective in 1940, and I can't imagine things have got any better since. We found that it was far more effective to remain on the ground on standby, and be vectored in to attack specific threats."

"Did you indeed?"

"Yes, Sir. I'm more than happy to draw up a plan…"

"I don't think you understand, Cornwall, so let me be crystal clear. You'll fly your standing patrols as a squadron, and you'll keep a Flight on standby at other times, and you'll do that every day between daybreak and nightfall. Outside of those times, you'll remain out of sight and out of mind. Are we clear?"

"Crystal..." Harriet squared her shoulders and looked forward, as the full reality of the situation became clear.

"Good. Now, I think that's everything. I expect your reports on my desk at the end of each day, and you'll supply personnel for duty roles on the Station. Good day."

"Sir…"

"What is it?"

"Sir, I need spares and stores for my squadron. We fly Hurricanes, and the stores on the station are minimal. Enough to keep us flying a week at the most, less if we encounter the enemy."

"I suspect you'll need more than stores and spares should that happen, but see Section Officer Shannon on your way out." He waved her away dismissively.

"There's also the accommodation block allocated to my officers."

"What about it?"

"I'm informed that it's damp, has no hot water, and is in a state of disrepair."

"Then you'd better repair it before my inspection. You should think yourself lucky. The Typhoon boys are in tents. Now, I suggest you get back to your squadron. You're operational from first light tomorrow morning, and I expect your first patrol to be in the air and over the coast for sunrise."

"Sir," Harriet replied firmly, squaring her shoulders again, before saluting and heading for the door.

"Send that clog wearing idiot in on your way out." She didn't reply, just marched out and closed the door behind her, before taking a deep breath to compose herself.

"How did that go?" Jan asked as he stood and walked over to her.

"I'm not sure, but I think I just regressed a few years…"

"I'm not sure I understand?"

"You know I said that I'm accepted in my squadron?"

"Yes?"

"Maybe that's the only place I'm accepted."

"Ah, I get it. I did warn you…"

"You did. Anyway, it's your turn. Good luck."

"Thanks. I just smile and pretend my English isn't too good."

"I should have thought of that before I told him I was English..." she frowned.

"Tough luck." He gave her a smile, then disappeared into the office, leaving Harriet to make her way from room to room in search of the tall strawberry blonde Section Officer she'd seen leaving Stanley's office.

"Shannon?" Harriet said, as she looked around the door of a small office.

"Yes, Ma'am. Niamh Shannon," the WAAF officer replied, with a soft Irish accent.

"I'm Harry Cornwall, 508 Squadron CO."

"You're a…"

"Girl? Yes, I know. Mind if I come in?"

"Not at all, Ma'am." She jumped to her feet and stood to attention as Harriet closed the door quietly behind her.

"Sit, sit," she waved her hands, a little embarrassed at being received so formally. "I'm told you can help me sort the stores and spares I need for my squadron?"

"Yes, Ma'am. Of course."

"Good, I'll get my Adjutant to give you a call. I'd be grateful if you could do what you can to expedite delivery. We'll be in trouble if we don't get what we need soon, and I'm not prepared to put my girls in harm's way because the Air Force is slow. You know how things can be with stores."

"Your girls?" Shannon asked, looking focused and intrigued.

"You seem surprised?"

"I am…"

"You didn't know we were coming?"

"I was told a transit squadron was coming through for a night or two."

"That makes sense… I don't suppose you could do me another favour, could you?"

"If I can?"

"I'm told there's no hot water in our accommodation, and that it's a bit of a dump."

"Honestly, the whole block was condemned, but the Station Commander insisted it be allocated."

"That makes sense, too." Harriet rolled her eyes. "Is there anything you can do?"

"We don't have any alternatives, but I'll see what I can do about the place you're in. Leave it with me."

"Thank you." Harriet gave her a warm smile. "I'll buy you a drink in the Mess to say thanks."

"I don't go in that often, but I'll remind you of that if I see you there."

"You don't? It used to be the centre of activity when I was last here."

"Let's just say it's not really a place for the ladies. We have an anteroom allocated to us, but otherwise, we tend to go to the local pubs."

"It sounds like I'm in heaven." Harriet frowned again.

"Yes. Or the other one..." Niamh gave her an awkward smile.

"Quite… Right, I should get back to the squadron. We have some work to do."

"I'll see what I can do about the accommodation."

"Thank you. Before I go… I don't want to pry, but what was going on with the Station Commander before you came out of his office?"

"Oh, that…"

"Yes…"

"Honestly, it's nothing to worry about. I just try and ignore it. It's how he is."

"Apparently… If you want to talk about it, you know where to find me. It's not OK for people to talk to you like that."

"I'm grateful, thank you… Ma'am. If I may, just be careful with him, he can be spiteful and cause problems for people who challenge him."

"Thanks, I'll keep that in mind." Harriet left the office, and HQ, fully understanding why the mood was so dark. Dutch was there to pick her up, and soon had her back to the squadron. She checked the aircraft status with Jo, then headed down to the accommodation block, where she'd been allocated a small individual room on the second floor of the building. It was the traditional type of accommodation used for enlisted personnel. A long dormitory type room on either side of the entrance, each with twenty beds, and a block of communal showers, washbasins, and toilets in the centre of the building. The set up was duplicated upstairs, so potentially the building could accommodate eighty people, plus the small individual rooms at the entrance to each dormitory. The enlisted ranks accommodation was similar, but often had bunk beds, doubling the occupancy and making it a very busy place. Harriet looked around the small room. There was space for a narrow, wire framed single bed, a locker, and a small desk. That was it. The walls were a dull shade of white, and the floor was cold and polished. It was the least homely place she'd been in, with the possible exception of the Gestapo cell, though it was a close run thing. She unpacked and made her bed with the cardboard like sheets and coarse military blankets; coming home was going to be a different experience from that she'd remembered.

"Alright, everyone, keep your eyes open," Harriet said as she squadron climbed into the dark morning sky. The sun hadn't yet risen, but the eastern horizon was turning a silvery blue as the morning twilight signalled the arrival of another day. It had been two weeks since they'd arrived in their new home, and the dawn patrols had started, rigidly following the Kent coast from Dungeness to Margate, then Whitstable, and back again. The exact same patrol route they followed every morning, noon, and night, at the exact same times, much to Harriet's frustration. She'd pleaded with Stanley to be allowed to change the route, or the timings, or preferably both, knowing full well that after the first two days, the Luftwaffe scout aeroplanes would have been fully aware of where they'd be, and when, but he wouldn't be moved, and even threatened to have her relieved of command if she continued to question his orders.

"Aircraft, nine o'clock low," Nicole said over the radio. Harriet quickly looked over to see a couple of squadrons of Typhoons skimming the ground and heading east towards the Channel, going over to raid the French coast and cause headaches for the Germans. She'd talked with Jan a couple of times since their first meeting, and he'd told her how they were over France every day, hitting a mix of fixed positions and targets of opportunity, and generally making a nuisance of themselves. They paid the price for it, and they had their fair share of casualties, but it left Harriet annoyed that she and her squadron were flying a patrol line and contributing nothing meaningful to the war. It also had her feeling jealous, not that she'd admit it to anyone. Ultimately, she'd got what she wanted. Command of a squadron, recognition of female pilots, and the safety of England so she didn't need to risk any more of her nine lives, which she was well aware of long overspending already. At the same time, her recent experiences in France had changed her. She'd seen just how bad things were for the French, and how truly evil the Nazis could be, and she wanted to do something about it. Something more than flying along the coast of Kent.

"We may see them coming back again before we land," Harriet replied, as she went back to focusing on her patrol line, which she knew like the back of her hand, and was so ingrained that it took very little effort to follow. They circled over Herne Bay, and she thought back to her swim in the Thames Estuary after being shot down by a marauding raid of 109s, and how her new friend Atwell had been most annoyed at getting her permanently perfect hair wet. Not that it took any of the sparkle away from her natural glamour. They were supposed to be meeting in London for drinks once Harriet moved south, but she hadn't had a day off since arriving in Kent. Stanley had worked the squadron continuously, despite the understanding by all that pilots should be rested regularly, and given time off to rest so they could perform at their best when it mattered. It wasn't the Battle of Britain, or Malta, and the Luftwaffe wasn't knocking on the door. There was something of a mini blitz, where the Germans had returned to night time bombing raids over the southeast, but that was the night. Occasionally, a fighter sweep would come in during the day, and 109s or 190s would swoop in over the sea and drop small bombs on whatever targets were the closest, and shoot up the place before running back to France, but there hadn't been one since Harriet had been patrolling. Not in Kent, at least. Something which Stanley used as an excuse to keep the squadron flying the patrol lines every day without fail. In his mind, the strategy was a success. The Germans saw fourteen aged and tired Hurricanes flying up and down, and decided not to attack. Despite being able to outrun the Hurricanes without breaking a sweat. They could fly right past within reaching distance without even thinking about it, and nothing much would bother them.

The patrol ended, and the normal routine commenced. A Flight would be on standby until the late morning patrol, B Flight until the afternoon patrol, and then C Flight until the last patrol of the day, after which the entire squadron was debriefed, prepared for the following day, and then dismissed. Nobody went off the station, mostly because they were tired from the flying, which had them on edge even if the enemy didn't show up. Up to ninety minutes at a time of scanning the horizon and waiting for combat was exhausting, especially when flying in low light, as they did twice each day, and during bad weather, which there was plenty of. After a meal in the Mess, most just got cleaned up and fell into bed. Some would play cards, and sometimes they'd brave the Mess for a drink, though they weren't exactly welcomed by pilots from the neighbouring Spitfire squadron they shared the airfield with, so they rarely stayed. With Harriet's blessing, the pilots had taken over one of the unused rooms upstairs in the accommodation as their own Mess. There wasn't a bar, but they'd managed to scavenge chairs and board games, and on an evening, it was a nice place for them all to relax. Nicole would visit Harriet most nights, often with AP, Ginny, and Lexi in tow, and sometimes Jo would join them for a game of cards. They'd talk about the squadron, and the war, and Nicole would complain incessantly about their lot. Mostly, they were all happy to be flying, they were just annoyed at the way they were being treated, despite them all having been treated much worse at one time or another since they'd been pilots. The consensus was that at least they were all together to share the experience.

## Chapter 6

## The Clash

"How long will we do this?" Nicole asked, as she walked with Harriet towards their Hurricanes. She'd been on standby since the dawn patrol, and after weeks of the same mindless task, and the growing fatigue of not having a day off, her irritability had been replaced with a forlorn sadness that made Harriet uneasy. She was used to Nicole being prickly and argumentative, and it didn't sit well that her friend was so downhearted that she couldn't even argue, almost to the point that she seemed defeated. The others weren't that much better. AP was as stoic as ever, and at the same time, she'd mentioned more than once how much she missed flying her reconnaissance Spitfire. She'd been generally accepted where she was. Reconnaissance squadrons being what they were, the home of pilots who flew alone, she'd been left to get on with it, with nobody really caring whether she was male or female, as long as the job got done. She missed the solitary lifestyle, and the opportunity to get on with something other than flying around in circles. Lexi was the most positive of the flight commanders. She kept spirits up with her typically American confidence and swagger. Though despite the neglect she'd been shown in the desert, she voiced in private to Harriet that she missed the freedom she'd enjoyed there, and that the stifling rigidity of her current life was suffocating. It all made Harriet concerned and disappointed. Her excitement at forming an all female squadron was being squeezed out of her day by day, to the point that she couldn't imagine the squadron lasting.

"Until we've won the war," Harriet replied with a confident smile.

"If they let us actually fight in the war, we'd win it much quicker."

"What we're doing is important, you know that. Somebody has to be here if the Germans come over."

"The Germans do come over, at night, or in fighters we wouldn't catch even in a dive."

"You know what I mean. Come on, smile; it could be worse. We could be back in Malta flying biplanes against the best of the Luftwaffe."

"That would be more fun."

"Don't be ridiculous. You nearly died!"

"I'm nearly dying of boredom here." She gave Harriet a smirk, then headed off to her Hurricane.

"I'll try and find you something to break the boredom. I hear the Station Commander needs a new Adjutant…" she shouted, then smirked to herself as she walked around her own aeroplane and checked it over, before climbing the wing and lowering herself into the cockpit and onto the parachute she'd left on the seat after the dawn patrol. She pulled on her flying helmet and checked the instruments, then fastened and tightened her harness before starting the mighty Merlin engine, which coughed and spluttered into life as it sent flames flickering from the exhaust stubs and a cloud of blue smoke into the air, which Harriet sniffed at and smiled, before the propeller blew it away. Once she'd gone through her checks, she looked up and down the line of Hurricanes to make sure they were all ready to go, then led them to the end of the runway, where they lined up behind Harriet and Carrie in their flights. Once she was sure they were ready, she looked over to Carrie and gave a nod, then slowly eased the throttle open until the aeroplane was straining to be let go. One last check, and a clearance from the tower, and she released the brakes and started the Hurricane sprinting along the runway and climbing into the clear blue sky. Her tummy flipped as she left the ground, as it always did, and she couldn't help smiling again.

The patrol went as it had every other time, until they were approaching Dungeness on their return trip, where Harriet noticed vapour trails and smoke out over the Channel. Her heart raced immediately. She knew a battle when she saw one, and while the smoke was distant, it was enough to suggest that the fight was still raging.

"Moonbeam, Vixen Leader. Enemy aircraft sighted over the Channel and engaging friendlies, angels fifteen to the southwest of my position.

Going to have a look!" Harriet called as she looked around for signs of other aircraft, while preparing to move the squadron onto an intercept course. "Vixen Squadron, standby!"

"Vixen Leader, Moonbeam. Negative, hold your position," the Controller replied. His voice was steady and calm, to the point of being void of any emotion. Harriet's heart squeezed a little as she processed the reply she'd just heard.

"Moonbeam, I repeat. Enemy aircraft engaging friendlies south west of my position."

"Vixen Leader, hold your position. Intercept has been dispatched."

'I can see them from here!" she bellowed in reply, as the smoke trails were joined by black dots, wheeling around the sky as the distant aircraft came into view. It was like an uncoordinated swarm, with more dots than she'd imagined. "Moonbeam! Friendly aircraft being chased by thirty plus enemy fighters. Going to intercept!"

"Vixen Leader, hold your position!" Came the forceful reply, now brimming with emotion. "Spitfires dispatched to intercept. You are ordered to maintain your patrol line!"

"Vixen Squadron, Vixen Leader. A Flight on my port wing, B Flight to Starboard. C Flight, get upstairs and watch our tails, and turn south west on my mark. Three, two, one, mark!" The squadron took their positions, with the flights scattering into loose pairs exactly where Harriet had told them to. Together, the fourteen Hurricanes turned to face the distant battle.

"Vixen Leader, Moonbeam. Maintain your patrol line, and do not engage! I repeat, do not engage enemy aircraft!"

"Sorry, Moonbeam, your transmission is breaking up," Harriet replied as she focused on the rapidly closing battle. "OK, everyone, keep your eyes open, and don't break until you're told. Stay in your pairs, and watch each other's backs. Stay off the air if you don't need to talk, and shout out the threats. You've trained for this, and you've done it before."

"Vixen Leader, you are ordered to return to base immediately!" the increasingly agitated Controller ordered, almost shouting over the airwaves.

"Repeat please," Harriet replied while totally ignoring him and focusing on the battle ahead, which was quickly taking shape. Typhoons were rolling and diving all over the place, each with two or more 109s on their tail. Some were smoking, others were burning, and the sky quickly became a mesh of smoke and trails of burning tracer. "Vixen Squadron, break now!" She shouted, and like clockwork, A and B Flights peeled off left and right, in wide, arcing turns that would bring them back on the battle like pincers, while C Flight pulled up into a steep climb, ready to drop down on the battle, once they'd secured the sky above. "Carrie, stick on my wing, and shout if anything gets close!"

"Wilco!" Carrie replied.

"Moonbeam, Vixen Leader. Am engaging enemy fighters, Tally Ho!" She pushed her throttle through the gate, driving the engine to maximum power, and feeling herself being pulled tight into her seat as the Hurricane surged forwards. She focused on the nearest Typhoon, and the 109s chasing close behind. The Typhoon was smoking as it twisted left and right to avoid the streams of tracer, which glanced past it and headed straight for Harriet, making her weave and dip to dodge it. She focused, waiting for the right moment, and as they closed, the Typhoon pilot pulled up hard, and the 109's followed. Harriet pulled up and pushed her fire button, sending her own tracer in the opposite direction as her four 20mm cannons roared into life and ripped into the chasing 109, blowing it apart with a huge explosion as the fuel tanks erupted. The second 109 pulled right to avoid her fire, and got its left wing clipped off by Carrie. "Good shooting!" Harriet shouted as she pulled up and rolled, just as another stream of tracer cut in front of her from a dropping 109, which quickly started burning as it dived past her before she could respond, being shot apart by a chasing Hurricane.

"Yeeha!" Lexi shouted as she followed the 109 down with the rest of her flight, who were quickly getting stuck into the fight, while A Flight and B Flight closed the trap, hitting the already distracted 109s from the left and right, and quickly opening up the battle, which was already stretched across several miles.

"Skipper, bank left!" Carrie yelled, and Harriet instinctively rolled to her left and pulled back on her stick, dragging her Hurricane into a tight left turn that greyed and narrowed her vision, leaving a 109 to race past her in a turn that was nowhere near as tight. Carrie dropped in after it and gave it a shot, having turned tighter than the 109 was capable of, and blasted into the space just in front of it, rattling it with her cannons in the perfect deflection shot and almost cutting it in half. It instantly burst into flames and dropped in a steepening dive towards the sea, giving the pilot just seconds to slip from the cockpit and tumble away before deploying his parachute. Harriet reversed her turn and came back around as a Typhoon passed below her, skimming the waves and racing towards home. She'd lost a lot of height, and opened up the engine again as she pulled back on the stick and rocketed upwards in the direction of what looked like a whole mess of fighters spinning after each other. Before she could reach them, her Hurricane shuddered as a 109 came down at her from above and behind, attacking from her blind spot and rattling her fuselage. A heavy thud behind her made her heart jump, as a cannon shell hit the armour plating behind her seat, and then another, both knocking her forward despite the g forces of the hard climb pulling her into her seat. She rolled, then pointed straight up and closed her throttle, and waited for the stall. The controls got sloppy, and as the wing dropped, she kicked the rudder bar, throwing the nose downwards and the tail up, then she spun and opened the throttle again as the 109 skimmed past, narrowly missing her and having to roll to avoid a collision, before diving away in panic. Harriet was left trying to catch her breath as she took control of her Hurricane, and pulled it out of the descent. The controls were still sloppy, despite the speed, and she looked out over her wings. The left was shredded, with the control surfaces badly damaged, and she could only imagine what the fuselage and tail were like. She levelled out close to the sea and checked her mirror, there was nothing following, and a spin of her head showed she wasn't a target, at least not right at that moment. She throttled back and went through her checks. The engine seemed to be fine; it was just the controls that were a bit off. After composing herself, she opened the throttle again and pulled up, then circled back towards the battle, or at least that was her intention. She couldn't justify leaving the battle, not when her squadron were going head to head with 109s, but in a stark reminder of her last time fighting over the south of England, the battle had gone. She swept around in a wide turn, but all she could see were black dots in the distance to both the north and south. As quick as it had begun, the fight was over. The sky was still full of smoke, and there was wreckage on the sea. Her first thought was to climb and circle, to check for downed Hurricanes so she could call for a launch. Something caught the corner of her eye as she looked up, and her attention was drawn to the sun and the 109 she just about made out a split second before it opened fire on her. She pushed the stick hard forward, and the Hurricane immediately dropped into a dive, flipping her stomach as it did, but also changing the angles and making sure the 109 would overshoot. As the 109 followed the stream of tracer, she pulled up and left, starting a tight turn while the 109 did the same, trying to come back on her for a second chance. She backed off the throttle a little and pulled harder on the stick, keeping her eye on the airspeed indicator to make sure she didn't lose so much she stalled while dragging the Hurricane into a turn so tight that the 109 quickly came around to her side, not able to follow and get behind her. As he came level and started to pass, she opened the throttle and rolled right, putting her gunsight on his tail and getting off a couple of shots, one of which cut through the fuselage of the 109, and passed straight out of the other side without causing too much damage. The pilot was clearly flustered though, and pulled hard right into another turn. He was still carrying his speed from the dive, and quickly pulled out of Harriet's range before racing around to try and get on her tail again. She kept her eyes on him, watching as she timed her turn so that by the time he completed his turn, she was just about coming onto his tail again. She gave him another blast, this time making him roll away, before flipping onto his back and starting a steep dive. She went after him, knowing full well she wouldn't be able to catch a 109 in a dive, not even a Spitfire could do that, but it didn't stop her letting off a couple more shots at him, catching him in the wing and making him roll slightly as bits flew off it, before steepening his dive and pulling away to the south west. For a moment, she planned to give chase, but he was going all out to get out of her range, and it was the moment she needed to get away, if she was sensible. So, she decided that discretion was the better part of valour and pulled around to the north and opened her throttle, while dropping to the waves to try and make it difficult for him to see her if he decided to come back and have another go. She knew that if he did, she'd be in trouble. Coming at her straight from behind would give her nowhere to run. Whichever way she turned, he'd be able to adjust and fire, and knock her straight down into the water. If he'd done that on his first attack, he would have finished her off. Even his second pass could have done the job if he approached from a way out, instead of trying to outturn her. Whoever the pilot was, she was grateful that he didn't seem to know how best to take on a Hurricane.

Her heart raced as she sped across the Channel and raced towards home, with one eye on the rereview mirror above the canopy, while spinning her head to check left and right, up, and forward, searching for signs of other enemy aircraft. The sweat that had run down her back in rivers was starting to cool, and she felt a shiver run up her spine as she licked her lips and tried to get some moisture in her dry mouth again. It had been a long time since she'd been in a proper fighter to fighter dogfight, and her head was still running at maximum speed as she tried to think through what had happened. Her instincts were still there, but she was slower than she'd liked to have been, both in her responses and the speed of her aeroplane, though her faithful old Hurricane had saved her life. Being slower and able to turn tighter had made all the difference when up against the 109, and she was thankful. A squadron of Spitfires passed high overhead as she approached the coast, heading in the direction she'd come from. She shook her head at the thought that they may be the squadron sent up to intercept the Luftwaffe and rescue the Typhoons. She hadn't seen any other friendly aircraft, so if it wasn't them, she couldn't think who else would have been sent, and whoever it was, they would never have gotten there in time. The excitement started to ease a little, and irritation started to take over from pure adrenaline once she knew that she was more or less safe. She couldn't think of a single logical reason why she'd been told to hold her patrol line when she could see the enemy, especially when the enemy were getting stuck into other RAF aircraft. She shook her head and tried not to let it get stuck in her mind. She still had a job to do, and being angry could wait. She approached the airfield and dropped her wheels. Unfortunately, her flaps weren't responding the way they should, and when she dropped them, the aeroplane lurched to the left, suggesting the hits on her right wing had taken out the flaps, so those on the left were now acting as a one sided brake, which ran the risk of pulling her out of control if she tried to land. She raised the flaps again and dropped her speed, but was still coming in faster than she usually would, especially with so little headwind to slow her. She slipped over the perimeter hedge, feeling it scrape her undercarriage as she passed, then touched down at the very beginning of the runway and did her best to slow, braking a little at a time, so she didn't overheat the wheels and risk blowing the tyres. She eventually slowed, to her relief, then taxied towards the dispersal, swinging left and right to see ahead of her, while trying to count the Hurricanes parked on the grass amongst a flurry of activity. She slowed to a halt and shut down the engine as Nicole appeared on her wing.

"Where have you been?" Nicole demanded. "Are you OK?" She looked both worried and relieved at the same time.

"Why? Did you miss me?" Harriet replied with a smile.

"Idiot!" Nicole blustered, then gave Harriet a smile, and helped her out of the cockpit. "We thought you'd gone down…"

"What?"

"Your Number Two saw a 109 blow chunks out of you, and when you didn't come back… Well, we naturally expected the worst."

"Did everyone else get back?"

"Yes, we haven't been back long. A few got shot up pretty bad, but not enough to put them out of the war."

"Thank God."

"God? You should thank my training programme. That's what kept them alive."

"Of course," Harriet sighed while rolling her eyes. "As you mention it, where is my Number Two?"

"Over there." She pointed at Carrie, who was sitting on the grass by her Hurricane as the ground crew climbed over it, and not joining the other pilots in getting drinks from the tea urn and talking excitedly outside the dispersal hut. "She wanted to go back up to look for you, and I had to tell her no. I think that if the ground crew got her Hurricane refuelled and rearmed before you got back, she'd have gone anyway. It's why she's waiting. I'll get you a cup of tea." She gave Harriet a smile and squeezed her shoulder. "Well done today, Ma'am. You were a real leader."

"Thank you..." Harriet returned a smile as she squeezed Nicole's hand, then walked off towards Carrie, who slowly got to her feet and stood smartly to attention as Harriet approached. "What are you doing over here by yourself?" she asked, giving Carrie a smile as she did.

"Just talking to the ground crew, Ma'am."

"The ground crew are over there on your Hurricane, and you're sitting in the grass. It's hardly what I'd call talking."

"Ma'am…"

"Harry. We've been through this. So, you're not over here waiting for them to refuel and rearm it, so you can disobey orders and go back up to look for me?" Harriet asked mischievously. Carrie looked away and blushed. "Come on, let's go and get a cup of tea."

"I can't…"

"What's wrong? Are you OK? You weren't injured, were you?" Harriet frowned nervously and looked her up and down.

"No. I just… Well, I only have one job in the squadron, and that's to keep you safe."

"I'm here, aren't I?"

"Only just."

"It doesn't work in degrees of safe. I'm either dead or alive, and I'm alive, mostly because you warned me when there was a 109 on my tail. Without your warning, I wouldn't have been able to roll, and I'd have gone down there and then instead of just getting hit in the wing." Harriet smiled warmly, and Carrie blushed again. "Look, we're at war, and that means we're inevitably going to be in situations where we can't control all of the variables. All we can do is our best, and hope that's enough. Today it was, and that's the only thing that's important. OK?" Carrie nodded.

"I was embarrassed that I'd come back without you. I thought you were with the other Hurricanes, but when I got to them and found out you weren't, I turned back and searched for you. I couldn't find you anywhere, and then Flight Lieutenant Delacourt found me and brought me home."

"It's a good job she did. You don't hang around by yourself over the Channel; that's how you get dead."

"She said the same."

"It's true. We learned the hard way in the Battle of Britain."

"You got back OK."

"Sheer luck. Now, that's us done, no more thinking about it. I need a cup of tea, and I'm sure you do too." Carrie nodded, and Harriet put her arm through her young friend's, and they walked together towards the excitement of the dispersal. "I saw you get one and damage two. Any more?"

"No, that's all." Carrie smiled.

"All? You've been in two fights with us since you arrived, and you've knocked down two enemy aeroplanes and damaged three. Anyone else would be pretty happy with that."

"I suppose… How many have you knocked down?"

"Enough," Harriet replied with a smile. She'd stopped counting in Malta. The number had stopped mattering to her. If she came back alive, that was all that counted. If she knocked one of the enemy down and they had one less in the fight, it was a bonus. It was that simple.

"Tea," Nicole said as she handed Harriet a mug. "Three cheers for Squadron Leader Cornwall. Hip, hip!" A huge cheer went up from the gathered pilots, ground crew, and anyone else who was passing the hive of excited activity. Ginny had handed out combat report forms so she could collate the information and hand it over to the Station Intelligence Officer, and the pilots were doing their best to fill them in while talking through their actions with each other. Some were smeared with smoke, others looked like they'd stepped out of a Savile Row tailor, but there was one thing common to them all, their big smiles and bright eyes. They worked hard and took their jobs seriously, and since they were together, she'd only ever seen them so animated three times. After both combat sorties they'd been involved in, and during their night in the Mess to celebrate the attack on the bombers before they moved south.

"Everyone's OK?" Harriet asked Ginny after making her way around all of her pilots and congratulating them on their work, and taking the time to hear their stories.

"I think so. Some of the aeroplanes are a bit shot up, but the pilots seem unscathed."

"Good. I've heard eight confirmed and five probables so far."

"Not a bad result."

"Not at all. Everything OK?" Harriet asked, as Jo made her way through the pilots to join her.

"Two are going to need more than we can do for them, and another five are going to be out for a while."

"How long?"

"Your guess is as good as mine..."

"Parts?"

"Parts... We still don't have what we need. We've got the basics, but the engines are running tired, and after today some are almost shot entirely, having been pushed to the max. We're already using the reserve aeroplanes, so after today I can give you six or seven."

"There's nothing you can do for the others?"

"I can try, but they won't be at their best..."

"No. They're not flying if they're not right. I'll sort out the stores." She frowned as she headed for her office. She'd asked for the spares the squadron needed on the day she arrived, and every day since. Shannon had done her best and put in the orders repeatedly, but nothing happened, and the squadron had been running on the bare minimum for days. One of the Hurricanes had given up mid flight a few days earlier when the overworked engine seized, forcing the pilot into an emergency landing in a farmer's field. It was getting dangerous. "Dutch, get me Group Headquarters on the phone."

"Ma'am," Dutch replied as she quickly got to work, then handed Harriet the phone.

"Flight Lieutenant Wright," the voice came over the phone.

"Squadron Leader Cornwall, 508 Squadron."

"Yes?"

"Yes, Ma'am..." she said forcefully.

"Yes, Ma'am?" came the questioning, yet unfazed reply.

"508 Squadron is currently not operational, and won't be until we receive the spare parts that have been requested for weeks."

"Not operational?" He sounded rather surprised at her announcement.

"Not operational. Good day." She put the phone down and gave Dutch a smile.

"That's one way of doing it, Ma'am," Dutch said with a shrug.

"It's a day for fights; why stop with the Germans?" At that, the phone rang. "That was quick..." She smiled as she picked up the phone again. "508 Squadron, Squadron Leader Cornwall."

"Harry, it's Niamh," the young Irish officer said, her voice signalling that something wasn't quite right. "He wants to see you right away."

"OK, I'll be right there."

"Harry, he's turning the air blue. Just so you're warned."

"Thanks..." She put the phone down and rolled her eyes. "Word gets around fast these days," she sighed. "Dutch, if I'm not put against a wall and shot, I'll be back in a while. Make sure everyone gets to lunch, no standby flight."

"Ma'am..." Dutch smirked.

"Where are you going?" Nicole asked, as Harriet left the dispersal hut and walked over to her car.

"To be shouted at. What's our final tally?"

"Eight and five. Seven damaged."

"Thank you, see you soon." She jumped in the car and revved the engine into life, before speeding around the air station while thinking through how she was going to explain ringing Group headquarters direct and telling them her squadron was stood down, and in doing so, totally circumventing the chain of command. She was prepared for an argument, though. She was ready for it before she even got in the car. It was bad enough that the squadron were being treated like pariahs, but not giving them the supplies they needed to stay safely airworthy was too far. She marched through the headquarters building and up the stairs, where she heard the ranting long before she got to Stanley's office.

"He hasn't stopped..." Niamh said as she met Harriet. "I'll let him know you're here."

"Don't worry about it; I'll let him know myself." Harriet smiled confidently, then hammered her fist on his door.

"What is it?" Stanley shouted.

"Squadron Leader Cornwall, Sir," Harriet said confidently as she entered the room. He slammed down the phone and pointed in front of his desk. She closed the door, then stood to attention where he'd pointed, and waited in silence. Standing to the side of his desk was the Station Adjutant, a Flight Lieutenant called Fraser, with thinning red hair, a man who was known as the Station Commander's flying monkey. He was sent to deliver and enforce Stanley's orders, and seemed to take great pleasure in the power he wielded. It was he who'd provided the substandard accommodation, and took great pleasure in making life generally uncomfortable for Harriet's squadron, all in the name of the Station Commander. There was also a WAAF Sergeant sitting in the corner taking notes.

"You're out of uniform!" Stanley said firmly, while looking at Harriet with disdain.

"Sir?" she replied, while looking down at herself.

"You know the Station Standing Orders, Cornwall. Flying clothing is not to be worn away from the dispersal. In Headquarters and around the station, pilots are to wear service dress only."

"Sir, I've only just landed, and was told to report to you immediately." She could feel her frustration building, and it was taking all of her energy not to let go at him.

"Orders are orders, Cornwall, though it seems that's a concept you struggle to grasp!" His voice started to rise in volume as his face reddened. "If your ignorance of dress regulations was the only issue, we'd be having a different conversation, but as it happens, there's something much more serious we need to talk about, specifically your deliberately disobeying direct orders!" He looked at her sternly. His face was twitching a little as Harriet waited for what was to come next. France had changed her. She was looking at him and waiting for the tirade she knew was coming, but she wasn't bothered in the slightest. He wasn't going to hang her, or beat her, and as such, she wasn't afraid. "So, what do you have to say for yourself?" he bellowed.

"Friendly aircraft were being overwhelmed by enemy fighters, Sir, so I made the decision to intercept."

"Made the decision to intercept?" he asked In disbelief. "You made the decision to intercept?"

"Yes, Sir."

"You don't get to make that decision! You get to follow orders! You were tasked to maintain your patrol line. You were ordered to maintain your patrol line. You made the decision to intercept, and in doing so, you disobeyed a direct order, deserting your post and leaving us vulnerable to enemy action. Lives could have been lost because of you, Cornwall!" He thumped his fist on the desk as he shouted. "Your inability to follow orders put lives at risk!"

"Lives were already at risk, Sir! Those Typhoons were out of ammunition. They were sitting ducks for the thirty or so Messerschmitt 109s that were getting stuck into them. If we hadn't intervened, we'd have lost valuable pilots and aeroplanes."

"Were you tasked to fly an escort mission?"

"No, Sir. We were tasked to patrol the coast, which a large force of enemy aircraft were rapidly approaching. We did our job."

"You disobeyed orders."

"We did the right thing!"

"You deserted your post! You opened the door to incoming raids and put lives at risk. A squadron of Spitfires had been tasked to intercept the 109s; there was absolutely no need for you to be involved. You deserted your post, you put lives at risk, and for what? So you and your gaggle of silly little schoolgirls could pretend to be fighter pilots for the day!" He thumped his desk again, making Harriet twinge involuntarily. She wasn't scared; she was furious. It was taking every effort not to jump over the desk and punch him in the nose, but she knew that if she did, it'd all be over. He'd been looking for an excuse since the day she'd arrived, and hitting him would give him exactly what he needed.

"We did our jobs, Sir. We did not desert our posts."

"You're an embarrassment, Cornwall. You and your circus. Unfortunately for me, that's part of my problem. You should be put in front of a court martial for what you did today, but that would bring more shame on this station than I'm prepared to accept. So, we're going to deal with this internally. Your squadron will be taken out of the line at your request, citing a requirement for further training, a request which I will reluctantly authorise. You'll then be transferred north, away from here and out of my hair. Then maybe we can get on with this war, without any more bloody silly experiments. I'll expect your written request to be stood down on my desk this afternoon. That's all."

"Sir?" Harriet's heart was racing. She wasn't afraid of him physically, but she was quickly becoming afraid of what he was trying to do to her squadron. She could take his shouting, and even his misogynistic behaviour, but he was threatening to not only punish her squadron, he was going to destroy it. She knew full well that if she requested the squadron be taken out of the line for more training, everyone who had a reason not to let women fly would jump on the opportunity to make sure they never flew again. Weak, scared, incapable, they'd accuse them of everything they could.

"You heard." He sat back in his chair and smiled as his voice dulled to a soft, almost happy tone. "Look, Cornwall, just get the request written, and it's done. It works for both of us. You don't want to be here flying up and down on pointless patrol lines, and I don't want you here. Write the request, and you'll be back in Yorkshire by this time tomorrow."

"No thank you, Sir," she replied, while squaring her shoulders and looking him in the eyes.

"Excuse me?"

"As an officer, I believe it's my right to request trial by court martial in the face of your accusations."

"What?" He leant forward, the smirk dropping from his face as he heard her words.

"I gave the orders to intercept the 109s, Sir, and I accept full responsibility for the actions of the squadron, who did nothing but follow the orders of their Commanding Officer. As such, I request trial by court martial on the charges of disobeying orders and deserting my post." She raised her nose in the air as dismissively as she could, and stared forward.

"Don't be ridiculous, Cornwall; it'll be the end of you. Write the bloody request, and let's get this over with. There's no need to ruin your career and get yourself thrown in prison, when for the sake of five minutes of writing, you can keep your precious squadron flying."

"No thank you, Sir. I'll take the court martial." She stepped forward and took a pen from her pocket, then wrote on a sheet of paper she took from his desk, requesting trial by court martial for the stated charges. She signed and dated it, and pushed it in front of him, looking him in the eyes as he trembled with anger.

"Get out…" he hissed. "You're a disgrace to the uniform! Get out of my office!" he bellowed, while standing from his desk. "Fraser, Squadron Leader Cornwall is under Mess arrest. You're to escort her to her quarters, and place an armed guard outside. Nobody comes or goes, other than meal deliveries or to use the ablutions."

"Yes, Sir," Fraser replied with far more enjoyment than was appropriate.

"You want to play with the big boys, Cornwall, fine!" Stanley raged.

"This way…" Fraser said, as he stood beside Harriet.

"Ma'am or Squadron Leader. I'm still a higher rank than you, Flight Lieutenant Fraser."

"Yes, Ma'am. Indeed you are, for now."

## Chapter 7

## Winds of Change

"Squadron Leader Cornwall," the Flight Lieutenant said as he entered the small room where Harriet had been waiting, staring at the walls and contemplating her future since she'd arrived at the Air Ministry that morning. After five days of Mess arrest, during which she wasn't allowed to talk with anyone in her squadron, and leaving it in Nicole's capable hands in her absence, she'd been summoned to London. Word had got out, thanks to Niamh Shannon, and all of the squadron's officers were paraded outside in their best uniforms when Harriet was escorted from her room to the staff car waiting outside. Nicole opened the car door and gave a smart salute before whispering a 'bonne chance,' and sending Harriet on her way to face her fate.

"Yes," Harriet replied, as her attention was pulled back to the room and out of her daydreams. She'd gone over the events again and again in her mind. She was confident she'd done the right thing in going to the aid of the Typhoons, and she was confident she'd done the right thing in not complying with Group Captain Stanley's plan, which would have seen the squadron demoted to ferry pilots before they knew it. They were better than that; they'd proved it. Two actions, fifteen enemy aircraft shot down, and no losses. They needed to be fighting, not ferrying aeroplanes around the country, or flying patrol lines. They'd earned the right for her to stand up for them, even if, in all likelihood, she would no longer be with them. She'd considered the options for days. However the court martial went, she'd be finished, she knew that much. What her fate would be, though, was anyone's guess. It could be anything from prison to the long threatened posting to Balloon Command. Whatever it was, she was convinced it was worthwhile if it saved the squadron.

"If you'd follow me, they're ready for you." He half smiled, not that it reassured her in any way, and she stood and straightened her uniform before following him along a long corridor with high ceilings, to the equally high office door. "I'll announce you. March in, and halt in front of the desk to the right of the other officer, and salute." He gave her another half smile as she nodded and took a deep breath. He opened the door and stepped inside. "Squadron Leader Cornwall," he announced loudly and formally, before giving her a nod. She squared her shoulders and marched into the office, and immediately wished she was back in Malta flying an obsolete Gloster Gladiator biplane against an overwhelming enemy raid. Sitting behind a long desk was an Air Marshal, with an Air Vice Marshal sitting either side of him. Away to his left, a Squadron Leader sat behind another desk, with a WAAF Section Officer sitting beside him. Standing in front of the desk in his best uniform was Group Captain Stanley. She felt herself start to shake as she marched. It was quite involuntary, and she had absolutely no control over it. She'd prepared herself, but couldn't have imagined a room so daunting. She halted and saluted, then stood in the silence and waited.

"Right, what's this about disobeying orders and deserting?" the Air Marshal asked. He was a tall and athletic looking man in his early fifties with salt and pepper hair, and he both looked and sounded irritated to be there.

"Sir," Stanley started. "Squadron Leader Cornwall was ordered to fly a patrol line along the Kent coast, and despite orders to the contrary, she left her post to fly out over the Channel. She was ordered repeatedly to hold her position so as not to interfere with another operation, and told in clear and unmistakable terms to maintain her post protecting our shores against enemy incursion. In disobeying her orders, she left our defences open and led a poorly trained and equipped squadron into extreme danger. The fact that an enemy raid didn't slip in through the gap she'd left in our defences, or that there weren't losses of her pilots to accompany the significant damage to her squadron's aircraft, was nothing more than sheer luck. As it is, the squadron was out of the line for almost two days due to the damage done to their aircraft, which in turn has left the burden on other squadrons to fill the void. Altogether, Sir, it was nothing more than criminal neglect on the part of Squadron Leader Cornwall, and when I tried to save the blushes of both her pilots and the RAF by suggesting more training, she demanded a court martial, being unable to accept the constructive criticism and guidance of an experienced superior officer, Sir."

"Very well… Anything else?"

"If I may offer a personal observation, Sir?"

"Go on."

"It's my opinion, Sir, that Squadron Leader Cornwall has something of a chip on her shoulder. Since arriving under my command, she's done everything possible to take offence, and even gone as far as seeking to segregate her squadron from the rest of the station by ordering them not to use the Mess bar. Far be it for me to question the Air Ministry's decision to let females fly, Sir, but after working with Squadron Leader Cornwall, I do question whether they have the emotional temperament for the job."

"I see…" He looked to the officers either side of him, then over to the Squadron Leader to make sure he and the Section Officer were keeping up with the documentation before he continued. "Is that all?"

"Yes, Sir."

"Good, then we'd better continue." He shuffled his notes and flicked through the pages for a moment before looking up again. "We don't have all day, and I'm pretty certain I have all I need to confirm my decision."

"Sir…" Harriet said quite involuntarily. Hearing her voice echo around the cavernous room before she even knew she was talking.

"What is it, Squadron Leader?" The Air Marshal asked.

"Sir, I'd like to give my version of events, if I may?" She took a deep breath to compose herself.

"You may not," came the stark reply, which quickly had her heart in her mouth. "Air Vice Marshal Lewis, if you'd like to continue?" He looked to the man on his left.

"Yes, Sir," Lewis replied. "I received a combat report from one of my Squadrons in the Second Tactical Air Force, stating that while over the Channel on their return from a raid over France, they were jumped by between twenty and thirty enemy fighters. The squadron commander immediately made radio contact with Group to request support, and I have evidence to confirm that this request was passed direct to 11 Group, and then to the Sector Controller, where a squadron of Spitfires was dispatched to come to their aid."

"As would be expected."

"Quite. However, Sir, if I may continue?"

"Please do."

"The Typhoon squadron had expended their ammunition over France, and were quite defenceless when they were set on by the enemy. They had their speed, though many aircraft had been hit by flak while attacking their targets, and weren't at their best, and it's a fair assessment to say that that left on their own, they'd be knocked down quite easily. Their squadron commander reports that just when they thought they'd had it, with German fighters among them and causing significant damage, a squadron of Hurricanes came out of nowhere and got stuck into the Germans with determined aggression, shooting down several aircraft and forcing the enemy to retire. The squadron commander went on to state that it's his opinion that if it wasn't for the Hurricanes, he would have lost half, if not all of his squadron."

"I see… And it was definitely Hurricanes, and not Spitfires, that came to his rescue?"

"Yes, Sir. He was adamant in this, as he was so surprised that Hurricanes had been sent to his aid, what with them being obsolete and retired from that particular role."

"Indeed they are. When exactly did the Spitfires arrive?"

"The squadron commander couldn't say, Sir. He didn't see them. However, the officer commanding the Spitfires scrambled to intercept stated that the only aircraft seen during his sortie was a single Hurricane crossing the coast. No Typhoons were found, and no enemy was intercepted. I should add that there was only one flight of Spitfires on standby; the rest of the squadron was on fifteen to thirty minutes warning, and had to be recalled from the Mess before they could be scrambled. Other squadrons on standby in the area had already been scrambled to investigate other potential raids."

"Thank you." He turned to the other officer. "Air Vice Marshal Reid?"

"Thank you, Sir. My investigation makes for uncomfortable reading in parts, and while I'll spare the details in the interest of brevity, I'll provide the points pertinent to this case."

"Please do."

"First, it would appear that despite standing orders to the contrary, 508 Squadron were issued Hawker Hurricane fighters with which to fly fighter sorties over south east England. An aircraft type obsolete in that role for some years. Second, despite that quite debilitating handicap, 508 Squadron have engaged in two combats, with a tally of seven enemy bombers and eight fighters confirmed shot down, a total of seven probables, and thirteen damaged. All without the loss of a single 508 Squadron pilot. Third, despite standing orders to the contrary once again, 508 Squadron were instructed to fly rigid patrol lines around the coast of Kent at set times of the day, not only giving the enemy an overt indication of our movements, but placing the squadron itself at risk of being ambushed on their predictable route by superior enemy aircraft… Fourth, I have a statement from the Commanding Officer of the supply depot claiming that orders for spares and parts for 508 Squadron were frequently countermanded by the Station Adjutant, a Flight Lieutenant Fraser, acting on the express orders of the Station Commander, Group Captain Stanley. Fifth, I have statements from numerous sources stating that 508 Squadron were placed on continuous duty without relief or rest, once again in contravention of standing orders. They were also issued substandard accommodation, requiring them to do their own maintenance and cleaning work to make the quarters liveable, and they were actively discouraged from using the facilities of the Officers' Mess, all of which they were being billed for." He sighed and looked to the Air Marshal. "Should I go on, Sir?"

"Thank you, that'll be all for now," the Air Marshal replied before turning back to Stanley. "Now we have all of the evidence, shall we get this court martial underway?"

"Sir…" Stanley stammered. "Sir, I hardly think it's appropriate to be discussing hearsay in this forum!"

"Hearsay? Group Captain Stanley, are you accusing two highly respected Air Vice Marshals of lying?"

"Not lying, Sir. Maybe misled."

"By?"

"The gentlemen they received their reports from, who clearly didn't want to discredit a lady, and therefore protected her with some more creative reporting of the actual events."

"As I understand it, Group Captain Stanley, the officer commanding the Typhoons had absolutely no idea which squadron came to his aid, and wouldn't know whether they were male, female, or a herd of flying cats. As for the other statements, it doesn't really matter. You weren't part of the decision to equip Cornwall and her squadron with Hurricanes; responsibility for that crime lies elsewhere, and is being addressed in a different forum. You are, however, responsible for the delaying of parts, the issuing of orders in direct contravention of standing orders, and the mistreatment of officers under your command. All of which have significantly increased threat and risk to this country, and reduced the effectiveness of our air defence. You're also responsible for instructing Sector Control not to vector 508 Squadron to aid the Typhoons in their moment of need, further risking the lives of even more pilots. Ultimately, Group Captain Stanley, your actions are nothing less than disgraceful, and that's without considering the frankly disgusting way in which you seek to bully, manipulate, and generally abuse females of all ranks under your command, instances of which are very well documented in the numerous witness statements we've secured, which are damning, to say the least. You're vindictive, and you're dangerous, and you have absolutely no place in the RAF. Now, I know that you're close to retirement, Group Captain Stanley, and that after your long service, you'll be looking forward to collecting your pension."

"Yes, Sir..." Stanley muttered.

"Well, I wouldn't get too attached to that idea... There will be a court martial, Group Captain Stanley. Yours. The Flight Lieutenant outside will show you to a room, where you'll wait under close arrest. Understood?"

"Yes, Sir." Tears rolled down his cheeks as he saluted. "I've given my life to the RAF..."

"And in doing so, you've made the lives of others absolute hell. Now, get out."

"Sir." He didn't look at Harriet as he turned and left, though she couldn't help looking at him. He was broken, and she didn't feel an ounce of sympathy for him.

"Will our witness statements suffice for providing your version of the events, Squadron Leader Cornwall?" the Air Marshal asked as the door closed.

"Yes, Sir," Harriet replied. She was more than a little stunned at what had just happened, having fully expected things to go very differently. After days under Mess arrest, and the opening statements, all she expected would happen was a whitewash at best.

"Good. You'll get your say in Stanley's court martial." He let the slightest smile curl his lips upwards for the briefest moment while he shuffled his papers again. "Now, what to do with you..." The smile left, and a frown replaced it.

"If the supplies have been received, I'm happy to get back to work, Sir. I can have the squadron operational in no time."

"Your squadron is already operational under the leadership of Flight Lieutenant Delacourt. She appears to be a very competent squadron commander, which is quite fortunate as it's not a post you'll be returning to after this situation."

"She is, Sir, and if I'm no longer going to be leading the squadron, Flight Lieutenant Delacourt would be the perfect choice to replace me. She has the experience, and the pilots like and respect her." It was difficult to talk. The bombshell he'd dropped had knocked the wind from her as much as any punch at the hands of the Gestapo. Her head was spinning, and she felt sick. With the evidence against Stanley, she thought it was over; she thought she'd be going back to get on with her job.

"Perhaps, but that'll be a decision for her Commanding Officer. In the meantime, let's get back to you."

"Yes, Sir." It was taking every effort to stop herself from shaking, again.

"In light of what's happening, the Air Chief Marshal commanding the Second Tactical Air Force has requested 508 Squadron be posted under his command. They'll be joined by 507 and 509 Squadrons, which will be formed in the coming weeks." He was stopped by the door opening at the back of the room, and he gave a nod before continuing. "Your new CO will give you the rest of the details." Harriet frowned, then looked at the figure that had arrived next to her. Cas. In his best uniform, and wearing the rank of a Group Captain. "Congratulations on your promotion, Wing Commander Cornwall. Run 13 Wing as well as you did 508 Squadron, and the Germans will be on the ropes."

"Sir?" Harriet's mouth was open in shock.

"Any questions, Group Captain Salisbury?"

"No, Sir. I'm quite sure we've got it all covered."

"Good. You're stood down operationally for the time being. Get your second and third squadrons formed, and get your training up to scratch. You're needed to take the fight to the enemy over in France."

"Yes, Sir."

"Dismissed."

Harriet followed Cas in saluting, then together, they marched out of the office. She was shaking for an entirely different reason as she pulled the door closed behind her.

"Alright?" Cas asked casually, smirking as he did.

"You knew?" she gasped.

"Knew what?"

"About this. About all of it?"

"I was called in yesterday and briefed, promoted, and given the job of wrangling a particularly fiery and troublesome Squadron Leader."

"Troublesome?"

"Is there ever a time when you're not in trouble?"

"Shut up!"

"Come on, let's go and have a cup of tea. You can let me know what I'm getting into, and I'll bring you up to speed with the RAF's plans."

"I can't believe you knew about all of this and didn't tell me," she frowned as they walked.

"You were under Mess arrest with no visitors. Besides, we needed to give Stanley the opportunity to sink himself entirely. He's a nasty little bully with an unglamorous career of sucking up to those in a higher position, while making life hell for those he commands. Nobody's had the courage to do something about him before now. He's always held the threat of their careers over them, largely because he's been protected by those above who seem to fall for his charades. Speak up, and your career stops in its tracks. Seems he hasn't come up against a female Squadron Leader before, though, especially not one who likes a good fight."

"You could still have told me."

"I went to the AOC as soon as Nicole called me to let me know what was happening. How do you think the investigation started?"

"Thanks..." She felt herself blushing with embarrassment for giving him a hard time."

"Anyway, better behave yourself. I hear your new CO can be even worse."

"I know, I've met him..." She gave him a mischievous smile, before he casually nudged her just enough to have her walk into a door frame, much to his amusement. "Idiot!"

"Idiot, Sir," he laughed. "We should probably go and visit Ralph while we're in town. You're going to need some new rank braid on your sleeve, Wing Commander." He gave her a wink, making her blush again before she climbed into his Aston Martin, ready for the short trip to The Savoy for tea.

"So, what's the plan?" Harriet asked, after taking a sip of Fortnum's best tea. Cas had ordered an enormous pot, and two small rock cakes, which were as solid as the name suggested. Wartime rationing was still making ingredients scarce, and food quality questionable, even at the most exclusive of restaurants.

"It's quite simple, really. Stanley's out, and we're taking over the station. The two Spitfire squadrons will be moving out in the next few days, and we'll replace them with the two new squadrons we're forming. You'll also be switching over to Hawker Typhoons. The wing's primary role will be causing trouble over the French coast. Either flying escort to bombers, or striking targets of opportunity."

"My squadron commanders?"

"Your call. You're Wing Commander flying, so you'll lead the Wing day to day, while I look after the administration."

"What? You mean I don't have to do the paperwork anymore?" she asked excitedly.

"There's still a few routine bits and pieces, combat reports mostly, but otherwise no. You've managed to dodge that particular bullet." He rolled his eyes in mock dismay.

"Promotion, pay rise, and no paperwork! Considering how it started, today's turning out quite well!"

"Better for some than others. I get to do the paperwork for three squadrons, while trying to keep you out of the wrong type of trouble."

"It's what you're good at."

"I know. That's why they sent for me!"

"Harsh!" She looked at him in shock. "You're not supposed to agree with me!"

"I'm serious. Apparently, I've had experience commanding female pilots, you especially, and I'm therefore the right person for the job. Which is why I've been dragged from the comfort of my job as a controller, and forced back onto a flying station."

"And forced to accept a promotion, and a pay rise…"

"And you…"

"Shut up! Anyway, I'm assuming you won't have any problem with me promoting Nicole to command 508?"

"I'd have more of a problem if you didn't. Can you imagine the noise she'd make?"

"She's not like that as much these days."

"No?"

"I mean, she can still be a handful, but since being a flight commander, she's really stepped up. She looks after her pilots, and spends lots of time teaching them and supporting them."

"Sounds like she's the ideal replacement for you."

"Yes, though God help anyone who crosses her."

"Quite… Look, your pilots haven't had a break since they were posted in; I know that much. Why don't we stand them down for a few days so they can let their hair down?"

"Sounds like a good idea to me. I think they'd really appreciate that."

"OK. I'll make some calls while we're in town and see if we can get a few bottles of something nice, and we can have a bit of a celebration in the Mess later. We'll talk to Ralph and get some rank braid while he's doing your uniform, then when we get back, you can make your promotions, and we'll have a proper party. How about that?"

"Even better!"

"Then we can have a few days getting ready for the new arrivals, and planning your training on the Typhoon. Our first deliveries arrive the day after tomorrow, and I've arranged for a Test Pilot friend from Hawker to come down and spend a few days with us bringing everyone up to speed with your new aeroplane."

"I can't believe this is all happening…"

"Well, you'd better. It's all your fault."

"What's that supposed to mean?"

"Look at what you did with the squadron. You were given every handicap possible, outdated aircraft, poor leadership, no supplies, and you still outperformed some regular squadrons who have been in the line much longer. Hardly any German raids come over in daylight these days, and you not only caught two of them, you knocked half of the buggers down. If you hadn't done such a good job, there wouldn't even be a squadron of female pilots, let alone an entire wing. You should be proud."

"Wait. 507 and 509 are female squadrons?" Her heart raced at the news.

"Do you ever pay attention?"

"Shut up! Nobody said they would be female!"

"Nobody said they wouldn't be. You shouldn't make assumptions, you know. Women can fly and fight every bit as well as men. You should get with the times."

"Hilarious."

"Indeed. Anyway, yes, they'll be all female. At least they will be once we've formed them. I don't have the details yet, but the RAF has pulled every female pilot with experience flying single engine fighters, and they're on their way to us. That said, I expect there'll be many who haven't seen combat, so we're going to have to train them hard."

"We can do that."

"You know, the spotlight's really going to be on. It appears that the intention was to hide 508 and keep them out of harm's way. Sending three squadrons of women into the fray over France is a different matter. There's going to be lots of people watching, and I don't need to tell you how many will be waiting for a mistake so they can say 'I told you so', and have the wing sent somewhere nobody can see them, or even have you disbanded altogether. It's not right, but it's how it is."

"I know, and I promise you we'll be the best we can be."

"I don't doubt it."

"I'm happy you're there to watch over us. I wouldn't trust anyone else."

"Well, you haven't actually had me as your CO before, despite all the time we've worked together. You may not be saying that once you see what an ogre I am."

"I hadn't thought of that; good point." She smirked, making him frown in mock disappointment.

"Right, we'd better go and see Ralph. I want to be at the station this afternoon, we've got a lot of work to do, and a party to plan."

After a pleasant lunch with Ralph, which he'd insisted on while Harriet's tunic was adjusted with the new rank braid while she waited, and a trip to Harrods and Fortnum's for some shopping, Cas drove Harriet back to her station on the south coast of Kent, following the winding roads which were increasingly busy with military vehicles of all types. Trucks, tanks, and everything in between. The army had been more active since the start of spring, with training exercises taking place almost continuously, and they'd slowed the roads of Kent to the point where Cas complained endlessly until they finally reached the station. Harriet had teased him as much as he'd complained, reminding him how grumpy he was, and questioning whether he was going to be the same as the old Station Commander. Despite the challenges on the roads, it was a pleasant trip that they both enjoyed, and it gave them the opportunity to catch up.

"Good afternoon, Ma'am," Niamh said as Harriet led Cas to his new office.

"Come with me," Harriet said with a smile, nodding her head in the direction of the Station Commander's office.

"Who's this?" Cas asked, as he threw his service cap on the hatstand and turned to face Harriet and Niamh.

"Section Officer Shannon, Sir. She knows the station inside out, and knows how things work. I thought she may be helpful to you while you're settling in."

"Sounds like a good idea to me. Salisbury." He smiled and held out his hand, which Niamh looked at for a moment, unsure of what to make of his friendliness. He looked at her, and then at his hand, and she shook it politely. "There, wasn't that bad, was it?" She shook her head and blushed a little. "What do you say, fancy the job?"

"Which job, Sir?"

"Station Adjutant. I need somebody with a feel for the station, and who knows the people on the ground. It's long hours, hard work, and comes with all the Fortnum and Mason tea you can drink. Maybe some nice biscuits every now and then if we can get our hands on them, but no promises."

"In that case, how could I refuse, Sir?"

"Good show! Welcome to the team, Niamh. I'm assuming you don't mind me calling you Niamh?"

"Not at all, Sir."

"That's a relief. Right, we'll need to find an office for Wing Commander Cornwall while we're at it. Any ideas?"

"There's one next door that your predecessor used as a lounge?"

"A lounge?" Cas raised an eyebrow.

"Yes, Sir. He liked to take a snooze in the afternoon."

"I see… Well, we'll be far too busy for snoozing, so we may as well turn it back into an office. Can you sort the furniture?"

"Not a problem, Sir."

"Great. Now, if you could rustle up some hot water and cups for us, I'll make us some tea. Don't forget to bring yourself one, and better bring a pen and paper; we need to start planning."

"Yes, Sir!" Niamh replied confidently. It was the most she'd smiled since Harriet had known her. "Ma'am, I just wanted to congratulate you on your promotion," she said to Harriet before she left the office.

"Thank you, Niamh, and thank you for all you did to support me. Things are going to be different around here; I can promise you that." She gave the young Irishwoman a reassuring smile. "Oh, and don't let anyone know I'm back just yet."

"Yes, Ma'am." Another big smile spread across her face, and she left, closing the door behind her.

"She seems nice," Cas said after watching her leave.

"She is... Though I think that's the first time I've seen her smile."

"I have that effect on people." He gave her a wink as he leaned against his desk.

"If you say so," she replied while rolling her eyes. "Though on this occasion, let's not let it go to your head. It's more likely she's just relieved to not have you scream at her."

"Why on earth would I do that?"

"You wouldn't, but your predecessor did. Four times a day, at least, she was in front of his desk being yelled at for one thing or another. Never for something she had any control over, but that didn't stop him. If he was feeling that way out, he wouldn't stop until he got tears, and if not from her, he'd go find a WAAF clerk to take it out on."

"Sounds delightful."

"Very. There's a lot to undo around here. Between him and that snitch of an Adjutant, they ran the place on fear. Except for their friends in the Spitfire squadrons, that is. They seemed to get an easy ride. Oh, and there's a couple of Typhoon squadrons down the end of the airfield living in tents. Just in case you didn't know."

"I did. They're moving out tomorrow, going to another field further west."

"Still in their tents?"

"Yes, I expect so. Many of the Tactical Air Force squadrons are tent bound at the moment."

"Rather them than me."

"Quite. I've never been one for camping; it reminds me too much of the trenches. I'd much rather have a roof over my head, with hot and cold running water if possible."

"Obviously. Can't have pensioners sleeping out in the cold."

"Don't you have somewhere to be?"

"Not particularly; my boss hasn't given me any orders yet."

"Orders? I didn't realise you followed them…" he shrugged.

"Can't we just be nice?" she sighed, knowing she was taking the conversation into a dead end that she couldn't get out of.

"Let's get your office sorted, then we can get onto the accommodation problems. We also need to make sure we're ready for the Typhoons when they arrive. Tools have been ordered, and the Engineering Officer from one of the other wings is coming over to brief on maintenance. We have a number of specialists being posted in to bolster the ground crews, too, so that'll make things easier."

"There are lots of things we're going to need if we're to be fully operational; we don't even have an Intelligence Officer on the squadron."

"Don't worry, all in hand."

"You only found out about this yesterday?"

"About my role in it, yes. Why?"

"You seem to have a lot in hand..."

"I'm efficient; that's why they gave me the job."

"I thought they gave you the job because you're the only one who can keep me in line?"

"If that was the sole requirement of the job, nobody would get it!"

"It's going to be hard working with you..."

"You've missed me."

"You can't prove that!"

Towards the end of a very busy afternoon, an American truck had turned up with a special delivery for Cas. Harriet had helped him unload it, along with Niamh, and both were amazed at the treats they were handling. Steaks, sausages, bacon, flour, butter, sugar, chocolate, and everything else that was desperately rationed everywhere in England except on American bases, where all the goodness of home was flown in from America almost daily. There was even a small mountain of cigarettes and bourbon whisky to go along with it, along with a selection of tinned and fresh fruits. It was like Christmas. Niamh couldn't believe it, and even Harriet was a little surprised at quite how resourceful Cas had been. Once unloaded, the goods required for the evening meal were delivered to the chefs, along with some cigarettes and whisky as thanks for their work, and the rest was spirited away for the night's celebrations. The dining room had been booked, and Nicole had been sent a message by Niamh telling her that the squadron's mealtime had been pushed back to seven. It wasn't an unusual change; Stanley messed them about all the time, so it wouldn't have been an out of the ordinary surprise to Nicole, and it bought time for the dining room to be set up ready for a squadron dinner. All the tables were pushed together to arrange one long table, which was dressed appropriately with candelabras, silverware, and glasses. Niamh had even quietly arranged for WAAFs from the Station Headquarters to act as waiting staff for the night, making sure each would receive extra pay and treats for their efforts, as was usual for formal dinners. The pilots started to arrive at seven o'clock, and Nicole grumbled irritably while the Mess Manager kept them waiting in the anteroom, explaining that the dining room wasn't quite prepared. Finally, when everything was ready, they were allowed to enter the room. Harriet was waiting for them at the head of the long table, standing with her hands behind her back as she watched them file into the room, with Cas by her side.

"What's going on?" Nicole asked as the pilots gasped and chattered loudly as they walked into the room. She glanced at Harriet, and then Cas, while frowning at them suspiciously.

"You'll see," Harriet replied. "Ladies, your names are on the place cards; please stand by your seats," she said loudly. Nicole stood behind the seat to the right of Harriet, with Ginny next to her. AP sat to the left, with Lexi and Jo Bird, and all the others finally found their places and fell silent, while looking up the table to Harriet, who stood smiling, hardly able to contain herself.

"Good evening, ladies," Cas said as the WAAFs passed along the table, filling up the Champagne flutes in front of each seat. "For those who don't know me, I'm Group Captain Salisbury, and I'll be the new Station Commander for the time being." Nicole looked at him, and at the braid on his sleeves. "Following your recent action over the Channel, where pilots from the Typhoon squadron you assisted have provided confirmation of no fewer than eight enemy aircraft shot down by you, I've been instructed by the Air Ministry to support 508 Squadron in its move to the Second Tactical Air Force, and help you prepare to transition from defence to offence, so you can take the fight to the enemy." A collective gasp came from the gathered pilots as they stared at him in excited disbelief. "As of this evening, you're stood down for a period of refitting with new aeroplanes fresh from the factory, but before that, starting tomorrow morning, you'll all be taking two days leave in London. Passes have been signed, and transport has been arranged to leave at eleven in the morning. The ground crews and support staff will also be taking leave, and I don't expect any work to be done during that time. Do I make myself clear?"

"Yes, Sir!" came the unanimous and confidently delivered response.

"This dinner is my way of thanking you for all you've done so far, and of welcoming you to the Second Tactical Air Force." An excited buzz went around the table as the pilots whispered to each other, confirming what they'd just heard. "Now, before I stop boring you all and let you get on with your meal, I'd like you to raise your glasses." He lifted his Champagne from the table and raised it in front of him, gesturing for the others to do the same. "In addition to commending you for your actions, and celebrating your transfer to the Tactical Air Force, I'd like you to join me in congratulating Squadron Leader Cornwall on her promotion to the rank of Wing Commander. Let's have three cheers, Hip hip!" The pilots cheered loudly while Harriet blushed, just about managing to smile at her friends as they cheered her. "Right, Wing Commander, I'll leave you to it." He gave Harriet a wink, and walked away. It hadn't been part of the script. She was supposed to have been telling everyone herself in a quiet and subdued way when they noticed the rank on her arm.

"Three cheers for Group Captain Salisbury," Nicole shouted. "Hip hip!" Another three cheers went up as he left the room. When the noise had finally died down, the traditional loyal toast to the King was made, and Harriet gave the signal for everyone to take their seats, grinning so much that her jaw was aching. She gave a nod to the chef, and the starter of French onion soup with large crispy croutons was brought out while the pilots chattered noisily.

"So, where are you going, Wing Commander?" Nicole asked.

"Excuse me?" Harriet replied.

"Y'all just got promoted to Wing Commander," Lexi said. "You ain't commanding a squadron at that rank."

"Which means that you're leaving, and somebody's replacing you commanding the squadron," AP added. "So, where are you going, and who do we have to put up with in place of you?"

"Nowhere," Harriet shrugged as she continued eating."

"Stop playing games!" Nicole demanded.

"Careful, you could get into trouble talking like that."

"You're not funny, Ma'am…"

"So, what's really going on?" Ginny asked.

"Not you as well? Can't we all just have a nice meal?"

"We could if you told us what you're up to."

"You'll have to wait until after the meal." She gave them a mischievous wink, then took a big mouthful of the Champagne that Cas had managed to find so much of. Eyes rolled, and sighs were loud, but they conceded and went on to grill her about what had happened at the Air Ministry and how Cas was now the new Station Commander. She toyed with them, giving them bits of information here and there, and they were satisfied enough that Stanley was gone and not likely to be able to retire into obscurity. Their questioning stalled when the main course arrived. The steaks silenced the entire table. Nobody had eaten steak for years; they hadn't even seen steak it was so hard to get hold of. The fine French wine that was served with it caused just as much of a stir, as did the chocolate cake that came after, before the cheese and port. Harriet sat back for a moment and watched. Her pilots were the happiest she'd ever seen them. They were laughing and joking as though they hadn't a care in the world. Their happiness made her happy. She was proud of them. Every single member of the squadron, from the most experienced pilot to the newest mechanic, they'd all worked tirelessly to make sure the squadron was a success. Not one of them had complained, despite the way they'd been treated; the only thing that was important to them was making sure the squadron succeeded. Every one of them knew how important it was not to fail, and not to be seen to fail. Their work was perfection, and their uniforms pristine. They were as proud of their squadron as she was of them.

The pilots made their way to the Mess bar once the meal was over. Harriet's head was spinning a little, despite doing her best to try and pace herself with the drinks. Before she got pulled into the party, she asked for Nicole, AP, Lexi, and Ginny to join her in the empty anteroom that had previously been reserved for the females on the station, to keep them segregated and out of the Mess bar. They pulled their chairs around the fire and got comfortable with a large whisky that had been sent to them without ordering. Cas' work, Harriet assumed, but she didn't complain.

"So, what's really happening?" AP asked.

"You're right," Harriet said as she looked at them in turn. "I'll no longer be commanding the squadron; that decision was made at the Air Ministry today without me having much say in it."

"Where are they sending you?" Nicole asked.

"To command 13 Wing, an old Royal Flying Corps unit that's been reactivated to fly Hawker Typhoons."

"Typhoons?" AP asked. "Have you even flown one before?"

"Not yet..."

"So, what does that mean for us?" Lexi asked. "Who are we getting stuck with?"

"A newly promoted Squadron Leader."

"Great," Nicole sighed as she slumped in her chair. "Some idiot we have to babysit until they learn what we do here."

"Sorry, but yes. I'm sure you'll do your best, though." She pulled a sealed envelope from her inside pocket and handed it to Nicole, who frowned as she took it.

"What's this?"

"A consolation gift."

"What?" Nicole pulled at the envelope and tipped out the Squadron Leader's rank braid. "I don't understand?"

"Congratulations on your promotion, Squadron Leader Delacourt."

"Don't tease me…" Nicole wasn't sure where to look, or what to say. She fiddled with the braid, then looked back at Harriet.

"I'm not teasing. You're 508 Squadron's new CO…" She smiled as she stood and offered her hand. Nicole stood and shook it. She had a tear in her eye, and couldn't stop herself from grabbing Harriet and hugging her tight. "I mean, the others are going to have to babysit you for a while until you work out what we do here, but I'm sure you'll get by." They all laughed and toasted Nicole before returning excitedly to their seats.

"Idiot was an understatement, but I'm sure we'll be able to whip her into shape," AP said.

"You won't get the chance," Harriet replied. "You're being posted."

"What?"

"You too…" Harriet looked at Lexi. They both looked confused, and hardly reacted when she handed them an envelope each.

"Honey, either you've had too much to drink, or I have, because I ain't got a clue what's going on," Lexi said.

"Oh my God!" AP said as she tipped her own Squadron Leader's braid from her envelope. Lexi's eyes opened wide, and she quickly ripped hers open to find the same. "Where? AP demanded.

"509 Squadron," Harriet replied. "You're their new CO. Lexi, you'll be commanding 507."

"I'm gonna need a bigger drink," Lexi said, before downing what remained of her whisky.

"Where are they based?" AP asked. "509 Squadron, I mean."

"Right here. Or at least they will be two days from now. This is now the home of 13 Wing RAF. You get a squadron each, and your new Typhoons start arriving tomorrow." They looked at each other in amazement. They were silent, lost for words, while Harriet sat smiling and sipping her whisky. "The paperwork's in, and you'll be gazetted shortly, but the promotion's effective as of today, so you'll need to get the rank on your sleeves before you go on leave tomorrow."

"What about the pilots? We have enough for a squadron, maybe one and a half if we don't have reserves."

"The RAF have thought of that, apparently. They start arriving two days from now. It's up to you, of course, but I thought that you'd each take your flights with you to your new squadrons; that way, you'll have a core of experienced pilots to build around. Then we'll distribute whoever turns up between you." They all nodded in agreement. "You can choose your own flight commanders, of course, but whatever you do, make sure that after your leave, you're ready to go. We're going to have to convert onto the Typhoons quickly and safely, then get ourselves up to combat readiness. It's going to be dangerous work, more than flying patrol lines in old Hurricanes. We need to be sharp."

"Ginny, you get the short straw. You're going to be the new Wing Adjutant." She handed Ginny the final envelope.

"Well, I'm not sure I want the job," Ginny said with a frown, while folding her arms across her chest and refusing to take the envelope.

"What?" Harriet's heart squeezed a little; it wasn't the response she was expecting.

"Unless there's a Wing Commander's rank or better in that envelope, you haven't got a hope of getting me to take a job looking after all four of you. It's been pain enough looking after you."

"Fair enough, you can stay as Nicole's Adjutant; I'll give somebody else the job." Harriet shrugged, as she pulled the envelope away,

"Not too fast," Ginny said as she grabbed the envelope. "If it's promotion and all of you, or staying with just her, I'll take the promotion and put up with the pain."

"You're cruel," Nicole frowned.

"And accurate in my assessment of you. You're a damn good pilot, but you're an administrative nightmare. I don't think I could cope. Better somebody else gets the job, and I look after them from a distance. Unless you need an Adjutant?" she asked AP, who shrugged while considering the offer.

"That's enough, Harriet said. Right, now that's all been decided, you'd better go and tell your pilots what's happening. You should probably get some more drinks, too. It's not every day you get promoted to Squadron Leader."

"What about you?" Nicole asked as they stood to leave.

"I'll be through in a minute. Send Stone through, would you?" Nicole nodded and smiled, and the four newly promoted and quite ecstatic officers left the anteroom. AP paused before leaving and gave Harriet a warming smile. She didn't need to say anything. Their friendship had grown and come a long way since they'd first met, when she wouldn't even acknowledge Harriet, let alone give her the time of day. Now they didn't need to say how they felt. They'd risked their lives to save each other; that was enough.

"You asked to see me, Ma'am?" Carrie said as she stepped into the anteroom.

"Carrie, come in and sit down." Harriet gave her a smile as the young woman walked over and handed her a very large brandy.

"Group Captain Salisbury said to bring you this, Ma'am."

"He's in the bar?"

"Yes, Ma'am."

"Sit down, and stop calling me Ma'am. We've known each other long enough for us to not keep having this conversation."

"Sorry... Congratulations on your promotion."

"Thank you."

"Does that mean you'll be leaving us?"

"Not quite, though I will be leaving the squadron, and that's why I want to talk to you."

"Me?"

"Yes. You'll find out when we go back through to the bar anyway, we're forming two new squadrons, and with 508, they'll come together to make up 13 Wing. I wondered if you'd like to take the post of flight commander in one of the squadrons? You've got the experience, and you're more than competent enough. The squadron commanders will be fighting over you."

"Flight commander?"

"Yes, with a promotion to Flight Lieutenant."

"Will you still be flying?"

"Try and stop me!"

"Don't you need a Number Two anymore?" She frowned, making her disappointment more than visible.

"I'm not sure I'm allowed one...."

"Aren't you a Wing Commander now?"

"Yes..."

"Then can't you give yourself permission? I mean, if you need one, that is." She blushed a little.

"There you go," Harriet said with a smile as she handed Carrie an envelope.

"What is it?"

"Your promotion to Flight Lieutenant."

"You're sending me off to be a flight commander?"

"Apparently not. You'll be staying as my Number Two. Though you should know that by giving up the flight commander position, you'll be unlikely to command a squadron anytime soon. You need to do that if you want to move upwards."

"I just want to fly."

"Looks like we're staying as a team in that case."

"Thank you." Carrie's face lit up. "You're sure?"

"Positive. Come on, let's go and join the others. She stood, then clinked her glass against Carrie's. "Congratulations on your promotion, Flight Lieutenant Stone."

## Chapter 8

## Getting Acquainted

"My God, it's huge…" Harriet said to herself as she stood in front of her new steed, a brand new Hawker Typhoon, fresh from the factory with only a brief stop at a maintenance unit to be prepped for action. She'd seen them from a distance, but never got up close enough to appreciate their size. It was almost three times her height, with a giant four blade propeller that was twice as tall as her at least. With the cannons on the wings, and massive air intake slung under the engine like an open mouth, it was a beast of an aeroplane that dwarfed both the Spitfire and Hurricane, and while she was excited to see what it could do, she felt a little nervous about the size of the thing.

"Big, isn't she?" Jo Bird asked as she joined Harriet looking up at the Typhoon.

"I was just thinking that…" Harriet replied.

"You'll get over four hundred miles an hour out of her on the flat."

"Four hundred?" Harriet's eyes opened wide.

"Easily. Probably four fifteen all out, maybe a touch more. In a dive, you can get well over five hundred, though you're not recommended to go much over five fifty. Otherwise, you risk structural damage."

"Structural damage?"

"Typhoons used to have a problem with compression. Basically, the tail would fall off once they went above a certain speed and the tail boom started to crumple. They'd come apart at the join, making them an out of control missile, and the pilot would be dead shortly afterwards."

"You're not selling it to me."

"It's OK, they fixed the problem. Fish plates around the join, and reinforcement on the inside seems to have done the trick. However, go above the speed limits, and all bets are off."

"Thanks for the warning…"

"You're welcome."

"Any other gems of advice to fill me with confidence?"

"Only that you should try not to let the tail hit you on your way out if you have to take to your parachute. It's thicker than most, and will take your head clean off."

"Great. At least it'll be quick."

"That's something. Anything else you want to know?"

"You're the expert. Is there anything else I should know?"

"Just make sure you keep your mask on, and start using oxygen as soon as you start the engine. They leak carbon monoxide into the cockpit from the engine, it's clear and odourless, and it'll kill you before you know it if you don't take care. They've done some work to resolve it, and while it's not as bad as it used to be, it's still a thing, so better safe than sorry."

"You know, I was excited when I found out we were getting Typhoons. Five minutes talking to you, and I'm starting to regret letting the Hurricanes go."

"You won't say that once you've flown it." Jo gave her a mischievous smirk as they walked around the wing.

"No, from what you've told me, I'll probably be too dead to say anything," Harriet replied as she climbed onto the wing and stepped into the cavernous cockpit.

"We'll see. You'd better get yourself strapped in."

"This is exactly the reason I'm doing this while everyone else is on leave. It won't do for them to see me end myself after being poisoned with carbon monoxide, then ripping off my tail before nose diving into the ground at somewhere over five hundred and fifty miles per hour…"

"Better than cutting your head off with the tail if you jump out. I can't imagine that would be nice. At least the carbon monoxide would be painless."

"Remind me where we got you from?"

"You didn't. The Air Ministry sent me here to make your life better."

"That's what you call it?"

"Stop complaining! Otherwise, I won't fasten your harness properly, and you'll do yourself a mischief." She pulled the straps tight, clamping Harriet to her seat, and making her gasp a little. "There you go, safe and sound. Now, don't forget it's a cartridge start. Prime the engine, then fire the cartridge, and it should kick start things into life. Don't prime too much, though, of you'll have an engine fire on your hands."

"Do you want to bugger off with your happy selection of ways for me to die?" Harriet frowned.

"Mask on, remember!" Jo winked, then pushed the bubble canopy closed above Harriet, who was busy pulling on her oxygen mask, before starting her checks. She waved once her mask was secure, getting an encouraging wave of the fire extinguisher in return, then she went through the switches and dials for the hundredth time. The first of the Typhoons had arrived that morning, and she'd spent hours going through the start up procedures and cockpit set up with the pilot's notes. It was designed by the same man who'd designed the Hurricane, so things had a familiar feel, yet there were stark differences. Not least the canopy, which was a teardrop bubble shape and made of clear Perspex, with none of the frames that obscured vision in the Hurricane. The visibility was even better than the Spitfire. The pilot who'd brought it in had talked her through the basics, and that was it, the standard RAF introduction to a new aircraft type. The prevailing philosophy was that a trained pilot should be able to get into any aeroplane and fly it with just the pilot's briefing notes for reference. It's what Harriet had done in her ATA days, and the RAF didn't veer from the strategy. The only time a pilot would get extra training was if they were switching from single to multi engines, or to seaplanes, but that was about it. A walk around, a kick of the tyres, and a quick once over from somebody who knows what they're talking about if you're lucky, and you're ready to go. Fortunately for Harriet, Jo had trained on Typhoons, and worked as an engineer on a Typhoon squadron, so she knew the aeroplane better than most. She'd even written a brief training manual for Harriet and her pilots, to try and help them avoid the more obvious pitfalls. Like not poisoning themselves, or killing themselves, or ripping off their own tails. Harriet looked around, then gave Jo a thumbs up before firing the first Coffman cartridge, which shot into the cylinder and kicked the propeller briefly. Nothing much else happened, and she shook her head as she remembered the instruction to prime the engine. She did this, then fired the next cartridge, and the monstrous Napier Sabre engine kicked into life with a roar.

All she could see was the nose of the giant aeroplane as she taxied around the airfield to the end of the runway, forcing her to swing left and right to make sure she didn't hit anything, not that she thought much would stand up to the Typhoon. She was confident she could crash into a tractor and come off better. The power checks made her smile, as she felt the engine vibrating the entire airframe as it strained to be let off the leash. Finally, she released the brakes, and the Typhoon shot off along the runway faster than anything she'd ever flown, pinning her back into her seat as it raced forward. She gently nudged the stick forward, and the tail came up into the airstream. Seconds later, she was rocketing upwards at almost three thousand feet per minute. Her smile was stretched cheek to cheek at the power of the Typhoon, so much that her jaw started to hurt. At fifteen thousand feet, she levelled out and watched as the dial crept above four hundred miles per hour. It was time to see what else it had to back up the speed. She pulled back on the stick and started a loop, which the Typhoon managed with ease while subjecting Harriet to extreme g forces. She rolled, and flipped, and turned, and while the controls were nowhere near as light as the Spitfire, and stiffened up a little at speed; and the response nowhere near as intuitive and smooth, the Typhoon was still a responsive aeroplane. She likened it to a heavy cavalry horse. A high speed flying tank that would crash through anything in front of it, whereas the Spitfire was a pure thoroughbred racehorse. She pushed the beast to its limit, and after nudging the speed to the upper end of the recommended maximum, she pulled up into a vertical climb. It was the fastest climb she'd ever experienced, and when the stall finally came, just short of thirty five thousand feet, she got to fly faster than she could ever have imagined when the Typhoon dived, and the needle passed five hundred miles per hour. It was a fight to take control and pull it back out of the dive, and the airframe shuddered as the needle passed the safe maximum. She quickly thought of the horror stories of compression ripping the tails off Typhoons, as Jo had kindly reminded her of before the flight, and she eased the throttle while pulling up the nose. Twenty thousand feet had gone in an instant. The Typhoon was fast, but Harriet was quickly realising how deadly it could be if the pilot wasn't wide awake. The speed and power could very easily be lethal, and not just for the enemy. An hour after taking off, Harriet was touching down on the runway again and rolling back to the dispersal. She had to fight the urge to pull off her oxygen mask and open her canopy, as she was used to doing both in Hurricanes and Spitfires. Finally, she shut down the engine and pulled open the cockpit. Off came her oxygen mask and helmet, and she was standing on her seat before Jo managed to get onto the wing to greet her.

"Well? Do you want your Hurricane back?" Jo asked with a smirk.

"I suppose I should probably keep the Typhoon now it's here... We don't want to Air Ministry thinking we're ungrateful."

"You'd better get out in that case, so I can get it ready for you."

"Isn't it ready enough?"

"Not quite..." She rolled her eyes and helped Harriet out of the cockpit. "When will you want to take her up again?"

"This afternoon, maybe. I've got some paperwork to do, and as much as I'd rather not, there's no escaping it."

"I thought that's why you kept Ginny around?"

"So did I, but she's in London living it up, like you're supposed to be…" Harriet shook her head with a smile, then jumped down from the wing and looked back at the giant Typhoon. It was an impressive aeroplane, and she couldn't wait to see what its offensive capability was like. It had the same armament as the Hurricane she'd been flying, two 20mm cannons on each wing, but it carried more ammunition. With its speed and power, it was going to be a handful for whatever the enemy put up against it. She climbed in her car and made her way back to her office in Station Headquarters, where she hung her flying kit on the hatstand and changed into her skirt, shoes, and tunic. Making herself presentable, knowing she had an example to set.

"Well?" Cas asked as he stepped into her office.

"Well, what?"

"You know what. The Typhoon! What's it like?"

"It's alright, I suppose," she shrugged casually and went back to her report.

"That's it? Alright? You get your hands on the latest, fastest, and most powerful fighter available, and the best you can manage is 'it's alright'?"

"Well, it's not a Spitfire, is it?"

"No, it isn't. There's no pleasing some people…"

"What about you?"

"What about me?"

"How's that new desk you're flying?" She smirked, not able to keep it in.

"You do remember I'm a Group Captain, don't you? Your commanding officer?"

"Of course, I'm not that new to the RAF."

"So you remember how it all works, then?"

"Obviously."

"Good, then you'd better get yourself down to the train station. One of your new arrivals is due on the eleven o'clock from London."

"Don't we have duty drivers anymore?"

"Of course we do, but I thought you'd fancy the drive, seeing as you decided to stay on the station instead of going into London. It'll be good for you to get out."

"Are you trying to get rid of me?"

"Yes. I have work to do, and can't have you hanging around making smart comments, and pretending not to be impressed with the new aeroplane I got you."

"You didn't get me it…"

"You've got it, haven't you?"

"Yes, and the RAF got me it, not you."

"My point exactly! I'm your CO, and therefore the RAF's representative, which means I got you it."

"You're impossible."

"Highly unlikely. Anyway, shouldn't you be heading to the train station?"

"Remind me again why you're sending me, and not the duty driver?"

"Because the Post Office in the village still has a stock of pear drops, and I've run out."

"Then why don't you go?"

"Because I've already been in to buy some this week. Besides, the Post Master likes you, so you're more likely to come back with some than me."

"So this is nothing to do with picking up a pilot from the train station; I'm just your skivvy?"

"Don't be ridiculous; a skivvy tends to do menial domestic tasks. You get to fetch me some pear drops. It's very different. Besides, I'll buy you whatever you want. For your trouble…"

"Why didn't you say?" She jumped from her chair and held out her hand as she walked over to him.

"You know you're a Wing Commander, don't you?"

"I do. I'm not sure I believe it yet, but I know."

"So you realise you're paid better than most?"

"Yes, I've never earned so much. I'm going to save as much as I can and buy a house in Hawaii after the war. Or California."

"Ah, bingo!"

"What?"

"That's why you want to spend my money instead of yours."

"No, I want to spend your money because you're finding reasons to send me into the village to buy boiled sweets for you."

"I did tell you to go into London with everyone else…"

"You did, but I want to get to know the Typhoon properly before they're back. Besides, if I'd gone, I wouldn't be here to go and meet people from the train station, would I?" She took the money from him, then grabbed her hat and walked past with a smile."

"Take my car, if you like." He threw his keys after her, which she simply reached up and snatched out of the air without breaking her stride. "Not even an argument..." he muttered.

"Your sweets, your car, your petrol. See you in a while." She marched happily through the headquarters, and jumped into Cas' Aston Martin. It was a beautiful spring day, so she took down the roof before whizzing through the station, and out along the open roads. She smiled as she felt the breeze on her face. She'd had breakfast, got lots of paperwork done, flown her new aeroplane, and was now racing along the country lanes in a big expensive car that she absolutely loved driving. After stopping at the Post Office, where she bought Cas' sweets, as well as a mixture for herself, she went over to the train station and waited. She was early, so she sat on the platform bench and listened to the birds. It was more relaxing than she expected it to be, and she soon found herself drifting off into her daydreams. It had been a long war. Almost four years since Sully's Hurricane had dropped into her sleepy little field in France, and started her on an adventure that had done its best to kill her at every opportunity. Things had been as bad as they could be, but it finally felt like things were changing. The Allies were fighting their way up Italy, and the Russians were pushing the Germans back on the Eastern Front. It seemed like the invincible German war machine was starting to run out of steam. Malta had broken them. They didn't knock the island out of the war, which meant that Rommel didn't get his supplies in North Africa, leading to him ultimately being kicked out. Years of war in the desert finally ended because of a little island in the Mediterranean. The desert fighting had also kept resources away from the Eastern Front, which ultimately meant the Germans were thrown back at the bloody battle of Stalingrad, and had been on the back foot ever since. There was still no obvious end to the war. While Italy had surrendered, and even switched sides once they were invaded, the Germans had rushed an army into the line to stop the Allies from marching in through Europe's back door, and they were putting up a hard fight. The war was so far from over that despite all that was happening, the Luftwaffe was still sending bombing raids over England. So many that it was being called another blitz, like that of 1940. As she got lost in her thoughts, she wondered what would come next, and how the war could ever end. There were rumours that if the army broke through in Italy, the Germans would negotiate a surrender to spare them the prospect of war on their own borders. It's what happened the last time, or so those from the previous war said. It made sense. As soon as the armies faced each other in Europe last time, they dug trenches and spent years massacring each other. Nobody imagined either side would want that again. She just hoped that it would come sooner rather than later. She'd be leading her pilots into harm's way soon, and while they were all keen to do their part, nobody could do it indefinitely. Despite the changes, she was still aware that she'd spent all of her own lives and was living on borrowed time, so she really did need the war to end.

"You with that lot down the road?" a gruff Yorkshire voice asked, dragging Harriet from her daydreams. She looked up to see the Station Master standing beside her. He was looking down at his fob watch, which he snapped closed and pushed into the pocket of his waistcoat before looking down at her.

"Excuse me?" Harriet replied with a smile.

"The fighter station, are you with them?"

"Yes, yes I am." She'd been so wrapped up in her thoughts she hadn't even heard him step out onto the platform, and his talking to her had taken her totally by surprise.

"Catching the train, or meeting somebody?"

"Meeting somebody. One of my new pilots is due in from London."

"Your pilots?"

"Yes..."

"Didn't realise they still let girls fly."

"Oh yes, they let us take the controls and everything," she replied as chirpily as she could, and trying not to roll her eyes.

"I should hope so as well. They don't give those wings you've got on your chest away for free." He nodded down at her tunic and gave her a smile. "Or medal ribbons, for that matter. You must be good at it." He was older than her, maybe in his forties or fifties, with blonde hair that was unusually long for men of the time, swept back under his hat and hanging just below his collar. He was handsome, with a ruggedness that matched his gruff voice, yet he seemed to have a friendliness about him. She looked at the medal ribbons on the chest of his smart railway uniform jacket. They were from the last war, and there were a few of them.

"You've got a few ribbons yourself."

"Them?" He looked down at his chest. "Nothing but a bit of coloured rag."

"Why wear them then?"

"It's what everyone does, isn't it? You see it everywhere a person wears a uniform."

"If you say so..." She gave him a smile, which he returned as he sat beside her on the bench.

"Why do you wear yours?"

"I'm in the RAF. Everyone does it because they have to."

"Aye, I suppose they do..." he laughed. "So, what do you fly?"

"Typhoons."

"No..." He raised an eyebrow as he looked at her.

"Don't be so surprised; I'm not bad at it."

"I'm not surprised. Just a bit jealous, is all. I always wanted to be a pilot."

"Oh?"

"Even put my papers in to transfer to the Royal Flying Corps in the last war... I'd sit and watch the aeroplanes fighting above the battlefields for hours; it fascinated me.

"What happened? With your transfer, I mean?"

"It was declined by my CO. I was needed on the ground, apparently. Destined to be a rifleman forever. I still watch them, though, even now when your aeroplanes come over."

"I'm sorry you didn't get to fly... I'm not sure what I'd do if they told me I couldn't."

"We're all here for a reason, I suppose. Yours is to fly."

"What was yours?"

"To fight the enemy the old fashioned way, with a rifle and a bit of cold steel." He gave her a wink and a smile. "The closest I got to an aeroplane, was when one of our pilots came down in the middle of no man's land between us and the German trenches during the last war. He'd come out of nowhere and shot up an enemy attack, machine gunning them and throwing bombs out of his cockpit, and sending them back to their trenches before they even got close to us. Lucky he did, too, otherwise they'd have been in amongst us."

"It must have been an incredible sight."

"It was. I'd never seen anything like it. Most aeroplanes we saw were up high, chasing each other about. This one was so low the Germans had to duck, just so he didn't hit them. Anyway, they got off a lucky shot, and he crashed, and I was sent out with a patrol to find him."

"What happened?" Harriet was feeling her heart race with excitement as she listened to the story.

"We found him, but the Germans had sent out a patrol at the same time, and we ended up having to fight them off until after dark. I still remember it like it was yesterday. The smell as much as anything. Burning castor oil from the engine, I could smell it on my uniform for weeks, and I spent hours with bad guts after. Anyway, the pilot was something else. A strapping six footer with a big moustache, and hair that he managed to check was still smart even in the heat of battle. The madman even pulled the machine gun from his downed aeroplane and ran at the Germans. At least until I tackled him, and pulled him back before he got his head blown off. Anyway, that was that. The closest I got to an aeroplane."

"That's a shame."

"Aye… All in the past, though. Now I get to make sure the trains run on time." He pulled his watch from his pocket again and checked it. "And the next one from London is due any minute. Can't sit around chatting all day." He leant forward and slapped his hands on his thighs. "You know, I haven't talked about that stuff for years."

"I enjoyed hearing about it."

"Don't humour me."

'I'm not. It's nice to just sit and talk."

"Aye, it can be." A whistle sounded, and they both looked down the tracks to see the train rumbling down the tracks. "Dick Vaughn, though everyone just calls me Vaughn." He held out his hand.

"Harry Cornwall." She smiled as she shook his hand, then stood to await the train.

"Your pilot another girl?"

"Yes, there's a few of us about."

"Never thought I'd see the day." He smirked at Harriet, who raised her eyebrow at him. "About time if you ask me. Nowt much more terrifying than a woman on a mission, and I reckon you terrify the Germans."

"Let's hope so," she laughed as the train pulled to a halt next to the platform. She looked along the carriages and waited. A couple of businessmen got off, and then, to her amazement, a familiar figure stepped onto the platform dressed in RAF blue.

"That your pilot?" Vaughn asked.

"Not quite," Harriet replied. She couldn't believe what she was seeing, and checked herself for a moment to make sure she wasn't asleep and dreaming.

"Why am I in England?" Robbie asked firmly as she marched over to Harriet.

"I have no idea…" Harriet replied, as she looked at the friend she hadn't seen since leaving Malta. "What are you doing here?"

"I was hoping you'd tell me! I was quite enjoying life until I was put on an aeroplane and flown to England. Without having a say in the matter!"

"I thought you said you'd never leave Malta?"

"I didn't have a choice! I was posted, and told that if I argued, I'd be charged with disobeying orders and thrown in prison. A prison in England, I should add. I was coming here either way, or so it seems, so thought I'd better choose the most civilised option."

"I still don't understand…"

"Posting to 13 Wing Royal Air Force as an Intelligence Officer, of all things, and to report to a Wing Commander Harriet Cornwall!"

"At least it's not Supply Officer. The RAF couldn't afford that."

"Not funny."

"Little bit funny."

"I should have known you'd be behind this."

"I swear I had nothing to do with it..."

"Oh really? Your name's on the posting."

"You should probably take that up with my CO."

"I will. As soon as you get me out of the cold. I swear England is always cold."

"We'd better get going in that case," Harriet smiled. "Want a hand with your bag?"

"Nope."

"The service has certainly changed since I was in," Vaughan laughed as Harriet turned to leave.

"Can you get off work tomorrow morning?" Harriet asked him.

"What do you mean?" he replied with a frown.

"Come by the airfield for ten. Ask for me at the Guardroom, and I'll show you around a Typhoon."

"I will." He smiled, and his face lit up. "I'll be there!"

"Come on, grumpy," Harriet said to Robbie, who sighed as she walked by Harriet's side. "I've missed you..."

"I haven't missed England," Robbie grumbled.

"You'll enjoy it here."

"I doubt that."

"Stop complaining. England is littered with several million Americans, so there are plenty of business opportunities."

"Millions, you say?"

"Millions... An entire army, and two whole air forces."

"Things are looking up." She gave Harriet a smile. "It's good to see you, Harry."

Robbie's arrival was enough to convince Harriet to leave work, and the pair went into London for dinner and a show, the tickets for which Cas somehow managed to get his hands on at short notice. Everything was usually booked by the Americans, but he seemed to know everyone, including contacts in the West End, and the tickets were waiting when Harriet and Robbie arrived at the door. His way of apologising to Robbie for her unexpected posting away from Malta, which he'd professed to having absolutely nothing to do with, despite the tirade of verbal abuse she sent in his direction when Harriet took her to his office from the train station. The night was great fun, and just what Harriet had needed after months of training and operations. Despite Robbie's annoyance at being away from Malta, she was in good spirits, and she managed to keep Harriet smiling all night. She looked much healthier than she had, more like when Harriet had first met her, and her bronze tan gave her a glow that made Harriet jealous. An English winter had bleached most of the North African tan from her skin, though there was still a hint of colour when she stood against Nicole. Back at the station, they had a drink in the Mess until Robbie started to fall asleep from her travels, and they decided to end the night and head to their rooms.

As she lay in her bed, Harriet's mind circled around recent events. She'd been a secret, mostly, or something to be hidden and kept out of the way, as had all of the female pilots. Those that made it to fighter squadrons were the dogsbodies, flying as reserve pilots at best, with the exception of Lexi's group, who'd been up to all sorts in the desert. Most of the female pilots, however, ended up away from combat units. Ferrying aircraft or flying transport missions, anything to keep them hidden away. Sometimes they were even sent to the desert, or a small island in the Mediterranean. Anywhere but home where people could see them. Almost overnight, they'd been recalled from across the world and pulled together into a unit that was now going to be taking the war to the enemy. It was incredible. Though to Harriet, the thing that was even more incredible was that she was leading them. In her mind, she was still a schoolgirl, even after all she'd been through, and each day she had to pinch herself and put on a facade that let her do the things she had. She just hoped she could keep it up.

Harriet went straight to the dispersal after breakfast, leaving Robbie with Cas for her induction to the world of military intelligence, something he referred to frequently as an oxymoron. Apparently, he had lots of paperwork to show her, which was Harriet's cue to make herself scarce. Her new job meant she had less paperwork to do than ever before. Mostly, she just had to fly and write a report here and there, which she was more than happy with, and while the wing was still on leave, she was intent on getting in as much flying time in the Typhoon as she could. As flying was one of her few duties, she had to do it well, especially as she was expected to be leading and setting an example.

"Good morning," Jo said, as Harriet stepped out of her car.

"Morning," Harriet replied. "I thought I'd get up first thing and have a bit of practice. Is she ready to go?"

"I thought as much. They're bringing her out for you now." She pointed over to the hangar, where a team of mechanics were pushing Harriet's Typhoon through the doorway.

"Good." Harriet's face lit up. She'd been buzzing with excitement since her first flight in the Typhoon the previous day, and couldn't wait to take it out for some more fun in the early morning sky. "What's that?" She asked, as she looked at the fuselage, at the large letters H and C painted neatly on either side of the roundel.

"Your initials…" Jo replied dismissively.

"I can see that. Why are they painted on the side of my Typhoon?"

"What else would you have us paint on there? You're not in any of the squadrons. Besides, the Air Ministry made it policy ages ago that Wing Commanders and above get to have their initials on the side of their aeroplanes. Your Wing Commander's pennant is painted on the cowling, too." She pointed to the light blue triangle, edged in dark blue, with two red lines running left to right in the centre.

"Oh, yes…" Harriet replied while blushing a little. She hadn't expected it. She then looked at the orange fox head painted on the cowling. Her personal mark. "How did you know about my vixen?" she asked Jo while narrowing her eyes. Just the sight of it made her heart race a little with excitement, as she thought of her time in Malta and Scotland.

"A little bird told me…"

"Put them on every aeroplane in the wing..." Harriet said with a mischievous smile. "If we're going to be taking the fight to the enemy, I want them to know who they're dealing with."

"Happily!" Jo replied with a smile. You know, I've had Squadron Leaders causing mayhem because they can't have their initials on their aeroplanes. You're a Wing Commander, and you look at me like I've painted the entire aeroplane pink when I put yours on for you."

"I wouldn't mind if you painted it pink."

"I don't doubt that. Where are you going?"

"Just for a familiarisation flight, maybe up north, somewhere out of the way."

"We checked her over, and everything's as it should be, and she's all fully fuelled. Oh, and armed. Just in case."

"Just in case of what?"

"Well, you do have a bit of a reputation…"

"For?" Harriet put her hands on her hips and waited for the answer.

"Finding trouble."

"I don't know who's been saying that, but it's certainly not true!" Harriet held her nose in the air as she marched away towards her Typhoon. "Who has been saying that?" she asked, as she stopped and turned to look at Jo again, who simply shrugged politely in reply. "You like Spitfires, don't you?" She continued on her way as Jo followed behind, smirking to herself.

"My favourite aeroplane."

"Good. The Russians have been asking for engineers to be sent out there to help them with the Spitfires we've loaned them. Don't think you're above a long cruise on an Arctic convoy to Murmansk."

"You wouldn't do that to me..."

"Try me." She gave Jo a smile, then jumped up on the wing, climbed into the cockpit and strapped in, with Jo's help. Having done her checks, she kicked the huge Sabre engine into life, and five minutes later, she was lifting into the air and heading north. It was another invigorating flight, and the Typhoon did exactly as she asked of it. At over four hundred miles per hour, it didn't take her long to get to Yorkshire, where she stopped by aunt Mary's house for a low flypast before heading back south. On her way home, she climbed up above thirty five thousand feet, pushing the Typhoon's service ceiling to see just how high she could get it, before diving to test how it was at the limits of its speed. Which she quickly found out was a bad idea as the needle passed five hundred miles per hour, and the controls started to get sloppy, just as her vision started to narrow and darken with the extreme g forces. She went far above the safe limits, and to her relief, the fuselage held together until she managed to level out at close to six hundred miles per hour, despite the buffeting almost shaking the rivets out of their holes. It took her a few minutes to recover, both physically and emotionally. She'd certainly learned her lesson, again, and made a point of not even thinking of pushing the limits for a third time. Once she was composed, she swept along the south coast before coming back in and rolling to the dispersal, where a cup of tea was waiting for her in her office.

"How was she?" Jo asked.

"As good as I'd hoped. Though..."

"Though what?"

"I may have gone just a little over the maximum speed in a dive. Not for long, I should add, but you may want to check her over just to be sure."

"Why would you do that? I told you how dangerous it could be!"

"Because I needed to know what was going to happen if I did it in combat. We don't just fly straight and level in a fight, you know? We sometimes have to dive hard when we're in trouble, and I wanted to know what it would feel like on the controls, and what it would be like to recover. All the pilots are going to have to get used to it."

"I know... You just need to be careful. They're not like Spitfires; they won't keep you alive and find a way to right themselves if you lose control. Typhoons are big, brutal killers. Seven tons flying four or five hundred miles per hour needs to be kept in its place, or it'll kill you."

"It won't dare try and kill me!" She gave Jo a smile that said she'd heard what was said, loud and clear, and Jo gave her a friendly nod. "Anyway, it knows its place now." While she sipped on her tea, she thought back to her time flying Spitfires in battle. She'd blacked out a few times due to the g forces, and each time she'd come around flying straight and level, like the Spitfire just knew how to fly. Many Spitfire pilots had said the same. It looked after the pilot, and it knew how to fly. There wasn't another aeroplane like it. "So, do we have all of our aeroplanes?"

"We do, and reserves, and enough spares to keep us in the war for ten years."

"Let's hope we don't need to fight that long."

"Indeed. Anyway, all we're missing now are the pilots. When are the reinforcements arriving?"

"Soon, I think. I hope so, anyway, we need to get training." The phone rang, and Harriet grabbed it. Vaughan was at the Guardroom. He was early, but that wasn't a bad thing. She'd had her breakfast and her morning flight, and she was ready for her day. She finished her tea, then grabbed her hat and drove down to the Guardroom, where Vaughan was waiting in his smart railway uniform, complete with medal ribbons and polished buttons. "You're keen," she said as he climbed into her car.

"Aye, well, five minutes before a parade is on time and all that. I mean, that's what we used to say in the army." He was a little embarrassed at being so keen, and sat uncomfortably while she drove.

"It's the same for us. Though you're about thirty five minutes before this particular parade." She gave him a smirk, which made him smile and relax a little. For a soldier who'd survived the trenches, he was more like a nervous schoolboy. "What time are you due back at work?"

"This afternoon. I've got somebody covering for me as a favour."

"Good, I want you to enjoy your visit without feeling rushed."

"I can't tell you how grateful I am for this. Just seeing one up close is more than most get to do."

"I just hope it lives up to expectation." She parked outside the dispersal and led him around to see her Typhoon, which was standing proudly outside the hut.

"Bloody hell…" he gasped as he stood and stared at it. "It's massive!"

"You coming?" she asked, as she continued walking and called back to him.

"Where?"

"You can't sit in it from down here."

"Sit in it?" He smiled as he ran after her. "Today's just getting better." He followed her instructions as she guided him up the fuselage and to the cockpit, which he sat in while she showed him around the many switches and dials, and talked him through moving the stick back and forth. They talked for thirty minutes as she answered his questions, before finally giving Jo a thumbs up after she'd joined them with her fire extinguisher. On receiving a nod to confirm the wheels were chocked, she talked Vaughan through starting the engine, which he did with her help. The propeller spun into life, and the engine roared. His eyes lit up with excitement for the few minutes she shouted into the cockpit, talking him through what was happening to the gauges, then she had him lean the fuel, close the throttle, and shut it down.

"So, there you have it. That's how you start a Hawker Typhoon," she said with a smile. "Noisy, isn't it?"

"It's incredible… And you say it goes four hundred miles an hour?"

"Over five hundred in a dive."

"I really don't know how to thank you."

"No need. It's my pleasure."

"Ma'am," Jo shouted. Harriet looked to see her pointing towards Cas' car pulling up at the dispersal. She watched and rolled her eyes as he got out and walked over. Of all the times he could have chosen for a visit, he came when she was giving a civilian a tour of her aeroplane.

"What's up?" Vaughan asked as he saw the look on her face.

"Nothing," she replied, returning to her smile. "Unfortunately, I can't let you fly it, but I hope that sitting in it and turning the engine over was enough of an experience for you?"

"Really, it is. You'll be getting bored of how much I keep thanking you, but I don't know what else to say."

"Don't mention it. Now, you can have another couple of minutes, but don't touch anything. Especially not that!" She pointed to the undercarriage lever.

"What does it do?"

"Raises the wheels, drops the aeroplane to the ground, and ends my career."

"Got it," he laughed.

"Harry?" Cas shouted up from beside the aeroplane.

"Sir?"

"What the devil are you up to?"

"Public Relations…"

"Well, can't it wait?"

"I suppose, what's up?"

"A group of your new pilots are due to arrive at one thirty; I thought I'd come and let you know the good news."

"That's great. I'll have a driver go down to the train station and collect them."

"Not at one thirty, you won't," Vaughan said.

"What's that?" Cas shouted.

"There isn't a train at one thirty," Vaughan said as he pulled himself up and looked down at Cas. "One o'clock or three. Nothing at one thirty."

"My God…" Cas said. "Dick Vaughan?"

"Well, I never! Cas!" Vaughan said as he looked at Cas.

"Know each other?" Harriet asked a little nervously.

"Remember I told you about a mad pilot crashing in no man's land, and charging the Germans with his machine gun?"

"You're kidding?" Her eyes opened wide with surprise.

"Nope... That's him."

"What are you doing here?" Cas asked, as he walked around to the trailing edge of the wing. "Harry, what's going on?"

"He's the Station Master at the local train station," she answered as casually as she could. "We got talking when I went to collect Robbie, and he told me how much he liked aeroplanes. I thought it would be good for him to see one up close."

"It was my idea," Vaughan said as he awkwardly removed himself from the cockpit, and climbed down to stand in front of Cas. "I talked her into it, really. She had no say in it."

"If you knew her half as well as me, you'd know that she has a say in most things, and the chances of getting her to do anything she doesn't want to do are next to zero," Cas replied while smiling at Vaughan. "Good to see you, old man. How have you been?"

"Oh, I've been worse. Good job that pays well, wife and two kids, though they're both grown up now and doing their own thing. You seem to have done well for yourself. Stayed alive, at least."

"Yes, I've been lucky... I really can't believe it's you, after all these years... You know, Harry, this man saved my life in the last war."

"He told me," Harriet replied. "He also told me you were shot down and crashed in the middle of no man's land."

"Yes... Gosh, it seems like so long ago," Cas laughed.

"It was." She rolled her eyes. "So long ago, you must have forgotten about it, because I'm quite sure that you've been telling me since we met that you've never in your life had an aeroplane shot from under you. In fact, it's something you use to tease me on a regular basis."

"I've landed every aeroplane I've ever taken off in. It's just that some of the landings have been a little rougher than others. Anyway, I think you'll find I said I never had to take to my parachute."

"You told me you weren't issued parachutes when I found you and asked why you didn't jump," Vaughan said.

"We weren't. The Generals thought we wouldn't fight as hard if we had a parachute and a chance to escape. A ridiculous and quite murderous strategy, of course, but at the same time, it still means I'm right, and I've never once parachuted from an aeroplane. Unlike some people." He raised his eyebrow at Harriet, who was busy rolling her eyes at his excuses. "Anyway, why are you really here?"

"Like she said, I told her how much I like aeroplanes, and that I'd never seen one up close except for yours, and she invited me to have a look around."

"Enjoy it?"

"Got to sit in an RAF aeroplane; not many get to say that."

"That's true... Are you going to hang around for lunch?"

"I have to be back at the station this afternoon."

"Fair enough. You'll join us for lunch, though?"

"I... Yes?" he shrugged.

"Good. In that case, let's help you get an appetite. Harry, do you have any spare kit lying around?"

"I'm sure I can rustle something up."

"That'll do. Get our friend here wrapped up and comfortable, and I'll go get the Argus. A jacket should do, maybe some overalls to keep his uniform clean." Harriet shrugged and nodded, and Cas turned and headed back to his car.

"What's an Argus?" Vaughan asked, "and why do I need overalls?"

"An Argus is a small, four seat aeroplane. We have one on the station's Communication Flight that Cas uses to travel around on business, and you need the overalls because it looks like you're going flying."

"I'm going what?"

"Flying. It's what you've always wanted to do, isn't it?" She gave him a smile and led him towards the hangar, where Jo found him some overalls and a flying jacket ready for Cas' arrival at the dispersal in the Argus. Harriet walked Vaughan out to it, and helped him into the seat next to Cas. "All strapped in. Hopefully, he doesn't have a 'rough landing' this time," she gave Vaughan a wink.

"Are you coming?" Cas asked.

"I'll follow you up," she replied with a smile. "Give you an escort, just in case the Germans turn up." Cas gave her a nod, and she closed the door before heading over to her Typhoon. "Did I break anything the last time up?" she shouted to Jo.

"Fortunately not. Going up again?"

"Just for a spin."

"Speed limits…"

"Yes, mum!"

The flight was a huge success. Cas took the Argus for a tour of the Kent countryside, while Harriet flew circuits around them in her Typhoon, rolling and diving, and giving Vaughan a close up display of what the aeroplane was capable of. It was too fast to fly alongside the Argus, so she'd have to pass close by, then roll away and come back on the other side, before diving or climbing again. Cas even let Vaughan take the controls and fly for a while when Harriet had gone up above to keep watch, and stop being so much of a distraction. After the flight, they had lunch in the Mess, where Cas and Vaughan talked about the old days, and the no man's land incident, while Harriet sat quietly, listening in amazement at the details of the story. Cas had always been contained and controlled since she d known him, and it was difficult at first to imagine him running at the German trenches firing the machine gun he'd pulled from the aeroplane he'd just crashed. Vaughan was convinced that the Germans thought he was a madman, because instead of shooting him, they jumped out of their cover and ran away to the safety of their trenches. It was only when one of their officers got a hold of them and gave them some discipline that they started fighting back. That's when Vaughan had jumped on Cas, and pulled him into a shell crater before their machine guns got him. She was fascinated, Cas was embarrassed, and Vaughan was deadpan in his storytelling, much to her amusement. After the meal, Cas offered to drive Vaughan back to the train station, and they arranged to meet for drinks and keep in touch. It was a happy reunion, and Harriet felt good that she was able to make it happen, even if it was entirely by accident.

"They should be here any minute," Harriet said as she stood beside Jo on the grass of the dispersal. It was a beautiful spring day, and the buttercups in the grass were glowing in the midday sun. It wasn't particularly warm, but it wasn't too cool either, and a welcome relief from the cold of winter.

"What are they arriving in?" Jo asked.

"I've no idea…"

"Helpful."

"Yes."

"Not like the RAF to be organised enough to gather them in one place and fly them in together. It's usually a rail warrant and a suggestion of which direction to head in at best."

"Is that what happened to you?"

"Pretty much. Fortunately, I'm from the south. Imagine what it would be like for a northerner to find their way."

"I'm a northerner..."

"Northerner, French, Norwegian, there's no keeping up with you." She gave Harriet a smile. They'd got on since the first day they'd met. Jo was a little older than Harriet, and had the confidence that came with a lifetime of working with engineers. Precise and smart, with a healthy dose of sarcasm, and a mind and mouth that worked in unison when holding her own in any conversation, especially when teasing and sparring.

"There..." Harriet said, choosing to ignore Jo, and pointing to the Dakota transport buzzing in the distance.

"A Dakota," Jo said with surprise. "They must have a lot of luggage with them... I was expecting something smaller."

"Skytrain," Harriet replied.

"Excuse me?"

"C47 Skytrain."

"Dakota."

"Same aeroplane, different markings. We call it the Dakota, the Americans call it the Skytrain, and that's got American markings..." She pointed at the large white star on the side of the fuselage as the C47 circled the airfield, and the unmistakeable drone of the twin radial engines echoed around the hangars.

"I told you it was too big. Maybe ours have been delayed somewhere?"

"Maybe," Harriet shrugged while checking her watch. "I wonder who that one's for?"

"They're all over the country these days; I'm sure there are more Americans here than there are in America."

"It feels like it when you're trying to book a restaurant or show in London."

"I wouldn't know; I haven't tried for a while."

"You should. It's sometimes nice to get out of the RAF for a while, and the war for that matter."

"Honestly, I'd rather be tinkering with an aeroplane."

"You need to get out more..." The phone rang in the dispersal hut, and Jo left to go and answer it, then returned a few seconds later as the C47 taxied towards them. "It's for you."

"Who is it?"

"Not on the phone. That." She pointed to the C47, which was rolling ever closer.

"Don't be ridiculous." Harriet frowned, then turned as the sound of the engines powering up as the C47 came to a halt. It was deafening. She watched as the rear door opened and a ladder was pushed out, before a member of the crew climbed down and stood below. A bag was thrown out, followed by stocking clad legs wrapped in a long black overcoat that swished left and right as the owner climbed down the ladders. Harriet's heart was in her mouth as the woman turned, dressed head to toe in United States Navy uniform, with two lines of brass buttons running down her long, unfastened overcoat, and gold rank braid on the epaulettes. "It can't be..."

"Who is it?" Jo asked.

"Bunny..." Harriet gasped as she felt her cheeks flush, then ache with the smile on her face. Bunny looked at her across the dispersal, and after checking the next pair of legs was following down the ladder, she grabbed her kit bag and marched over to Harriet.

"Commander Wilma Carrington reporting for duty, Ma'am," Bunny said as she stood smartly to attention in front of Harriet.

"How is this possible?" Harriet asked in amazement. She looked Bunny in the eyes, and got a warm smile in reply, then she looked around her to see Ness, Tiff, and some others she remembered from California.

"Our orders," Bunny handed Harriet a sealed envelope, which she quickly pulled open and read.

"By order of the Secretary of War, the officers of the United States Navy identified in this letter are to conduct flying duties on permanent attachment to the Royal Air Force for a period not less than twelve months, or until the cessation of hostilities in Europe, whichever is the longer..." Harriet looked down the list of twelve names, then back at Bunny.

"There's another letter in there from your Air Ministry, posting us to 13 Group Royal Air Force, under the command of Wing Commander Harriet Cornwall. I was handed them this morning when we landed."

"Landed? You flew over?"

"In the belly of a B17, and it was freezing!"

"You must be exhausted."

"That would be one of your typical British understatements."

"Have you eaten?" Bunny shook her head. "Jo, call the Mess and have them put on a late lunch for twelve officers, something warm, and give the stores a call; I want twelve rooms prepared. Bedding, towels, everything they need to make them liveable as soon as they've finished lunch. You'd better get the duty driver here with a truck while you're at it."

"Ma'am," Jo replied, then ran off into the dispersal hut.

"You'd all better come inside and have a cup of tea..."

That evening, Harriet and Bunny sat by the fire in the anteroom after their evening meal. The Americans had a few hours to sleep and freshen up after lunch, before Harriet knocked them up for their evening meal. They were tired, but she was insistent they got up and dressed so they could have a decent warm meal after their trip across the Atlantic. She knew from personal experience how tiring the journey from America was, and how important it was to eat and try and get into a normal routine right away. While they were tired and grumpy, they'd be better for being up and eating before a proper night's sleep.

"How did you sleep?" Harriet asked.

"Badly..." Bunny replied. "I feel worse now than when I went to bed."

"It could be worse..."

"I guess... So, you're running the show here?"

"I hope you're not going to say that's what could be worse."

"Would I dare?"

"Yes..." Harriet smirked while Bunny sipped on her whisky. "So, are you going to tell me how come I've got twelve US Navy pilots on my air station?"

"We were posted; you read the orders."

"I did, and while they tell me you're here, they don't tell me why. The last time I saw you, you were heading to Hawaii to deliver aeroplanes to the Pacific Fleet. In your letters, you said you were flying regularly."

"We were."

"Were?"

"Until this year…"

"I feel there's something you're not telling me."

"Because I can't quite say it without getting angry."

"Bunny, what is it?"

"They've had enough of us back home, so they've sent us out of the way to Europe. As far away as possible."

"I don't understand. I thought you had support?"

"We did. Right up until our army landed in Italy. Attitudes started to change, and by December last year, we had more male pilots queueing up to serve than anyone knew what to do with. Women in flight training were dismissed to other duties, and those of us already serving were put back into ferry pools, shipping airplanes around the mainland. No matter what we tried to get back into action, the answer was no, and things took a turn for the worse this year when even the ferry jobs were given to men. They just didn't need us anymore. Flying and war work was men's work. The misogynists finally won, with the loud support of angry women across the country who didn't like to see girls fly. Or, more realistically, didn't like girls flying with their husbands and boyfriends, like we're all members of some sort of flying harem. Anyway, we went from heroes in '42 and '43, to zeroes in '44. There's word they're going to disband the female ferry pools any day, just to finish us off. Dad talked with the General, and strings were pulled to send a few of us more embarrassing female pilots overseas. The RAF agreed to take us, and that worked out just fine for Uncle Sam. Oversees and out of sight."

"Why would you be more embarrassing?"

"Because those of us who arrived today are the only active surviving female pilots with combat experience. They pinned medals on us a couple of years ago, and had parties to celebrate how brave and wonderful we were. You can't exactly tell girls like that to go back to the kitchen sink so the boys can do the flying, can you? Not when you're gonna be running for office in the next few years, and half the voter base are women. You've got to be smart. Get the girls to retire or resign, or marry them off and see them pregnant. If all else fails, send them to England and hand them over to the British."

"I'm sorry… That's a terrible way to be treated after all you've done for your country."

"You saw it when you visited. We'd been kept under wraps for long enough because people wouldn't stand for girls flying warplanes, in both Congress and the public eye. Pearl Harbour changed things. People were scared, and focused on defence. It's the price of success, I guess. Our boys are fighting hard and pushing the enemy back in Europe and the Pacific. They don't need us girls as much."

"You're talking like the war's over."

"Isn't it? That's the way they talk back home. Have done since Italy surrendered last September."

"The Italians may have surrendered, but there's a whole army of Germans there keeping us out of Rome. It's not exactly a walk in the park. The losses are significant, ours and yours."

"That's not what our newspapers are saying. They're saying it'll be over by Christmas."

"They always say it'll be over by Christmas. They've been saying it since 1939. I actually read it in a French newspaper in 1939, and again in 1940, and here in England in '41 and '42. I can assure you, there's plenty of fighting left to do."

"Good. That's what we're here for."

"So, what's this experience you mentioned?"

"You didn't think you're the only one that got to have some fun, did you?" Bunny smirked.

"Bunny…?"

"We had our fair share of action for a while."

"Well, I hope you remembered what you learned. I expect we're going to be busy soon."

"What is it we're going to be doing here, anyway?"

"According to the last briefing, we're going to be heading out over France in the next few weeks."

"I'll take that."

"I thought you would. We'll be flying Hawker Typhoons. They're the biggest and fastest fighters we've got. Are your pilots up to it?"

"You know half of them; what do you think?"

"I think you're going to fit right in."

"That's what I like to hear." Bunny smiled and swirled her whisky before taking another sip, the way she always had when she and Harriet spent their evenings together in California.

"Bunny…"

"What's up?"

"It's great to have you here, but you need to know that you've given me something to think about." Harriet looked nervously at her friend.

"What?"

"I already have three squadron commanders. I know you're used to leading your pilots, and you'll hold a Squadron Leader's rank while you're with us, but…

"I wouldn't waste time thinking on it," Bunny said with a warm smile. "I'm here to fly and fight, not to lead. I'll fly under whoever you say, like any other pilot."

"That's very gracious of you."

"Beats being at home chained to the kitchen sink, right?" She gave Harriet a nod.

"I can't imagine you ever letting that happen."

## Chapter 9

## Going Home.

Two weeks after Bunny had arrived, along with the rest of the new pilots, the wing were sent to the island of Anglesey off the coast of Wales, where they were introduced to the new RP3 air to ground rockets, which their Typhoons were adapted to carry. The rockets were deadly, and while the training warheads were made of concrete, the real thing came with high explosive or armour piercing options, some of which had delayed fuses to make sure the rocket exploded inside whatever it had hit, such as a warship or tank. There was even a fragmentation option designed to take out troops and soft skinned vehicles like trucks. With four rockets and two 20mm cannons on each wing, it made the Typhoon one of the most deadly aircraft in the Allied arsenal, and Harriet's pilots quickly demonstrated their skill at using them. The American Squadron, as it quickly became known, were particularly lethal. Lexi used her ground attack experience from North Africa to great effect, and Bunny's pilots picked it up like naturals, thanks mostly to their experience dive bombing Japanese ships in the Pacific, something Harriet found out about over drinks in the Mess one night. She also found out about how her own Number Two, Carrie Stone, had been involved in action with the Americans not long after Harriet had left for England, claiming a number of Japanese aircraft shot down. Something Carrie had kept to herself since arriving.

Following the rocket training, the wing returned to their station on the south coast in high spirits. It had been a busy month of training, getting to know their aircraft, learning to fly it to the extremes, and recover it from danger, with many hours firing concrete rockets or glowing tracer at ground targets, in between hours of mock dogfights. Camaraderie in the squadrons developed quickly, and the pilots soon came to implicitly trust and depend on each other. Harriet was initially concerned at how awkward it would be for Bunny to serve under Lexi, when she and her pilots were put in the American Squadron. Bunny had led her pilots in combat, and was the same rank as Lexi, and it could be argued that she had much more experience as well as seniority. The worry was misplaced, though, and Bunny settled in without so much as a raised eyebrow. She didn't even take the post of Flight Commander when Lexi said she'd ask one of the others to make way for her, instead insisting that she start at the same place as everyone else. She and Lexi quickly became the best of friends, and when there was nobody around, Lexi would probe Bunny for information and advice, all of which was given freely. The only oddity was having one too many Squadron Leaders, but Cas made sure it was OK. Besides, the American government was still technically paying their wages, so most of the RAF wouldn't really care that much anyway. With the possible exception of those that obsessed over propriety, or just didn't like female pilots, but that was less of a problem now that they were all in one place, and nobody much bothered them.

"How did it go in Wales?" Cas asked, as Harriet stepped into his office. "I'm told those rockets can be a bit awkward to get on target."

"Nothing to worry about there. Well, not for us, at least. Any Germans in our sights may have a bit of a problem."

"Went that well?"

"Better than. The Americans are particularly good at it."

"So, you'd say you're about ready to be made operational?"

"I'd say so. There isn't much more we can do without on the job practice."

"Good, I was hoping you'd say that. Have a seat." He pointed to the chair in front of his desk, which she pulled out and sat on while he picked up the phone. "Robbie, come through, would you? Bring the charts." He put the phone down and looked at Harriet for a moment.

"What?"

"What?"

"Stop it! What are you looking at me like that for?" She watched as he pushed a letter across the desk to her. "What's this?"

"Thirteen Wing RAF is now operational, and for the first time since the last war, is about to go into action over France."

"You're serious?" Harriet's eyes opened wide as she read the letter confirming the wing's operational status.

"Deadly..." He looked at her for a moment, then switched his gaze to the door as Robbie joined them. She had a map rolled under her arm, and a few other sheets of paper clutched in her hands. "Ah, Robbie. Let's see what you've got." He pointed to the map board on the wall, to which she quickly clipped her unrolled map.

"Where are we going?" Harriet jumped up and stood beside Robbie, looking over her shoulder at the map.

"Patience is a virtue," Robbie said causally, without looking at her.

"I don't have any?"

"Virtue? Yes, I had heard the stories..."

"Shut up!" Harriet felt her cheeks tingle with the slightest blush, and she nudged her elbow into Robbie's ribs.

"Alright, behave before you get started," Cas said, as he joined them looking at the map board. "This is your target." He tapped the map on the French coast, about half way between Dieppe and Le Havre, two heavily defended ports where German ships operated from. "It's a radar site that's been causing us some problems recently. It has the Freya radar, which lets the enemy know our raids are coming, and it's directly connected to a Wuzrburg radar site just up the coast. Wurzburg is the gun layer. If that gets locked on to one of our raids, all of the anti aircraft guns in that area will follow, cutting our aircraft to pieces. You can imagine how much of a pain that is..."

"Radar controlled anti aircraft guns..." Harriet said as she looked at the map.

"Precisely, and it's your job to shut them up."

"What's the plan?"

"Have you got the photos?" he asked Robbie, who nodded and pulled the large monochrome images from an envelope, and pinned them to the map.

"Simple. You're going to go in with your rockets, and put the Wurzburg site out of business." He tapped at the photo showing the large, dish shaped antenna sitting on top of a concrete building. It was huge, bigger than a bus, and made of a metal frame meshed with cables. "Knock that out, and the guns won't be half as effective. They'll have to rely on the old fashioned mark one eyeball, and that evens the playing field a little. Get that out of the game, and we can hop up the coast and take out the Freya site a lot easier than we would if the guns still have radar.

"What are the defences like?'

"Anti Aircraft guns of all sizes surround the site, linked by trenches filled with infantry. Our PRU types were over there this morning having a look around, so the photos are as recent as we can get them." Robbie said as she handed them photos showing close ups of the site. "

"When are we going?" Harriet asked, as she looked at the photos.

"You're to strike at first light tomorrow. The low light may give you a degree of cover, certainly from any fighters sent up to meet you," Cas replied.

"OK, I'll need to take the map and photos to brief my squadron and flight commanders."

"Robbie's prepared a briefing pack for you, copies of the map and photos included."

"Right, I'll get to it in that case." Her heart was racing a little.

"I'm not finished yet..."

"What did I miss?"

"Another wing of Typhoons will be going after the Freya site almost simultaneously."

"We're a distraction so they can get the Freya site?"

"No, your mission is to knock out the Wurzburg, it's a vitally important target. However, should you pull it off, the chances of taking out Freya are significantly increased. They'll be crossing the coast approximately ten minutes behind you, in the hope that you've done the job."

"And if we haven't?"

"Then they'll go in anyway. That's their mission. Your putting the Wurzburg out of action for them is a bonus."

"I see..."

"Look, it's going to be a difficult job. Radar sites are notoriously well defended, and those attacking them undoubtedly suffer losses. You need to be sharp, and fast, and get in there and do your job, then get out. I won't tell you how to do it, that's your decision, but beware of the flak. It'll be murderous."

"Fighters?" Harriet asked, choosing to minimise the warning, externally at least.

"Possibly. You'll have a wing of Spitfires hanging around over our coast, ready to come in if you have any trouble. Group don't want to send them any closer while the radar is still effective. That means you'll be responsible for looking after yourselves."

"Understood..."

"You'll be on the same frequency as the wing going after the Freya site. If you're successful, you're to give the code word 'Harvey', understand?" She nodded her head. "It will let them know what they're getting into. If you're having to pull out and the radar is still intact, you're to use the code word 'Keystone'. Remember, the dish is what you're going after. Knock that down, and the site will be useless."

"I'll see what I can do."

"Is there anything you need?"

"Some luck?" She gave him a smile, then took the briefing pack from Robbie. Both of them looked nervous. At least as nervous as she was feeling inside, though they weren't saying it, while she was trying her best not to show it. "Would you both relax? It's not like we haven't been training for this, it's literally our job."

"Yes, of course," Cas said, forcing a smile. "I'll order some tea all the same. Shall I have it sent to the briefing room?"

"Thank you. Robbie, could you call the squadrons for me? Get the squadron and flight commanders to the briefing room without delay. Probably best to get Jo to come with them, too. We'll need an update on aircraft serviceability."

"I'll get on it."

"Anything else?" Harriet asked, trying to appear as composed as it was possible to be, and not showing the nerves that were raging inside. She knew she had a job to do, and she knew this was coming, yet she hadn't been prepared for how it made her feel. She hadn't had time to think, other than to be part excited about getting the opportunity to do what she was being paid for, and part nervous in hoping she, and her pilots, could actually do it. It was going to be a big test.

"No, I'll leave you to your briefing. We're up here if you need anything."

Harriet went down to the briefing room and prepared herself, pinning the maps and photos to the board, and thinking through her plan. It had already been forming as Cas was briefing her, and in the silence of the briefing room it started to take shape. She knew what she had to do, and she knew the pilots would do their best, but the outcome was in the hands of the gods. The others arrived just after the tea Cas had ordered, which came with a tray of biscuits he'd managed to find somewhere, which were quickly destroyed while she went through the planning. Everyone was confidently excited, and if there was any fear, nobody was showing it. It was agreed that they'd brief the squadrons after their evening meal, then send everyone off for an early night, ready for an alarm call in the early hours so they could get up and ready to cross the enemy coast at sunrise. An early breakfast had been arranged, along with tea down at the dispersal huts, so they could deal with any last minute dry throats before they set off. The meteorology was looking good, with not much weather around to get in the way, so there was absolutely nothing to stop the mission.

The night was the longest Harriet could remember having in a while. After eating with the wing, she'd gone to her room with the intention of getting a good night's sleep, a plan which fell apart the minute she turned off her lamp and her eyes opened wide, while her brain went into overdrive thinking of every possible outcome. Her two biggest fears played over and over. The first was a very personal fear. That of being shot down and falling into the hands of the Gestapo again. She hadn't recovered from her last trip to France, not emotionally at least. She'd still wake with nightmares every now and then, of being hung, or tortured, or sometimes of watching the Resistance man from Paris kicking and twitching at the end of his rope. She didn't want to be in that situation again, and on the same day she was put in charge of a wing which she was told would be heading over France at some point, she'd made the decision to carry the Walther pistol she'd been given by Carlyle for the Geneva trip. From her first flight in the Typhoon, she'd carried the pistol in a shoulder holster which fit under her arm quite snugly, without getting in the way of her parachute, or making it uncomfortable to fly. To double up on the fun, she always flew with her service revolver tucked in her flying boot, just in case. She knew she couldn't fight her way out of being captured, but it was enough to make sure she didn't get captured in the first place, with the added bonus of taking a few of the enemy with her, if she could. It was a morbid thought, but being tortured, or worse, being used to torture somebody else, was something she'd sworn to never let happen again. The second thought bothering her was one of failure. A lot of trust had been put in her and her pilots, and she knew that if she made a mess of the operation, there'd be a lot of powerful people not only waiting to point and laugh, but disband them on the spot. Stanley was evidence enough that there were still plenty of enemies on her own side she had to watch out for, and Bunny's story about the way she was treated in America wasn't exclusive to that side of the Atlantic. They were all together because somebody somewhere wanted to hide them, they were never supposed to be going into battle. A failure would make ugly reading in the newspapers. The chauvinists would say they should never have been there in the first place, and the mothers and fathers would say their daughters won't be in the future. Between capture and failure, the thoughts were enough to keep her awake all night, especially when they combined to become a failure that led to capture.

An hour before her alarm call, Harriet was up, washed, dressed, and heading down to 508 Squadron's dispersal, where she kept her Typhoon. She collected the tea urn on her way, and talked one of the cooks into giving her some freshly baked biscuits, which she had with a drink while standing outside the dispersal hut in the cold, and watching the stars.

"You're early," Jo said, making Harriet jump. "And highly strung, by the looks of it."

"I wasn't expecting you to be sneaking around in the dark."

"I wasn't sneaking. You just weren't paying attention."

"What are you doing here? Don't you sleep?"

"Not the night before an operation. I wanted to make sure the aeroplanes were OK."

"Are they?"

"Every last one of them. All armed, fuelled, and ready to go."

"Good… Thanks for making sure."

"That's what you keep me around for, isn't it? Well, that and my rapier like wit."

"Obviously."

"Anyway, I had company."

"Who?"

"All three of your squadron commanders were down here at one point or another during the night, all checking on their aeroplanes."

"Is that so?"

"Seems it's not just you that couldn't sleep."

"I slept fine. I'm just keen to get going, that's all."

"If you say so. I bet you're the only one who did…" She gave Harriet a reassuring smile. "It'll all be OK, you know?"

"I know… It's just, well, it's our first time going into action as a wing. There's a lot depending on us."

"As long as you do your best, what more can anyone ask?"

"I don't know. I'll tell you when they ask after we get back…" They talked as they waited. It was cold, but Harriet was keen to stand outside and enjoy the fresh air, knowing that it wouldn't be long until she was squeezed into a cockpit, strapped down tight, and breathing oxygen. The truck arrived on time, and Nicole led her pilots into the dispersal hut to brief them, while Jo went back to help the ground crews prepare the aeroplanes, and was replaced at Harriet's side by Carrie. "All ready?"

"Yep…" Carrie replied, in a casual and quite simple way.

"Just remember your training, and you'll be fine. Stay on my wing, and let me know if you see me doing anything stupid." She gave

Carrie a wink, which got a smile in reply. "There's some tea inside, why don't you get yourself some? We've got a few minutes before we set off."

"I can't, if I have anything else I'll be desperate for the toilet before we get to France."

"Fair enough." She checked her watch, it was twenty minutes before take off, and the pilots were starting to leave the dispersal hut, suggesting Nicole's brief was over. "Better go and get ready, I'll be over in a minute." Carrie nodded, and Harriet headed into the hut to see Nicole finishing off with her flight commanders. Once they were dismissed, she wandered over to see her friend, getting a 'good luck' from the pilots who were heading out. "All good to go?"

"It's too late if not," Nicole replied with a casual shrug, followed by a smile.

"You know the plan?"

"Like I've been up all night going through it in my head."

"You too?"

"Yes… It's a big test."

"One you're more than capable of handling."

"I won't let you down, Harry." In an unusual moment of vulnerability, Nicole looked at Harriet nervously. She rarely let her emotions show beyond happiness and irritation, and it took Harriet a little by surprise.

"You never could," Harriet replied, while putting her hand on Nicole's shoulder. "Just be yourself, and everything will be fine." Nicole nodded and smiled, then took a breath and shook her head.

"It's my first time in charge like this. Usually I get to leave it all to you."

"Well, you've got to earn the pay rise somehow."

"I still can't believe they pay us at all. Who else gets to fly a Typhoon and shoot Germans? We should be paying them."

"I'll remind you of that when the Germans start shooting back."

"They're bad shots, I'll be fine." She shrugged, back to her usual confident self. "Besides, you're coming with us. You're a magnet for German bullets, so they'll be coming your way if anyone is stupid enough to put up a fight."

"Thanks…"

"You're welcome. Shall we go?"

"Let's. Before you put me off the idea." They walked out of the hut and into the darkness, and after giving each other's hand a quick squeeze, they headed to their aeroplanes. Harriet climbed up the wing, where her ground crew were waiting to help her into the cockpit and strap her in, while she started her checks. The soft glow of the dials made her smile. The anticipation was gnawing at her. She wanted to get on with it. Every minute was feeling like an hour, and despite having no sleep, she was more awake than ever. The adrenaline had started early, which meant it was going to be a long and exhausting day. She waited once the ground crew had jumped down, and checked her watch repeatedly, until finally she gave a shout of 'clear prop' and got a thumbs up from below, then fired the Coffman cartridge into the engine after giving it a prime. The huge Napier Sabre engine immediately roared into life, and the giant four blade propeller spun. The gauges were where they should be, and she went through her power checks, making sure everything was ready for a quick getaway. There were three squadrons due to take off, and they needed to be off quickly with no messing about. Even a minute of delay could be disastrous for the wing attacking the Freya radar station, and she was determined to give them every chance. She looked around, the eastern sky was starting to turn a royal blue, with a hint of silver on the distant horizon. It was time. She waved the chocks away, then looked over to Carrie and gave her a thumbs up, which was immediately returned, and she let off the brakes.

Together they zigzagged to the end of the runway where, after a final check, it was time to get going. Harriet opened the throttle, inching it forward little by little until the engine was at full power. As soon as the green flare went up, she let off the brakes, and the Typhoon shot down the runway at a speed that would leave even a Spitfire standing. Out of the corner of her eye she could see Nicole's Squadron rolling to the end of the runway, with the others following close behind. She brought the tail up into the airstream with a slight push on the stick. Then pulled back as the Typhoon leapt into the air. Wheels up, instruments checked, and she started a steep climb, then turned into a wide circuit while watching Nicole's Squadron roll at the second green flare. They followed her in a climbing turn, and then came AP's squadron, and then Lexi's Americans. They were all up quickly, and soon they formed on Harriet, one Squadron behind the other, as they headed east along the Kent coast, before turning north. It was the first stage of Harriet's plan. She knew that German radars and reconnaissance had a good chance of seeing them forming over their airfield, so to throw them off the scent, she led her wing in the opposite direction. She slowly descended, leading the others down behind her, and at a thousand feet she started her turn south, lining up on a course that would take her out over the Channel at Dungeness, where she'd adjust her heading and aim right for the radar station. They crossed the coast at five hundred feet, then dropped down to the wave tops, racing across the serene and mill pond like water separating England from France. The first light of day was brightening the eastern sky, though the sun hadn't yet risen, but it was enough for the light to catch the water, and make avoiding it a little easier. When she'd been planning her attack the previous evening, she used her experience of flying Lysanders into France undetected as a way of hopefully sneaking up on the Germans unannounced. By flying low she and Nicole had slipped in and out of France without being seen by the enemy radar many times, and this time she was hoping that she'd be able to do the same with almost forty heavily armed Typhoons, which were racing along at four hundred miles per hour.

Harriet was focused and ready as she checked her watch again, knowing it was less than five minutes until they hit the French coast. If she'd got her navigation right, they'd arrive right in line with the radar site. If she hadn't, they were going to lose valuable time, and the element of surprise, by flying around trying to find it. As the coast came into sight, she was sure she was in the right position. It looked exactly as it did in the photos, so she gave her wings a waggle, the silent instruction for her wing to form battle positions, which they did. She'd insisted on radio silence until the shooting started, knowing that a radio transmission could easily give the game away, and let the German listening stations track their exact position, and everyone had stuck rigidly to her rule, not wanting to be the one that caused the attack to fail. The squadrons fell back into the predetermined places. Nicole's Squadron, 508, named The Marseillaise after the French National Anthem, were going to follow twenty seconds behind Harriet, and break left and right to support her in attacking the anti aircraft guns. Lexi's Squadron, the Yankees of 509, were then going to follow in ten seconds later, and go straight down the middle, aiming for the radar installation. As Harriet opened the attack, AP was going to lead 507, Dagger squadron, which Harriet had amusingly named at the look of daggers AP gave anyone who annoyed her, into a steep climb at maximum power, and circle as umbrella cover while looking out for fighters, before switching places with 509 and coming down with their rockets as soon as Lexi's Squadron had emptied their ammunition. Harriet's heart raced as she approached the coast. There was a light silvery layer of fog sitting over the fields, which made the radar mast stand out as clear as day. She'd found it. "Valkyrie Wing, target ahead. Tally Ho!" she called over the radio, then set her gunsights on the top of the cliff, directly in line with the radar mast, where she knew from the photos that a large anti aircraft position was hiding under the fog. As she closed, she pushed her fire button, and sent a stream of glowing tracer into the mist, lighting it up as she zipped a line along the cliff and onto the target, and Carrie did the same just to her right. As their tracer converged, Harriet released four of her rockets, and watched as they fired away from her, sinking as they raced forward, leaving silver trails of smoke behind them as they joined with Carrie's in turning the dawn darkness into a raging inferno, as the mixture of fragmentation and high explosive rockets ripped into the anti aircraft position. She pulled back on her stick as she hopped over the coast, and passed through the burning cloud of fire that had leapt into the air from the attack. As she did, the site lit up with tracer, as heavy machine guns barked into life from every direction, followed closely by more deadly anti aircraft fire. She snaked left and right, while climbing and leading Carrie into a steep ascent, before coming back down again in line with the road to the rear of the installation, where she saw a truck rolling innocently forward towards the radar site. She pushed her fire button, and ripped it apart with her cannons before banking around for another attack on the many anti aircraft positions. By the time she came back in, Nicole's Typhoons were all over the place, firing rockets in twos and fours, and letting loose with their cannons at everything that moved. Before she could pick a target and dive in to attack, Harriet watched as Lexi led the first wave of her squadron in for the attack, charging forward in pairs and letting their rockets fly. Harriet ignored the tracers stalking her inaccurately through the dark and smoky sky, mostly because she was so mesmerised by the trails of rocket smoke as they whistled towards the radar dish, which was suddenly and dramatically consumed by an inferno as rocket after rocket found home. By the time the last of Lexi's Typhoons released their rockets, the whole site seemed to be ablaze, with even the forest surrounding the site burning intensely. Lexi's squadron didn't hang around, they went straight up to relieve AP, so the murder could continue.

"Dagger Squadron, hold your position!" Harriet called over the radio, when she was finally able to get some moisture into her mouth, halting AP and keeping her up at height while she circled, searching the inferno to see if the job had been done."

"Look out, fighters!" an unrecognised voice shouted over the radio. Harriet instinctively searched above, not sure who had called, or where from.

"Dagger, is that you?" she called at AP.

"Not us. No fighters up here," AP replied. "Yankee?" she asked Lexi.

"Negative. No fighters," Lexi confirmed. Harriet was confused, she looked around again, watching as Nicole's Typhoons continued to circle the now almost entirely defeated radar installation, like Native Americans in the movies circling around the wagons. The occasional burst of tracer was still coming up, but as soon as it did, a Typhoon snuffed it out with a rocket or a burst of cannon fire.

"Fighters. Talon Wing, break, break, break," another unrecognised voice shouted, and the penny dropped. Talon Wing was the other attack, those heading for the Freya site further up the coast.

"Dagger, Yankee, form above and keep your eyes open. Marseillaise, can you see the radar?"

"It's down!" Nicole replied excitedly. Look! We got it!" Harriet banked hard as the smoke cleared for a moment, and she saw the huge radar dish blown into pieces and laying on the ground, with the concrete station below it all but obliterated.

"Marseillaise, disengage and rejoin," she ordered, and watched as Nicole led her Typhoons up to join the others. A trail of tracer leapt up and clipped one of them, incensing Harriet in the process, who dived and put a pair of rockets into the smoke and fog where she'd seen the tracer come from, blowing the ground into a firestorm, before leading Carrie up in a climb. "Watcher this is Valkyrie Leader. Harvey! I repeat, Harvey!" She waited patiently for the reply from control, while racing up to join her circling Typhoons.

"Understood, Valkyrie Leader. Beware of fighters in your area, Talon returning home. Recommend you do the same, and quickly. Well done!"

"Watcher, confirm Talon unsuccessful?"

"Confirmed, Valkyrie Leader. Approximately five zero bandits north west of your position," the controller replied. Harriet quickly pulled her map from under her thigh. The Freya site was just along the coast, and while she had no doubt the Germans knew they were in the area, they no longer had the Wurzburg radar laying their guns for them, so she was confident that the flak would be inaccurate.

"Valkyrie Wing. Any damaged or out of ammunition, get high and head home, everyone else form on me!" Nicole, Lexi, and AP gave orders to their squadrons, and soon there were twenty five Typhoons lined up behind Harriet, and following her along the coast. "OK, Yankee. You get to stay up top and watch for fighters this time, Marseillaise, follow me in and let's open the door for Dagger.

Dagger, no messing about, fire everything you've got at the radar mast. You can't miss it, it looks like a giant fly swat, just don't get hit! Split into loose pairs, don't make an easy target for the flak." Confirmations came in reply, while Harriet searched the fog for the fly swat, which she soon found. "Watcher, we're going to have a crack at Talon's target. Valkyrie Wing, tally Ho!" She pushed her nose down and opened the throttle, and soon she was charging down towards the second radar site at over five hundred miles per hour. She remembered her previous experience, and as the g forces were starting to crush her, and dull her vision, she was able to back off the speed until things were just about manageable. As she did, the sky filled with a wall of flak, as fluffy little black dots formed a mesh in front of her, then quickly exploded into a screen of fire that hid everything below. She held her breath and closed her eyes as she passed through, just as she had when flying through the air defence box over Grand Harbour in Malta. The Typhoon was shaken and thrown about, and shrapnel rattled off the airframe like hail on a tin roof, but she was quickly through, and just had time to fire her remaining rockets at the radar mast, before a line of tracer rattled her cowling and left melted gashes in her windscreen. She pulled left and put her cannons on a gun position, keeping the gunners occupied while Carrie rattled it with a pair of rockets, before turning right on to the next position, this time with Harriet flying as her Number Two, and shooting at anything that moved while her young friend lined up her final two rockets, which hit the target and obliterated it. Other Typhoons dropped through the curtain of flak, firing cannons and rockets while diving at ever steeper angles. Anti aircraft gun positions were ripped apart, and the whole site was turned into just as much of an inferno as the last, though the giant fly swat was still standing. As Harriet was about to call off the attack, a sole Typhoon dived down right above the radar mast, coming at it almost vertically. It was on fire, having been hit more than a few times by Flak, but the pilot was unwavering. Harriet's heart pounded as she watched in slow motion, desperate to shout a warning, but all she could see was the Typhoon going to collide with the mast. Before it did, to her amazement, the pilot let all eight rockets go, sending them streaming down in a perfect bullseye, and throwing pieces of twisted metal in every direction, as the giant fly swat broke apart and fell into the concrete building below it. Miraculously, the Typhoon pulled up just before the ground, and skipped up and over the cliffs, blowing out the flames on its wing with the sheer speed. "That's it, Valkyrie Wing, break it off. Home and watch for fighters!" A chunk of Harriet's wing was blown off as she reversed her turn, ready to follow the Typhoon over the cliffs, making a hole so big she could see daylight through it. Before she could respond, Carrie let the flak site have a burst of cannon, which silenced it immediately, and the pair slipped out over the Channel, leaving a second burning radar installation behind them. "Thanks!" she shouted to Carrie, and gave her a wave. "Come on, let's get out of here before they get any closer!" Harriet looked around as soon as they were over the water, there were Typhoons everywhere, and some of them had been shot up quite badly. Fortunately, nobody seemed to be shooting at them. She composed herself, and caught her breath for a moment, while checking to make sure they weren't still being shot at. Once she was sure they were safe, she checked her instruments. Fuel was lower than it should be, but that was understandable considering they'd gone off course to go and shoot up a second target, but there was certainly enough to get them back to England. She looked over her wings. The right had a huge hole in it, but the aeroplane was still flying, and the controls still responding as normal, so she wasn't too fussed. She then checked around the other aeroplanes. They were scattered all over as they raced home, and that made her nervous.

"Dagger and Marseillaise, reform. We're not home yet!" she barked, and the scattered aircraft of AP and Nicole's squadrons started to come together.

"Fighters, nine o'clock high!" Lexi said, and Harriet quickly followed her directions. "Focke Wulf 190s, twenty plus. We'll hold them while you get home."

"Marseillaise Leader, take the wing home. Full power. Valkyrie Two, go with them."

"Wilco!" Nicole replied, as Harriet opened her throttle full, and turned hard left while pulling into a climb. The Napier Sabre engine screamed as she squeezed every last breath of power out of it, while climbing to intercept the swarm of dots which were closing quickly. She scanned the sky ahead, to make sure there wasn't another swarm following, then she picked her target as the 190s started to dive from twenty thousand feet, coming straight down at Harriet, and totally ignoring the squadron of Typhoons coming down at them from fifteen thousand feet higher, invisible to their prey as they dived out of the sun. Harriet held her course, luring the enemy in, while her heart almost pounded out of her chest. Inside she knew it was one of her more reckless and stupid decisions, to go headfirst into twenty of the enemy's most advanced and deadly fighters, but it was working. They were so fixated on her, that they weren't paying attention to what was above them, a cardinal sin in the world of fighter tactics, and they quickly paid the price as Lexi's squadron caught them, ripping into them and knocking three 190s down on their first pass, with two more damaged and heading home. The leaders didn't change course, keeping their focus on closing with Harriet. As they started to come into range, Harriet adjusted her position to correct for the speed and drop, and pushed on her fire button. A spurt of cannon shells lanced upwards, and then stopped. She pushed again and nothing happened. She pushed again and again, and still nothing. Either all four cannons had simultaneously jammed, or she was out of ammunition. She cursed herself as her mind raced through the options in a split second. Before she could act, a burst from the leading 190 passed down the left side of her cockpit and rattled the fuselage. She was about to roll right when four streams of tracer zipped past her from behind and ripped into the leading 190, making it burst into flames and steepen its dive, before spiralling down to the Channel. The firing continued, and the other 190s scattered, just as two of Lexi's Typhoons caught up with them, hitting them from behind and splitting them up. Harriet looked to her right and watched as Carrie pulled alongside her, and gave another 190 a blast of her cannons, severing its tail and sending it down in flames, passing between them as it fell. Harriet's mouth was bone dry with fear and adrenaline. She gave Carrie a nod, then turned back to see the remaining 190s turning in every direction and racing towards France.

"OK, let them go!" Lexi said over the radio, and her Typhoons broke off the action, and joined Harriet and Carrie in heading home, just as a squadron of Spitfires passed above them, giving chase to the 190s.

"Good work, Yankee leader," Harriet said once she'd composed herself. She looked around as the Typhoons formed to her left. A few were worse for wear, but they were flying, and that was the important thing. She checked her fuel and engine temperature, and as the coast of England came into sight, she breathed a sigh of relief and started to descend, leading her pilots home, where she circled overhead, with Carrie by her side, while she watched Lexi's squadron land. Finally, when she was sure that everyone was down, she landed, and bounced to the dispersal, wishing she could have flown with her cockpit open and mask off so she could compose herself with fresh air after the battle. Unfortunately, the Typhoon's carbon monoxide vice meant it was impossible, not if she wanted to stay alive, but as soon as she'd shut down her engine, her mask and helmet were off, and the canopy was pushed open so she could gulp in the air, and let the sweat cool.

"Are you OK?" Ginny asked, as she appeared on the wing by the ground crew.

"I don't know, am I?" Harriet frowned in reply.

"Your aeroplane suggests it could go either way." She helped pull Harriet to her feet.

"Fair point," Harriet replied when she stepped out onto the wing and saw what Ginny's talking about. The whole aeroplane was like a sieve, scattered with shrapnel and bullet holes from nose to tail. "A bit of effort and I'm sure that'll all bluff out."

"I'm sure… You're OK, though? Nothing on you that needs to be buffed out?"

"Not that I know of. Everyone back OK?"

"Not yet. Come on, let's get you a cup of tea. Cas is on his way down."

"What for?"

"Apparently, some maniac went off the rails and decided to do somebody else's job for them as well as their own. It's caused a stir."

"What on earth are you talking about?"

"You're impossible."

"Anyway, what do you mean, not yet?"

"Three unaccounted for."

"Excuse me?"

"Three haven't come back yet, but there's time."

"Who?"

"Two from 508. Jenny Jones, and Pippa Devereux; and Emma Poppleton from 507."

"Oh…" Harriet felt like she'd been punched hard in the stomach, and it was all she could do to keep herself upright. "Can you have a ring around the local airfields and see if they've turned up? Maybe check with the launches and see if anyone came down over the Channel?"

"I will, as soon as I've got you a cup of tea."

"I hardly think that's the priority right now."

"Well, I do." She led Harriet into 508's dispersal hut, and poured her a cup of tea from the boiler, which she loaded with sugar.

"I don't…"

"Here." She pushed the mug into Harriet's hand, which she sipped while Ginny pulled a small bar of chocolate from her pocket and opened it. Before Harriet could argue, a couple of squares of chocolate had been pushed into her mouth. Ginny gave her a warming smile, then nodded towards the CO's office, while handing Harriet another cup and the rest of the chocolate, then opened the door and guided her in. Nicole was sitting on the desk with the phone pushed to her head.

"Call me the minute you hear anything." She slammed the phone down and looked at Harriet. Her eyes were red and wet with tears. "Two lost!" she snarled between clenched teeth, as Ginny pulled the door closed and left them to it.

"I brought you some tea," Harriet said, as she handed Nicole the cup.

"I don't want tea! I want my pilots back!" Nicole snapped furiously. Harriet put both cups down without a word, then put her arms around her friend and held her tight.

"Of course you want them back, so do I, but this is war and losses happen. You can't control that. Now, there's a time for tears, but not here, not now. The pilots you brought back need you," she whispered in Nicole's ear. "Have this, and get some tea in you, then we'll go outside and make sure they're OK." She pushed the chocolate in Nicole's hand, then stood back and handed her the tea. Nicole did as she was told, then dried her eyes on the handkerchief Harriet passed her.

"I don't know how to do this… I wasn't expecting to lose anyone."

"It happens to all of us sooner or later, it's the price of command."

"How long until I get used to it?"

"You don't. You just learn to live with it."

"All these years… I knew it was hard on you, but I didn't realise how bad it was to lose somebody you're responsible for. What do I do?"

"You bury it deep inside, and you get back to work. Two didn't come back, the rest did. They need you to be their leader."

"How?"

"Be yourself. That's what they know, and what they're relying on to get them through this."

"Thank you, Harry." She kissed Harriet on the cheek, then ate the chocolate. Harriet drank her tea, and realised that the words she'd used to reassure Nicole were just as important to her. Ginny knew that. It's why she'd pushed the chocolate in her mouth and given her the hot sweet tea, then sent her to deal with Nicole. "Now, let's go and do our jobs." Nicole squared her shoulders and put on a smile, then stepped out of the office with her cup in her hand. Harriet smiled as she watched her leave, then followed behind. By the time Harriet was back outside the dispersal hut, Nicole was already talking with her pilots, congratulating them on their skill and fighting, and listening to their stories. Robbie had arrived with a stack of combat reports, which she was busy handing out to the tired but excitable young women, who were still wearing their Mae West life jackets while drinking their tea.

"I'm going to go over and see the other squadrons," Harriet said to Ginny, who was looking out of the open window while holding a phone to her ear. She nodded, and Harriet walked away, just as Cas' car rolled to a halt.

"Wing Commander Cornwall," he said loudly, over the noise of the conversation. She changed direction and walked over to him. She was feeling nervous for some reason, like she was in trouble and about to be told off.

"Sir," she said as she stood smartly to attention in front of him.

"Going somewhere?"

"Heading over to the other squadrons to see how they got on."

"I'll give you a lift if you wait a moment. He gave her a slight smile and nodded his head for her to follow him, then walked over to Nicole, who was standing surrounded by her pilots. She called them to attention when she saw him, and the dispersal fell quiet, apart from the voices of the ground crew, calling to each other as they climbed over the battered and beaten Typhoons. "Squadron Leader Delacourt, I'd like to address your pilots, if I may?"

"Of course, Sir," Nicole replied, and all of the pilots turned to face him.

"I've just had a call from the top, and they send their thanks and congratulations to you all. Both radar sites are reported as completely out of action, thanks to your efforts." The pilots smiled proudly as they listened. "I'd also like to add my own congratulations. Some of you may know that 508 is my old squadron, when your CO, the Wing Commander here, and I were fighting the Germans in France back in 1940. Back then it was the highest scoring squadron in France, with more victories over the enemy than anyone else. Not bad for a squadron known as the black sheep, because nobody wanted them. That said, I couldn't be any more proud of your efforts upholding the squadron's reputation for being the best of the best. Well done to you all, I'll stand each of you a drink in the Mess the next time you're off duty." The smiles grew among his audience. "I'd also like to offer Squadron Leader Delacourt my particular thanks for her work in leading you. I saw her in action in these very skies during the Battle of Britain, you're lucky to have her. Let's have three cheers for Squadron Leader Delacourt and the fighting 508. Hip hip!" Three loud cheers went up, and Nicole visibly grew with pride. Cas gave her a nod, then he and Harriet walked over to his car.

"It's not a long walk, you know…" she said as she got in.

"Got something against me driving you?"

"No…"

"Good, you can close your door in that case."

"Yes, Sir."

"That's better, at least you're starting to remember how all this works."

"All what works?"

"The RAF… Though you seem to have forgotten it for a moment when you were instructed to return home after you knocked out the Wurzburg site…"

"I wondered when this would come up."

"What?"

"This… Anyway, it doesn't matter because I wasn't instructed to do anything."

"I'm quite sure you were. The duty controller told me as much."

"Then he needs to have his memory checking, because I distinctly remember him recommending, not instructing, that we return home."

"Is that so?" Cas smiled.

"It certainly is. I don't disobey orders. Anyway, stop complaining. We got the job done, didn't we?"

"You did, and command are incredibly happy with what you achieved. Not so much the CO of the wing who didn't get there, but that's not our problem."

"So I'm not being told off?"

"You're a Wing Commander in the RAF, you don't get told off, that's not how it works."

"I'm pretty sure I do."

"Disciplined, advised, warned, yes. Told off, no."

"It feels like I'm being told off now."

"Advised."

"Shut up."

"Anyway, you did so well that they want you to do it again."

"What?"

"This evening. Right before sunset. The Germans will be doing their best to repair the damage, and they won't be expecting another raid quite so soon. HQ want you to go in and make sure that the radar there never works again, and hopefully catch their repair crews in the act. It takes specialist skills to get a radar site up and running, and if we wipe some of them out, we'll set back other repairs. That's the theory, at least."

"OK."

"OK, that's it?"

"What was you expecting?"

"I don't know… For you to be annoyed at having to go back and do the same thing again right away?"

"I have three pilots missing, and four in the hospital, not to mention half of my aeroplanes have been shot up. Having been caught napping, I wouldn't be surprised if the Germans were sitting at thirty thousand feet and waiting for us. What's there to be annoyed about?"

"You'll have Spitfire cover this time, if that'll help?"

"We had Spitfire cover this morning, too. They arrived just as we were leaving, long after the other wing was attacked, and we were practically home. I'm not convinced…"

"You have my word; they'll be where you need them to be. Now the Wurzburg site is out of action, the enemy have a blind spot, and that's where the Spitfires will be hiding. Right above you, so you can get on with your job in peace."

"You don't need to sell it, it's our job." She gave him a smile, which clearly gave him a little relief.

"Did you say it's three pilots you lost?"

"That I know of."

"I'm sorry… I know it's not easy."

"It's the job." She forced another smile as they stopped outside AP's squadron dispersal. She jumped out before they could say anything else, and met AP, who'd walked over to meet them. "Any news about Poppleton?"

"No…" AP shook her head. Her eyes looked sad, but otherwise she was as expressionless and as hard to read as always. "She was shot up pretty bad when she attacked the Freya mast, it was a miracle she managed to pull up at all."

"That was her? The one that came down near vertical and finished the job?"

"Yes… She must have gone down in the Channel after she hopped over the cliffs. Nobody saw anything of her."

"I'm sorry."

"It's war." AP shrugged dismissively. It was obvious she was upset by the loss, but she was determined not to show it. "I've got two others injured, they're in sick bay."

"Injured how?"

"One took some shrapnel to the leg, and another got some shrapnel in her face when a shell took her canopy off. They'll be OK."

"Good job today, AP," Cas said as he joined them.

"We got the Freya, that's what's important."

"Mind if I address your people?" He asked. She shook her head, and he gave a speech similar to the one he'd given to 508, but more personal to the pilots he was addressing. Many of them were new to the wing, and had come from across the country when the new squadron had been formed. They'd hardly flown together previously, but they'd outperformed all expectations. He promised them all a drink in the Mess as well, then left them to continue with their tea and talking. "Thanks, AP. I'll call in the medical centre and see how your pilots are doing."

"Thank you." She gave him a slight smile.

"Mechanic to Squadron Leader pilot… Not bad, AP. Not bad…" He gave her a wink, and her smile grew, lighting up her face. "Make sure your pilots have everything they need. Brunch in the Mess, then get some rest."

"Sir." She stood smartly to attention, and Harriet and Cas left, climbing back into the car for the journey to the American Squadron."

"Two more down…" Harriet said.

"At least they're alive."

"That's three missing and six wounded in one action. If we keep going like this, you're going to have to go find us some more female pilots." She looked at him for a moment, but smiled when she saw how awkward he looked. She was feeling every loss and injury, and she knew he was too. It wasn't fair to take it out on him, and she knew it. It wasn't even deliberate; the words were just falling out of her mouth. "I'm sorry."

"What for?"

"Being snappy about the losses. It's not your fault."

"No, it's the fault of that madman in Berlin who started all this in the first place, and the madmen in London, Washington, and Moscow who want to keep it going."

"Who? What madmen?"

"Hitler, of course!"

"Yes, I know that one… You said madmen here."

"Well, we're the ones demanding an unconditional surrender. The last time that happened, we pillaged their country, starved their people, and created an environment where perfectly rational people welcomed an angry little man with a questionable moustache as their saviour. The Russians are pushing them back in the east, we're pushing them back from the south, and their cities are being bombed day and night. If surrender wasn't unconditional, and they could retain control of their country while removing the current government, I dare say there'd be a military coup and the war would be over tomorrow."

"I don't know…" Harriet frowned.

"Oh?"

"When I was in France I got to see them up close. They're looting the place, and killing without a care in the world. I don't think surrender's even occurred to them."

"Maybe…" He gave her a pained smile. They'd talked about her time in France, though not in any detail. It upset him to think about it, and her to talk about it, so they just left the details alone.

"They take thousands of bottles of Champagne every week, and demand the good stuff. The Resistance know when there's a major offensive coming, because the Germans order the celebratory Champagne in advance.'

"Really?" He raised an eyebrow at her.

"Yep. They've put a commissioner in charge to control the region, and when there's an offensive, he summons the heads of the Champagne houses and puts in his order. The crates are stamped with the destination, the Champagne house tells the Resistance, and the Resistance tell us. We knew they were heading into Russia before their infantry did."

"How do you know all of this?"

"The Resistance… Where do you think I stayed while I was there? Before the Germans got their hands on me."

"Every day's a school day."

"I'm not sure you remember that far back. Didn't they write on slates with sharp stones when you were at school?"

"Shouldn't you still be at school?"

"I would be, if you hadn't put me in a uniform and signed me up for the RAF."

"We learn from our mistakes… Here we are." He gave her a wink as she gave him a stern look, then climbed out to be met by Lexi, who'd pulled herself away from her loud and excited pilots when she saw the car pulling up.

"Sir…" she said mischievously, while standing to attention and giving him a smile. "Ma'am," she added as she gave Harriet a smile.

"How are your pilots?" Cas asked.

"All present and accounted for, and all on a high."

"Any damages or injuries?"

"A few cuts and scratches from shrapnel here and there, but nothing to write home about."

"What about the aeroplanes?"

"I'm talking about the aeroplanes, we're fine."

"Good to know it. Mind if I talk to your pilots?"

"Anytime, come on, I'll hush them for you." She gave Harriet a wink, then turned and led him to her pilots, who were all stood to attention.

"At ease…" he said, asking them to relax so he could talk with them. As he did, Bunny side stepped out of the group, and walked over to stand by Harriet's side.

"Are you OK?" Bunny asked quietly, while Cas talked.

"Yes, are you?" Harriet whispered a reply.

"Yes, but I'm not the crazy woman who turned and climbed head first into a swarm of enemy 190s."

"They can't shoot straight; I was perfectly safe."

"Only because your Number Two got them before they got you…"

"Shut up. They needed something to keep them distracted while you did your thing. Anyway, did you get one?"

"Sure did." Bunny gave her a confident smile.

"Good. Well done."

"The whole squadron fought like tigers. You'd be proud of them."

"I am."

"They're proud of you, too."

"What?"

"The first female fighter pilot leading from the front. You inspire them."

"Whatever… Just make sure they don't get overconfident. It's important they keep in mind how dangerous it is, we were lucky today."

"I know. Got to let them have their moment though, right?"

"I suppose. Do me a favour, will you?"

"What is it?"

"Both of the other squadrons lost people. Maybe let your pilots know once Cas and I have gone?"

"Oh… How many?"

"Three missing, six injured. Everyone's doing what they should, closing ranks and moving forward, but I don't doubt some will be a little raw."

"I don't doubt it. Thanks for the warning."

"You're welcome. I just don't want any of your girls feeling awkward, that's all."

"I get it, we'll be considerate."

"Don't pacify them too much, you've still done great today. You need to celebrate and be proud."

"Oh, we will." They were distracted by the usual cheers, and Cas returned to the car, while Bunny made her way back to her friends.

"Done?" Harriet asked.

"Yes… We should give them a while before briefing them for this evening's job. I'll get the meteorology reports for you while you make your plans."

"Thanks."

"Want a ride back to headquarters?"

"No thanks, drop me back at 508, would you? I want to see what our aircraft availability is like."

"I think I can do that. Jump in."

The rest of the morning was spent doing paperwork, despite being promised that she wouldn't need to do any now she had Ginny. All the combat reports were put in front of her to check and sign off, as were the aircraft serviceability reports, spares reports, and every other report imaginable. It was all an appropriate distraction for her from the three letters she knew she had to write. They'd been in the back of her mind since she found out about the losses, and she'd gone over the content in her head again and again. She'd written letters to the families of lost pilots before, but it felt different this time. Worse, somehow. So she avoided the job, and buried herself in reports instead, at least until Nicole, AP, and Lexi arrived, and sat with her drinking tea while she briefed them on the evening's plans. They were all up for it, and Jo had managed to move spare aircraft around enough to ensure that each squadron had enough for the job, so once they were briefed, she sent them to their squadrons to do their own briefings before lunch, and have an afternoon resting in preparation for the task ahead of them. Harriet stayed in her office for the afternoon, and put pen to paper writing the dreaded letters. She made them as personal and sensitive as she could, knowing that the parents of the missing pilots would be reading them at the toughest time in their lives, knowing their daughters were dead. There were more than a few scrunched up versions thrown in the waste paper bin, ready for her to take back to the accommodation and burn in the stove so they were never found.

"Yes?" she shouted, after a knock on her office door dragged her from the final letter.

"Shouldn't you be having a nap or something before this evening?" Ginny asked, as she brought Harriet a cup of tea, and sat herself by the desk.

"Shouldn't you be bossing somebody else around?"

"This is what you get when you drag me from the tranquillity of Scotland. We haven't had venison or good whisky since I arrived."

"Have you really come in here just to give me a hard time?"

"No, I'd come to give you some news, but if you're going to be all prickly I'm not sure I'll bother."

"Does that mean you're leaving?"

"Does that mean you don't want to know what I came to tell you?"

"OK, I concede," Harriet said, as she threw down her pen and picked up the cup of tea she'd been brought. "Surprise me."

"I bet I can, too..."

"Ginny Russel!"

"Jenny Jones was picked up in the Channel an hour ago, paddling around in her dinghy. She's in the hospital being treated for a bad shrapnel wound and a case of hypothermia, but she's going to be OK."

"You're serious?" Harriet felt her chest tightening as she heard the news.

"Very much so. What's more, Emma Poppleton crashed at Cowes.

"Crashed into cows?" Harriet frowned.

"At Cowes. On the Isle of Wight. Do keep up."

"She's alive?"

"For now. The Royal Navy pulled her out of the water when her Typhoon made a splash in the harbour. They thought she was a German trying to sink the fishing fleet at first, but once they'd established that a petite blue eyed girl wasn't that much of a threat without her aeroplane, they took her to the Wardroom and started to drown her in rum. Word has it she hasn't stopped talking about aeroplanes since they pulled her out of the water, and they wondered if we wouldn't mind sending somebody to collect her?"

"She's OK?"

"She won't be if we leave her there much longer, the hangover alone will finish her off if she's not rescued from the rum. Their doctor has looked her over, and nothing more than a few cuts and bruises."

"Thank you," Harriet said, as she felt the tension in her shoulders release a little.

"Thought you'd be happy to know. Saves you so much writing." She nodded at the papers on Harriet's desk.

"Devereux?" she asked, hopefully.

"No news, I'm afraid. Still, two out of three isn't bad?"

"A lot better than it could have been." She stood and straightened her clothes.

"Where are you going?"

"To collect Poppleton. I'll take the station hack."

"Don't you have something to be preparing for?"

"I'll be back in plenty of time." She marched across the office and pulled her door open, then stopped in her tracks as she almost walked into Cas.

"Going somewhere?" he asked.

"The Isle of Wight."

"I don't think so." He twirled his finger in the air, suggesting she turned around and went back into her office.

"But?"

"But nothing. You have something to be preparing for."

"Have you two been planning this?" she asked, as Cas followed her back into the office and closed the door behind him.

"Planning what?"

"Never mind. Look, the planning for this evening is already done, and I can be there and back in no time."

"No need, it's already taken care of. Besides, if the planning's already done, you can get off to your bed for a while and have a snooze."

"There's really no reason why I can't go and do it. She's one of mine. I'm responsible for her, and I should really be the one that goes and collects her."

"You're also the Wing Commander leading the mission in a few hours. What are we going to do if you crash, or get shot down by a marauding German fighter sweep? What are you still doing here anyway?" He looked over to her desk, and frowned as he saw the letters. "Get the one written that you need?"

"Yes..."

"Good. Ginny will take care of it for you. Now, bed. You were up in the middle of the night for this morning's raid, and you'll need to be awake when you go up again. Even an hour will help."

"There's no point in arguing, is there?"

"Not really. Get some sleep, then you'll be awake for a drink in the Mess later. I've got a rather large round to buy for you and your pilots, so you'd better make sure you're there."

"Yes, Sir..."

"There we go, progress. See you later."

The evening strike was another success, with Harriet leading the wing in low and fast, coming out of the setting sun and hitting the Freya site hard. She arrived ahead of the main force again, to lure any anti aircraft gunners into giving themselves away, which they did, making perfect targets for AP's squadron, who were following close behind. Lexi then came in with her pilots, and hit everything above ground level with rockets. Cas had been right. The enemy had repair crews around the site, and they were blown apart with everything else at the Freya site, putting them, and it, out of use forever. The Wurzburg site suffered the same fate, though it was mostly deserted. There were a few trucks, and a handful of guns, but they were quickly silenced. It was a fast and furious strike, all with the cover of Spitfires overhead, which got stuck into a squadron of 109s that dared to turn up, and sent them home before they even got close to the Typhoons. Harriet was the last to leave the radar site, circling to make sure there was nothing else stirring, and to be sure that all of her pilots were away safely, then she and Carrie followed them back to England, touching down on the runway just after sunset. It had been a long day, their first in action, but when she finally fell into her bed exhausted, Harriet was proud of what the wing had achieved.

## Chapter 10

### Summer Sun

"It's June. It's supposed to be summer..." Harriet muttered to herself, as she led the wing across the Channel just above the turbulent waves, while heavy rain hit the cockpit in sheets like a giant was throwing buckets of water at her repeatedly. May had been glorious, and when they weren't working, most of the pilots had found time to sunbathe and enjoy the warmth. By the end of the month, they were all feeling the strain of relentless sorties over France, during which they'd lost five killed or missing and eight injured, three bad enough to be sent home to convalesce, and the sunshine was one of the few things that helped keep them going, Harriet especially. She'd had enough of the cold when she was last in France, and she noticed that grey skies quickly brought her mood down, so when an early summer arrived at the beginning of May, she couldn't have been happier. Then June happened. It was the first of the month, and already it felt like the world had slipped back to February. The temperature dropped, the skies turned grey, and the rain poured, making flying more of a chore than a pleasure, if for no other reason than she was half soaked before she even started the engine, which made the job just that bit more uncomfortable. If that wasn't enough to make her miserable, water would find its way into the cockpit while flying, as well as onto the clothes of the pilots, and as the temperature changed, the beautifully clear bubble canopies which usually gave such good visibility clouded with condensation.

She shook the misery from her mind and checked her watch; they were just a couple of minutes from the French coast, and she needed to be focused on the job. The wing had quickly developed a reputation as radar killers since their first venture into the war over France, and more than a few radar sites, Wurzburgs and Freyas, had been reduced to smouldering craters by the Typhoons of 13 Wing. Tactics were tweaked, but the format was generally the same. Harriet and Carrie would go in ahead of the main force and start shooting things up, and without fail, the enemy flak would open fire and chase them around the sky, giving away their positions to the following squadron, which would cut them apart while the next squadron came in to take out the radar, before going up to keep watch while the third squadron came down to finish the job. It was lethal, and brutally effective. The Luftwaffe turned up every now and then, but the Spitfires were usually waiting for them, and able to stop them getting close to the Typhoons. The flak, however, was murderous, and it was that which accounted for the wing's losses of both pilots and aircraft, many of which were literally flying sieves by the time they got back to England. It was during their last mission, when they attacked a particularly well defended Freya site, that Harriet had watched in helpless horror when one of AP's squadron had her propeller blown off by a burst of flak which set the nose of her Typhoon on fire. AP had screamed at the pilot, Sally Timpson, to use her momentum to climb high enough to jump, but instead, the young woman simply asked AP to say goodbye to her mum and dad, and tell them she did her duty, then flew her Typhoon nose first at the base of the radar mast, firing cannons and rockets as she went. A fireball engulfed the site as the seven ton aeroplane hit the concrete structure at over five hundred miles per hour, igniting gallons of aviation fuel as it did. It was the bravest thing that Harriet had ever seen, and the most sickening and upsetting. Cas had tried to tell her that Sally was likely already hit, and knew she wouldn't get out alive. Choosing to make sure she took some of the enemy with her instead of crashing into a field, or jumping and dying on her way down. It was little consolation, and it didn't make AP feel any better either. They'd earned a reputation for being radar killers, but the price had been high.

"Enemy coast ahead, skipper!" Carrie called over the radio and sharpened Harriet's thoughts. Harriet looked at the port and the town ahead. Dunkirk. The place she'd desperately escaped four years earlier. She'd had a strange sensation in her stomach when Cas had briefed her on the target, fortified gun positions and concrete defensive bunkers of the 'Atlantic Wall' that overlooked the beaches, built at Hitler's command to defend Europe from Allied invasion. It was like going home, in a way, back to where it all started, and she wasn't sure how to feel about it. A mix of nerves, fear, contentment, and fate. She'd survived long enough to come back and fight. Four years earlier, she was bloodied, defenceless, and desperately trying to escape the beaches before the Germans rolled over them. Almost everything she did was pure instinct as she fought desperately to stay alive. Now she was flying over the same place in a death machine, trained, experienced, and committed to fighting back.

"OK, everyone, you know what to do..." Harriet said coolly over the radio, before starting her run at a command bunker just a little inland from the defences. "Tally ho!" She fired a couple of cannon rounds to get her eye on the target, then let rip with all eight rockets, watching them ripple and shoot away from under her wings in pairs, streaking menacingly down towards the bunker, which was surrounded by a scattering of wooden buildings, mostly accommodation blocks and workshops, with trucks and cars parked outside. As she watched the glowing white trails snaking behind the rockets, she saw German soldiers pointing up at her in amazement. Seconds later, the whole scene was engulfed in fire and smoke. She rolled, giving way to Carrie, who followed her in and unloaded her rockets in a similar fashion, obliterating anything above the ground and scorching the concrete bunker, before following Harriet, rolling and banking, as they started a long, wide, circle so they could come back in again. Harriet looked along the defensive line and watched briefly as the squadrons started their attacks. Each flight had a target. A gun position, a bunker, a supply depot, and all were hit almost simultaneously, before the flak guns could even get started. Content that everyone was doing their jobs, and not overly worried by what was above, knowing that the Spitfires were keeping watch, Harriet turned back inland and headed for a building identified by the Resistance in their communications as being where German engineers were billeted. It was her secondary target, something to hit if she had the time and ammunition, with the intention of slowing down any repairs to the damage done by the raid. She strafed it with her cannons, as did Carrie, and the pair of them swooped and circled, shooting up trucks and stores, and the accommodation, before heading back to the coast, where the squadrons were flying low through the flak that was crisscrossing the sky, and shooting up anything that moved. Every German gunner that fired made an instant target of himself, and seconds after a stream of tracer leapt into the sky, a Typhoon shot at the source. Soon the Germans that had any sense were running or hiding, and the whole coastline was burning and smoking. "That'll do, everyone; let's go home," Harriet said. "Into the clouds, and out the way of any fighters that may be coming to see what all the noise is about. Marseillaise, lead the way."

"Roger, Vixen Leader," Nicole replied. " Marseillaise Squadron, form on me." Nicole's Typhoon circled, and then shot upwards with her squadron on her tail. Lexi and AP did the same, and Harriet and Carrie followed behind, after doing one last circuit of the site to survey the damage. It was complete. Nobody was shooting back, and nobody was moving. The section of Hitler's Atlantic Wall that overlooked the beaches she'd escaped so long ago was now blackened and burned, and she felt satisfied. Payback for the British soldiers who'd been shot up while waiting to escape four years earlier. She even allowed herself a smile as she climbed up into the cloud and joined the rest in racing back to England.

June's autumnal weather continued for the next couple of days, with rain, wind, and varying shades of grey sky to keep spirits up while the wing continued its raids on the French coast, ravaging everywhere from Calais to Ostend, and reaching inland to attack German army depots, communications lines, and any other enemy position that could be hit by the type of fast and furious airstrike that the Typhoons specialised in. To increase the number of targets that could be attacked at the same time, something easier done with the radar stations out of the way, each squadron would go in escorted by two squadrons of Spitfires. They attacked in stages, the first squadron would go in and do its job, pulling any German fighters or mobile flak units to that location, and some fifteen or thirty minutes later, the next squadron would strike somewhere else, and then the next. It kept the Germans guessing, and caused chaos all around the Dunkirk area. German fighters tried to intercept a couple of times, but they didn't get through the Spitfires, leaving only the flak to worry about; and while the enemy didn't have their radar laying the guns, the accuracy was still deadly, and another of the pilots was injured after her Typhoon was shredded in the crossfire of what seemed like every gun the German had. She managed to get her Typhoon home, just, before passing out from blood loss, and having to be rushed to the medical centre.

"That was some good work, well done, everyone," Harriet said before leaving the 508 Squadron dispersal hut, having flown with them on a raid. "Have you got a minute?" she asked Nicole, who nodded and joined her walking outside.

"What is it?" Nicole asked.

"You're doing a great job at leading the squadron." Harriet gave her friend a warm smile as they walked. She took it in turns flying with each of the squadrons, and all of the commanders were doing an exemplary job. They had a respect for their pilots which bordered on devotion, and each had grown in their posts, especially Nicole, who took her responsibilities very seriously. She'd regularly take her newer pilots up to practice their dogfighting skills, and made sure everyone had every opportunity to practice their tactics, navigation, and general skills. She was just what they needed, to the point that Harriet considered Nicole to be a much better squadron commander than she ever had been.

"I know this," Nicole shrugged, in a typically French way that only she could. "You didn't need to bring me out here to tell me."

"Of course, how silly of me..." Harriet rolled her eyes. "Anyway, your worship, I wanted to tell you that I've twisted Cas' arm into talking to HQ on our behalf, and we're going to be stood down next Friday for a long weekend off."

"You're serious?" Nicole's eyes opened wide with excitement.

"Absolutely. It was either a squadron at a time staggered over the week, or if we could keep doing what we're doing until the end of the week, we could stand down as a wing. I know squadron spirit is strong, but lots of the girls have friends across the wing, so I thought it better for everyone to have some time off together."

"It's about time; we've been at it every day for as long as I can remember."

"I know... You've all done a fantastic job, but you're overdue a couple of days off to let your hair down."

"And enjoy this beautiful English summer."

"You know it's miserable in France as well, don't you? I mean, we're over there every day, and the weather's exactly the same as here."

"It never used to be. When we were young, I mean. Do you remember? The summers always seemed golden and warm."

"When we were young..." Harriet smiled. She was in her early twenties, and felt at least forty. The French summers she remembered were beautiful, but they seemed like a lifetime ago.

"A long time ago, wasn't it?" Nicole smirked, knowing what Harriet was thinking.

"Thirty years ago, wasn't it?"

"At least! Thank you, Harry; the girls will appreciate the time off."

"They've more than earned it."

"Will you have some time off too?"

"I certainly hope so! I'm thinking of maybe a night in London, then heading home for a couple of days, if you'd like to come? We can fly up and see Archie on the way."

"I'd love to!" Her attention was distracted by the sound of approaching engines. "Lexi's squadron," she said as she watched the first of the approaching Typhoons coming into land.

"How many?" Harriet asked, her heart racing instantly as she started to count the aircraft.

"They're all there, mother hen..." She gave Harriet a knowing smile. "You'll age yourself even more than you already have if you keep worrying like this."

"Shut up."

"It's true. You wouldn't think we were a similar age."

"I can always cancel your leave and make you duty officer next weekend..."

"You wouldn't."

"Try me."

"Aunt Mary wouldn't forgive you. She misses me."

"If you say so..." Harriet rolled her eyes again, and let out an exaggerated sigh, then looked over at the airfield just as the landing gear collapsed on one of the Typhoons that had just touched down. The lighthearted humour turned to horror in an instant as the aeroplane hit the ground, the propeller striking as the nose tipped down. It was like watching in slow motion as the huge air scoop under the nose caught the ground, and the momentum of seven tons of aeroplane still moving close to a hundred miles per hour flipped the tail in the air, and just seconds later, the Typhoon was upside down. Harriet and Nicole were already sprinting side by side as the hulking aeroplane finally slowed to a halt in a mass of sparks and smoke. The fire truck was quickly racing across the airfield, with the ambulance not far behind. The horror deepened as a neat string of flames sparked from the engine cowling and zipped downwards, following the stream of leaking fuel and igniting the upturned wings. Harriet dived under the fire and crawled across the ground, which was quickly soaking with petrol, and started pulling at the cockpit. The pilot was desperately pulling at the release, but it was holding the weight of the aircraft and jammed tight closed. Harriet yelled as she rived and kicked at the cockpit hood, trying in vain to shift it as the flames started to lick at the inside the cockpit. Another scream and pull, and the cockpit shifted a little, enough for her to get her fingers inside and lever it better. The pilot was desperate. She was fighting hard to get her fingers into the gap Harriet had created and helped to try to pull the canopy open, in between slapping dawn the flames that were beginning to burn the sleeves of her jacket. Nicole dragged Harriet out of the way as the fire truck arrived, and an airman replaced her and started hacking at the canopy with an axe, supported by another who started levering hard with a crowbar, while the others ran out the hoses. Nicole held Harriet's hand as the screams from the cockpit cut through the air, and a giant fireball engulfed the entire aeroplane.

Harriet watched helplessly, feeling like she wanted to be sick as both she and Nicole staggered backwards in the face of the blaze. To her amazement, the firemen appeared dragging the pilot. The hoses went into life, and the burning Typhoon was covered in a thick creamy foam which doused the flames, while a fireman with a carbon dioxide extinguisher doused the flames burning the pilot's burning uniform. She was laid on a stretcher the ambulance crew had brought forward, still shaking and crying. Her flying jacket was charred, and her trousers burned. Harriet ran over and knelt by her side, holding her blackened leather flying glove as she was lifted and carried to the ambulance. "It'll be OK," she said. "It'll be OK; you've just got to keep fighting. You've made it, OK?" The young woman nodded. Her flying helmet was burned and blackened, as were the oxygen mask and goggles she was still wearing. "I'll go with her, let Lexi know…"

"Of course," Nicole said as she watched Harriet climb into the ambulance.

Two hours later, Harriet finally returned to her office physically and emotionally exhausted, and wishing the long weekend off wasn't still several days away. She hung her flying jacket on the coat stand before slumping on her chair and closing her eyes. She could still smell the petrol and smoke, and all she could think of was getting back to her room and scrubbing herself. It had been a horrific morning.

"How is she?" Cas asked as he stepped into her office carrying a tray loaded with a teapot, cups, and biscuits.

"She'll live," Harriet replied with a forced smile.

"That's the important thing…"

"She kept her oxygen mask and goggles on, which saved her life when the flames got into the cockpit. Fortunately, she had the good sense to shut off the oxygen and fuel when the undercarriage gave way, otherwise even they wouldn't have helped."

"It sounds horrible."

"That's one way of describing it. She's stable, so they're going to move her to the specialist burns unit."

"How bad is it?" He passed her a cup of tea, which she gratefully accepted.

"She inhaled a lot of smoke, and the fire got to her legs. She's in a lot of pain, but you've got to be alive to feel pain, right?"

"That's the theory…" He gave her a pained smile as he sat and sipped on his tea. "We had a lot of it in the last war; it used to scare the hell out of me."

"Fires?"

"Yes… I'm sorry you had to see it the way you did."

"Sadly, that's not the worst I've seen." She thought back to her friend in Malta, Whisky, and how she'd seen him burned alive when his Hurricane came down. Being in Malta, he was flying in shirt and shorts, as they all did, and didn't have a thick jacket to protect his torso. He hadn't been wearing his oxygen mask or goggles either, and there wasn't a part of him not burned.

"Malta?"

"Malta…"

"Who was it? Today, I mean."

"Van der Windt. Commander of B Flight, 509."

"I'll make sure we get word back to the Dutch government in London; maybe they can do something to support her through her recovery."

"Thank you."

"It's the least we can do. I'm just happy she's alive."

"Me too." She sipped on her tea and felt it washing the smoke from her mouth, making her feel slightly more human again. "So, what's the mission for tomorrow?"

"I'd expect more of the same."

"Expect? Don't you usually know by now?"

"Usually. Though with the amount of damage you've done to the Dunkirk area in the last few days, they may just be running out of targets." He gave her a wink, which brought a smile to her face. "Well, I should probably leave you to get on with your reports. You should have them done by this evening if you get started now."

"You really know how to fill me with enthusiasm."

"I can help if you like?"

"You're going to write them for me?"

"Don't be ridiculous; why would I do that?"

"Because you like me?"

"You inhaled too much smoke..." He smirked as Harriet's mouth opened wide in mock disgust at his reply. "Besides, this is much more likely to motivate you." He pulled a folded piece of paper from his pocket and handed it to her. She snatched it from him with a frown, then smiled as she read it.

"This'll do."

"I thought so; I'll get Niamh to make the calls. Enjoy your paperwork..." He stood and headed for the door, taking his tea with him. "Drink in the Mess later?"

"I don't think we can avoid it, do you?" She smiled as he left, then read through the paper again, before putting it on her desk and starting on her reports with a renewed enthusiasm, which saw them finished a lot quicker than they usually were.

"Flight Lieutenant Stone for you, Ma'am," Niamh said, after knocking on Harriet's door and sticking her head inside.

"Send her in, would you." Niamh nodded and stepped aside, and Carrie marched into Harriet's office and stood to attention in front of her desk, saluting smartly and staring straight ahead.

"Flight Lieutenant Stone reporting as ordered, Ma'am," Carrie said in a very formal manner.

"Flight Lieutenant Stone," Harriet said as she sat back in her chair. "Do you remember our first mission as a wing, when we attacked the two radar sites?"

"Yes, Ma'am."

"Good, then you'll remember that on the way back to England, you were given a very specific direct order, which you chose to disobey."

"Ma'am…" Carrie looked nervous, and her cheeks turned pink.

"Care to remind me what the order was?"

"To return to England with the others, Ma'am."

"To return to England with the others… And what did you do?"

"I chose, Ma'am, to stay and cover you."

"We haven't talked about this since, though I'm sure you expected we would sooner or later."

"Yes, Ma'am."

"Do you have anything to say for yourself?"

"Yes, Ma'am. Only that I did what I did because I'd been with you since the start of the raid and estimated that you'd be low on ammunition, if not out altogether. I knew I had maybe four or five seconds left in my cannons, and as your Number Two, I felt it was my duty to cover you when you turned to take on the enemy fighters."

"Is that so?" Harriet choked a little, having not anticipated the reply. Knowing that Carrie had been watching and calculating her ammunition expenditure was entirely unexpected, and she was a little embarrassed that she hadn't done such a good job of it herself. She thought her young friend was just being dutiful and stubborn, and hadn't even considered her motives.

"Yes, Ma'am. In California, you taught us to watch each other closely, and to count our shots."

"So I did...What did I say about disobeying orders?"

"I don't remember you mentioning it, Ma'am."

"You don't?"

"No, Ma'am."

"I seem to remember collecting you from an American military stockade and warning you that if you ever stepped out of line again, there'd be consequences."

"Yes, Ma'am." Carrie blushed fully, and looked increasingly nervous.

"Good. In that case, you'll understand why I've done what I've done."

"Yes, Ma'am."

"Very well, Flight Lieutenant Carrie Stone, by order of His Majesty the King, you've been awarded the Distinguished Flying Cross." She held out a paper and nodded, while finally letting herself smile as Carrie took it and read it. "You'll be gazetted in a day or two, so you can wear the ribbon right away, and we'll arrange for a formal presentation in due course." She then handed Carrie a small envelope containing the purple and white diagonal striped ribbon of the DFC that Cas had ordered from Ralph. "Better get that sewn on... I'll expect to see it on your tunic in the Mess bar this evening. The first round's on you, Flight Lieutenant Stone, DFC."

"Yes, Ma'am. Thank you, Ma'am." She tried hard not to let the smile fully onto her face.

"Well done, Carrie, and thank you for saving my life. If you hadn't done what you did, that 190 would have knocked me out of the sky. Your flying is exceptional, and your loyalty and commitment to duty make me proud to know you." She stood and walked around her desk, offering Carrie her hand.

"I don't know what to say, Ma'am."

"Don't tell anyone else until I mention it in the Mess later, but we've got next weekend off. You can go home and see your family, and tell them the news in person."

"Thank you, Ma'am."

"For the hundredth time, Carrie, it can be Harry when nobody's about." Harriet rolled her eyes mockingly. "Go on, you've got some sewing to do." She opened the door, and Carrie saluted again before leaving excitedly, and being replaced by Niamh.

"Poppleton, Ma'am?"

"Send her in."

"Yes, Ma'am."

"Flying Officer Poppleton reporting as ordered, Ma'am," the short young officer said as she stood in front of Harriet's desk and saluted.

"I'm told that you convinced the Royal Navy you were one of ours when they pulled you from the water, by giving them the full lowdown on the Hawker Typhoon's specifications, performance attributes, and limitations. In fact, I hear that you carried on with the Hawker Hurricane specifications as a follow up act in their Wardroom, then spent a couple of hours soaking yourself in rum while answering rapid fire questions on almost every British aircraft currently in service."

"That's not technically true, Ma'am," Poppleton replied.

"Oh?"

"It was the Navy who soaked me in rum, Ma'am; I had no say in it."

"No say at all?"

"No, Ma'am. The Captain ordered me to have the rum; he said it would help warm me up after being in the cold water. It'd be rude not to obey orders, Ma'am."

"Yes, I suppose it would…"

"Yes, Ma'am."

"Anyway, that's not exactly why you're here." Harriet changed the subject before she found herself laughing out loud at Poppleton's conviction. She was short and full of life, known as Poppy to the pilots, and an absolute whirlwind of energy and knowledge. There were rumours that she'd stood on her toes during her medical just to meet the minimum height criteria, and could only fly sitting on two cushions so she could see out of the cockpit; but what she lost in height, she made up in character. She was an instinctive pilot, and had both a passion and a skill for hitting her targets with her rockets, not to mention a determination to press home the attack at all costs, as she'd demonstrated when attacking the Freya radar. "I've been meaning to talk to you about that near vertical dive on the Freya radar not so long ago."

"Yes, Ma'am," she answered confidently. "It was steep and fast, but fully within the Typhoon's operational parameters."

"It was dangerous."

"It was all I could do, Ma'am. I was already heading down, and the target was right in front of me, so I thought it better to have a go."

"You were lucky not to follow your rockets right into the target, you know that, don't you?"

"You taught us how to fly, Ma'am. I was confident I could get away."

"Anyway…" Harriet said, seeing that the conversation was going off on a tangent, thanks to Poppy's inability to see the slightest thing wrong with what she did. "As a result of your actions in attacking the Freya radar station, putting your own life at great risk to secure the objective while showing the highest standard of flying skill, you've been awarded the Distinguished Flying Cross."

"Ma'am?" It was the first time since she'd entered the office that Poppy was lost for words.

"Apparently, HQ think your craziness should be recognised with the DFC." She handed Poppy the paper confirming the medal, and a small envelope containing the medal ribbon. "On your uniform by tonight, or you'll be improperly dressed."

"Yes, Ma'am!" Poppy replied excitedly.

"You'll already have to get a round in for your squadron; you don't want to make it two for not having your ribbon sewn on, so you'd better get going."

"Yes, Ma'am." Poppy saluted and marched away.

"Poppy," Harriet called after her.

"Yes, Ma'am?"

"You're a good pilot, but try and stay alive long enough for the medal to be presented, won't you? No more close calls."

"Yes, Ma'am." Poppy smiled, then left the room, closing the door behind her and leaving Harriet to smile for a moment. Cas was right; it had picked her mood up no end to give out such coveted medals to two of her pilots. She'd put the recommendations in the day they first attacked the radar sites, and was happy to see her recommendations confirmed. After a while of reflecting on how lucky she was to have such good pilots, she went back to her paperwork with a new sense of determination. It had already been a long war, and it was only going to get longer, but despite the challenges, and the pain of the losses, her new job was the best she'd had. The pilots of the wing were making a name for themselves, and showing what women could do when given the opportunity to fight. It's what she'd wanted from the start.

## Chapter 11

## Stripes

"Where's Cas?" Harriet asked Ginny, as she joined her in the very busy and very loud Mess bar. After their evening meal, the pilots had rushed to celebrate Carrie and Poppy's medals, and they were already three drinks into the night. Harriet had given strict instructions to limit the drinking. They still hadn't received any orders for the following day, and she didn't want hangovers if they were sent off first thing in the morning. That didn't stop the pilots singing around the piano, to tunes that Harriet recognised, but not necessarily the new words that had been created to go along with them. It made her smile while she stood talking with Nicole, AP, and Lexi, trying to lift Lexi's spirits. She was down after her Dutch friend, who she'd been through the war in the desert with had been badly burned when her Typhoon flipped, and despite putting a brave face on it, she wasn't her usual full of life self.

"Headquarters," Ginny replied, while waving at the barman and ordering a drink.

"Put it on my tab," Harriet said to the barman, then turned back to Ginny. "You could have dragged him down here with you. One drink wouldn't hurt."

"Not our headquarters, Second Tactical Air Force Headquarters. He got a call summoning him this afternoon, and we haven't seen or heard from him or Robbie since."

"Great. Looks like we're not getting tomorrow off after all," Nicole sighed.

"Did you really think we would?" Harriet asked as she rolled her eyes. "You've been in the RAF long enough to know better."

"Amateur," AP said casually, getting a scowl from Nicole and a laugh from the others. "Hurry up and wait is the RAF's favourite game. If you haven't learned that by now, you've got no chance."

"It's tiresome," Nicole replied. "I bet you they don't have anything for us tomorrow, and we spend the day sitting in the rain and going nowhere."

"How much?" Lexi asked, giving everyone a smile as she pulled herself out of her gloom and started a bidding war between the senior officers, which quickly escalated from a drink, to two, to the loser buying dinner at a restaurant in London.

"Bets are closed, ladies," Ginny said as she nodded over to the door. Cas was standing in the doorway and scanning the room. He set his sights on Harriet and made his way over to the bar.

"Whisky?" Harriet asked as he joined them.

"No... I want all pilots and senior officers in the briefing room immediately." He looked around the other senior officers, then turned and left. Harriet instantly felt a nervous twinge in her stomach. He looked distracted, which was unusual for him. He could carry a conversation whatever was happening; even in Malta, he'd been totally unflappable.

"Lexi?" Harriet asked after she'd watched Cas leave the room. Lexi nodded and gave an ear piercing wolf whistle that silenced the room, pulling everyone's attention to Harriet. "Drinks down, and everyone report immediately to the briefing room." The pilots didn't need telling twice, and the room quickly emptied with not even a mutter. "Shall we?" she asked the other senior officers, and they all followed her out into the evening air and over to the briefing room, which to Harriet's concern had armed RAF Police sentries posted outside. "Make sure everyone's accounted for as soon as you're inside." The others nodded as they stepped into the theatre like building, where the wing was usually briefed ahead of their missions. Harriet frowned as the door was closed and locked behind her.

"Good evening, ladies," Cas said from his place on the small, raised stage at the front of the room. It wasn't particularly high, but raised him just enough to see well across the room, which was full of chairs and nervous looking pilots. "Take a seat as soon as you can, please."

Harriet walked down the centre of the room and took a seat at the front beside Ginny. She looked up at Robbie, who was standing at the back of the shallow stage, by the curtain which often covered the large chalkboard which was frequently decorated with maps of the target. She half smiled at Harriet, looking nervous as she did, and not doing anything to settle Harriet's unease. Cas stood in silence as he looked around the room. Every pilot stared at him in anticipation, Harriet included, to the point where she couldn't bear the suspense, and felt herself starting to shake nervously. "I've just come from Second Tactical Air Force Headquarters, where I was briefed on your mission for tomorrow." He finally spoke, then gave Robbie a nod, and she pulled the small curtain open to reveal the intricately detailed map on the chalkboard. A gasp went around the room as the pilots stared at it, and Harriet's mind and heart started to race as she focused on the details and tried unconsciously to anticipate the plan. "At approximately six thirty tomorrow morning, over one hundred and fifty thousand British, American, and Allied soldiers will go ashore in Normandy, France, and it'll be our job to protect them. As of now, all leave is cancelled, and all personnel are confined to base. No telephone calls, no climbing over the fence, no games. I don't have to tell you the importance of secrecy around this mission, and now you're being briefed, we can't risk a word of the plan getting back to the Germans." The room was silent. Harriet looked at Cas, then looked around the room at the other pilots, who were gobsmacked by what they'd heard. Everyone knew that something was coming, there was no hiding the sheer numbers of troops, trucks, tanks, and stores in the south of England, or the ships tied up in ports along the coast, but nobody could have imagined it was the invasion of Europe. With all of the activity around Calais and Dunkirk, there was money on a Dieppe type raid, a relatively small affair to see if strategy and training had improved any since that particular disaster. A full invasion wasn't even in the running when it came to the bets that were being taken. "You'll be over the beaches shortly after the invasion goes in, and you'll operate in this area." He tapped the map between Ouistreham on the coast, and Caen inland. "Keep out of the way of Caen's anti aircraft defences, they're particularly nasty, and we've got too much on to worry about that just yet." He looked around the room again, letting a smile break onto his face. "As of tomorrow morning, we're going to be in the fight of our lives. It's been five long years, but finally, we're going to finish it. The invasion's on, and you'll be at the sharp end. Get this right, and Hitler's days are numbered. Get it wrong, and we could have another five years to come. Are there any questions before I leave you to have a look at the maps?"

"What's our target, Sir?" Harriet asked.

"I thought you'd ask..." he replied with a mischievous smile. The simple answer is that you'll be doing what you do best. Flying around at low level and looking for trouble. As soon as the Germans realise the invasion is on for certain, they'll throw everything they have at the beaches to try and push us back into the sea. Shortly after midnight tonight, the 6th Airborne Division will be dropping to the east of Sword Beach, the beach on the left flank of the invasion, to take out key enemy positions, capture bridges, and secure the area so the 3rd Division can come ashore relatively unmolested. Your mission is to stop anything German that you find approaching the flank. Tanks, trucks, even trains if you see them. The French Resistance have been warned, so the local population will be staying out of harm's way, which means that most of what you see above ground and moving is fair game. In addition, your secondary targets are any fixed defensive positions. Pillboxes, artillery positions, trenches, whatever it is that could be useful to the enemy defence. The objectives of our paratroops are marked on the map, so avoid them unless you're called on to give them direct support. Once over France, you're to contact the Forward Air Controller with the Navy, who will have received any requests for help from the paratroopers. If tasked, the targets will be marked with smoke." He looked around again, then took a drink from the teacup he had on the small desk beside him. "Now, a few points to note. First, stay away from the ships. They're tasked with getting our troops ashore, and that's it. They'll shoot first and ask questions later if they see anything flying near them, so be warned. To help with identification, the ground crew are painting black and white invasion stripes on your aircraft as we speak. Second, intelligence suggests that the Luftwaffe have pulled back recently following our raids on their airfields. Don't believe a word of it. The only chance the Germans have of stopping the invasion is if they can stop it right away, so keep your eyes open! They'll throw everything they have at us, and that includes the Luftwaffe. That said, there'll be an umbrella of Allied fighters watching over Normandy, so any Luftwaffe excursions will be dealt with long before they get to the coast. Remember the invasion stripes. The Germans don't know about them, and everything Allied that will be flying will have them. If it doesn't have stripes, shoot it down!" He looked around the room and smiled again. "It's going to be a long and bloody day tomorrow, and if we get a foothold, I suspect the days to follow will be much the same. Study the maps, make your preparations, and I'll see you all in here for an intelligence and meteorology brief before sunrise. I've asked the cooks to have an early breakfast ready, and there'll be tea down at your dispersals. That's all." Robbie brought the room to attention as Cas stepped off the stage, then dismissed them. "Can I have a word?" he asked Harriet as he walked over to stand in front of her.

"Normandy?" Nicole asked him excitedly before Harriet could answer. "We're really invading France?"

"We are…" He gave her a warm smile, knowing how important it was to her to be part of the mission to free her country from German occupation. "We'll have you home soon enough." He gave her a wink, then led Harriet out of the room and into the cool evening air. "Are you OK?" he asked as he lit a cigarette.

"More OK than you'll be if you keep smoking those things. They're not good for you," Harriet replied.

"You're about to take part in the biggest military invasion in history, and you're telling me off for smoking?"

"You shouldn't smoke, then I wouldn't have to tell you off."

"I'll make you a deal… You get through this safely, and I'll stop smoking."

"Get through what?"

"The invasion!"

"Oh, that. Why wouldn't I get through that safely?" she asked casually.

"Did you miss the part where I said it was the biggest military invasion in history? Thousands of ships and aircraft, hundreds of thousands of troops, and the Germans doing all they can to make sure it doesn't happen?"

"No, I got that part. I just don't get why you're so worried about me now. Malta was worse, and France, and the Battle of Britain for that matter. We were outnumbered and on the defensive. They were all much more dangerous than this."

"And how did we fare in those battles?"

"We won. Don't you remember? Is your age playing tricks in your memory again?"

"Hilarious... We won because our backs were against the wall. Cornered animals can be dangerous, you know? And we're just about to go and punch a huge beast right on the nose. It's not going to be a walkover."

"If this is your confidence building speech, you need to work on it some more."

"Harry!"

"Cas!"

"All I'm saying is that it's almost done. If the invasion goes well, the Germans will be on the back foot, and it'll only be a matter of time before they give up."

"I know that."

"Do you also know that I'd rather not lose you when we're this close? You've made it through four years; let's just make sure you get to the end."

"Shut up!" she said firmly, as she felt herself start to blush, and instantly wished it was darker than it was.

"I'm serious."

"Me too. Shut up! I'm going to be absolutely fine. I was when we invaded Sicily."

"You were shot down over Sicily, and only managed to escape because you were able to glide your wrecked aeroplane to Gozo."

"Shut up!"

"Again."

"Yes, again!" She shot him a fierce look, then smiled. "I'll do my best to be safe, I promise. Better?"

"Better… You should get back inside and check the maps over, and go through a plan with your squadron commanders. Robbie has all of the intelligence information you'll need."

"Thank you. And thank you for caring."

"Nobody said I care… It's just a nightmare having to do the paperwork for a missing Wing Commander. Besides, who would I choose to replace you? It'd be far too much of a headache having Nicole do the job, and I wouldn't dare argue with AP. Lexi, however… Maybe I could work with her..." He gave her a smirk, knowing full well how annoying he was being.

"I have absolutely no doubt you could. I'll leave you to think it over while I go and get ready for work tomorrow." She rolled her eyes and sighed, then gave him a smile before turning and heading back to the briefing hut.

"Get some sleep."

"You too, old man." She laughed to herself, then straightened up as she came back into view of the armed sentries, and hoped they hadn't heard her insulting the Station Commander.

After a couple of hours studying maps and agreeing on the plan for the following day, Harriet finally made her way back to her room, having already sent her pilots back ahead of her to get some rest, while she talked things through with the senior officers. Everyone was full of nervous excitement; it was the biggest day of their lives. The invasion of Europe. Sicily and Italy had gone well, until Italy stalled as the Allies pushed north and came up against well prepared German defensive position, and Dieppe had been a disaster in 1942, when a large force made up of mostly Canadian soldiers landed in France and were massacred. France wasn't Italy, it would be much better defended, and no matter how many thousands of men stormed the beach, she couldn't imagine the Germans just letting them march in the front door without a fight. The thoughts stayed with her through the night while she tossed and turned, unable to sleep as she processed what was to come. Despite Cas' teasing, she didn't even think of coming through it safely herself. She had three squadrons of pilots to think about, and in her mind, it was more important that they got to the end of the war than it was her. She'd accepted some time ago that she was living on borrowed time, but her pilots were different; they had their time to come. Eventually, she got out of bed, got cleaned up, then got dressed in her flying kit before heading down to the dispersal, where she found Jo and her ground crews putting the finishing touches to the Typhoons. All of which had been painted with three white stripes and two black on both the wings and the fuselage. She checked on the aircraft state, then had a cup of tea and a short conversation with Jo about the coming day and the need to be refuelled and rearmed quickly when they came back, before she headed over to the met and intelligence briefing with Cas and Robbie. The news wasn't good. The weather was still overcast, cold, and miserable, but not as much as it had been, though worse than that was the news that the airborne drop overnight had been just as chaotic as Sicily, with paratroopers being scattered all over the place. It didn't fill her with confidence. Sicily wasn't that heavily defended in comparison to France. In recent weeks she'd been in continuous attacks against German targets along the French coast, as had many other British and American squadrons, yet there was still a very strong force awaiting the invasion.

After being wished good luck by Cas, who'd toured all of the squadrons to see them off after the morning briefing, she strapped herself into her Typhoon and went through her checks. It was like any other day, and at the same time, like nothing else. The consequences of what was about to happen were huge whichever way it turned out, yet she couldn't feel excited about it either way. It just felt like another sortie over France, and she was a little disappointed at the lack of emotion she felt. For years she'd dreamed of the day, in one way or another, and imagined how she'd feel taking the war into Europe. She'd never thought she'd be so apathetic about it. She shook her head and checked her watch, and smiled as the pre dawn glow caught its face and made it shimmer like a rainbow for the briefest of moments, then she switched on her oxygen and started the engine. The vibrations from the Napier Sabre engine made her smile. It was time. She looked around, then gave Carrie a thumbs up and waved the chocks away. Following behind her and Carrie came Nicole and 508 Squadron, with 507 and 509 coming after, and in pairs, they climbed into the royal blue dawn sky, circling and forming, until the whole wing had come together over the airfield. There was no need to worry about any remaining German radar this time. A wing of Typhoons was the last of their worries, or at least she hoped that would be the case when she got to France. If not, something had gone badly wrong. They levelled out at five thousand feet and cruised out over the Channel, where she was soon met with an unimaginable sight. Ships, as far as the eye could see, nose to tail between England and France, like a giant bridge. Barrage balloons dragged above them for air defence, and higher above were swarms of aircraft of all description. Heavy bombers, light bombers, fighter bombers, transports, fighters, everything was there. The emotion that Harriet had been missing hit her like a tidal wave as she saw the might of the Allied war machine heading for France. She turned the Squadron parallel to the huge shipping lane, which was guarded by torpedo boats and destroyers, and headed for the French coast, watching in awe as they got closer, and she could see battleships firing their huge guns and streams of rockets at targets inland. The coast came quickly, and already there was fighting on the fire and smoke strewn cliffs overlooking the beaches. Harriet tried to focus on the beach to get an idea of what was going on, and how well things were going. There were lots of dark specks scattered about, with columns of troops rushing off the sand from the landing ships. It was only when they passed directly overhead that she realised that the specks were the bodies of those who'd gone ashore in the first wave. It made her stomach squeeze.

She called up the forward air control frequency as they crossed the coast, and received a report from the British paratroopers that a lightly armoured German column was heading directly towards them, consisting of trucks, halftracks, and armoured cars. The location was given, and the wing was tasked to take care of it. It was game time, and her focus snapped away from the raging battle below, that stretched right up the Normandy coast. She turned the wing and followed the given bearing until she saw the trees where the airborne troops were dug in and fighting the lead elements of the German column. Once she was sure of their position, she looked up the road to find the main body of the convoy stretched into the distance. It was a substantial force of reinforcements. The paratroopers had attacked a small number of halftracks and motorcycles that had been scouting ahead of the main force and were holding them off quite well, but they'd never last against what was coming down the road. If the Germans broke through the paratroopers, which they inevitably would, there wasn't a great deal to stop them between there and the coast, and the whole force would quickly be on top of the troops coming ashore.

"OK, Valkyrie Wing, let's get to work. Marseillaise, hit the front. Dagger, hit the back. Yankee, take the middle once the column's stopped and trapped. Valkyrie Two, stick with me. Let's climb and keep a watch out for trouble." Confirmations came over the radio, and the wing split. AP taking her squadron left so she could bank around and hit the rear of the convoy, and Lexi going right, ready to line up and come in at the middle. At the same time, Harriet and Carrie pulled into a steep climb above the convoy, attracting all manner of light anti aircraft and machine gun fire, which zipped up after them, turning the sky into a mesh of tracer. The bullets got closer and closer, but weren't enough to bother Harriet, who knew full well that trying to shoot from a moving vehicle at a Typhoon travelling over four hundred miles per hour would be hard work for even the best shot. She dragged the tracer higher, keeping their attention until Nicole led her Squadron in at the front of the convoy. One by one, her Typhoons came down and released their rockets two at a time, blasting vehicles apart and sending fiery explosions into the sky.

Seconds later, the same explosions rattled the rear of the convoy as AP got started doing exactly the same thing. The long stretched outline of vehicles was trapped between the fences and hedgerows of the narrow road, making perfect sitting targets as Lexi's squadron came in at treetop height and hit the middle of the convoy. The anti aircraft fire faded as the trap closed, and vehicle after vehicle was blown apart by the Typhoons, which came in at the convoy again and again, cycling out after their strike, and lining up to come back in for another go. Some of the gunners continued to take pot shots here and there, the brave or the crazy, or those trapped with nowhere to hide, but they weren't effective, and certainly not enough to shake any of the Typhoons off their attack runs, even when they managed to get shots on the fast moving aeroplanes. "Break it off and reset," Harriet called, when she could see nothing left but a long line of burning vehicles. The squadron commanders immediately gave their orders, and the squadrons formed by flights before climbing up to join Harriet circling the scene. It was a massacre. The entire convoy had been ripped to pieces, with the exception of a few vehicles and groups of soldiers here and there who were scattering left and right, escaping into the surrounding fields. A quick scan of the area and Harriet estimated that there was still quite a force among the escapees, so she dispatched the squadrons into sectors. 508 to the left of the convoy, 507 to the right, and 509 to the rear. They dispersed quickly and split into pairs, hunting down their prey over the Normandy countryside, and quickly starting their rocket and cannon attacks. "Valkyrie Two, look to the front of the convoy, heading for the trees," Harriet said, as through the smoke she caught a glance of a couple of halftracks and maybe fifty soldiers heading for the paratroopers.

"I see them!" Carrie replied.

"Good. Go and get them; I'll be right behind." She watched as Carrie tipped and dived, coming in from the side and lining up perfectly with the halftracks. Harriet followed close behind and watched as Carrie opened up with two pairs of rockets, the first pair hitting the first half track dead on and blowing it apart, and the second pair doing the same to the other. Harriet came in afterwards, cutting up the soldiers with her cannons, knocking them down or sending them running. She followed Carrie up into a high turn, before coming back down again to finish them off. She glanced briefly to her left and saw the paratroopers waving and cheering, and gave them a wave and a smile before pulling up again into a steep climb, ready to retake her position overseeing the destruction, which was by now complete. Once reformed, she led the wing down low over the convoy, flying at treetop height over the smoking and burning vehicles. Nothing had survived. There were groups of soldiers here and there, some injured, some hiding, but nothing worth attacking, and certainly nothing that would make any sort of force able to attack the paratroopers. Once she was sure the column was stopped, and the threat to the invasion's flank minimised, she took the wing on a tour of the sector to look for targets of opportunity, which were found in abundance. The last of the rockets were used on an artillery position and supporting infantry, and with their cannons, they hunted pockets of troops here and there until finally they'd used all of their ammunition. "Valkyrie Wing, home for tea," she called, when she knew there was no more to be done, and after a quick check of the sky for enemy aircraft, who were uncharacteristically absent, she led the wing home, where they landed by sections before she and Carrie landed side by side and taxied to 508's dispersal.

"How was it?" Cas asked nervously as she jumped from her Typhoon, which the ground crew quickly went about checking over.

"We stopped an enemy column heading for the left flank," she replied excitedly, "and hit an artillery position. All for no losses!" Her adrenaline was running, and her senses and emotions were fully awake.

"That's great, well done! Show me." He handed her a map, which she studied for a moment before tapping on it.

"Convoy here, artillery position here. There were a few groups of infantry here and there, nothing major."

"The convoy and artillery are the important things. Good show!"

"What's next?"

"Cup of tea, then back over as soon as the kites are refuelled and rearmed. Same area, but extend further north and east. I'll get the initial report to HQ while Robbie debriefs you and gets the combat reports." Harriet nodded and shrugged. "Harry…"

"Yes?"

"What's it like over there? Is it working?"

"I don't know… The beaches look like hell on earth, but I've never seen so many ships and aircraft. Something's gone badly wrong if it doesn't work."

"Good." He gave her a smile. "Remember what I said about the smoking…"

"You'd better keep your promise."

"I wouldn't dare break it! Right, I'll see you in a while." He ran off to his car while Dutch pushed a cup of hot tea into her hands.

"There you go, Ma'am," Dutch said.

"Thank you. Anything to worry about here?"

"No, Ma'am. Everyone's back OK."

"Good." She looked around the dispersal, and couldn't help smiling as she heard the excited pilots talking to each other. They were full of themselves, and rightly so. It was the invasion, and they'd played their part, wiping out an enemy force before the sun had fully risen. She walked over to Nicole, who was sipping her tea and watching. "Well done," she said. "Your squadron did a great job."

"Thank you," Nicole replied warmly. She wasn't her usual boisterous self, and was more calm and collected than Harriet had seen her in years.

"Everything OK?"

"It's happening, Harry. We're going to liberate France; can you believe that?"

"Feels good, doesn't it?" She smiled as she joined Nicole leaning against the dispersal hut.

"I never imagined it would feel this good. All that power we unleashed today, and we're just one wing. There's no way the Germans can resist us, can they?"

"I hope not."

"I didn't think it would happen. From the day we left grandpa in 1940, I thought that was it. We'd never get the Germans out, not in my lifetime, but did you see all of those ships?" Nicole's excited talking was making Harriet smile even more, the words she was hearing were exactly what she was thinking, and it was exciting to hear them said out loud.

"You'd better get everyone ready for round two. We're going back once the aeroplanes are refuelled and rearmed."

"We'll be ready."

"I know." Harriet left her and visited the other squadrons, checking in that all were OK, and briefing them that they were due to go up again. They hadn't lost a single aircraft, with only a few bullet holes here and there that were being patched, but nothing mechanical to worry about. What's more, every single pilot was ecstatic, and feeling ten feet tall.

An hour later, and the wing was over Normandy for the second time. The fighting around the beaches was still as intense, and it seemed like the entire coastline was on fire, while more and more men and machines poured onto the sand from the steady stream of landing craft queueing to drop their cargo before rushing back to the bigger transport ships to reload. It was an incredible sight. The patrol didn't bring much joy, and the forward air control had no trade for them in their sector, so Harriet led them closer to Caen, where she was positive there'd be some business. The anti aircraft gunners nervously fired at them from a distance as they approached the city, and she kept them just out of reach as the wing circled like vultures, looking for targets of opportunity, which finally came in the form of a line of light tanks breaking cover from the trees, and making a sprint in the direction of the beaches. It was a fatal mistake, and as soon as they hit the open fields, the Typhoons were on them, swooping down a squadron at a time and putting tank after tank out of action, while turning the ground around them into a field of burning craters. It was another massacre, followed by more hunting for defensive positions closer to the beaches, which resulted in what looked like a headquarters being attacked and reduced to rubble. Another successful sortie with no losses, which was celebrated just as well as the first when they all touched down again back in the Kent coast.

The day continued much the same, with the wing going up five times before their final trip of the day, a sunset patrol over their sector for one last sweep before leaving the many thousands of troops that had now landed on the beaches to their first night on French soil. From what Harriet could see, and from the information she was getting from Cas and Robbie, the invasion was going well. The Germans hadn't responded quickly enough to stop it in its tracks, and thousands and thousands of soldiers, hundreds of tanks, and tons of equipment, had got ashore in over twelve hours since the invasion had landed. As the wing crossed the Channel, heading for the eastern flank of the British and Canadian advance, Harriet watched the last of the day's sunlight skipping over the still turbulent water while the distant sky started to darken, highlighting the fires that lined the coast, and the flashes of the ships' guns as they continued to fire in support of the landings. She felt privileged to be part of it. Her adrenaline had been flowing since she'd seen the mighty armada first thing in the morning, and despite the fatigue of near constant sorties, she couldn't wait to get back to France and continue her work. The wing had found targets every time they crossed the Channel, and she wanted to do more before last light, knowing that every German soldier they put out of action was one less for the troops on the ground to face. Her hopes were answered when a message from the forward air control sent the wing to the east of their sector, in search of an airfield where a reconnaissance Spitfire had reported movement, and Harriet wheeled them around and spread the squadrons out, ready for a quick attack if they found anyone hanging around in the shadows.

"Eleven o'clock low!" AP said over the radio, and Harriet's eyes snapped to the position. She squinted for a moment, searching the ground for tanks or troops. "190s! Four of them!"

"Got them!" Harriet shouted as she finally caught sight of the four black silhouettes skimming the ground and heading for the airfield. Their wheels were down, and while they were moving fast, it wasn't fast enough; all four had slowed ready to land. "You saw them, Dagger. Go and get them. Yankee, swing left and look for more. Marseillaise, get up top and keep watch. Valkyrie Two, follow me in and have a look around the airfield." AP led her squadron straight at the 190s, Charging at them from the side at full speed, while Harriet tucked in behind them as the other squadrons broke left and right. Long lances of tracer shot out from the Typhoons, each section taking a 190 and knocking them down in seconds. The German fighters had nowhere to go. They were committed to landing and didn't have the speed to escape, and one by one, they exploded as the cannon fire found its mark. In a heartbeat, they were down, and AP's squadron were overhead and receiving fire from heavy machine gun positions. The enemy shooting was a long way off target, missing the Typhoons as they screamed over at treetop height, moving over four hundred miles per hour and making themselves a very difficult target. "Carrie, hit the gun position on the left of the buildings; I'll hit the right! Marseillaise, come in and shut the place down." She put her sights on one of the gun positions that had given itself away and let loose with a pair of rockets, while Carrie did the same to her target. Seconds after they crossed the airfield, Nicole led her squadron in, coming down in pairs and hitting every gun position, truck, building, and hedgerow, obliterating everything in sight.

"Skipper, we've got movement to the east. Three tanks, Tigers, by the looks of it," Lexi said from her position up above.

"Stop them!" Harriet replied as she pulled back on her stick and climbed above the burning, and now silent airfield.

"Yes, Ma'am!" Lexi replied, then commenced her attack, diving down at the giant steel beasts that were crawling slowly along a narrow road. Harriet rolled and watched as rocket after rocket went into them as Lexi guided her aircraft down in a perfect attack, hitting the tanks from behind and exploiting their weak spot, enveloping one after another in flames and smoke. Harriet pushed her stick forward and kicked her rudder, and raced down towards the tanks as the last of Lexi's Typhoons streaked past, then let go with her remaining rockets as soon as she could see the leading burning hulk. The crew were jumping from it as she fired, and they disappeared in the flames. Carrie came in afterwards and did the same, finishing off what remained of the tanks.

"That'll do," Harriet gasped as she pulled up tight and looked down at the mess below. Whether or not anyone could survive the attack didn't matter. The Tigers were immobilised, possibly destroyed, and even if they could be repaired, they wouldn't be going anywhere quickly. She circled while the wing came together, and looked over the airfield. It was in ruins; there was movement here and there, but no action. It was wrecked, and nothing would be landing on it. She led the wing back towards the Channel.

"What the hell…?" AP said over the radio, making Harriet look around in confusion. "Look out!" she yelled. "Break, break, break!" Harriet instinctively pulled hard right and dived, just as a stream of tracer came down at her, followed by a streak of silver. She spun her head, looking right as she pulled around tight, and got her eyes on her attacker, an American P51 Mustang.

"Mustangs!" she shouted, while watching the wing scatter as more Americans dived down through them. She contacted the forward air control and shouted at them to get a message to the American squadron. Her heart raced as she searched for a target, hoping to try and intercept and let them know they were friendlies, but the Mustangs were already racing away at full speed. "Check in! All squadrons, check in!"

"Yankee Leader's down," Gabi, the Polish pilot, and one of Lexi's flight commanders, said.

"Say again," Harriet replied. Her heart was squeezing so tight that she thought it would explode, and her pulse was thundering so loud in her ears that she wasn't sure what she'd heard.

"Yankee Leader and Yankee Blue Three are down," Gabi replied.

"Parachutes?"

"Negative."

"Understood... Let's go home…." Harriet felt a tear roll down her cheek as she led the wing out over the Channel. Her heart was breaking, and it was all she could do to keep her mind on her job. She felt sick, and all she wanted to do was pull off her oxygen mask and suck in the air, but she knew that if she did, she'd risk gulping in carbon monoxide from the engine, and the last thing the wing needed would be to lose another leader. Losing Lexi was enough.

"How was it?" Cas asked as she jumped down from her wing, as he had after every mission that day.

"Four 190s, three Tigers, two Typhoons, and Lexi," she replied, while fighting hard not to burst into tears.

"Lexi? What happened?" Cas looked as shocked as she felt.

"We were jumped by American Mustangs on our way home…" Her voice trembled a little.

"Americans… What?"

"I know…"

"Harry, I'm so sorry. I don't know what to say…"

"It's war." She forced a half smile.

"It'll be war when I find out which squadron attacked you." His face turned to thunder. "That's us done for the day; do you want a ride back to HQ?"

"No, thank you… I need to go and talk to her squadron."

"I'll come with you."

"No… It's something I want to do myself."

"I'll be at HQ finding out who's responsible. Come and see me when you're done." He gave her a half smile of condolence, knowing full well how bad she was feeling, then put his hand on her shoulder. "Are you going to be OK?" She nodded, and he turned and left, marching away quickly towards his car, furious and on a mission. Harriet headed for her own car, not looking at anyone as she walked past 508's pilots. She saw Nicole out of the corner of her eye, watching her closely and giving a smile of support that Harriet just didn't have the energy to return. Instead, she just jumped in her car and drove away, sucking in the cool evening air as she did, and trying hard to compose herself on the short drive to 509's dispersal.

"Who else did you lose?" Harriet asked as she stepped out of her car to be met by the flight commanders, all of whom were looking both upset and angry.

"Erica Carney," Bunny replied. "One of my girls, from Chicago."

"Everyone else OK?"

"A few were shot up, but got back in one piece with no injuries to report.

"That's something, at least. How is everyone?"

"Wanting to declare war on the Americans," Gabi replied angrily. She then looked uncomfortably at Bunny, who forced a smile in reply. "You know what I mean."

"Group Captain Salisbury is on the phone to HQ trying to find out who's responsible. He'll make sure they know about it." The others nodded, though she knew that it didn't change things even remotely for her, and likely wouldn't for them either. "That's us done for today, but we need to be ready to go again at first light. Talk to your pilots, get their heads where they need to be, and prepare them for whatever comes tomorrow. Lexi was a close friend and a fantastic leader, but we can't let her loss distract us from our mission. Not now. I don't want to sound hard and uncaring, but If we focus on her loss, we'll lose more. I can guarantee it. Get some food in them and get them to bed, then close ranks and move forward. Understood?" They all nodded. "Bunny, I want you to look after the squadron. Come and see me once you've talked to your pilots and stood them down, and I'll brief you for tomorrow."

"Me?" Bunny asked, looking at Harriet in amazement.

"Problem?"

"I just..."

"I'd choose you," Gabi said bluntly, and Alice the Australian agreed with a nod and a shrug.

"We're here to protect democracy, not practice it, but it's good to have you both on board," Harriet said to them both with a smile, breaking the dark mood a little. "You're a Squadron Leader, Miss Carrington, time to earn the pay."

"Yes, Ma'am." Bunny stood smartly to attention, as did the others.

"That's all. Oh, and tell your pilots well done today. Despite the losses, they did a hell of a job and saved a lot of lives on the ground. That's what this is all about; remind them of that." She gave Bunny a smile and received a nod in reply, then the three turned and walked away to join their pilots, leaving her standing by her car in the dimming light and swallowing down her tears to stop herself from falling apart.

## Chapter 12

## Relentless

"Shouldn't you be in bed?" Cas asked, as Harriet joined him in his office and slumped into the comfortable armchair he kept in the corner of the room, which she'd taken over on the day it arrived, and sat on almost every time she visited. She was still in her flying kit, not having had the energy to go to her room and change before reporting in after another hard day of sorties flying over France, and fighting the many counterattacks on the ground and in the air that the Germans were throwing forward in their now vigorous defence, which had only really got started properly on the night of the invasion, over twelve hours after the first Allied soldiers had stepped onto French soil, and almost twenty four hours after the airborne troops had landed. The Germans had been caught totally off guard, and while the coastal garrisons fought hard throughout the day of the invasion, there didn't seem to be a real strategy to the defence, and their actions weren't coordinated. That had all changed, though. The British 3rd Division was supposed to have captured the town of Caen on the first day of the invasion, but due to German counterattacks and bottlenecks at the beach which slowed down the landing of supplies and troops, they still hadn't captured it days later, meanwhile the Germans had rushed forward their own reinforcements, including many armoured divisions, and squeezed an entire army into the area, making the fighting slow and bloody.

"I could sleep for a week," Harriet replied. She'd taken her wing up over France six times per day, every day for a week, and there wasn't one of them that wasn't exhausted. They'd found targets every time they crossed the Channel, and done their part to support the invasion, but the renewed vigour in defence had made life hard. There seemed to be a million anti aircraft guns scattered across Normandy all of a sudden, and despite the umbrella of fighter cover, the Luftwaffe were launching more and more sorties from airfields further inland, sending bombers to attack the fleet, and fighters to cause trouble, which they were doing a very good job of. They were still overwhelmingly outnumbered, but that didn't seem to stop them, and they were becoming a nuisance. Between the Luftwaffe and the flak, the wing had lost another two Typhoons badly damaged, though the pilots managed to get them home safely, and one more was lost to the northeast of Caen. One of AP's pilots, who was brought down by a storm of flak. A parachute had been seen, which had many in the wing feeling positive, Harriet excepted. She thought of her own experience at the hands of the Gestapo, and the thought of one of her pilots being captured made her sick to the stomach, not that she shared that with the others.

"Then why are you sitting in my office?"

"Because this is where you keep the best whisky, and I could do with a drink." She frowned at him from across the room as he smiled, then, with a sigh, pulled a bottle and two glasses from his desk.

"You know this isn't the Mess bar, don't you?" he asked as he poured a drink and walked around the desk to hand it to her.

"If the Mess bar had good whisky, I wouldn't be here."

"And there was me thinking you visited for my company."

"Well, the whisky isn't my only reason to visit." She gave him a smile, before taking a sip of the whisky and feeling it burn her throat and mouth. She didn't even like whisky that much, but sometimes it was just the right thing.

"Oh?" He leant against his desk and sipped his own whisky.

"Yes, you told me you had some information for me?"

"Oh yes..."

"Your memory's getting worse."

"Must be my age..."

"Must be." She smirked at him for getting it in first. "Anyway, what's so important that I'm here in your office instead of sleeping?"

"The Americans have sent over several cases of whisky by way of apology. Apparently, their pilots mistook your Typhoons for Focke Wulf 190s in the low light, and attacked thinking you were a raid heading for the fleet."

"They thought we were Focke Wulfs?"

"Yes… It's not the first time, I'm sorry to say. The Americans have been shooting at everything and anything. Even this evening, they had a go at a squadron of our Spitfires. If it was just Typhoons, I could understand it, just about; in the heat of the moment it would be easy to make a mistake. Spitfires, though. They're quite unique looking… Anyway, a message of sincere apology came from their CO, especially when he heard we'd lost two pilots, and he sent over some whisky by way of apology. Good stuff, too."

"I'm not sure I want it… It feels like taking blood money."

"It does, and at the same time, it shouldn't go to waste. I was thinking of splitting it between the squadrons, and handing it out when we're next stood down."

"I don't like it. They killed Lexi; whisky doesn't change that. It'd leave a bitter taste in the mouth."

"I suppose…"

"Robbie."

"Excuse me?"

"Give it to Robbie and see what she can get for it in trade? If it's the good stuff, she'll probably be able to get enough for a party when we're next off duty. If we're ever next off duty."

"I think we can do that."

"Wait… This isn't?" She cringed as she looked at the glass she was holding.

"It isn't. The stuff I get is much better. I'd have thought you'd know that by now."

"It's not bad." She drained her glass then jumped to her feet. "I need my bed. Any change in orders for tomorrow?"

"Nope. Just keep doing what you do, causing trouble and looking for a fight."

"How's it going? The invasion, I mean?"

"Precarious. There's an entire German army in Caen, including the SS and a number of armoured divisions, and they're putting up a hell of a fight. Practically all of the tanks they have in France are exactly where we want to be. If they get us on the back foot with a coordinated counterattack, they could have us pushed back to the beach before we know it."

"Great. So no chance of a weekend off yet?"

"Not yet."

"Goodnight, in that case."

"There's one other thing I wanted to tell you."

"Yes?"

"That first radar job you did, when the other Typhoon wing was turned back, and you decided to take out their target for them..."

"That feels like a lifetime ago... What about it?"

"The AOC apologises for the delay in letting you know, but you've been awarded the Distinguished Service Order for your action in leading the attack."

"The what? Why?"

"The DSO. You already have one, which means you'll be getting a bar to add to your medal on this occasion, so stop pleading ignorance."

"I know what it is, thank you very much; I just hardly think it's warranted. We had the ammunition, and we were already there. We didn't do anything that anyone else wouldn't do."

"You had limited ammunition, the enemy had been alerted to your presence, there were fighters in the area, and you decided to put yourselves at significantly increased risk to push home the attack and complete a mission that wasn't even yours. In doing so, you saved lives. The AOC's words, not mine, though I happen to agree with him." She fought a blush as she looked at him, and thought back to the day. It was the wing's first operational action, and it was etched permanently in her memory, every detail as clear as if it had only just happened. "Your squadron commanders have also been awarded the Distinguished Flying Cross for their part in the action, if it makes you feel any better."

"Thank you," she said with a warm smile. Appreciating the recognition that had been shown to her pilots. Her own award wasn't important. She already had a complex relationship with medals at the best of times, but knowing that her friends had been recognised for making her decisions a success made her smile. "I wish Lexi was here to see it..."

"Me too..." He forced a pained smile. "Details of the award have been given to the American Ambassador, and forwarded to the President. I'm told that the Medal of Honour has been recommended, and will be presented posthumously to her parents, along with our DFC. It doesn't bring her back, of course, but it's nice to know that her name deeds won't be forgotten."

"It is. Thanks, Cas. I'll let Nicole and AP know." She smiled for a moment as she thought of Lexi, her golden American friend, then locked her away in the back of her mind again, with all of the other painful memories she didn't need to think of while the war was still raging.

"Goodnight, Harry."

The next morning they were back at it, with five sorties flown by mid afternoon, each time hitting targets around Caen. An anti aircraft battery was put out if action, and what looked like a supply convoy of soft top trucks was shot up on its way to resupply a forward defensive position, which itself became a target in the next sortie, under the direction of troops on the ground who marked the enemy positions with red smoke, as they had done in Sicily, and making it an easy target for the rocket laden Typhoons that left a scorched landscape of craters and rubble behind them. The last mission of the day was something a little different; they were sent further inland to look for a supply train that was rumoured to be heading for Caen. The message had come urgently via the Resistance, who passed it to the British army on the ground, and in turn, they got it back to the forward air control. An armoured and we'll defended trainload of tanks and ammunition was on its way direct from Germany, and Harriet's wing were the closest Typhoons.

"There it is. Twelve o'clock," Harriet said as she saw the train in the distance, so long that it looked like it was snaking almost all the way back to Germany. It was making a desperate run to the front. Going in daylight was suicide, and as Harriet surveyed it for a moment, she was quite sure that the wing could do a good job of helping it on its way. "Control, this is Valkyrie Leader. Target spotted."

"Good work, Valkyrie Leader. You're clear to attack at your leisure. Do what you must to ensure it doesn't get to Caen," came the reply from the forward air controller.

"Valkyrie Leader, Wilco." She scanned the surrounding area, while fine tuning the plan that she'd had in mind since she was given the mission. It was the same as usual, a pincer movement with a squadron coming from the left at low level, and another from the right shortly afterwards, following a head on attack to stop the locomotive and make the tank laden flatbed carriages an easy target. "Dagger, left. Yankee, right. Come in after our pass. Marseillaise, follow me in. Tally Ho!" She pushed the stick forward and started her dive, as the squadrons took their positions, ready for their attack.

The train was racing along a long straight stretch of track, making it the perfect target as the black smoke from the locomotive streaked into the sky, drawing a nice line for anyone to see and follow. The train's anti aircraft guns burst into life as she dived, filling the sky with tracer and explosions, which bounced and rocked the Typhoon until she dropped so low she was out of their view. A couple of seconds later, she fired her rockets. All eight streamed down towards the locomotive, flying off in pairs and leaving long white smoke trails behind them. The real danger came when she pulled up hard to avoid the blast, and the train's many gunners got a perfect view of her Typhoon's underside. They quickly threw everything they had at her, rattling the fuselage with shrapnel and bullets as her rockets found their target, blowing away the track and ripping apart the locomotive, rolling it off the tracks as the boiler exploded and sent a thick jet of steam upwards, and dragging the leading carriages with it, flipping them as the others behind crashed into each other. Carrie went in right after, sending her rockets into the pile of wrecked carriages, then following Harriet in a steep climb while the squadrons went in and finished the job. The train was a sitting target, and the gunners were quickly silenced as Typhoons attacked in pairs. First from the left, and then from the right, destroying the cargo of tanks and their crews, the ammunition, and everything else on the train. Explosions lit up the sky in blinding flashes as ammunition carriages were hit, and less than a minute after the attack had begun, the train was shrouded in thick black smoke, its position only given away by the intense fires burning along its length, making perfect guide lights for Nicole to follow as she led her squadron along the length of the train, flying in one at a time and releasing their eight rockets each, just to make sure that anything still moving below the smoke wouldn't be moving for long. It was another absolute massacre, and as much as Harriet could imagine the hell below, she was comfortable with what she'd done. The tanks would have caused chaos had they got to their destination, and hundreds, maybe thousands of Allied soldiers could have been killed trying to stop them. Her job was a very necessary evil. She circled while watching the destruction, and just minutes after she'd fired her first rockets, she was climbing past twenty thousand feet and leading the wing back towards the coast in the late afternoon sun.

"Watch out!" Carrie shouted unexpectedly, as an unusual looking aircraft dived down in a green blur of speed with cannons blasting, forcing her to pull hard right, then flip and dive to avoid being blown out of the sky, while Harriet instinctively pulled her stick to the left, as she took a hit which clipped off the end of her wing.

"Valkyrie Wing, break, break, break!" Harriet yelled as she rolled away, catching sight of more of the curious looking aircraft as she did. She came around in a tight turn and dived after her attacker, but even with the Typhoon dropping at full speed, passing five hundred miles per hour, she couldn't keep up. The aircraft pulled away, leaving her in its wake as she looked on in disbelief. As her Typhoon started to shake with the speed, she pulled out of her dive and looked up to see the whole wing scattered, diving and turning as more of the unidentified aircraft dropped on them. Voices called out warnings, frequently cursing as the enemy aircraft got among them. Harriet desperately raced up to get back in the fight, and just managed to get close enough to fire her cannons as an enemy aircraft passed in front of her and got shots off on the Typhoon it was chasing, rattling the fuselage and starting it smoking as it dived away. Her own shots dipped behind the fast moving enemy, which roared away in a fast turning dive that she knew she wouldn't catch. She rolled again to bring herself into another fight which had three Typhoons twisting and turning, as another of the beasts closed fast on their tails. It was impossible. She pushed her engine to the maximum as she gave chase, and took a long shot as soon as the enemy aircraft came into sight, just clipping his tail briefly and throwing the pilot off his aim, making him flip and dive, fearing that she was closer than she was. Her heart was pounding, and her mouth was dry. This new enemy aircraft was literally running rings around the Typhoons, and getting into a firing position was almost impossible. "Turn as tight as you can!" she shouted over the radio. "Don't try and outrun them; they're too fast. Use your turns; fly like you're in a Hurricane!" She watched as a Typhoon instantly pulled into a climbing turn that was so tight the pursuing enemy aircraft shot past, unable to follow. She was looking left and right, shouting instructions, warning her pilots of the enemy on their tails, and trying to get there to help them, but it seemed impossible; everything was moving too fast.

"Harry, look out!" Carrie shouted, and Harriet spun her head away from the enemy aircraft she was watching as it turned with a Typhoon over to her left, and looked forward to see another of the enemy coming straight at her. It was a mottled green and grey colour, and from head on, it looked like a shark as it charged towards her. She was mesmerised as she looked at the engines, one on each wing, and neither had a propeller. A flash of gunfire from the shark faced aeroplane sent a shiver down her spine. He'd got her. Before she could roll away, a Typhoon cut in front of her, banking hard and presenting its underside to the shark, and taking the full force of the cannon fire intended for Harriet.

"Carrie!" she yelled, as the Typhoon that had saved her life was now smoking badly and flickering with flames as it dived away. She pushed on her fire button and rattled the shark with her cannons, ravaging its nose and right wing, and making the rocket like engine smoke. It fired one last burst before rolling onto its back and dropping into a vertical dive, and a cannon shell passed through Harriet's propeller and shattered it before burying itself in her engine with a thud. Grinding vibrations quickly shook through her seat and controls, and a pall of black smoke scattered with fiery orange sparks erupted from the exhausts. Her mind spun as she tried to control the aeroplane while gauging the damage. There were more and more sparks, and the smoke was becoming denser while the instruments were showing temperatures rapidly climbing. She quickly shut off the fuel and pushed the stick forward, starting a dive which she hoped would put out the flames before they started. The remains of the shattered propeller windmilled as the smoke thinned, and the sparks stopped, and Harriet scanned the horizon to get her position. She knew that there was no getting home, but she was desperate to try and get over the front lines at least. Coming down in German held territory wouldn't end well, especially not after the hell she'd just visited on the German train. For a brief moment she looked up at the battle, but it had passed. Typhoons were running for the coast, and the shark like German fighters were nowhere to be seen. The only remnants of the battle were wisps of black smoke coming up from the ground where aircraft had met their end. She didn't have time to count the wisps, or to think about what had happened; she had much more pressing concerns.

The speed started to rise as Harriet continued her dive towards the coast, so much that she had to pull up a little and slow to prevent any damage to the wings, which had received their fair share of shrapnel in the battle, and weren't in the best condition. The engine fire had gone out, so the chance of burning alive had been reduced, which was something, and with that worry reduced she was able to focus on what to do next. She wasn't thrilled at the idea of taking to her parachute, at least not just yet, but she started to prepare for it just in case by pulling her harness tight. Machine gun fire came up at her briefly, making her swear as she flinched, unable to do anything other than roll her wings left and right to try and dodge the bullets coming up at her. To her relief, the shooting didn't last, and she was soon over what she thought to be the front lines. At five thousand feet, she caught sight of one of the newly constructed advance landing grounds, ALGs as they were called. Hastily built runways bulldozed flat and covered with pierced steel planks, the same as those she found in Malta, put together by combat engineers who came ashore with the invasion. They were run by RAF Commando units, defended by the RAF Regiment, and stocked with fuel, ammunition, and spare parts, so fighters could land after a sortie and get right back up again, without having to waste time making the return trip to England. She circled, shallowing her dive and scrubbing off her speed, while descending towards the ground and keeping her eyes on the runway below.

"You've got to be kidding me!" she shouted as a fluffy black cloud appeared in the sky to the right of her wing, and quickly erupted into a ball of flames. Flak, and she couldn't do anything to avoid it. Turning would slow her enough to risk stalling, and diving would make her too fast to land, so all she could do was continue her circuit and hope for the best while the sky filled with bursts of anti aircraft fire. "That's right, a bit closer next time!" she shouted angrily out of her cockpit, having ripped off her face mask and pulled the cockpit canopy open. The lack of a working engine made the risk of carbon monoxide poisoning significantly less of a worry, and if she didn't vent some of her anger, she'd likely fire what remained of her ammunition at the nearest anti aircraft gun, regardless of how much doing so would risk her landing. She looked down as she shouted. The ALG had a ring of anti aircraft guns around it, all of which seemed to be firing, much to her dismay. She'd managed to escape the Germans, only to be blown out of the sky by her own side, and it didn't sit well.

A blast rocked her wings as she came in on her final approach, slowing her a little as she fought to keep the aeroplane level while nervously watching the speed drop, and feeling for the dreaded stall. She'd been shot up, and there was every chance that her undercarriage had taken a hit, which increased the risk of it giving way when she landed, if it came down at all, and her Typhoon flipping. Something she was keen to avoid, so she pulled her harness tight and lowered her seat, to make sure she didn't crush her skull if she was flipped. Undercarriage down, flaps down, and she descended to the ground, holding her breath as the wheels bounced hard on the steel runway, then letting out a gasp as they held, and sent a reassuring rumble through the cockpit while a cloud of dust was thrown up as she started to brake the best she could. She was down, and relieved. A khaki clad figure appeared in front and waved her to follow him off the steel runway and onto a patch of barren, dusty ground, where she finally came to a halt, then pulled off her helmet, and laid her head back on the rest.

"Don't just bloody sit there!" the Sergeant shouted as his shadow blocked the sunlight. He reached into the cockpit and unfastened her harness, then grabbed her by the shoulder and dragged her roughly up out of her seat. "Move, for God's sake!" He all but dragged her from the cockpit and onto the wing, where she stopped and tried to compose herself before he jumped off the leading edge of the wing and pulled her with him. They crashed down onto the hard ground side by side, just as spouts of dust jumped into the air in a neat line that zipped all the way across the planking and not an arm's length from Harriet's head. She buried her face in the ground and wrapped her arms around her ears as the cannon shells thudded into her Typhoon, hitting the engine and cockpit, before running down the fuselage. The hits were followed by a Messerschmitt 109 flying so low that it would have taken her head off with the propeller if she wasn't laid flat on the ground. "Come on!" The Sergeant stood and grabbed her by the collar, then started running before she was even off her knees, pulling her along as she staggered awkwardly behind him. She'd only just got into her stride when he pulled her headfirst into a deep slit trench, just as another 109 passed over and put some more rounds into her Typhoon, and filled the trench with dust and stone chips as its cannon shells ripped into the sandbags lining the edge, and skipped off along the ground. "Welcome home, Sir," the Sergeant gasped, while Harriet looked up at him from the floor of the trench, and tried to stop her heart from beating out of her chest.

"Ma'am," Harriet wheezed in reply.

"Ma'am?" he asked in amazement as he looked at her in shock.

"Wing Commander Cornwall..." She gave him an exhausted nod and smile. "Thanks for getting me out of my aeroplane."

"My pleasure." He pulled her to her feet, then took a pack of cigarettes from his chest pocket and lit one before offering it to her.

"No thanks, those things will kill you." She looked at him for a moment, then smiled as he let out a laugh.

"So will the Germans, but you didn't seem that bothered about them!" He took a deep drag on his cigarette before blowing out the blue smoke. "Wait there... Ma'am." He lifted himself and looked over the top of the trench. "Just a welcoming committee."

"A what?"

"They like to have a go every now and then, usually when they see an aeroplane on the ground." She stood and joined him in looking out. "Made a mess of your nice Typhoon, Ma'am."

"It was a mess before I landed," she sighed. "The propeller was shot off, and I took a cannon shell to the engine."

"Lucky you were in a Typhoon. They're built like tanks. Anything else would have fallen out of the sky long before you got here."

"Yeah..." She gave him a smile of resignation. Her ears were ringing, but the anti aircraft guns she'd been convinced were shooting at her, and had cursed loudly and repeatedly, had fallen silent having chased away the 109s. She ran her fingers through her hair and tied it back, then put her hands on the lip of the trench, ready to pull herself out. "I'd better go and look at the damage."

"No you don't," he said, as he put his hand on her shoulder and kept her in place.

"What?" She fired a frown at him.

"Wait for it..."

"For what?" A whistle filled the air, and he pulled her down into the bottom of the trench just as a loud explosion shook the ground, followed by another, and another."

"What the hell is it now?" she yelled, as she sat in the bottom of the trench with her arms wrapped around her head to protect from the shower of stones and clumps of dirt that were raining down on her.

"German artillery," the Sergeant shouted in reply. "Welcome to France, Ma'am!" The ground shook for a few more minutes as they were rocked by the deafening artillery barrage, which then stopped as suddenly as it had started. "Sergeant MacInnes, Ma'am." He held out his hand, which she shook, having taken her arms from around her head. He took a tight grip, then stood and pulled her to her feet, before looking out over the top of the trench again. "That'll probably do it for now." He jumped from the trench, then bent down and gave her a hand out above ground and onto the airfield, which was already a hive of activity with engineers rushing to fill holes and check the runway surface.

"Is it always like this?"

"Pretty much. The front lines are only a couple of miles in that direction." He pointed east across the airfield. "They were further away when we first landed and set up the airfield, but the Germans counter attacked yesterday, and now they're mixed in with the hedgerows and proving a pain to dig out."

"Great..."

"Yes, Ma'am. It can make it difficult to have a nap." He gave her a wink, which put her at ease a little and made her smile. "I'll show you to our CO, so we can see about getting you home. I doubt you'll be flying that anywhere." He pointed to her Typhoon, which was now flat on the ground and smoking, having had its wheels knocked from under it by one of the closer artillery shells. She nodded and followed him towards some tents camouflaged along a row of hedges and trees. "Wing Commander Cornwall, Sir," MacInnes said as he led her into the command tent, where an RAF Wing Commander dressed in army khaki, with his blue rank braid on the shoulders of his battle dress, was giving instructions to his radio operator, who was sitting at a folding table loaded with heavy radio sets.

"Who?" the Wing Commander asked as he turned and looked at Harriet.

"Cornwall," Harriet replied. "13 Wing. I had tc put down on your airfield when my engine was shot out."

"George Valance," he said as he walked over and offered his hand. "What're the ATA doing out here in Normandy? Little dangerous for deliveries, isn't it?"

"I wouldn't know; I'm an RAF Typhoon pilot," she said as she shook his hand. "I need to get a message back to HQ right away."

"Oh?" He looked a little confused, and unsure how to take her.

"Yes, we were just attacked by a new type of aeroplane, something I haven't seen before. Twin engines, no propellers, and went so fast it made my Typhoon look stationary."

"That sounds like something out of a fantasy."

"More like a horror story. Anyway, HQ need to know about it right away. Can you get a message out?"

"Write the details down and give them to Corporal Wright." He handed her a pencil and pad of paper, and nodded in the direction of his radio operator. "He'll pass the message up through the forward air controllers; they can probably get the information out quicker than anyone else, and warn our pilots while they're at it."

"Thanks..."

"I can't guarantee anyone can look at your Typhoon, I'm afraid, we're a little busy at the moment."

"I wouldn't bother; the Germans took care of it as soon as I landed."

"Yes, they can be like that around these parts at the moment. Oh well, you can hang about here for the time being, if you like, and I'll try and get you a ride home later."

"Thanks."

"Sergeant MacInnes, take the Wing Commander over to the Mess tent, would you? Get her a cup of tea and something to eat.'

"Sir," MacInnes replied, as Harriet quickly scribbled down a message and handed it to the Corporal at the radio.

"Try and find her a tin hat as well, would you?"

"Something I'll need?" Harriet asked.

"You've been here more than five minutes; what do you think?" Vallance gave her a smile. "Don't wander too far, and if the shooting starts, get yourself into a trench. Come back as soon as you've had a drink and something to eat, and we'll see about that ride home. I'll let your people know you're safe."

"Thanks." She followed MacInnes to a tent hidden away in the woods to the rear of the airstrip, where she was given a tin mug of hot, sweet tea, and to her amazement, a corned beef sandwich in a thick white sliced bread, with proper butter and a huge chunk of corned beef. MacInnes found her a tin helmet then showed her back to the airstrip. She found a tree and sat underneath it, and closed her eyes for a moment. It had been a hell of a day, and the adrenaline was still running through her body and keeping her on edge. After taking off the uncomfortable helmet, she started on her sandwich, which tasted far better than a corned beef sandwich had any right to. She noticed as she ate that her heart was still racing and showing no sign of settling. It had been pounding since the new German aircraft had jumped them, and there hadn't been a moment to relax since. It had been a blur of adrenaline inducing danger from the first break, to being pulled out of the trench after the artillery barrage. Even sitting and eating, she couldn't fully relax. There was gunfire in the near distance, rifles and machine guns, accompanied by the occasional explosion, and it kept her nervous as she wondered when the next artillery barrage would start. While the nearby fighting was keeping her adrenaline flowing, it was also keeping her mind off Carrie, for the most part. She thought briefly of what had happened, but couldn't let herself give in to it too much. Just the brief glimpse in her mind of Carrie's Typhoon being shot up as she put herself between the enemy and Harriet was enough to make her want to cry; but she knew she couldn't. While she was in the relative safety of what seemed like a heavily defended RAF unit, she was in Normandy, and the Germans were putting up a fight not a few miles away; there wasn't time for emotions. So, Carrie was pushed to the darkest recesses of her mind, with Lexi, Sully, and everyone else she'd grown to care about, and then lost.

A flight of four Spitfires came in while she waited and sipped her tea, and were quickly refuelled and rearmed before the German artillery could start up and get shots in at them. The pilots stayed strapped in and ready to go, and as soon as the job was done, they were in the air again and heading east. It was a fast turnaround. The ground crews didn't mess about, and as soon as the first four were gone, another flight came in, and the operation was repeated, then again with another four. An entire squadron of Spitfires in and out, refuelled, rearmed, and back into the fight, without having to waste time going to England and back. It was an impressive thing to watch, though as the final Spitfire took off, she found herself wondering where her air cover had been for the mission to stop the train. They'd been promised an umbrella of fighters while they were operating, and she couldn't help but get annoyed when the thought popped into her head that had the Spitfires been overhead as they were supposed to have been, the new German fighters wouldn't have got through to her Typhoons. Once the thought was in, it was hard to shift. There wasn't a single fighter there to support them when the enemy struck, and that had cost lives, not to mention at least three Typhoons that she could be sure about, though the smoking aircraft she'd seen in her desperate attempts to stay alive in the battle had suggested there were many more damaged.

"Squadron Leader Cornwall?" a voice asked, pulling her from the vicious cycle of thoughts that had run around her mind for over an hour, doing nothing more than making her angry.

"Wing Commander!" she barked as she snapped out of her trance, and looked to an officer standing above her in the shade of the tree.

"Wing Commander? Oh… Sorry, Ma'am. My mistake." He frowned for a moment, as though he was unsure what to do next. He was a Flight Lieutenant, in his early thirties and wearing an Observer's single wing brevet on the left breast of his khaki battle dress jacket.

"Is there something you wanted?" Harriet asked irritably.

"Yes. I mean… Yes, Ma'am. Flight Lieutenant Hooper." He knelt beside her, getting a look of suspicious disdain from Harriet as he did.

"I'm hoping you've come to tell me you've got me a ride home?"

"What? No," he replied unexpectedly firmly. "That's not my department, I should say. No, I'm from Intelligence."

"Oh?" She raised an eyebrow, while fighting the urge to make Cas' joke about military intelligence being an oxymoron.

"Yes. We received a message saying a pilot had been knocked down by some unusual aeroplane, and I was sent to ask you about it."

"What do you want to know?"

"Everything you can tell me, I suppose?"

"Two engines, no propellers, and the fastest thing I've ever seen. Will that do?"

"Anything like that?" He showed her a grainy photograph of the shark like aeroplane she'd seen up close.

"That's the one. What is it?" she asked as she sat forward and took the photo from him. He'd grabbed her attention, and her irritation at him was quickly put aside.

"Messerschmitt 262, we think. A new German jet engine fighter. I say new; we've known about them being in development for a few years, but didn't realise they'd got this far beyond prototypes... How many were there?"

"I don't know, half a dozen or more? They dropped on us so fast that we didn't have time to respond properly."

"How fast?"

"I chased one in a dive at over five hundred miles per hour, and it left me standing. In level Flight, they were maybe a hundred miles per hour faster than us. Maybe more." He scribbled furiously and whistled at what she was describing.

"It sounds like something else."

"Like nothing I've seen."

"Guns?"

"Four, I think. Cannons, by the feel of it."

"Anything else useful?"

"Not really, it was over in seconds. Others in my wing that got back to England may be able to give you more." She frowned as she thought through the brief yet violent combat. "Oh, they can't turn."

"They can't turn?"

"They move too fast. The only chance of getting away is to out turn them. You'd be lucky to get on their tail unless they slowed down to try and turn with you, but then they'd be like any other aeroplane... That's all I've got, I'm afraid."

"It's incredibly useful, thank you. I'll get the information back and make sure we let people know about them."

"Has nobody come up against them before?"

"Never. The Focke Wulf 190 has been the best they've put up against us until now. This is something entirely now. You're lucky enough to be the first to see them." He smiled excitedly.

"I'll make sure I mention that in the letters I write to my pilots who were shot down by them…"

"Oh… Yes. Sorry." He stood and pushed his notebook back into his pocket. "I just mean it's an exciting development for us, that's all. In terms of aircraft and performance, that is. Not…"

"Is that everything?"

"Yes, Ma'am." He stood looking awkward, and she gave him a nod that suggested he leave, which he did after smiling nervously, then stumbling a little as he quickly walked away.

"Lucky…" she muttered as he left, while shaking her head. "We were lucky that any of us escaped alive!" She leant back against the tree and closed her eyes again. It was early evening, and the day's activities were starting to take their toll. With the adrenaline finally wearing off, and having no aeroplane to fly or job to do, there was nothing left to keep her awake, and she quickly fell into a deep sleep.

"Ma'am…" MacInnes' voice pulled her out of the dreamless sleep with a jolt, and she gasped as she sat up and looked around, not quite sure where she was. "Everything alright, Ma'am?"

"Yes… Yes, I must have dropped off for a minute. What's up?" She smiled sheepishly in the pink and orange glow of the early evening, and hoped she hadn't been snoring.

"Your ride home's here. They're ready for the off, so we need to get you over there as soon as." He pointed over to the C47 Dakota twin engine transport that was parked just along from the wreck of her

Typhoon, with its engines roaring and propellers spinning, as it blew up a huge cloud of dust that covered the entire airfield. She'd been so tired she hadn't even heard it come in, and from its position on the runway and the wind direction, she knew it must have come right past her when it landed, and she hadn't even flinched. MacInnes held out his hand and pulled her to her feet. She winced as her tight muscles screamed at her. They'd been tensed solid since being jumped by the German jets, and her sleep against the tree had left them to stiffen uncomfortably. "OK?"

"I will be… I must be getting old."

"Yes, Ma'am," he replied with a raised eyebrow and half a smile. He was forty at least, and looked like he'd been around a bit, and the thought of a young woman half his age frowning and complaining of being old clearly amused him. "You'll be back in your bed tonight, Ma'am, after a long hot bath back in England. You'll be alright."

"Thank God! Us pilots don't do roughing it, you know…" She smirked at him, knowing full well he'd been living in a hole in the ground since he'd landed in Normandy, with the Germans throwing artillery at him in between air raids, and she knew he wouldn't be likely to see a hot bath or soft bed for quite some time. "I'll have a drink for you in the Mess."

"Appreciate it, Ma'am." He shook his head and laughed as they started to run side by side along the hard ground to the side of the steel planked runway towards the C47. She frowned nervously at the sight of an army ambulance speeding away from the aeroplane, and she felt herself desperately hoping that whatever had happened to warrant the presence of an ambulance wasn't enough to stop her from getting on board and going home. She'd half expected a seat on a truck heading to the beach, and a miserable trip to England on an uncomfortable boat of some sort when she'd first been told she would be getting a ride home. A C47 would have her home in an hour, or in the safety of Kent at least, she could always arrange a lift back to her own airfield easily enough once she was back in England, and away from the front lines of the war. "Hang on," MacInnes shouted as he waved at one of the crew, a Corporal who was in the process of closing the large cargo door on the side of the aeroplane.

"What is it?" the young woman demanded as she turned to look first at MacInnes and then Harriet. She was short with neatly tied brown hair, and was dressed in an RAF blue battle dress tunic and a yellow Mae West life jacket, with her blue trousers tucked into her flying boots; and she was wearing a fierce frown. The sight took Harriet by surprise; she wasn't expecting to see another woman in Normandy, and certainly not one crewing a Dakota. She looked down at the young woman's rank stripes on her arm, and the wide white armband just below them, with a large red cross in the middle.

"Wing Commander Cornwall is to go back with you. CO's orders." He pointed to Harriet, who smiled awkwardly, unsure of what to make of the young woman.

"Very well..." The Corporal replied while looking Harriet up and down. "Ma'am, if you'd like to climb on board?" she shouted over the noise of the engines, with an exceptionally polite change of tone from her initial response.

"Thank you," Harriet said to MacInnes. She held out her hand, which he shook warmly. "I'll have that drink for you in the Mess tonight."

"Good luck, Ma'am."

"We need to leave!" the Corporal shouted. Still remaining polite, but her voice and the sternness in her eyes suggested she wasn't in the mood for being messed about. Harriet gave her a nod, then pulled herself up through the door. As she held onto the fuselage to steady herself, the young woman jumped in after her and pulled the door closed. "Better have a seat right there, Ma'am." She pointed to the loadmaster's seat that was folded away against the rear wall of the cabin, then turned and gave a thumbs up towards the cockpit. Harriet pulled down the seat and took her place as the Dakota started rolling into life. She looked down the cabin as she got comfortable and was amazed by the sight, and the smell of blood, smoke, and burning flesh, which quickly became almost overwhelming. Stretchers lined either side of the cabin, slung at waist height from supports protruding from the fuselage, with other non stretcher cases laying and sitting below them.

"Where are they from?" Harriet shouted as she pulled on the young woman's sleeve, while the engines started to whine as the Dakota slumped forward.

"The front lines, Ma'am. We're an aeromedical evacuation flight, sent to take the worst injured back to England for urgent care. Better sit tight, Ma'am. I need to go make sure they're comfortable for take off." She gave Harriet a smile, then went off and started tending the stretcher cases. Checking dressings, wounds, and even their breathing as she went from stretcher to stretcher, walking and standing perfectly balanced as the Dakota bounced and rocked along the runway. Harriet looked out of the window as she felt the aeroplane swing around, ready for take off. It was just before sunset, and the sky was beautiful. She focused on it, rather than the many wounded filling the aeroplane, while she waited impatiently for the engines to run up to maximum power, the sign that they were ready to leave. She couldn't wait to be back in England. It had been one of her hardest days. Before her mind could get stuck on Carrie again, which it was about to, the engines roared, and the brakes were let off, and she was dragged back into the moment as the airframe vibrated and the Dakota started to sprint along the runway. A sense of relief passed over her as she felt the wheels lift from the ground, followed by a sense of confusion, and then horror, as beams of light cut through the fuselage, leaving a smoking trail behind them that quickly expanded and filled the cabin with a swirling haze of light. Screams overwhelmed the sound of the engines, as a fine red mist filled the air, filtering the light to a soft pink. A split second later, the wheels were crashing down to earth again, and Harriet was bounced onto the floor from her seat. She grabbed at it as she rolled, thrown around by the swerving Dakota. She looked up as she steadied herself and saw the flicker of flames outside the right side of the fuselage. It was a fight to pull herself up as the brakes were desperately applied, and the Dakota was slowed, while the ground beneath the wheels became increasingly rough, bouncing her relentlessly. Along the cabin, the young Corporal was holding onto a stretcher with one hand, while plugging the bleeding shoulder wound of one of the screaming injured with the other. Harriet took a breath, then staggered down the cabin to join her, determined to help. If for no other reason than to focus on anything that would distract her from the terror she was feeling.

"What can I do?" Harriet shouted as the Corporal looked up at her.

"Press hard!" came the reply, as the Corporal took Harriet's hand and pushed it into the bloody wound she'd been plugging. Harriet nodded and did as she was told, grabbing a handhold above to steady herself while she did. The Corporal knelt and stuck a dressing on a wounded soldier sitting on the floor below them, before running off to the back of the cabin and pushing the wide cargo door open. Seconds later and she was back at Harriet's side. She pulled Harriet's hand away from the wound, stuck another dressing on top of it, then grabbed the soldier's hand and pushed it against the dressing. "Hold this in place, or you'll bleed to death!" she ordered.

"I can't..." he yelled. "It hurts too much."

"Quit your bitching, and get on with it! There's more than you on this aeroplane!" the Corporal shouted firmly. He stopped screaming in an instant, and held the dressing against his wound just as he'd been told. "Come on, Ma'am. We need to be quick." She led Harriet to the stretcher closest to the door, then between them, they lifted it from the racking and headed back to the opening, where already a shocked looking member of the ground crew was peering in the doorway, ready to jump in. "Stay there; we'll pass them out!" She lowered her end of the stretcher for the airman to take, then went back to help Harriet lower the other end to the next waiting man. "Get him to a safe distance, then back here for the next." She turned and was back inside the fuselage in a heartbeat. "All men not in a stretcher, get shuffling to the door. Now!" She yelled, and the walking wounded burst into life, while she and Harriet grabbed the next stretcher and moved to the doorway to hand it out. When they went back in for a third time, the pilots were carrying another stretcher down the cabin, and the navigator and radio operator had another. Harriet pushed herself up against the fuselage as they hustled past. It was hot and uncomfortable, and the air was thick with smoke. She looked out of the window to see the fire raging along the starboard wing; they didn't have long. The next stretcher was hurried out, and the next, and the next, while the fire found its way into the cabin, licking its way out of the cockpit and churning out black smoke which rolled along the roof. "That's it. That's everyone!" the Corporal shouted, and everyone ran for the door, and the flight crew jumped out and started to run.

"Hey! Where are you going?" Harriet shouted, as she got to the door and turned to see the Corporal running back into the burning cabin. She took a step back into the cabin, ready to grab the young woman and drag her out by the collar if she needed to, but she needn't have worried. The Corporal was soon running back towards her and dragging a large backpack. "Anything else?"

"Just my medical kit." She grabbed Harriet's arm, and they jumped from the Dakota together, joining the others in running to the nearby trees, where the wounded had been laid out by the ground crew. Harriet slowed and turned to look at the Dakota; it was engulfed in flames as it lay among the bushes it had finished up in after leaving the runway and crashing through the boundaries of the temporary airfield. It was a miracle anyone had escaped at all, let alone the entire crew and their load of wounded passengers. The sound of the Corporal giving out instructions pulled Harriet back into the moment, and she turned to see the rest of the Dakota crew helping the wounded, all given jobs and guidance, while the Corporal herself went about dealing with the new wounds.

"What can I do to help?" Harriet asked again as she knelt by the Corporal's side, hoping she wouldn't have to put her hand in a bloody hole in somebody's body again.

"Get around the other side, Ma'am." She pointed to the end of the stretcher she was kneeling behind. "You're going to have to lift him and roll him towards you, so I can check the exit wound and get a dressing on him." Harriet nodded and got into place, and put her hands exactly where she was told. "OK, Ma'am. On three." She counted down, then they rolled the man towards Harriet. He groaned and gasped and screamed in agony while the Corporal went about her work. "Not too bad. Hold him while I dress it, Ma'am." It was the same man she'd told to be quiet in the Dakota, and to his credit, he'd done a good job of holding it together. He was already severely injured; the new wound was a final straw.

"I think we can dispense with the Ma'am, don't you?" Harriet replied, lost for anything else useful to say. The Corporal looked up at her for a moment, then gave her a half smile while getting to work dousing the wound in sulphur powder, then dressing it so he could be laid flat again. A morphine syrette was then pushed into his thigh, and with the blood from his wound, the Corporal drew a letter M on his forehead with her finger, before checking her watch and adding the time. Without stopping to think, she grabbed her pack and headed over to the other man who'd been hit, and Harriet followed close behind. He was leaning against a tree and breathing deep, his arm was in a slung, and his head was bandaged, but those were his old wounds, the ones that were sending him home. The new wound was his lower leg, which the Dakota pilot was holding a dressing against.

"Let me see," the Corporal said as she knelt beside the pilot. She took the dressing and pulled it away to reveal a gaping gash across the outside of his lower leg, showing his shinbone and making both Harriet and the Dakota pilot look away from the gore. The Corporal didn't miss a beat. She had the wound covered in sulphur powder and dressed by the time a small convoy of trucks, Jeeps, and an ambulance arrived. Harriet had assisted the best she could, mostly by cutting pieces of the soldier's trousers away with scissors from the medical pack, and being handed blood soaked dressings to dispose of.

"Who's in charge here?" an army doctor shouted as he ran from the ambulance.

"She is," the Dakota pilot said as he stood and pointed to the Corporal.

"What's the situation?" the doctor asked. He was a Captain in the Royal Army Medical Corps, and had a Sergeant by his side.

"All as you left them when you signed them over to me, Sir," the Corporal replied as she stood and faced him. "With the exception of these two." She pointed to the two she'd just worked on, and gave him a brief rundown on their injuries and what she'd done to help them.

"Good work, Corporal. Very good work!" He gave her a nod, then turned to the Sergeant. "Right, let's get them all loaded on the trucks.

Get those two in the ambulance; we'd better get them into surgery right away." The Sergeant went into action as only a sergeant could, and anyone standing and able was soon carrying a stretcher or giving a shoulder to the walking wounded, and getting them onto the trucks. Harriet helped again, taking one end of a stretcher and helping get one of the wounded onto a truck. It was a quick operation, and soon the convoy was rolling away at speed, leaving the Dakota crew, Harriet, and the few ground crew that had arrived on the scene in a jeep when the Dakota had gone down.

"Are you OK, Ma'am?" the Corporal asked as she joined Harriet watching the convoy race away.

"What? Yes. Yes, thank you. Are you?"

"Yes, Ma'am."

"Are you going to keep doing that?"

"Doing?"

"Calling me Ma'am? I clearly remember telling you to stop it."

"Sorry, Ma'am. Just doesn't seem right. You're a Wing Commander, and I'm only a Corporal. I'm supposed to call you Ma'am."

"We've both just had our hands inside a man's body. I think we can dispense with the formalities. Harry Cornwall." She offered her hand, then frowned as she realised it was filthy with blood.

"Anna Outwood," came the reply, as the young Corporal put her equally bloody hand in Harriet's. She smiled for the first time since they'd met, and her brown eyes lit up. "Sorry if I got a bit bossy back there. We needed to act quickly to keep people alive."

"Don't even mention it. You did a fantastic job of keeping us all alive. Those men owe you their lives."

"I don't know about that; I was just doing my job."

"Which is what, exactly? I didn't realise WAAFs were over here in Normandy?"

"Aeromedical evacuation."

"Aerowhat?"

"Flying ambulances. We've been coming in since the airstrips were built, to collect the bad cases that need a proper hospital back home in England."

"You're a medic?"

“A Flying Nightingale."

"A what?"

"A Nurse. They call us the Flying Nightingales, as in Florence, because we fly into battle to pick up our patients."

"I should have known… Every nurse I've ever met has been bossy." She gave Anna a wink, which got another smile in reply.

"Can we give you a ride, Ma'am?" One of the airmen asked as he started the jeep. The rest of the Dakota crew were already in it, and they quickly made space for the two women as they climbed into the back for the short trip back to the airstrip command tent.

MacInnes had provided them both with hot water and a bar of soap and towel between them when they arrived back at the HQ, so they could clean up and get the blood from their hands, before having a mess tin of stew and cup of hot sweet tea from the Mess tent. Instead of taking Harriet home to England, the entire Dakota crew were now joining her in staying on the airstrip for the night, and after being given some more tea and some chocolate and boiled sweets, they were shown to some trenches dug into a small, wooded area. Their new home. Harriet and Anna were given their own trench to share, and MacInnes had managed to find them a blanket, which he delivered at last light, just as the orange sky was fading to royal blue, and the pair wrapped it around their shoulders and stood side by side while sipping tea as they looked out over the airstrip. They stood in silence, each lost in their thoughts. Harriet's mind went around and around as she tried to make sense of the day. The Messerschmitt 262 jets had given her nightmares in combat. She was a confident pilot; she'd got through so much air combat that she thought she could fight her way out of anything, but coming up against jets had been something new for her. A skill she hadn't learned yet. She'd taken on 109s when flying the old Gloster Gladiator, and the speed difference was about the same, though it wasn't as high. Nothing moved as fast as the 262s did. The unknown of fighting them had led to her losing Carrie, which was something she wasn't yet ready to process. For brief moments, her mind had latched on to her accountability, and how Carrie would still be alive if Harriet had been fully immersed in flying and fighting, instead of being so distracted by the jets. To top off a bad day, she'd been told that the reason she almost died for the second time that day was that the Dakota had been shot up by a low level raid by a pair of 109s that had come in skimming the trees, so low that the anti aircraft gunners hadn't seen them, and even the portable radar that had been moved into the area hadn't picked them up. They hadn't hung around. Just got their shots in, put the Dakota down, then disappeared before anyone even had the chance to fire back. The Dakota crew had performed a genuine miracle by getting the aeroplane down again, by all accounts. They'd been going so fast that they left the steel planks of the runway and continued into the fields, but it could have been worse. They'd been hit just as the wheels left the ground, any higher, and there would have been no escape. The wheels would have been up, and it would have got very messy, very quickly. Technically, it was the second time Harriet had been shot down that day, and a small part of her was happy to be staying on the ground for the night. She didn't want to risk it a third time.

"This is the closest I've been to the actual war," Anna said quietly, as they watched the skyline flashing with artillery and gunfire, and listened to the endless sound of explosions and shooting that drifted on the evening breeze.

"It sounds quite far away," Harriet replied in a reassuring whisper. Not sure whether she was trying to make Anna feel better or herself. As the darkness settled in, accentuating the flashes of battle, she started to feel more vulnerable, with memories of 1940 making their way to the fore of her mind.

"It's closer than it was in England."

"You're from Yorkshire, aren't you?"

"My accent gave me away, then?"

"Just a little."

"Yeah... South Yorkshire. I'm not a total stranger to the war; I remember the air raids when they used to come, and the big one that hit Sheffield. You could see the glow in the sky from the fires for miles around. It was exciting at the time, hearing it and watching it from a safe distance. We knew London had got it bad, and places like Hull and Liverpool, but it brings it home when it happens to your own area. Fortunately, I could still go to school throughout. I'd have been furious if it had been bombed."

"School..." Harriet smiled as she thought back to her own time at school. She'd have been more than happy to see it bombed. "How old are you?"

"Nursing school."

"The question stands."

"Twenty one... Anyway, what are you doing here? If you don't mind me asking?" She changed the subject expertly, and while Harriet was quite aware of what was going on, she let it go. "I wasn't expecting to see a woman out here."

"I wasn't supposed to be out here. I'm supposed to be in a hot bath in Kent about now."

"Then how come you're sharing a trench with a Corporal in darkest, noisiest Normandy?"

"Because earlier this afternoon, before I was being shot down while getting a ride home on your Dakota, I was shot down all by myself."

"You're a pilot?"

"Yes. They do let us girls fly too, you know?"

"I know they used to."

"Used to? They still do, thank you very much. I'm living proof of it. A mystery in itself, considering that I've been shot down twice today."

"You may still fly, but it's closed to new applicants."

"What?"

"A few of us wanted to train as pilots, but we were told no. It's closed to female applicants. Has been for a while. This year at least. Apparently, they've got enough male pilots going through training these days. Unless they were just giving me a line because I was a nurse, and they wanted to send me to do that instead of flying, though a few of my friends who aren't nurses tried, and they were knocked back for the same reason."

"Is that so…?" Harriet felt herself frowning. She knew nothing of the change, and it made her feel uncomfortable. "You know, if you're still keen to be a pilot, I can ask a few questions when we get back to England…"

"Thank you, but I'm OK where I am. I kind of went off the idea of being a fighter pilot."

"Why, what's wrong with us?" Harriet frowned again. Other than Ginny, who had very firm opinions about being a pilot, almost everyone she know would snap her hand off at the chance.

"Nothing's wrong with pilots, as such..." She paused for a moment as she looked for the right words. "I evacuated a pilot who was burned alive when he was shot down. He was still alive when I got to him, somehow, but I've never seen anything like it. Even his eyelids had burned off…" Harriet winced a little as she listened to Anna talk, and thought back to her friend Whisky in Malta. She could still see his badly burned face as if it had happened only yesterday, and the smell of his burning flesh came back to her as though she was back kneeling over him. "It traumatised me so much that I still have nightmares about it..." Anna continued, then gave her head a shake and forced a smile. "Anyway, I decided that it would be a much better use of my skills to try and help the wounded and ease their suffering a little. It's why I volunteered for this unit. It gets me in the war and doing my bit. Though, as I said earlier, I didn't expect to be quite this close to the war."

"Don't worry, I'm sure the Germans are occupied with more than coming and getting us. Anyway, we should probably get some sleep." As the words left her mouth, the sky lit up with an explosion just the other side of the airstrip, and almost instantly, the whole world seemed to burst into life. Rifles and machine guns cracked and rattled, but the anti aircraft guns remained silent, and while Harriet searched the sky each time it was lit by an explosion, she couldn't see any sign of enemy aircraft.

"Stand to!" A loud shout echoed around the airstrip, and the order was repeated everywhere. Harriet's heart was racing as she reached under her arm and pulled out her Walther pistol she'd been issued by Carlyle for her Geneva trip.

"What does that mean?" Anna asked nervously. "And why do you need that?" She nodded and stared at the pistol.

"Did they issue you a weapon?"

"No. Why, do I need one?"

"It's looking more likely than it was thirty seconds ago." She reached into her boot and pulled the issue revolver she had carried as a backup since getting home from France. After checking it, she pushed it into Anna's hand. "Safety catch is on the side; push it, point, and pull the trigger. Only shoot when they're right in front of you, or you won't hit a thing."

"You're serious?"

"I don't want to be." She peered out across the airstrip, and in the flash of explosions, she saw the silhouette of a tank surrounded by soldiers heading slowly for the runway. "Down." She yelled as the tank's muzzle flashed. She grabbed Anna and pulled her down into the bottom of the trench as the tank shell exploded over to the right, right where a defensive machine gun had burst into life, sending a plume of dirt and debris into the sky, which rained down into the trench.

"What the hell was that?" Anna yelled.

"A tank..." Harriet replied nervously, feeling herself start to shake.

"A bloody tank? What the hell's a revolver going to do against a tank?"

"Just shut up and stay down!" Harriet lifted herself again and peeked over the lip of the trench. The Germans were on the runway, close enough for her to hear them shouting orders to each other as they advanced. The distant battle was now right in front of her, with ever closer silhouettes being lit by muzzle flashes. She turned and looked behind, looking for an escape route. There were other trenches in the small copse of trees, but she didn't know where they all were, so jumping out and running could just as likely end up with her falling into another trench headfirst as anything else. They needed to move, though. The Germans were moving quickly, and if they kept coming, they'd soon be amongst the trees. She reached into the bottom of the trench and grabbed Anna, pulling her up and holding her finger to her lips. "We need to get out of here," she whispered. Anna nodded nervously while turning to look in the direction of the battle. "Hey..." Harriet pulled at her sleeve, focusing her attention. "We need to slip out of the trench, staying as low as we can so we don't make a target of ourselves, then we crawl on our bellies to the back of the trees and into the ditch. I'll lead the way; you need to stay right behind me. OK?"

"We can't stay here?"

"You want to?"

"Let's get out of here!" a voice shouted from another trench. Harriet turned to watch two shadowy figures jump out of the ground and start to run. Anna went to follow, and Harriet instinctively grabbed her and pulled her back into the trench, just as a long burst of machine gun fire let rip, accompanied by other guns, sending a wave of bullets ricocheting through the woods and cutting down the runners in their tracks. Harriet held on to Anna while listening to the Germans shouting, and working out from their yells that at least a few of them were now heading towards the trees.

"What now?" Anna whispered.

"Well, you wanted to stay..." Harriet checked her pistol, then lifted herself up and looked out of the trench again, and quickly ducked back down at the sight of a group of Germans almost right in front of her. She pulled Anna face down into the bottom of the trench and dropped on top of her, hiding their pale faces and hoping the Germans wouldn't look too close. "Not a sound," she whispered in Anna's ear as the crack of branches breaking under boots echoed around the trees from right above. She could feel her heart pounding so hard she expected the Germans could hear it a mile away. She held her breath and pushed tight into Anna as a nearby German called out, asking his friends if they could see anything. Before anything else could happen, a machine gun rattled away in long bursts from the rear of the trees, supported by rifle fire, and a loud cry of 'charge' went up. Harriet opened her eyes and lifted up, pulling herself up to the edge of the trench and peering over as a strong British counterattack swept through the trees, and into the flank of the advancing Germans. The tank that had been sitting in the middle of the runway, shooting into anything that moved with its main gun and machine guns, was lit up as it was targeted by anti aircraft guns and hit from three directions at the same time. Anna was quickly by Harriet's side, watching as the Germans were pushed back by a fierce bayonet charge. It looked like the entire British army was running across the runway, chasing the Germans off into the fields beyond. It was a deafening battle, with casualties on both sides falling everywhere, but the enemy were quickly overwhelmed, leaving only cracks of rifle fire and shouts in the distance, while the tank on the runway burned fiercely.

"Ma'am…" a voice said from behind the trench, and Harriet spun around with her pistol at the ready. "Ma'am!" MacInnes repeatedly desperately, with his arms held in the air.

"Don't sneak up on people!" Harriet scowled in an angry whisper.

"Lesson learned… Are you OK?"

"Yes. Yes, some others didn't make it, though."

"OK, well, you'd better stay put for now. The RAF Regiment lads are off chasing the Hun. It looks like they've had enough for now, but we won't be sure for a while. I'll come back later." He gave Harriet a nod, and she smiled in reply as he ran off through the trees.

"You OK?" Harriet asked Anna.

"Yeah… What do we do now?"

"Watch and wait."

"Have they gone?"

"Hopefully."

"OK, good." Anna threw her backpack out of the trench and jumped out after it.

"What the hell?" Harriet seethed, then jumped out after the young woman and followed her through the trees. "Get back here; it's not safe!" She hissed in a loud whisper. She looked around, pistol at the ready, as she followed Anna in a crouched walk until finally, they came on the bodies of those who'd tried to run. She dropped to one knee and leant against a tree trunk, keeping watch while Anna checked them over. It was the Dakota crew. The pilot and co pilot were dead, shot in the back as they ran, and laid out side by side. The Navigator was nowhere to be seen, but after moving a little further through the woods, they found the Wireless Operator slumped against a tree with a hole in his chest. He'd made it a little further than the others, having taken a bullet in the back which passed straight through him and blew a hole in his chest, but the shock and blood loss from such a wound was always going to get him, and he'd finally sat down and quickly bled out. Anna checked his wound repeatedly, but even from her position on watch, Harriet could see that he was already dead. "Come on…" Harriet whispered as she knelt beside Anna. "He's gone." She put her arm around Anna's shoulder for a moment, then stood and pulled her to her feet before leading her back to their trench. They climbed back in and leant against the wall, pulling the blanket around their shoulders again, then looking out over the airfield and watching the tank burn. "I'm sorry," Harriet said after a while of silence.

"What for?"

"Your crew."

"They should have stayed in their trenches."

"They weren't to know. They were just scared, that's all. It's human."

"I know… I'm lucky I had you to keep me in line. If I was in their trench, I'd be with them now."

"Don't be so sure. I was about to do the same if you remember? They were just unlucky in their timing."

"You were going to crawl on your belly, so you weren't seen."

"I'm not sure that would have made any difference."

"I'm pretty sure it would, so thanks." She looked at Harriet and gave her a rare smile. Something that must have been difficult considering she'd just seen her crew massacred. Harriet smiled back, then went back to watching the tank burn as its ammunition started to cook in the heat and explode, round by round. They both shuddered each time one blew, and for a moment, they marvelled at the firework display in front of them, before coming down to the reminder that they were in Normandy and in harm's way. They stood watching for the entire night, with a brief interlude spent hiding in the bottom of a trench when an air raid came in and caused more havoc, just a few hours after the last of the German soldiers had been chased from the airfield. It was terrifying, and the scattered bombs shook the ground and filled the trench with dirt and branches. It was a brief attack by a handful of bombers, and it was over in minutes, though for Harriet, it felt like hours, with every blast fraying her nerves. It took everything she had to keep her composure, to try and be a rock of confidence for Anna, who stood firm the entire time and refused to succumb to emotion, much to Harriet's continued surprise and admiration. As much as Harriet tried to compose herself for Anna's sake, it was working both ways, and the stoic young woman kept Harriet's confidence up throughout the night.

Daybreak brought a fresh challenge, as the German artillery started a deadly morning chorus to shake the airfield. Harriet and Anna sunk down to the bottom of their trench once again as the explosions shook the airfield. It was like an unending headache of thumps, bang, bang, bang, as the guns fired, and boom, boom, boom, as the shells landed haphazardly, not hitting any target in particular, which made Harriet even more nervous in knowing that a random shell could land right on top of them. As she sat in the bottom of the trench huddled close to Anna, she thought of the stories Cas had told about his time in the trenches during the last war, and how the artillery barrages would go on for hours, or sometimes days. Hundreds of guns firing almost constantly. She couldn't begin to imagine what it had been like. The Germans had only been going a short while, and she was already considering jumping from her trench and running to the beach, ready to swim home if she couldn't find a boat. A thought that was only put out of her mind by the sound of Sabre Napier engines roaring overhead. She jumped to her feet and watched as a Squadron of Typhoons crossed the airfield at treetop height, heading in the direction of the artillery.

"What is it?" Anna asked, as she stood by Harriet's side.

"Typhoons..." Harriet replied excitedly, and they watched as smoke spiralled into the air some miles away while the Typhoons circled and dived, and silenced the artillery for good. Watching them do their job had Harriet smiling, and feeling even more desperate than ever to get back home. An eventuality made all the more possible several hours later by the sound of Spitfires, two of which flew along the length of the runway in the late afternoon. Harriet and Anna had spent the entire day in their trench watching the fighters come and go, refuelling and rearming, before heading back up to continue their fight. The Spitfires climbed and circled to cover a Dakota, which quickly swooped in and ran up to the same place the last had landed. "Home time!" Harriet said as she looked at Anna and smirked.

## Chapter 13

## Murder

The trip back to England was a fraught one for Harriet, who sat at the back of the Dakota loaded with wounded soldiers, some of whom had been on the aircraft that was shot up the previous evening, including the two whose wounds Anna had dressed. While some of the passengers were the same, it smelled the same, too, reeking of smoke, cordite, blood, and burned flesh, which didn't make the flight any more pleasant. The take off had been a nervous time, and Harriet had kept her eyes firmly closed until she felt the aeroplane banking east and heading for the coast. The pair of Spitfires that had escorted the Dakota in had stuck around to escort it home again, which was a slight relief, but all the same, she couldn't wait to be back on the ground in England. She didn't like not being in control of her own fate. At least in a fighter, she could see what was coming, and take action to avoid anything dangerous. Sitting in the back of a Dakota with no view of the sky around her was terrifying. Anna had gone to work as soon as the supplies had been unloaded from the Dakota, helping the Nightingale that had come in with the crew to pick up the wounded. She hadn't slept all night, neither of them had, but she looked as fresh and energetic as when Harriet had first met her the day before, as she went about checking dressings and making the wounded comfortable for the flight home. Being back on a Dakota didn't seem to bother her in the slightest, and Harriet took some comfort in seeing how the young Nurse threw herself into her work. If she was scared, she wasn't going to let her patients see it. She marched up and down the cabin confidently, giving comfort where it was needed, and the occasional stern words to those making a nuisance of themselves.

When they finally touched down in England, just as the sun was setting, and the wounded had been unloaded into a fleet of waiting ambulances, Harriet and Anna walked over towards the control tower. It was a beautiful summer's evening, with warm orange and blue skies. It was a world away from the trench where they'd spent their night praying the German artillery didn't get them, and that another counterattack didn't come in at dawn. They were both exhausted.

"Here you are," Anna said as they stood by the door into the control tower. "The Duty Officer should be able to get you a ride back to your airfield."

"Thanks…" Harriet replied with a smile. "What is it for you now? Bath and a good sleep?"

"I'll find out when I report to my CO, I suppose. Hopefully, I'll get another crew and get back out to France as soon as I can."

"In that much of a hurry to go back?" Harriet raised an eyebrow in surprise at how keen Anna was to put her life back on the line.

"It's my job. As long as the fighting continues, there'll be wounded soldiers we need to get back home. I'm no good to them here."

"I suppose…"

"You'll be going back, won't you? Into combat, I mean?"

"I'll find out when I report to my CO…" She gave Anna a mischievous wink.

"You're a Wing Commander; I'm sure you'll be fine."

"It's not the first time I've been shot down. There's every chance I'll be given an Iron Cross for destroying another British aircraft." She smiled as Anna let out a laugh. "Good luck, Anna Outwood. Stay safe, and keep on being a good nurse. Your patients are lucky to have you." She held out her hand, which Anna shook warmly while fighting a blush.

"Thank you, and good luck to you too. Don't get shot down again."

"I'll do my best." Harriet smiled again, then turned to head into the tower.

"Wait!" Anna said, as she pulled the revolver from her belt and handed it to Harriet, who took it and looked at it for a moment. "Thanks for the loan."

"Hang on…" Harriet replied, then handed it back. "You'd better keep a hold of it. If the RAF aren't going to issue you one, you may as well have this. Just in case."

"I'm a Nurse… I shouldn't be armed. I can't..."

"Put it in your kitbag, and nobody will know. It's not for you to go around starting wars, but you need to be able to defend yourself if you're in harm's way again."

"But…"

"Or defend your patients..."

"I suppose… Won't you get into trouble? Isn't it issue?"

"Yes, but I lost it when I was shot down. Shame..." She gave Anna a nod. "I can make it an order, if it makes you feel any better?"

"Would you mind?"

"If anyone asks, you were issued it in Normandy when you were forced to defend yourself after being shot down. Orders of Wing Commander Cornwall, 13 Wing. Second Tactical Air Force."

"Yes, Ma'am." Anna stood smartly to attention and smiled, then marched away, stuffing the revolver into her battle dress jacket as she went. Harriet smiled to herself as she watched her go, still looking as confident and energetic as when she'd started.

Just minutes after entering the control tower, she was sitting in the co pilot's seat of a Dakota and heading to her home airfield on the Kent coast. She'd struck lucky with her timing when asking the Duty Officer if he could arrange a ride home for her. She was half expecting a train warrant and a long night of travelling, but instead, she was offered a ride by a Flight Lieutenant going up on a last minute air test after his Dakota's engine had been overhauled. It was needed for a dawn mission, so he had to make the most of the last light of day to make sure it was OK. He was confident, yet overall engaging and pleasant for the short journey, despite his amusingly respectful attempts at flirtation. Despite her exhaustion, Harriet found untapped reserves of enthusiasm when he offered her the controls once they were up and cruising, and she thoroughly enjoyed throwing the giant American built transport aeroplane around the sky. It wasn't a fighter, but it was a dream to fly. A typically American aeroplane, big and powerful, with instruments and dials easy to read and where they needed to be. Taking the controls passed the trip and had her smiling, but she handed over when it came time to land. She hadn't landed one before and was in no hurry to injure herself, not after surviving what she had.

It was a quick turnaround, and the pilot was taking off again the moment she'd jumped out onto the runway, in a hurry to get back home before last light. Harriet stopped and watched the Dakota climb away, and as its engines faded to a distant hum, she headed across the airfield, making her way back to Station Headquarters and thinking through what had happened. She had a letter to write, but for the first time in a while, she didn't have a clue how to write it. She hadn't even begun to process what had happened to Carrie, who'd selflessly and bravely sacrificed herself to protect her from what would have been certain death. Even the thought of it made her stomach spin and her breathing race with a feeling of deep and painful guilt that made her nauseous. She knew as she walked that it wasn't the time to write the letter, and a large whisky or two and a long sleep would help. Or at least that's what she hoped. She was exhausted and starving, and emotions were close to the surface. She drifted through the quiet headquarters building and made her way to her office, where she slumped into her chair and let out a sigh of relief to be home. There was an instant feeling of regret, and she cursed herself for sitting down. Going straight to her room would have been the better decision, and she quickly found herself struggling to keep her eyes open as she felt dizzy with tiredness. She leant forward and put her head in her hands, resting her elbows on her desk and closing her eyes for a moment, and drifting into a deep and instant sleep, until a sharp scream shocked her awake. She sat up with her eyes wide open and her heart racing.

"What the hell are you doing here?!" Nicole shouted angrily from across the room. She was standing in the doorway and shaking visibly.

"Hello to you, too!" Harriet replied with a scowl.

"Idiot!" Nicole shouted as she ran across the room while Harriet stood from her desk, still more than a little shell shocked and struggling to join the dots in understand what was going on. The daze was knocked from her as Nicole slapped her hard across the face. "Idiot!" she repeated, then wrapped her arms right around Harriet and started crying. Harriet put her arms around Nicole and held her for a moment as she sobbed.

"Nicole, are you OK?" Cas asked as he ran into the office. He stopped in his tracks as he saw Harriet, and stood silently staring for a moment. "What the hell are you doing here?" he asked, echoing Nicole's sentiment.

"Well, that's some welcome!" Harriet blustered in reply, as Nicole released her from the hug and stood looking her in the eyes. "She slaps me across the face, and neither of you has taken a minute to ask me how I am!"

"Harry, we thought you were dead..." Cas said as he walked over to her. He was genuine, his eyes said as much, and seeing her was clearly something he hadn't expected.

"What? Don't be ridiculous! I sent a message yesterday saying I was alright!"

"I can assure you it didn't get as far as us; we thought you were lost over Normandy when you encountered those 262s. My God, Harry. It's good to see you." He let himself smile as he put his hand on her shoulder to make sure she was real.

"You're still an idiot!" Nicole said angrily, trying hard not to smile. "I thought you were a ghost!"

"Sorry..." Harriet replied. "Honestly, I sent a message. My engine was shot through, so I put down on an advance landing ground in Normandy. I got a ride back on a Dakota this evening."

"Don't worry about that," Cas said. "We're just happy to have you back. The wing are going to be relieved!"

"Not just the wing," Nicole said, as she finally let herself smile while drying the tears from her eyes.

"Is everything OK? With the wing, I mean?" Harriet asked nervously.

"Yes..." Cas replied. "Your replacement has been during a fine job." He nodded at Nicole.

"My replacement? I was gone five minutes, and you replaced me?"

"You were gone long enough, and reports saw you blown out of the sky..."

"That wasn't me..." Harriet said as a wave of sadness hit her again. "I don't suppose anyone's heard from Carrie Stone?"

"No..." Cas replied with a sympathetic half smile. "We lost three to the 262s, you included, and four damaged with one wounded. Unfortunately, young Stone was one of those that didn't come back."

"Have you written the letter yet?" Harriet asked Nicole.

"Yes... Though I haven't posted it." She sorted through her papers and handed the letter to Harriet, who quickly read it through.

"Your words are beautiful..."

"Thank you. She was a brave pilot. I wanted her family to know that."

"Would you mind if I wrote my own to go with it? I'd like to go and deliver them by hand; her parents don't live far from here."

"Of course. You don't need mine; I won't be insulted."

"No. No, I think it shows how well she was thought of to get one from both of us."

"When did you last sleep?" Cas asked.

"Not since I was last in my bed."

"You should probably get some rest in that case."

"I could do with a drink first."

"I think I can help with that. Come on, both of you. I've got just the thing for the occasion."

"The occasion?" Harriet asked, as she and Nicole followed him to his office.

"The prodigal daughter's return, of course. Not every day somebody comes back from the dead... Though in your case, it's more frequent than most."

"Shut up!"

"He's got a point," Nicole added.

"You can shut up, too! It's not like I had any say in it!"

"You're back; that's what's important," Cas said as he handed her a whisky, poured from a small bottle he'd had hidden away at the back of his desk cupboard. "Welcome home." The three clinked their glasses, then Harriet took a mouthful of the whisky. It was incredibly smooth, better than most she could remember having.

"That's good... Why haven't you shared it before now?"

"That bottle of whisky is older than you; it's for special occasions."

"I was literally a prisoner of the Gestapo not so long ago; you'd have thought getting home after that would be enough!" she blustered.

"Does this mean I'm going back to the squadron?" Nicole asked, ignoring Harriet's complaining.

"Sorry…" Cas replied.

"No, don't be. She's welcome to the paperwork and late nights; I'll be back at my squadron tomorrow morning!

Harriet fell exhausted into her bed, her body and mind switching off in unison the moment her head hit the pillow. She hadn't even had the time to get cleaned up, or even out of her clothes. She sat on her bed to kick off her boots, and didn't wake until the next morning, stiff and cold, to the point that it was the shivering that woke her. It took a moment for her to recognise her surroundings, but as she dragged herself to her feet and started pulling off her filthy uniform that stunk of smoke, sweat, and dirt, the recent memories returned and reminded her exactly why she felt as rough as she did. It was early, so after scrubbing the smoke and dirt from her hair and pores, she headed to her office to get on with the letter that she knew she had to write, despite not knowing what to say, or how to say it.

"Morning," Harriet said as she stepped into Cas' office. She'd heard him in the corridor while putting the finishing touches to her letter, which she signed and folded into an envelope. There were a number of screwed up balls of paper in her wastebasket, and she knew if she read through this one, she'd find a reason for it to join them. She'd said all that needed to be said; rewording it wouldn't make the news any better.

"What are you doing...?" he started.

"Don't!" she stopped him before he finished, making him smile and nod at the point she was making.

"I just thought you'd be sleeping in, that's all. The weather's miserable over France, with cloud down to the ground. The met types are saying it's set in for the day, so I'm going to stand the wing down, give them chance to get their aeroplanes overhauled, and let the pilots catch up on their sleep."

"Very decent of you."

"I know, I'm considerate like that." He returned her smirk. "That means you can knock off, too, of course. I can't imagine you got much sleep in Normandy."

“I'm fine…"

"But?"

"If you're standing the wing down, I need to go off station for a while to visit Carrie Stone's parents."

"I see…"

"I need to do it in person. She literally died saving my life; it's the least I can do."

"OK…" he replied, while standing purposefully from his desk. "Let's go and do it."

"You're coming?"

"And you have absolutely no say in it." He gave her a look that she knew meant that arguing would be pointless, so she nodded and smiled, knowing that having him with her for support would be exactly what she needed. "I'll drive." He walked across the room and took his service cap from the hatstand. Together they walked through Headquarters and down to his Aston Martin, which he soon had roaring through the country lanes, and heading along the coast to the village where Carrie's parents ran the village shop. On the way, they passed the hospital where Harriet had recovered on her return from Dunkirk, and she smiled briefly at the memories. It all seemed so very long ago, and so many things had changed since then. She'd had no idea what lay ahead when she'd returned to the strange country that used to be her home, and she could never have imagined that she'd be having to let her friend's parents know that their daughter was dead, shot out of the sky over France. Her stomach started to churn as Cas turned into the Main Street, and pulled up outside the shop.

"Do you want me to come in?" he asked in a soft and considerate tone, knowing what was about to happen.

"No, I should do it alone," Harriet replied while shaking her head. She gave him a nervous smile, then after taking a deep breath, she got out of the car and straightened her uniform. "Here goes," she said to herself, then marched over to the shop and stepped inside.

"Wing Commander Cornwall!" Carrie's father said as he looked at her from behind the counter. They'd met before, when Harriet had brought a letter home from America for Carrie, along with some bits and pieces from America that were hard to get in England. "Elizabeth, it's Wing Commander Cornwall!" he called excitedly into the back of the shop. "Congratulations on your promotion," he said as he turned back to Harriet. "Carrie told us all about it, and how you'd promoted her, too!" Every word was like a knife in Harriet's heart, and it was all she could do not to turn and run out of the shop.

"Wing Commander! Please, come in and have a cup of tea, won't you? We were just about to have one; the kettle's just boiled!" Carrie's mum said as she came through to the front of the shop. "Close up and lock the door, Michael. Put the sign in the window asking them to come back later." She waved Harriet in and hurried into the back room. Harriet nodded uncomfortably and walked slowly and painfully, feeling like she could pass out at any minute, while Michael hurried past her to lock up the shop before joining them in the kitchen, and showing Harriet to a seat at the table.

"What brings you into this neck of the woods?" Michael asked, as he took a seat at the table while Elizabeth poured from the large teapot that had been sitting on the table when she entered the room. Harriet's stomach twinged, and not for the first time she wished she was in battle somewhere. In her innocence, a small part of her had hoped she'd just be able to break the news and run, despite knowing full well that she'd never have been able to do that, as preferable as it may be to the torture she was currently enduring. She swallowed hard and composed herself, then sipped the tea to wet her mouth. Whatever she was feeling wasn't anywhere close to what the people who were so happy to see her were about to feel, and she knew she had no right to be thinking of herself at such a time.

"There's something I need to talk to you both about," Harriet said, as Elizabeth sat at the table beside her husband. Their smiles were starting to look more than a little nervous.

"It's Carrie, isn't it?" Elizabeth asked.

"No…" Michael gasped painfully.

"I'm sorry…" Harriet said. They were both instantly crushed, but stoically stayed upright and fought the tears while staring silently at Harriet, waiting for more. "We've been over France supporting the invasion since the first day, intercepting German reinforcements and taking out tanks to try and help our troops on the ground secure a beachhead and get a foothold on the continent. We go over three or four times a day sometimes, and Carrie has been on every sortie, leading the way fearlessly, and playing her part as only she could. It was on one of these missions that she was shot down by a German fighter." She felt her heart squeeze tight as the words left her mouth. A wave of nausea swept over her, and she felt cold sweat on the back of her neck. "I can't give you all the details, not yet, but I can tell you that in her last moments she saved my life, and…" She felt a tear run down her cheek, and the words just wouldn't come out. "I'm so sorry." She put her hand to her mouth and tried to compose herself. She took the envelope from her inner pocket and slid it across the table. Elizabeth opened it and took out both letters, Harriet's and Nicole's, and handed one to Michael. They read them closely, and swapped, all while Harriet sat in silence and tried to breathe, despite feeling like there was a huge weight on her chest that was crushing the life from her.

"She loved flying with you, you know," Elizabeth said as she lowered the letter. Her hands were shaking, but she was managing somehow to remain composed. "She loved everything about you, had done since the day she met you in the hospital, and you told her what it would take to be a pilot."

"She did as you said," Michael added. "She studied every night, she ran, she exercised, and did everything she could to give her a chance. She was so happy when she got selected for pilot training, she wanted to find you and tell you, but you'd long moved on, of course. Malta, wasn't it?" Harriet nodded. It's all she had; she couldn't speak. "Then you turned up in America. She wrote to us when she could, and she said you were there, and that you'd made her an officer. Proud doesn't begin to describe it." His voice started to waiver, and Elizabeth held his hand.

"The only thing that made her more proud was when she joined your squadron, and you made her your number two…" Elizabeth continued. "She wrote, she always wrote… We have so many letters from her, and almost every one of them talks about how great you are. She worshipped you." She forced a smile, and Harriet felt herself shudder as tears flooded down her cheeks. She screamed at herself inside to get control, and pull herself together. She had no right to be crying, not while they were suffering so much.

"I…" Harriet tried to talk, but she couldn't find the words. She just wanted to tell them how sorry she was. It was the only word in her head. Elizabeth stood and walked around the table, then helped Harriet stand and gave her an unexpected hug.

"She'd have flown without you if roles were reversed. She wouldn't have liked it, but she'd have got on with it and continued to do her duty, and you've got to do the same, understand?" she said softly as she held Harriet. "Now, come on. You take a deep breath and dry those tears." Michael joined them and handed Harriet a handkerchief, which she took and dried her cheeks, having let go of Elizabeth.

"I'm sorry… I didn't mean to get so upset in front of you," Harriet said as she tried to compose herself. "I just wanted to be the one to tell you, and I wanted to do it in person."

"We're truly grateful that you took the time; we know you're busy."

"Not too busy for this," Harriet shook her head while still drying her eyes. "I'll bring you her things, her uniform. I'll make sure her medals come, too, and her DFC."

"You're welcome here any time. Any time at all. There'll always be a cup of tea and a friendly face waiting for you."

"I'm proud of her," Harriet said. "She was the best pilot, and more devoted to her duty than anyone in the wing."

"She was devoted to you." Elizabeth smiled and nodded.

"I'll give you some space alone," Harriet said, having taken a deep breath.

"You're welcome to stay for tea?"

"I'd better go," Harriet shook her head. "I'll come back with Carrie's things as soon as I can..." They both nodded, grateful for her giving them the space to grieve privately. They'd held it all in, and the tension in the room was close to breaking point. "I'll show myself out." She smiled, then quickly turned and marched away, through the shop, and out into the gloomy fresh air, which she desperately gasped in.

"Are they open yet? I need my shopping!" one of a pair of middle aged women queueing outside asked, as Harriet almost marched into them. She fired daggers at them, not able to speak, and they both backed up.

"Oh..." the other said as the penny dropped. "It's their girl, isn't it? Young Carrie?" Harriet ignored them and simply climbed into Cas' car.

"You OK?" he asked as he started the engine.

"Is it too early for the pub?"

"That bad?"

"Just drive... Please, just drive." She looked out of the window at the shop, and Cas did as she asked, taking off down the street quickly.

"Do you want to talk about it?"

"I told them that their daughter was dead, and they told me how much she loved flying with me. I've never felt like such a fraud in my life!"

"You're not a fraud," he replied softly, and reached over to put his hand on hers to comfort her. "She did love flying with you; they all do. Which means that while it's a genuine tragedy she died, she truly loved and lived while she was alive, and her parents know it. That'll be a great comfort to them."

"Thank you..." She gave his hand a squeeze as she forced a smile. "All I could do was sit there and cry like an idiot."

"If it was me in their place, I'd be reassured knowing that losing her was so painful for you that you cried."

"This is exactly why I asked you to come with me today..." she smiled.

"I'm pretty sure I didn't give you any say in it..." He gave her a wink, going along with the game.

"Is it really too early for the pub?"

"Yes! Besides, I have something better in mind."

"What?"

"How about we take off into London for Lunch? Nobody will miss us for a few hours. Besides, who are they going to report us to?"

"The Savoy?"

"Do you think I'm made of money?"

"What? You're paying too? I'm in!"

"Walked into that, didn't I?"

"Can we go to Fortnum's while we're there? I want some tea."

"You go through more tea than the rest of us put together."

"Nonsense! I can only buy a bit of the good stuff at a time. It doesn't last, and that dishwater the cooks send isn't even deserving of being called tea. You'd think the Station Commander would do something about that."

"You'd think the Station Commander would make Fortnum's tea standard in all messes? Again, I ask, do you think I'm made of money?"

"You're buying the tea, too? This London trip is sounding better and better! Where else shall you take me while we're there?"

"I'm not saying another word..." He gave her a smile, which was returned. Her eyes were red from the tears, but the bickering was helping her get over what had just happened, temporarily at least. It continued all the way to London, until they had to put on a public display of professionalism while shopping. It wouldn't do for two senior RAF officers to be seen bickering playfully in public, the Air Ministry would frown on it, and while the public information posters on the walls said 'walls have ears', warning the public that careless talk could get back to the Germans, it wasn't the Germans that were the problem in this case. The Air Ministry had ears and eyes everywhere in central London. There would be a department somewhere who knew that the station's two senior officers were shopping in London instead of marching their pilots up and down a parade square while they waited for the low cloud to clear.

After shopping, a very nice lunch at The Savoy, and an unscripted trip to Harrods, where Cas bought Harriet the surprise gift of a small bottle of her favourite Chanel perfume, they headed back to their station. The weather had stayed miserable, with very low cloud hugging the ground, and back in the office, they had tea while working through some paperwork that needed doing. Cas tried to get Harriet to go back to her room and get some rest, but she insisted on staying and helping. She didn't want to be alone with her thoughts, and they both knew it. Cas didn't mind, he enjoyed the company, and

Harriet welcomed the distraction of having Ginny and Robbie coming and going, passing comments, and generally complaining about the easy lives of pilots, who were able to sleep in and lounge around when the weather was bad, while the non flying types still had to work. Harriet simply shrugged and told them both that they had no right to complain at her for their poor career choices, something that made her laugh, and them gasp in shock at her mischievousness, which simply prompted them to have other comments when they next saw her. It passed the day, and kept Harriet's mind from going to gloomy places, as did the drinks they all had in the Mess that evening. Most of the pilots had slept the day away, and caught up on writing letters home and other personal admin. It had been a long stretch of fighting without a day off, and another wasn't looking like coming any time soon. The previously agreed long weekend had been cancelled as soon as the invasion started, with every Typhoon being needed to fly air cover and keep the Germans under the cosh so they didn't have time to reorganise and counterattack, at least not effectively.

The day off was to be the last the wing had for the next two months. The invasion of the continent had been a success, just about, though the Germans were still fighting hard to keep the Allies in Normandy. It had been brutal, in the air as well as on the ground. The Luftwaffe were still attacking from airfields further east, though Spitfires and Lightnings tended to be the ones who dealt with fighter and bomber incursions, leaving the Typhoons to continue their work attacking ground targets. 13 Wing flew a mix of missions, either pre planned targets such as depots and garrisons, or marauder operations, where they'd fly around their area of responsibility shooting up anything German that moved. Cab rank missions started to become a more frequent assignment as the weeks rolled on, and the armies on the ground established their tactics. Squadrons of ground attack aircraft would patrol designated sectors until they were called down to attack a specific position by the Forward Air Controllers, usually RAF officers attached to the infantry, and speaking directly to the squadron commanders by radio from their armoured cars. It was an effective strategy that had worked well in Sicily and Italy, and was doing just as well in Normandy. The call would come in, and the enemy position would be marked with smoke, then minutes later a section, flight, or even a squadron of Typhoons would descend with their rockets and obliterate the target, leaving the position burning and smoking, weakened ready for the infantry and tanks on the ground to finish off. Occasionally the entire wing would be called down, when the enemy where a holding a particularly strong position, or were spread over a wide area. When it happened, it was tremendous, and devastating for the enemy. The anti aircraft guns weren't as numerous as they had been, either, even around the reinforced positions, and those mobile units that did put up a fight usually did so at great risk to themselves. Whenever they shot at one Typhoon, they could be sure there was another one watching, which would quickly descend and wipe them out.

The carnage continued until early August, when the American 3rd Army finally broke out of St Lo, which they'd planned to capture in the first days of the invasion, and pushed behind the German lines in Normandy. The Americans had been held by a defence much fiercer than had been anticipated, something that took a great deal of breaking. Fortunately, the British and Canadians kept the majority of the German armies in Northern France, and almost all of their tanks and other armour, tied up around Caen, so they couldn't head for St Lo to push the Americans back. Those that tried were picked off by Typhoons, P47 Thunderbolts, and P51 Mustangs, who were just waiting for them to move. Had they got through, there was a danger of the entire Normandy offensive stalling, or even being pushed back. Reinforcements were still being rushed up to Caen by the German high command, but they couldn't break out any further. It was make or break, and every pilot was exhausted from the endless missions over Normandy, but not one of them would give up. They couldn't. The army needed them.

"Harry, you need to get the wing ready to go before first light in the morning," Cas said as he stepped into her office. It had been a long day, and after her evening meal, she'd headed to her office to finish off some paperwork before heading to bed for an early night.

"Go where?" She perked up a little from her drowsiness, and sat up in her chair.

"Normandy. Falaise, to be precise. The Germans are making a run for it." His voice was full of urgency.

"Caen's finally fallen?" she asked excitedly. It was supposed to have been captured on the first day of the invasion, and would have been had the Germans not placed some of their toughest and most battle hardened divisions there, including fanatical SS divisions who fought to the last man, and refused to give up even the smallest piece of ground. The fighting had been bloody, to say the least, and the wing had flown in support of the British and Canadian armies there a number of times.

"Not yet, but it's virtually surrounded, and could go at any time. The Germans are trying to get as many of their trapped armies out and across the River Seine before they're cut off and wiped out, and the SS divisions are trying to open a corridor for them to escape."

"Orders?"

"You'll be going in to support the 1st Polish Armoured Division; they're there attached to the Canadians. Reports are coming in tonight that the SS are hitting them hard." He handed her a map with the Polish positions marked on it. "If they can hold through the night, you'll be the first on the scene as soon as there's enough light for you to make out your targets. "The forward air controller will give you your targets once you're over Normandy."

"We'll do our best."

"I know you will. You'd better get yourself to bed; it's going to be an early start." He gave her a smile, and she nodded in agreement. "This could be it; you know. If we can stop them from breaking out, Hitler will lose two entire armies, and it'll open the door to the rest of Europe."

"No pressure, then…" she frowned.

"Well, if you could get it all wrapped up and finished by Christmas, I'd be grateful. The whole thing has dragged on a bit." He smirked, as did she, as she stood from her desk and grabbed her flying jacket and service cap from the hat stand.

"I'll do what I can... Though I could do with a holiday," she sighed as they walked from her office.

"It wasn't that long ago you were sunning yourself in Hawaii while the rest of us were busy fighting a war."

"That was literally years ago!" she scowled. "Besides, you may have heard about that big battle that happened in Hawaii while I was there... It wasn't exactly a stress free week at the beach! Well, not entirely... Anyway, you can't complain. You had a few months off in the sun, too, if I remember right."

"I was a prisoner of war!"

"Still..."

"You're impossible."

"And I'm right!" she laughed. "It's OK; I won't make you say it."

"Thanks!"

"I really could do with a holiday, though. We all could. The girls have been at it constantly for months; they're flying half asleep at times."

"I know..."

"We need a refit, our Typhoons are worse for wear, and I need more pilots. We're on the last of our reserves already, any more losses, and we won't be able to put up three complete squadrons."

"I know..."

'I'm just saying!"

"I know, and I'm not arguing. I'm meeting with HQ to discuss just that tomorrow morning."

"It's not that we don't want to fight; we do, more than anything."

"Harry..."

"What?"

"I'll take care of it. Go and get some sleep."

"I know you will. You know, we really couldn't have asked for somebody better to look after us. You do a great job."

"If this is your way of showing me you're so tired that you're delirious, it's working..." he replied with a frown, not used to her saying something so openly complimentary. Usually, it was teasing, and bickering, and genuine compliments said so openly were rare.

"I mean it. It takes somebody with a lot of experience, and years behind them, to be able to do the job you do," she said with a smirk.

"And there it is!" He shook his head as they stepped out into the warm evening air. "Get to bed."

"Goodnight!" She walked away with a bounce in her step, smirking to herself as she went. She looked over her shoulder to see him still standing and watching her leave and gave him a wave, which he returned before smiling and walking away.

Despite living on the edge of near exhaustion, sleep didn't come easy that night. Before going to bed, she briefed her squadron commanders on the early start, which involved some excited conversation about the possibility of the Germans being pushed back, especially from Nicole, who'd been on fire with French passion since the invasion had started. She was as exhausted as everyone else, but the thought of kicking the Germans out of France once and for all gave her a near unlimited source of energy. Gabi, the Polish pilot, was another that was fired up for a fight, especially when she heard that they were to fly in support of the Polish army. She rarely smiled, but news of the mission did the job, and she was the happiest she'd been since Harriet had met her in 1940. Whether it was the excitement, or the burden of worry she'd felt since the day she'd been given the job of leading an all female wing into battle, there wasn't a thing that Harriet could do to get to sleep. She spent the night tossing and turning, until she finally gave up and dragged herself out of bed to get ready for the day. It was August, first light wouldn't be too far away anyway, at least what was her reasoning when she left for the dispersal, where she talked with Jo about the aircraft availability before having a cup of tea and watching the starry sky, and finally feeling tired enough to sleep. Much to her annoyance.

The wing were in the air as the eastern sky turned royal blue, with a silver slither of light heralding the approaching dawn running low across the horizon. They climbed and crossed the Channel, passing over shipping lanes busy with the constant stream of ships passing back and forth between France and England, ferrying stores and supplies to the beachheads, and returning the wounded. Soon they were over the beaches, and Harriet called up the forward air controllers while heading in the direction of the artillery flashes surrounding Caen, suggesting battles were already raging in every direction. She picked out the hill where the Polish were holding their position, and received the light signals from the ground identifying friendly forces, then watched as a flare lit up a whole line of German tanks parked side by side on the edge of a tree line facing the Poles.

"Valkyrie Wing, standby and watch my targeting," Harriet said as she arrived over the target and flipped her Typhoon upside down, then pulled back on her stick and dived at the tanks Her tummy flipped, and she steadied her gaze on the closest tank, not flinching when lines of machine gun tracer came up towards her in the inky blue pre sunrise darkness, coning around her aeroplane and somehow bending away as though some sort of shield was pushing the bullets from her. She took a deep breath, then as she pulled out of her dive, she let go with her first two rockets. There wasn't time to see if they hit their target; she was moving so fast that she could only pass the line of German tanks firing her rockets, pair after pair, before finishing off with her cannons as the world around her was turned into golden daylight by the explosions leaping into the air from behind her. "Alright, Marseillaise, your turn," she called as she pulled up and right, getting her first view of the burning carnage she'd sewn along the line of tanks. Nicole led her squadron down, sending her rockets into the tanks, which were now rapidly trying to disperse. One after another, all twelve of her Typhoons came down and hammered the German position while Harriet circled and kept watch. "Dagger

Squadron, check the artillery at the rear of the German position. That's your target!" she called as she saw the muzzle flash of heavy guns.

"Understood," AP replied. "Dagger Squadron, targets three o'clock. Tally Ho!" Her squadron dropped the same as Nicole's, one after another in a long line, and ripped the German artillery position to pieces. There was tracer zipping into the sky from every direction, but it was still before dawn, and while Harriet and her Typhoons could pick out targets on the ground, it was hard for the Germans to see the aircraft until it was too late, their dark shadowy silhouettes merging with the dark western sky, which is where they all attacked from, making themselves hard targets. "Yankee, your turn. Side by side, light up everything in between." She watched as Nicole and AP's squadrons climbed and circled, while Bunny led her Typhoons in by flights, flying wingtip to wingtip in three waves of four, and firing indiscriminately at everything and anything between the burning front line of tanks and the blazing artillery positions to the rear. Harriet's eyes opened wide as her instincts were proved to be right, and the explosions of the rockets showed hundreds, if not thousands, of German soldiers either running or being blown into the air by Bunny's attack. Just minutes after Harriet had started the attack, it was over, and she led the wing to a large ALG close to the coast, where the entire wing was rearmed and refuelled within half an hour and were back over the target area as the sun started to climb over the horizon. It was easy to find; the destruction of their previous visit was still sending palls of black smoke into the sky from the burning tanks, trucks, and whatever else they'd managed to hit. As they approached, a desperate call came in from the forward controller, advising that SS infantry units were advancing on the most forward Polish positions. "Yankee, get down there and hold them off. Cut the grass!" she ordered, sending Bunny in with her Americans, still the wing's best at low level flying. She watched as Bunny's Typhoons attacked in pairs, running along the line of attack below treetop height, and shooting up the advancing Germans with cannon fire and rockets, scorching a deadly accurate line in the ground between them and the Polish positions, which were only a stone's throw away from the attack. AP was sent in next to hit the Germans further back, the halftracks and trucks coming up with infantry support, which were quickly turned into a scattering of funeral pyres for their occupants as

AP led her squadron in a discriminating and considered attack, making sure each rocket was well spent, and getting the maximum return in terms of destruction for each. While AP did her work, Harriet sent Nicole to take care of a small convoy approaching from the direction of Caen, which she did expertly, leaving Harriet to fly along the road firing her rockets at anything moving to finish the job. With the second attack complete, they headed back to the ALG for rearming and refuelling, where they had to circle and wait while two other wings were refuelled and rearmed. Water canteens were passed to the pilots while they waited in their cockpits when they finally got on the ground. Not able to get out and stretch their legs, even if they wanted to. Allied aircraft were queueing for refuelling and rearming, and in the short time they were on the ground, Harriet was amazed at the number of aeroplanes she saw. Typhoons and Spitfires filled the sky.

On their return to their target, they were informed that the German attack on the Polish positions had been broken, though the fighting during the night had forced open a narrow corridor, and German units were making a run for safety. The wing was sent to help stop them, along with other Typhoons and American P47 Thunderbolts, which took it in turns to attack by squadrons along the length of the corridor. It was carnage, and Harriet's wing had to wait a while for their turn. When they were finally allowed into the fight, Harriet led her wing along the escape route in pairs, heading for Caen. Everything that moved was shot at. Trucks, tanks, horse drawn carts, and units of infantry. She led, firing her rockets and guns simultaneously, then pulling up and out of the way while the squadrons carried on the run. By the time they'd finished, a mile long stretch of land was burning, along with everything on or around it, and they were soon heading back to the ALG and making way for an American squadron.

The rest of the morning was much the same, with the wing refuelling and rearming, before being tasked back into what had quickly become known as the Falaise Gap, the place where the besieged German army was trying desperately to escape the now fierce assault on Caen by the British and Canadian armies. Caen was almost broken, and Normandy was almost won. The wing had gone back to England for lunch, and were back for more fighting in the afternoon, this time with Cas flying a spare Typhoon. He'd insisted on coming over and seeing the destruction for himself after Harriet had reported what was happening. He would often tag along with the wing on their trips to France, flying as an observer, and staying out of the way, but happy to jump in and shoot up the Germans if Harriet gave him permission, which she always did. For the afternoon trip to Normandy, he'd volunteered to fly as Harriet's Number Two. She'd declined the offer previously, choosing to just fly alone after losing Carrie. She wouldn't admit as much, but she couldn't put herself in a position where somebody would think they had to die for her again, and even the thought of having a Number Two made her stomach turn. Something had changed, though. Seeing Normandy that morning, she knew things were different. They hadn't seen a Luftwaffe aircraft the entire time, the Spitfires were keeping them well away, and she was confident that Cas wouldn't do anything stupid. Or at least she hoped. Once across the Channel, they were tasked to search the countryside for targets of opportunity, of which there were plenty. Tanks and groups of infantry were everywhere, and the only frustration Harriet had was having limited ammunition. The wing split into flights and marauded around Falaise, hitting anything and everything that moved before reforming and heading to the ALG for ammunition and fuel. While they waited, they were told by the local Intelligence Officer that the Americans were pushing to close the gap, and they expected the remains of the German army to be fully encircled by the end of the day. They were tired but enthused, and the news fired them up for their afternoon of work, both around the gap where the Germans were trying to escape, and around Caen, where defenders were in a desperate battle to hold back to the Allied forces while their countrymen escaped. It was exhausting work, and it was bloody, yet each time they went back, Harriet was eternally grateful not to be on the ground. The thought of it gave her chills, and made her all the more careful not to get shot down in the middle of it all.

As the sun started to set, the wing was given the job of flying one last sortie over Falaise to see if any Germans were still stirring, before heading for the perimeter of the now closed encirclement that saw tens of thousands of German soldiers surrounded by the overwhelming power of the combined Allied armies. British,

Americans, Canadians, French, Poles, all had divisions waiting for the orders to finish the defenders.

"Follow me in," Harriet said as they arrived over the target area. "Shout out if you see a target, and keep your eyes open for German fighters." She checked over her shoulders to see the squadrons forming behind her, and after hearing from Nicole, AP, and Bunny confirm that they'd received and understood her instructions, she pushed the nose of her Typhoon down and headed for the ground. Cas stayed on her right wing, and slightly behind, and followed her down to treetop height. "My God..." she muttered as she followed the road of destruction, flying over a seemingly endless line of burned out tanks and trucks, with the corpses of German soldiers scattered between them like a carpet. It turned her stomach to see the destruction. Not able to pull her eyes from the gruesome scene, she estimated as they reached the American positions some miles later that she could have walked the whole route she'd just flown standing on nothing other than dead bodies. She'd done her job, and she'd done her best, and she knew that if she hadn't, the escaping Germans would set up defensive positions elsewhere that would eventually have to be breached, either by air power or the infantry on the ground, and at the same time she knew that she'd been involved in nothing more than murder. The Germans weren't even fighting back by the afternoon, just desperately running in the hope of having another night of being alive, and they'd been cut down in their thousands with the rockets and cannons of the Allied air forces, and a blanket of artillery from the ground troops slowly encircling them. While the Germans were the enemy, and had been responsible for the deaths of millions as they looted Europe, they were still human beings. She felt deeply despondent as they circled around to head back across the battleground in search of prey, as if there could be anything still alive in the hell below them. The bodies below were husbands, fathers, and sons, and while the Nazi regime was the embodiment of evil, she couldn't imagine the majority of the ordinary soldiers below wanting anything more than to keep their country safe, and protect their wives and children from whatever imagined threat their government had put in their minds. Hitler and his Nazi fanatics were the ones with the blood on their hands, and Harriet felt herself getting angry at them as she passed over the hell of Falaise, angrier than she'd ever been, even when she'd been in the hands of the Gestapo. They'd started a war that had killed millions, and ruined the lives of millions more. They'd forced people on all sides to do things they'd never do. They'd dragged her from the peace and innocence of a field in France, and thrown her into a war that had consumed the entire world. They'd made her a killer.

Sitting by himself in the middle of all the destruction, she saw a lone German soldier. He looked up at her as she approached, not bothered by her being there, not running, just watching, and waiting for the coming death.

"Let's go home..." she said as she pulled up and away, leading the wing into the blood red sky. She'd had enough of the war.

**The End.**

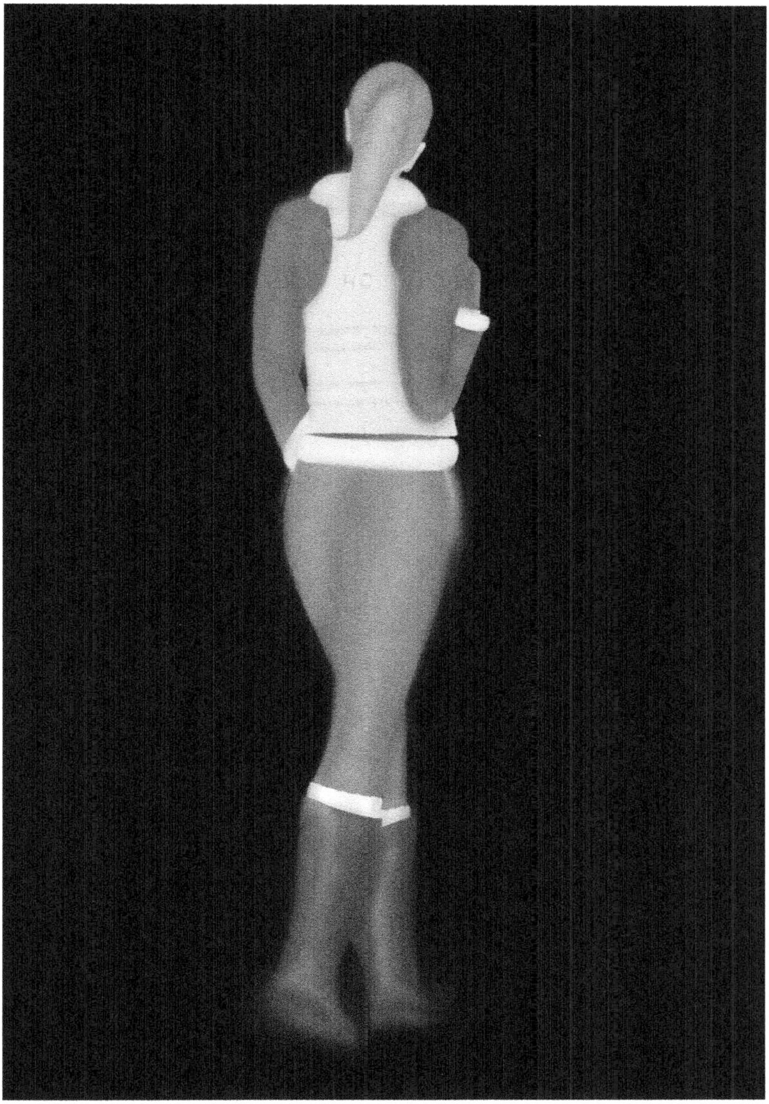

**HARRIET CORNWALL WILL RETURN**

**IN**

**'HARRY'S GAME – LAST OF THE FEW'**

## Titles in the Harry's Game Series

**Harry's Game – First of the Few**

Published in November 2019

**Harry's Game – Hell's Corner**

Published in February 2020

**Harry's Game – Shadows and Dust**

Published in May 2020

**Harry's Game – Sleeping Giants**

Published in January 2021

**Harry's Game – Blue Skies and Tailwinds**

Published in July 2021

**Harry's Game – Sands of Time**

Published in November 2021

**Harry's Game – Moonlight Serenade**

Published in February 2022

**Harry's Game – Winds of Change**

Published in May 2022

**Harry's Game – Last of The Few**

Published in August 2022

If you enjoyed this book and would like to drop me a message, it would be great to hear from you!

Please contact me by email at the address below, and I'll do my best to get back to you as soon as I can.

Karl

karl@harrysgame.com

Printed in Dunstable, United Kingdom

73038706R00184